"In the tradition of novels like Kingsley Amis's *Lucky Jim*, Cole gives us a flawed protagonist facing a crisis, then ratchets up the comedy as the protagonist digs himself in more deeply. . . ."
— *Winnipeg Free Press*

"Cole belongs to the Truman Capote school of stylists; his prose is clear as a mountain stream. . . . I have a feeling that *Norman Bray* is just the first of many novels Cole will write. I hope so." — David Gilmour, *Toronto Star*

"Trevor Cole's great accomplishment is to write seductively and sympathetically about someone as narcissistic and bullying as is actor Norman Bray, leaving the reader in a wonderfully uneasy state of delight and horror. Tightly structured, funny, poignant – this wonderful novel delivers the pleasure of seeing that Norman is, under the correct circumstances, capable of leaving himself behind."
— Jury citation, Governor General's Award

"Cole deftly manipulates tone, diction, and point of view to create a brilliant study of Norman's persecuted artist persona and the peculiarly endearing person who hides behind it. The narrative voice is agile and witty. . . . Cole accomplishes something extraordinary." — *Quill & Quire*

"*Norman Bray* is so smart and funny, and it moves along with such speed, you're almost tricked into thinking it's a comedy. But this book is more than that – Cole has written a layered, resonant novel, full of surprises."

– Sarah Fulford, *Toronto Life*

"There are delicate, subtle shadings of characterizations, hidden pockets of humour and observations of the human condition that make *Norman Bray* a rewarding read. . . . Cole has written a punchy, frothy first novel that rings true on many levels."

– *Edmonton Journal*

"This is a very, very funny book. . . . Trevor Cole knows how to tell a story of the I-couldn't-put-it-down variety; Norman's performance is filled with giddy surprises and wonderful set pieces. The book is smart and deft; it zips along. This is fine writing, with a light and generous touch. . . . Just delicious!"

– *Globe and Mail*

"Trevor Cole, in his debut novel, has created a character as complex, infuriating, unpleasant and funny as any we've seen in a long time. . . . Somehow, though – and this is Cole's real coup – Norman retains a tattered nobility. In his unsparingly charted decline, the reader finds a rubber-necker's glee but also real sympathy. . . ."

– Montreal *Gazette*

"A terrific read. . . ."

– *Hamilton Spectator*

# TREVOR COLE

# NORMAN BRAY

# IN THE

# PERFORMANCE

# OF HIS

# LIFE

EMBLEM EDITIONS
Published by McClelland & Stewart Ltd.

Cloth edition published 2004
First Emblem Editions publication 2005

**Library and Archives Canada Cataloguing in Publication**

Cole, Trevor, 1960-
Norman Bray in the performance of his life / Trevor Cole.

ISBN 0-7710-2263-8

I. Title.

PS8605.O44N67 2005        C813'.6        C2004-905948-3

We acknowledge the financial support of the Government of Canada through the
Book Publishing Industry Development Program and that of the Government of
Ontario through the Ontario Media Development Corporation's Ontario Book
Initiative. We further acknowledge the support of the Canada Council for the Arts
and the Ontario Arts Council for our publishing program.

The lyrics on pages 70, 71, and 179 are from the song "Man of La Mancha" from
the play *Man of La Mancha*; the lyrics on page 340 are from the song "The
Impossible Dream" from the play *Man of La Mancha*; the lines on pages 62, 323,
324, and 342 are from the play *Man of La Mancha*. Songs by Joseph Darion and
Mitch Leigh. Book by Dale Wasserman. Copyright © 1965. Reprinted by permission.

The lyrics on pages 248 and 249 are from the song "Sixteen Going On Seventeen"
by Richard Rodgers and Oscar Hammerstein II. Copyright © 1959 Richard Rodgers
and Oscar Hammerstein II. Copyright Renewed.
WILLIAMSON MUSIC owner of publication and allied rights throughout the World.
International Copyright Secured  All Rights Reserved  Used by Permission.

SERIES EDITOR: ELLEN SELIGMAN

Cover design: Kong Njo
Cover image: LuckyPix Photography / Veer
Series logo design: Brian Bean

Typeset in Sabon by M&S, Toronto
Printed and bound in Canada

This book is printed on acid-free paper that is 100% recycled
ancient-forest friendly (40% post-consumer recycled).

EMBLEM EDITIONS
McClelland & Stewart Ltd.
*The Canadian Publishers*
481 University Avenue
Toronto, Ontario
M5G 2E9
www.mcclelland.com/emblem

1   2   3   4   5      09  08  07  06  05

For Fehn

# ACT I

Watch the man being seated at a table in the middle of the Skelton Arms pub. He has been shown a table to the side, but no, he prefers the one in the middle, so that is where he sits. His name is Norman Bray. You won't have heard of it before, although that fact might surprise him.

The waitress hands Norman a plastic-clad menu. "Ah." He smiles beneficently. "Thank you." He opens its leaves with practised dexterity. It is rather like a dance, he thinks, these habitual movements of hands in public places. Or a language. "Tell me," he says, "do you have a good brandy here?" He tilts the menu off to the side and awaits the young woman's answer.

She, in her jeans and mauve sweatshirt and distracted hair, considers this question for a brief flicker of time. Then she lifts her thin eyebrows. "Gee, I don't know. Most people just take the Courvoisier."

At this, Norman's chest fills and his smile grows more kindly. This is precisely the answer he expects. "Yes." His eyes twinkle. "You understand, though, that I mean brandy. Not cognac. The two are not really the same, and I prefer brandy."

"Right," she says slowly. "I'll have to go and ask."

"That would be wonderful."

Norman returns to his perusal; the menu of the Skelton Arms is new to him. His usual establishment in this part of downtown is the Windsor Grill, but when he goes to the Grill it's for a light dinner on Wednesdays before his evening's work, not for lunch. Lunch is a different matter, requiring different choices, because the Grill is not open for lunch. Norman is not used to eating downtown at this time of the day – is not, he doesn't mind saying, used to being out of bed before noon – but today it is necessary because Robert needs him, and so he must shift his pattern. Not that he considers himself to be a man of habit, but the Grill is easy because they know him and he feels comfortable there, and when one is working it is important to feel comfortable.

He is not quite comfortable in the Skelton Arms. For instance, the chair he is sitting in is cutting into his back in an unpleasant way. It is not something that would have bothered him as a younger man, but he is fifty-six now, and such things irk a bit more than they did. Still, he will have a brandy with his lunch – just one prior to taping – and all will be well. And he will ask the waitress for a different chair.

"We have Duff Gordon," she says on her return.

"That's all?"

"Yes."

It seems to Norman that the waitress is somewhat too satisfied with this answer. He considers her for a moment. She is a young girl, twenty or so. Perhaps, he thinks, she is new to waitressing. "You know," he confides, "sometimes the bartender keeps a better brand in a cupboard for special occasions."

4

"Not here," she says.

"Did you ask?"

He says this not meanly or aggressively, more as a helpful reminder – but the girl seems to be easily frustrated. She sighs loudly and rolls her eyes and hitches her weight from her left to her right leg. "That's all right, that's all right," he says, forcing a small chuckle. "It's not a problem, really. Actually, I'm surprised you don't have Winkelhausen or Miespejo. These are very good brandies and they seem like something you should have – you might want to suggest it – but anyway I will have the Duff Gordon with ice." He smiles, making the best of it. "And I would like the ice on the side, please."

Norman looks to see if his ice request has registered sufficiently in the waitress's eyes, and he thinks for a second that, despite her manner, and despite the difference in their ages, she probably finds him attractive. He is still a good-looking man. He was quite dashing in his twenties and thirties, but even now, well mired in middle age, he has the smooth skin and dark hair of someone in his early forties. It's a frequent delight for him to see pictures of people his age – or he will see them in the street, people he knew years ago in school, or during his tours – and be reminded again of how much younger he looks. They are flabby or grey or bald, and he, despite his weakness for brandy and cigarettes, is none of these. And so it is conceivable to Norman, as he regards the waitress, that, if he were to approach things just right, using all of his potent charms, she might at some point in the future agree to have sex with him.

By the time she sets his brandy and ice on the table – the ice is in a nice cut-glass bowl, with a small set of stainless-steel tongs, which Norman considers a special touch and takes to mean that she is not completely immune to his powers – he has almost decided on lunch. But first he has a question: "Can you tell me about the shepherd's pie?"

"What do you want to know?"

Ah, she is engaging him. This is just the sort of thing he enjoys. "Is it very meaty?" he asks. "I like lots of meat in a shepherd's pie. It's the way I make it myself."

"Oh," says the waitress evenly, "you cook, do you?"

This could not be going any better. She really is interested in him – there is even a small curl at the corner of her mouth. What might appear to someone looking on, someone unaware of the developing connection between them, as a slight sneer is in fact, Norman knows, a devilish grin.

"Absolutely. I love to cook. It's a kind of art, I think. I like to express myself with spices, with flavours." A smile, a wink. "I'm a man of many talents." It's like applying butter to loosen a ring. If you know what to do –

The waitress leans forward, her eyes wide. "Do you want the shepherd's pie or *what*?"

Norman's smile vanishes. He stares at the waitress, his brow corrugating in confusion, as if she has suddenly begun to speak in German.

"Look, I'm sorry, but I've got a full section." She sweeps her hand around to indicate five or six tables surrounded with customers. Norman notices these people for the first time, just as he begins to notice the clipped edge in the waitress's replies.

"Yes," he says dejectedly. "The shepherd's pie, please." She is not a very good waitress at all, Norman decides. And she is obviously a girl who doesn't know what she wants, doesn't know what sort of man he is, has no idea of his range of knowledge or experience. So, with some effort, he manages to feel sorrier for her than for himself. He will be satisfied with the shepherd's pie, even if it is slightly less meaty than he prefers. He will make a point of it. And he decides not to trouble her about the chair. More than that, he resolves to devote his energies to overcoming the discomfort the chair causes him. It will require a unique strength of will but, in his life and work, Norman has many times found it necessary to overcome discomfort, and so he has mastered the skill, a fact that he would be happy to share with the waitress, if only she were less grumpy.

For the remainder of his time in the Skelton Arms, Norman and the waitress say very little else to each other. He asks for an ashtray at one point, because he enjoys a cigarette or two after his meal, and she brings him one wordlessly. He almost comments to her about the hexagonal shape of the glass ashtray – he has seen it once before, in Halifax during an especially gruelling three-week run – but he decides against it, because whenever she comes near him she seems to be very busy.

When he is done, having enjoyed the shepherd's pie well enough – the potato tier was nicely browned on top, and the filling was passably meaty – he pays for his meal in cash, leaving a two-dollar tip. Then he rises and stretches out his back to ease the ache from the chair. Standing in the middle of a group of tables, he pulls on his shoulders one at a time, over and over, in an elaborate but necessary ritual, as one or two people nearby look on with expressions he reads as concerned. When he catches the eye of one man wearing the thick boots of a tradesman, he smiles wearily and pats the chair. "Badly designed,"

Norman informs him. The man nods very slightly, as if unsure whether Norman is actually talking to him. Then Norman pulls on his cream-coloured windbreaker, gathers his cigarettes and his wallet and slips them into his breast pockets, and heads for the exit. He makes sure to lean towards the waitress and smile graciously as he passes – "Thank you very much. Enjoyed the meal" – then pulls on the brass door-latch, and squints into the sunshine of November 7.

Outside, with the late-autumn air crisping his nostril hairs and the midday pedestrian traffic busying past him, Norman checks his watch, a flimsy digital thing made of plastic he picked up in a gas station, which he thinks looks more expensive than the ten dollars he paid. It is 1:46, if he can believe the time it gives, and he's due at the studio at 2:00 p.m. He clears his throat loudly and smiles at a passing elderly woman who looks up, startled. "Grand day," he booms at her, because he knows older people appreciate words like *grand*, and breathes in deeply.

Briefly he savours an image in his mind, of gently cupping his waitress's small, pale breast in his left hand, and squeezing her nipple lightly between his fingers. The thought gives him so much pleasure he nearly grins.

It truly is a Grand Day.

It is only a ten-minute walk to Jarvis Street, past the name-less office buildings Norman never enters, where people live the kind of life and do the sort of work that makes him shudder. "Lives of ledger," he sometimes says to his sister, Margaret. Of course, he appreciates the work these people do – there is a place and a need for people of limited scope, to attend to the papery drub of the official world. But appreciation is as close as he wants to get. Norman has lived a life devoted to the interpretive arts, and to the principle, based mostly on his own experience, that artists are different and largely misunderstood, except by other artists. It is a lonely kind of life, he thinks. Ah, well.

On the steps outside the tiny, bunker-like studio, Norman stops to have one more cigarette before subjecting himself to what he knows will be at least three hours of concentrated effort. Through the grimy, iron-barred window he sees Penny Curtis, the script assistant, then sees her notice him and disappear from view. A second later, with the metallic thunk of its lever being shoved down sharply, the studio's heavy door swings open and Penny leans outside.

"Norman, Robert's beside himself. Where've you been?"

"Oh, Penny." Norman flicks away an ash in greeting. "Hello." He watches a frond of smoke from the tip of his cigarette curl around her red-rimmed ear.

Penny is a soft-hipped woman in her late thirties, with narrow shoulders and a chin that slips away into her turtleneck collar. In Norman's view, she is a woman who works doggedly to be more than what she seems because, he suspects, to herself she seems very little. The effort involves being serious and busy beyond the immediate need, admonishing the slightest transgression, and worrying most when others worry least, as if part of her duty were to keep a balance of anxiety in the world. When she tries exceptionally hard the edges of her ears turn red and become hot to the touch.

Norman congratulates himself on his ability to understand all this about Penny and, in the amplitude of his understanding, to forgive her. What irritates him – indeed, strikes him as ungracious – is that she seems to chafe against this forgiveness, as if it were unwanted.

"Norman?"

"Yes?"

"Robert's livid. He's been waiting for an hour."

"Has he?" This news has Norman somewhat dumbfounded. He checks his watch. "But it's not even two."

"That's right," says Penny, nearly quivering with purpose. "But you were supposed to be here at one. We've only got use of the studio until four-thirty."

"No," he says, horrified. "Robert said two. I'm sure he said two."

"Want me to show you the call sheet?"

"Yes, I do."

He pulls on his cigarette as Penny lets the door shut, and imagines her rushing back at his behest over the threadbare grey carpet to grab the call sheet sitting on her desk, the desk she uses on Wednesdays and Thursdays when Chenowirth Productions has the studio booked, and which she can often be seen wiping down with a wet cloth because whoever uses it the rest of the week is, in her words, "an unconscionable juice-swilling slob," and he follows her in his mind as she races with the call sheet in hand, back to the front door, so that the door swings open just as he's stubbing out his cigarette with the narrow toe of his scuffed leather shoe.

"Here."

Norman accepts the clipboard and studies it carefully. There it is: *Norman Bray, 1 p.m.* "Well, obviously the time must have been changed and someone forgot to call and warn me, because I'm sure I heard two o'clock. I'm sure of it." He hands back the clipboard and looks hard at Penny to let her know he's just as sure she's the culprit.

Penny merely pushes the door open wider and backs up to let him in, and Norman steps through and heads down the dimly lit hallway. At the door to the studio he turns right and then left and continues through to the open doorway of the even darker control room, where he stands and holds out his palms and opens his mouth and creates for an instant the impression of a man about to leap into the first note of *Les Misérables*.

"You're fucking late, Norman." Robert Chenowirth, bald, lacquered with sweat, and aggressively unshaven, sits in front of an aging control panel on a swivel chair so flimsy that its ability to withstand his enormous bulk defies logic to the point of sorcery. His vast T-shirted belly (the T-shirt, black, features a startling woodcut of Liza Minnelli) is pressed into the ledge of the switching board, billowing above and below, but even so he has to extend his arms to rest his hands next to the yellowed controls. He is famous within his industry largely for having not yet died.

Kitty-corner to him the studio technician, Bink Laughren, glances over the top of his Dick Francis novel at a green oscillating-wave monitor. Norman hears Penny come up behind him.

"I'm sure you said two o'clock, Robert," implores Norman. "I'm positive. Whatever Penny says, I don't miss my call times. You know that. I'm a goddamn professional."

Chenowirth turns his head, an oiled ball dipped in metal filings, towards Norman for the first time, his threatening glare undercut just slightly by the feathery catch in his voice. "You missed this one."

"But not –"

11

Robert swings his fists as if he's pounding two sturdy lawn ornaments into the earth. "Oh *Jesus Mary*, Norman, just get into the booth. Somebody give him his *fucking* script."

It is unfairness to such a degree that Norman considers walking out in protest. It's what he should do. But instead – because he is a goddamn professional, and to some lesser extent because he needs the money – he takes the pages Penny hands him and makes his way back along the hall. He wrenches open the sound booth's outer door and pushes on the inner, which gives with a slurp of air, and he enters a tiny room fronted by a large glass window looking out into the control room.

"Hello, Judith." Norman nods at the actress already seated at one of two microphones and smiles to suggest that nothing is wrong, that he has had a perfectly reasonable conversation with Robert, an eminently reasonable man. Judith Fenwick, a matronly sort of woman smelling of hand cream and tea, regards him overtop pewter reading glasses tipped with tiny wings.

"I've had a very nice time going through this week's papers, Norman, which someone was kind enough to leave on the floor." She speaks with the vestiges of an elusive English accent, like so many other moderately talented actresses of middle age whom Norman has encountered. "I was about to start balancing my cheque book."

Norman nods distractedly and emits a short humming sound, because he is essaying the role of an actor concentrating on his script. It is, just as he expects, the script for episode #001 of *Tiny Taxi*, a fifteen-minute children's show produced on a delicately small budget for the new digital cable channel KidSpot. In concept and execution it is identical to *Timmy*

*Taxi*, which Chenowirth produced over the previous two years for another channel (and for which Norman provided the lead character's voice for all forty-two brief and brightly lit episodes) until Robert discovered an unnoticed clause in his contract that required him, after ten years, to relinquish his residual rights. Because he had planned to retire on the steady earnings of *Timmy Taxi*, and because the broadcaster's lawyers would not bend to his protestations that the contract was void because he'd been hopelessly adrift over a failed affair – and very likely drunk on gin toddies – when he'd signed it, Robert folded his company, established another one, acquired a new cable partner, and resumed taping in the same studio, with the same set, after only a month's delay. (Penny, whose employment contract calls for her to share in a percentage of the residuals in lieu of a decent salary, had tears in her eyes when she gathered the cast and crew to present Robert with a small celebratory taxi-shaped lemon cake.)

That *Timmy*-less month was an awkward one for Norman, who for these last two years has relied on his cheques from Chenowirth Productions more than he would care to admit. It necessitated visiting his sister on at least three occasions (it was four, to be precise, but one of those times she was at the doctor's seeing to polyps on her colon, so it didn't count) to negotiate the loan of sums so small they hardly warranted the inconvenience.

But yesterday, the first day in the life of *Tiny Taxi*, it was as though nothing had changed. The production process was the same: Wednesday afternoon, on a set no larger than an area rug, colourful toy cars with removable headlight eyes and toothy grilles were videotaped being pushed around the snap-together streets of Grandville by wires and unseen hands. On

Wednesday evening, from six until midnight, the actors arrived to give voice to their dreams and dilemmas. Having played the robustly cheerful Timmy for so long, Norman adapted easily, he thought, to the demands of playing the equally jolly Tiny, whose only bane in life is the mildly menacing Cab Calladay (formerly Ty Cab), who seems to lurk around every corner waiting to muscle in on his fares. Last night, in fact, Norman was noting to Penny and Judith, and Fred Trumble, who plays Cab, that he really understood Timmy/Tiny, that it was not a stretch to say their essential nature mirrored his own. "Each of us is optimistic at the core," he explained. "Willing to explore the unknown. Willing to embrace the new." It wouldn't have surprised him to find out that Robert had based the character entirely on him. As Timmy, Norman had even contributed the signature line: "Up the street or down the road, it's all a trip to me!" delivered with the eager chirp he'd perfected after only a few months. (For Tiny, Robert, who writes most of the scripts, had adapted the line to read, "You never know, you know, where the next turn will take you!" which Norman granted was snappy, but seemed to lack the texture of Timmy's sang-froid.)

Typically, after the Wednesday taping sessions, Robert and Penny and Bink spend Thursdays marrying the audio and video. They rarely need the actors, except for follow-ups necessitated by the occasional script change, which Norman invariably finds questionable but never complains about because it usually means an extra four hours' pay. Norman assumes this is why he has been called in.

"Did you know," says Judith, adjusting the folds of her oatmeal sweater, "that the Circle Stage is doing *Man of La*

*Mancha*? I believe they're updating it in some way. It's in the paper."

Norman thinks there's something odd about the script in front of him, he doesn't yet know what, but Judith has announced the *La Mancha* news without a note of horror or incredulity, and he considers this fact of more immediate concern.

"Up*dat*ing it, Judith?"

"Yes. I'm curious to see how."

"You're *curious* to see *how*?"

"Yes." She hesitates. "Aren't you?"

Norman presses his eyes shut, as if Judith's ignorance has become his sudden pain. "You can't update a classic of musical theatre."

"Why not? They do it to Shakespeare. I would say the sanctity of *Hamlet*, or *Henry V*, is far –"

But Norman doesn't hear what follows from Judith because he is troubled. Something about his script is nagging at him in a distracting way, and now there's the matter of having to explain something that shouldn't need to be explained. To a woman who is "of the theatre." The combination of vexations requires Norman to shake his head and exhale loudly through his nostrils. At some point in the midst of Judith's rebuttal he says, his voice draped in a lamé of consternation, "A musical is meant to be what it is. It is of this era. You can't update it because it is inherently modern. What you can do with a musical is fully achieve its potential, or not. Success or failure – those are your options."

"That's ridiculous."

"And it is not always immediately apparent which of those two things you're headed for. Sometimes what looks like success is revealed as failure only at the last minute, and only to an artist with the courage to recognize it and do something about it. I know what I'm talking about."

Judith has dropped her gaze to her script and now smoothes an arched eyebrow with the tip of her ring finger. "I'm so glad one of us does."

Norman watches her reach for a Styrofoam cup of tea on the ledge in front of her. The word *blithe* comes to him. Judith is *blithe*.

"You may not be aware of this, Judith, but I had the lead in a dinner-theatre production of *Man of La Mancha* just a few years ago. It would be fair to say I saved that production from humiliation. By being courageous and making hard decisions. That's what I'm talking about."

Judith regrips her tea with a Styrofoam rasp and does not look up. "No, I wasn't aware of that, Norman. They didn't mention you in the paper."

Penny appears at that moment on the control-room side of the glass and leans over Bink the technician to push the intercom button. "We're almost ready," says her voice, emptying through the speaker at their feet. "Norman, could you step out for a moment to speak to Robert?"

In fact, Norman would very much like to speak to Robert. There is the matter of the undefinably disturbing something relating to the script he has in his hands, and also the manner in which he was treated moments ago. But just now Judith must be attended to.

"I'm not sure I understand what you mean, Judith. What do you mean they didn't mention me in the paper?"

Judith droops slightly, as though softening in an oven, then sets her finger against a line of dialogue and lifts her head with a sigh.

"Actually, I was being facetious. But they do have a list of local productions in there – twelve in forty years, apparently not including yours. The mind can play tricks, though, so perhaps I'm wrong. Maybe you are mentioned. Did Penny want you, by the way?" She returns to her page.

Norman begins rummaging through the sections of newsprint at his feet. "What list? Where is this list?"

"Arts section. Just a small item off to the side. As I say, maybe I'm wrong."

She is likely wrong. Norman, snapping and folding papers, is quite sure she is wrong. He locates the arts section and scans the first page, finding nothing.

"No," he says, "I don't see it."

"*Inside*, Norman. It's hardly a front-page story."

He snaps and folds again and begins searching the smaller items, ever more convinced she is wrong. And see, here is a small item about *La Mancha*, the "sweetly tragic retelling of the *Don Quixote* saga," and the director's appalling plan to "update" its "reliable but naïve" sixties sensibility. Of course, neither he nor the Beverly Dinner Theatre production he saved from disaster are mentioned here, because this item is only alluding to the past and has nothing to do with past productions per se. So clearly, although Judith was right about the egregious "updating" part of things, she was wrong about everything else. Norman suppresses a triumphant smile and holds the paper out, tap-tapping the item and clearing his throat remonstratively.

"You must not have —"

Norman stops himself in the midst of correcting Judith because he notices an even smaller, boxed item below the story. He pulls the paper back sharply.

"That's the one," says Judith.

MUCHO LA MANCHA the item is titled. It is indeed a list of twelve local productions, dating back to 1967, showing in each case the theatre, the director, and the production's star, topped by a small block of text referring to the musical's enduring popularity. Norman reads the list twice.

"I'm not mentioned anywhere."

"No, I thought not."

The muscles of Norman's jaw flex and prowl as he inspects the list again. A sourness pools around his tongue that makes it difficult to swallow.

"Well, it's understandable," he says. "I wouldn't have expected them to mention it, frankly, since our production was outside the city, in Beverly."

"Five of those were outside the city, I think," says Judith, not looking up.

Norman sees them: Horace Theatre, 1967; Picton Stage, 1973, and so on. Productions listed not for their strength of vision, not for the acts of courage involved in their creation, but merely for having existed. Whereas his . . .

He folds up the paper with subject-changing vigour. "It doesn't matter. It's not important. I've already received all the recognition I need for my efforts in Beverly." He places the folded paper next to Judith, who is still reading her script.

She gives him a placid glance. "And what recognition is that, Norman?"

"I was given an award in Beverly. The Mirror Award."

A minimal smile. "Congratulations. I've never heard of it, but I have no doubt your performance was memorable."

Norman shifts in his seat. "It wasn't so much for my performance," he says, "as for my efforts in general." He picks up his script again and begins to read.

Judith looks at him steadily. "Meaning what, exactly?"

Norman finds himself getting irritated now and irritated is not what Timmy/Tiny needs. He ignores Judith and tries to concentrate on his script, striving for that lightness of spirit. *Good day there, Mailbox. How's it going, Lamppost? It sure is a sunny day, hey, hey, and I'm on the road to adventure!* But as he searches for the line changes he expects and finds not a one, he slowly realizes what it is about this script that has been troubling him. "This is the same script as before," he murmurs to himself. "We've done this script." He faces Judith. "We've *done* this script."

He's out of his chair. He yanks the booth's inner door open with another sup of air (it bangs into the back of Judith's chair – "Oh," says Norman; he hasn't time for "sorry"), pushes on the outer and he's bellowing as soon as he's in the hall. "Penny!"

He catches her outside the control room. "Penny," he says, his script raised and the index finger of his free hand rigid and ready for thrusting, "we've done this script. I've been given the wrong script!"

Penny turns halfway, not facing him. "No, it's the right script, Norman. Robert wants to talk to you about it." She begins to tug on the control-room door.

"But we've done this script."

19

"You should talk to Robert." She looks up at him, wincing. "I'll send him out."

Norman waits in the corridor's dull light, shaking his leg, charged with his own certainty. When Robert emerges from the control room, belly first, Norman tumbles at him. "It's the same script, Robert. It's the same script! You've –" But he stops when the producer holds up his hand and lets the door ease shut with a clump.

"I should have told you this before, Norman. I apologize. I've been derelict." Robert pulls at his fingers as if shedding extra rings. "But you arrived late and it was a bit mad there." Norman wants to jump back at that "late," but something tells him to wait. "You're right, it is the same script."

"Ah-hah! I knew it!"

"There is one change, though."

"Where? I can't find a thing."

Robert sucks in a quick breath and grimaces. "Sweetheart, they've decided they want a new voice."

"What new voice?"

"A new voice for Tiny."

Well, this is a very odd request. And remarkably ill-timed. "That's ridiculous, Robert, we've been doing it this way for two years –" But he sees Robert shaking his head, trying to interject, so he shrugs abruptly. "Well, all right, fine. I guess I can try something new. I've no idea what, but –"

"Sorry" – Robert lays a pillowy hand on Norman's arm – "I'm not being very direct." He smiles uncertainly at him. Unhappily. "Norman, they want to try someone else as Tiny."

Norman stares at Robert blankly. "What do you mean?"

"Hmmm." Robert frowns. "Well, *that's* what I mean. What they've said – this is the new group we're dealing with? KidSpot? – they said a lighter voice would work better for Tiny. I suspect they want to make a clearer shift from the whole Timmy thing. Which makes sense, really. So, what I thought you could do –" He's pulling the script towards him now, out of Norman's hands, but Norman grabs it away.

"No, wait." He narrows his eyes at Robert. "You are telling me I am no longer playing Tiny. A role I've been doing for *two years*, and now suddenly I am not doing it any longer. Is that right?"

"It's a shame. I don't agree with it myself, but –"

"Who's going to do it, then, if not me? Have they chosen someone already?"

"Well, yes."

"Who?"

Robert's gaze drifts towards the wall. "Judith."

Judith is a woman who does Little Theatre. Besides the odd fringe voice for *Timmy* – a lamppost, a stop sign – her single professional credit, as far as Norman knows, is a cat-litter commercial in which she was required to blurt, "Wow!" This can't be happening to him. "But" – he can't bring himself to say any of those things, so – "she's a woman, for Christ's sake. How can she play a boy taxi?"

"It's a high voice, Norman."

"Yes, but I can do the high voice. I have been doing it."

Robert holds up both hands. He shuts his eyes. "We need to begin again. All right?" He takes a deep, wheezy breath. "All right, Norman, I am saying this to you. The people we are working with now want Judith as Tiny. I'm sorry. They'd like you to play something else, and I was thinking about Cab Calladay . Freddy's been away a lot lately, I don't mind letting him go. And you can put that lovely baritone of yours to use."

It's all too clear to Norman. No need for explanation; he saw this coming. "They don't understand what I'm doing with him. They don't get it." He's jabbing his hard finger towards the general *theyness* of the hallway. "It's a complicated reading I'm giving this taxi. They think the kids won't understand, but they're not giving those kids enough credit."

"Mmmm."

"Why else if that's not it?"

Robert's rubbing his bristly cheeks now, looking towards the dark, warm haven of the control room.

"Why, Robert?"

"Boy, that's a thing. I wish –"

"Just say it, Robert. Just tell me!"

Robert closes his eyes again, as if he doesn't want to see Norman's face. "They said you sound forced."

There's silence for a moment as Norman stands back and observes this new information. He expected something absurd, and there it sits before him. It's an odd-looking object. "Forced?"

"That's what they said."

"When?"

"Last night. After recording."

"They came here after midnight?" Somehow these details seem important. When and where was this information delivered? What were they wearing? What sort of cigarettes did they smoke? How real is this opinion, this news, that he sounds forced?

"No. They – it was actually just this one young fellow who's in charge of programming, he's twenty-eight but he's very smart – he was sitting there in the corner the whole time. You didn't see him. He said you sounded forced."

"Well, what did you say?"

Robert tips his round head from side to side. Bip, bop, bip, bop. He sighs. "I agreed with him."

Norman is silent.

"Norman, really, play Cab. It's a fun part. You'll have a ball with it."

Norman can only stare back, his chest constricted, his throat burnt dry. "But, Robert," he says, in a voice not unlike Tiny's small warble, "I'm the *lead*."

◦━◦

It is a not insignificant truth about Norman that he has always, since the day he could reach a low G, been the lead. First in school productions, stepping over the slower and less talented, past the hopefuls who wanted to grow up to be watched and heard but who couldn't decide whether to be lawyers or teachers or actors (as if, Norman would say, the professions were variations on a theme), then later in regional theatres, working in earnest productions in front of approximated sets, beside actors whose talents were not quite striking enough to take them beyond their thick ankles and soft chins, Norman was always the hottest, brightest spot on the stage. Darkly handsome, not especially tall, but able to carry himself at a height, he held clear promise in his eyes and his smile. And the other actors, some who found it hard to rise to his standard, some who resented his obvious future, still wanted to bow beside him, feel the vibration in the air, accept applause in the warm, reflected glow.

Norman Bray. He was Heathcliff. He was Sky Masterson. Not *Streetcar*'s Stanley – not after Brando made the role muscular and brutal. And not Richard III – he was never that intellectually fibrous. Rather, he had a flair. He was light and dashing – he moved gracefully, kept his chin high – and this, along with his voice, led him to musicals. He had a bright, meadowy baritone, and by tweaking its tone one way or the other he could find the bravery or the melancholy in a character. He could achieve the heartbreaking stillness that romance required, when he would wait before a kiss, and the audience could only, could do nothing but, hold its breath. Women loved that. Certain nights, certain moments, you could look out into the audience and see a hundred women with their mouths open. One night, it was twenty-six years ago now, backstage at Calgary's Foothills Theatre after playing Hajj, the poet, in a touring production of *Kismet*, a woman from the audience – mid-thirties, short dark hair, firm lips, a green Chanel suit and a gold dragonfly pin – knocked on his dressing-room door. He had not yet showered, was wearing his cotton robe, still had traces of makeup and cold cream under his jaw and the damp of exertion on his skin. She said she was sorry, she hoped he didn't mind, but she simply had to come back and see in the flesh the man who had crafted such a spell. They chatted politely for a moment – he felt off tonight, she was here with friends, he was disappointed in the house, her husband was in Finland – but she kept looking at his chest hairs. She wondered whether it exhausted him, all that thrashing about, the singing. It must be exhausting, night after night. But she was looking at his chest hairs, and seemed to be tipping forward. And he finally, deftly, reached behind her and slipped the door closed.

At the height of his success, Norman was a man who assumed ownership of the air around him. On the day of a performance, as the curtain hour approached, he would begin to breathe powerfully, deeply, loudly through his nostrils, blowing up his gut with the bellows of his diaphragm, imagining himself onstage, girding himself. By seven o'clock, he would start filling the immediate environment with his sounds, clogging the nooks and crannies of a room with the exercises of his tongue, his palate, his vocal cords – the guttural, the nasal, the sudden fleshy orchestrations. And it was no use for others in the room to complain; if they did, Norman's sucking and bellowing only became louder, as if the task of entertaining an audience not only excused his exorbitance, but also made it necessary.

It was always theatre for Norman. Not the intimacy of film, and, with the exception of voice-over work and the rare commercial, not television. His presence was too big, his gestures too sure – his were performances assembled from large swatches of colour. He was an artist. You stood back from art.

And he didn't like those film and television people, or what they seemed to represent. They were mercenaries. Deal-makers. In a studio, in front of a camera, he was merely a cog in their construct. They could manipulate his performance, tamper with his timing, make choices he would never make. Hollywood? New York? They talked about markets, he said, about generating receipts, not creating moments, and he would not be a part of that. That's how he explained it when the inevitable questions came in his mid-twenties: Why doesn't he, shouldn't he, go, find his rightful place in the midst of it? But he wouldn't go. And by his mid-thirties, the pestering stopped. And then began the theories as to why he'd never gone. That he'd been scared. That he'd had doubts. That maybe – this was only whispered, by the bitterest colleagues – his talent had never really borne close scrutiny, that it was all, somehow, a mirage.

If any of these theories were true, Norman managed to ignore them. He had a nice run for a few years. From 1969 to 1985 he had the luxury of steady work. Maybe three productions a year, maybe two. It was all that any stage actor in a small country could ask. What did he need movies for? It was easier to work with theatre directors. He could make them accept his vision, because it was his vision that mattered. They weren't striding out onto the boards every night, he was. And if they objected or made things difficult, he waited, because once they'd had their say for six weeks of rehearsal, it was his show.

The rest of his time – he had more of it as the years progressed – he spent in his slippers. Tinkered on the piano. If they were calling, he didn't need to audition. If they weren't, it was just a matter of patience. His work was his calling card. They knew what he could do. The actors who ran from meeting to meeting, who steadily tried out for roles, were somehow, in his mind, diminished by it. And as long as he had a phone, and as long as his wife, Amanda, kept him in brandy and cigarettes, why did he have to worry? Then Amanda left him, after twelve years of childless marriage (childless because, as Norman repeatedly explained, he needed to be unencumbered, free to move where and when the work dictated), and though it was upsetting for a while, and though the calls became few, he managed. There was a toothpaste commercial in 1988 that had a four-year life span – he'd done a clever thing with his eyebrows on the second take that people seemed to enjoy.

Besides that, there wasn't much. But that was the industry's problem, Norman insisted. Political forces were moving against the arts – it was hard times all around. This line of argument, adhered to consistently, was enough to convince his aging sister, Margaret Bray, to share her disability pension with him for three of those in-between years, until he met Gillian Swain, Gillian the professor of medieval literature whose husband had left long ago, and who seemed grateful that a man as handsome and talented as Norman would be willing to share her life, her home, her income.

And now it is eleven years since he moved in with Gillian and her two teenaged children, and three years since Gillian died. He has reached the age of fifty-six, and he has not yet succumbed to the undeniable fact of what he has become.

⋯

He's home by 5:30, up the steps of the red-brick semi-detached on Sorauren Avenue, a hard-worn street they said was sure to be swept up in the waves of gentrification but which never quite managed to run with the concept beyond a few painted brickfronts. Gillian, who'd loved the man she sensed he could be, had misread the street's inertia too. When she died, her university pension went to her children, but the house she left in Norman's name. She did so hoping that, surrounded by the street's coming renewal, he might see the value, even the nobility, in a personal act of renovation. Today, unless you asked him, Norman wouldn't think to notice that neither event has come to pass.

He looks for mail and finds only the usual mercantile detritus, the bills and the flyers and the rest of the whatnot from the official, commercial world, the world that has failed to realize he does not buy things. His shoes and boots are scrounged from productions he has been in, his clothes are presents from Christmases and birthdays past. He has no use for electronic gadgetry – other than a reliable answering machine and a snowy TV – or for cars or other fashionable pieces of equipment. He does not blow leaves or snow with machines. He does not watch movies on disks or tapes. He does not go anywhere, nor does he want to. Norman Bray wakes at noon, he drinks and smokes and eats, he adjusts the rabbit ears on top of the television that was Gillian's and watches the four channels they receive. He reads books borrowed from the library in search of attitudes that support his own. Then he sleeps, and does it all again.

Detritus in hand, Norman opens the door, enters the dark house, and feels his way towards the kitchen. Forgetting that the ceiling fixture's bulb popped this morning he flicks on the kitchen switch and sees the continuing darkness as a further insult.

As a professional he would never have left them in the lurch. Though he was wounded – could they know how deeply? – he had done what was necessary. Robert had looked at him with basset eyes, pleading, "Play Cab, Norman. We need you." Yes, of course, they needed him. And it was a brilliant idea of Robert's – Norman knew exactly how to play the sly and smirking (though not truly evil) Cab. And there was even a line in the script that spoke directly to the situation at hand, which he read with bitter relish:

Why, Tiny, my word – your
grille seems tarnished. Are you
feeling quite yourself?

Yes, he was fucking marvellous, and they were full of praise, fairly gushing over him. But of course, Cab was a supporting character, with twelve or fifteen lines of dialogue per episode at most. It wasn't really the sort of character that could satisfy him. So in his moment of triumph, in front of Judith and Penny and Bink, Norman drew himself up, filled his chest, aimed his eyes down along his admittedly pronounced yet still heroic nose, and said, "Thank you, Robert. It has been a pleasure. But I'm afraid that is all I can do for you." Then he gave Robert a grave, knowing smile of farewell, a smile that said, *You will soon realize your loss*. And he left for good. He didn't bother to look at the tepid Judith on his way out. He didn't look at her because he knew she knew: her Tiny could never approach the heights his Timmy had achieved. Her joy would not be transcendent. Her trepidation would sound like timidity. Her courage would rarely come across as anything more than bluster. She would never *know* Tiny. And the children – God, he thinks of the children who will tune in next Saturday morning and feel unsettled, unsure. The four-year-olds who will see their favourite taxi and hear this strange new voice, and feel deceived!

He cracks out some ice cubes from the freezer, reaches into the cupboard beside the fridge for a bottle four-fifths empty. In the darkness, he pours himself a generous, healing brandy. It is, unfortunately, not his favourite brand, Miespejo Aguardiente, which he discovered many years ago in a small glass handed to him in a Montreal motel room by the wife of a Québécois car dealer. Only twice has he been able to afford his own bottle of Miespejo Aguardiente, and no one else has bought it for him. He has never been able to make anyone comprehend the distinction between Miespejo and an ordinary, undistinguished brandy. He can describe its label – the raised gold letters in an elegant script on a deep-red background – and try to make plain that the wrapping only hints at the wonderments within; a taste with layers, with progressions from sweet to bitter, light to dark, a taste that rewards experience and understanding. He can explain all this, and yet people attempting to do him a kindness manage to hear only "brandy" and buy him Duff Gordon. This bottle, for instance, is from Amy, Gillian's daughter, and every pour from its mouth is a reminder to him of how little he is understood.

As he swallows, he sees the mail he laid on the kitchen table, dimly visible in the light from a neighbour's porch coming through the back-door window. He reaches forward to take up three envelopes. The large blue one, full of grocery coupons, he puts to the side to be combed through later – there may be, among its special offers on Cradle Bras and central vacuums and free lenses with any complete pair of glasses, a dollar-off food coupon or two. The second he opens with a steak knife. It's a notice from Actor's Equity to pay his union dues. They could have drummed him out for taking half a dozen non-union jobs over the years, but no, they want his $135. He hasn't been to a meeting in nine years, knows none of the people in charge there now. They still want his $135. He refolds the notice and slips it back into its envelope, downs the

30

last of the brandy in his glass, and pours the bottle's remnants.

The third envelope is from some bank. Ordinarily he would toss it away – banks, impassive and monolithic, make Norman wary, and anyway it's not his bank; likely it's trying to sell him services he doesn't want or need. Why do they keep pestering him? He feels the envelope's thinness and almost decides to throw it in the waste can under the sink. But for some reason he pokes his finger under the flap and begins to break it open. Before he gets halfway, the phone rings on the wall next to him. He plucks up the receiver with a flourish.

"Hel-*low*."

"It's your sister, Norman." He knows the wheezy voice. It's not necessary for her to explain her relationship to him. She could simply say hello.

"Yes, Margaret." He can tell by her tone that she needs something. He straightens his back and forces himself into a heightened state of alertness.

"Norman, I need you to take me to the doctor."

"When?"

"Never mind when. I want you to take me. I want you to agree."

There is a chance that his sister, sixty-three years old and suffering for the past twelve from an insidious fatigue and mild agoraphobia, has figured out the trick of "when?" The trick of "when?" entails luring her into specifying a time for some errand or task she needs him to attend to – accompanying her to her doctor on Eglinton Avenue, for instance – so that he can then describe some conflict of schedules that stands in his way.

"I will if I can, Margaret," says Norman, proceeding undaunted. "Just tell me *when* you need me to be there." He thumbs the upturned flap of the envelope in his hand and hears her frustrated sigh. "Some days are better than others, of course." He eyes the pantry shelves in front of him. "Things aren't always in my control." He wonders what he will make himself for dinner. "But you know how I want to help." Then all he holds at his ear is a dial tone; his sister has hung up.

What to do about dinner? Freed of the prospect of spending two hours with his ever-expanding sister – 270 pounds now and picking up speed – stuck in a fume-choked bus while she wobbles on the next seat and berates him about his not owning a car, Norman's natural optimism is restored. He will go to the supermarket and buy something challenging to cook, a fillet of monkfish, say, such as might be served at a bistro in Paris. But he will need wine. He has no wine. He has almost no brandy for that matter. He will go to the liquor store and buy wine and brandy! His freedom knows no bounds.

It is only now, as he lifts his glass and finishes off his drink, that he sees the wall clock showing 6:05 and remembers Gillian's children, Amy and David, are coming for dinner. They will arrive in less than an hour and a half.

Norman tugs open his fridge, finds a carton of week-old milk, some bacon in a package bound up with an elastic band, a hunk of hardening Gouda. Below that, some limp celery and one pockmarked zucchini, half a lemon only partly enclosed in a bit of loose plastic wrap, and two onions, each of them sprouting what looks like a green serpent's tongue. On the lowest shelf, a tiny plate of butter flecked with toast crumbs, an apple, one jar of jam and another, unopened, of Jamaican jerk sauce a coupon convinced him to try, though he still hasn't. He presses the package of bacon with his finger, sees its rose liquid, vaguely biological, flow up and back through the clear plastic window. If the bacon is fresh enough, he'll make supper with what he has here. He knows he has some canned things, some rice, a small bag of pasta; it should suffice. In the light from the fridge he pulls off the elastic and checks inside the plastic pouch; the top two bacon slices have turned faintly grey, and that – he sniffs at them – leaves three slices to eat. Is it enough? He gauges his hunger. The taping, the issues with Robert, forcing himself to play Cab, it's all given him an appetite. And doesn't all that selflessness, the pride gulped back, warrant some sort of reward? He thinks it does. Goddamn it, Norman thinks, tonight I deserve steak.

He checks: there's ten dollars in his wallet, and he can make twelve if he scrapes up the quarters from his bedside table. If he wants wine with this meal – of course he wants wine, a Merlot perhaps, Chilean – he'll have to go to the bank. He has about eighty dollars in his savings account. Thirty dollars in total should do.

Norman marches briskly off to his bank at the corner of Queen and Calendar Streets. At the end of the block, by the last of the wedges of lawn fading towards a November khaki, he catches the heavy herbal scent of dog feces. He walks past and lights a cigarette, inhaling the first puff, as always, deeply, almost desperately. Around the last knee-high fence and down Queen Street, he passes a chicken-wings outlet he has never entered and, beside it – he exhales only now – a minuscule Korean noodle joint with laminated pictures taped to the inside of the window, photographs of unidentifiable dishes, faded to a sickish blue-green, that he convinces himself look appetizing, because he is a man of the world.

On the sidewalk opposite him, a pair of used-furniture dealers haul in the merchandise placed outside for the day. One of them carries an armload of brassware into his shop, but the other, an older, Hungarian-looking man, is struggling to lift a heavy oak chest of drawers over his threshold. "Here" – Norman raises a hand and jogs quickly across the street – "I can help you with that." Cigarette wedged in his mouth, he takes one end of the bureau and, before the white-haired man can say a word, heaves it over and wedges it through. "Oh," he says, seeing that this act has trapped the shop owner amid a forest of floor lamps. But the man waves him off, insisting his friend will help him get out. And Norman leaves, warmed by his own generosity of spirit.

⊷⊶

Inside the glass lobby of his bank, Norman walks past the automatic teller machines, pulls on the inner doors and finds them locked. It's barely 6:20; they can't be closed already. He can see people inside. Tellers moving silently behind the counters. They appear not to notice him, so he raps on the glass. "Excuse me!" he calls. One nearby teller, an East Indian woman in sleeveless blue, looks up. "Hello," bellows Norman, smiling. "Could you let me in? I need to make a withdrawal." He recognizes that woman; he's seen her before. But the teller shows no reaction. She seems to look through him, and then returns to her work. Norman can feel heat at the back of his neck. "Excuse me!" he calls, even louder. The woman in blue moves away from the counter. The others, farther off, vanish one by one, retreating to offices and desks beyond his view. "Hello!" he calls. He opens his hand and slaps it once against the glass, wobbling it

34

with the force of the blow. When nothing happens he slaps the glass again. Behind him, the three people standing in line for the ATM begin to murmur.

"Hello!" he shouts.

"What's your problem, man?"

Norman turns and sees the queue of people, at the end of it a thickly padded man in his twenties in a billowy windbreaker and Florida Marlins baseball cap, with a week's worth of wispy stubble on his chin. The man shrugs towards the locked door. "They're closed, right?"

"But there are tellers in there," says Norman, his hand throbbing. "I see people working." When he turns back, to his amazement, the woman in blue is standing before him, right there on the other side of the glass. Relief and vindication pour through him; she has seen him after all.

Her face, however, is unpleasant. She's frowning behind the glass. "We are closed," she says with emphasis, her voice sounding far away. "Use the ATM." And she lifts a hand above her head and points to the area behind Norman, to the people standing in line.

But Norman has no ATM card. Has never had one. He hates the machines. They give nothing but money, and he wants more than that. To the woman in blue he shouts, "But I want to deal with a person!" And the woman behind the glass sways back abruptly, as though she has caught a whiff of something sour, and walks away.

The man in the Florida Marlins cap is snickering. Norman turns to see him shoving his shiny card into the machine. He's alone now with Norman in the vibrating, aquarium light of the lobby, shaking his grinning head.

Norman's jaw stiffens. "Yes?"

The man stabs the buttons with a stiff thumb, still shaking his head, still grinning.

"Excuse me?"

The man holds out a palm to take the cash the machine slips him. "I don't know, buddy," he says, folding the bills into his wallet. "I think you got some issues."

Norman says nothing, watching, as the man begins to move away, until a streetcar's cranky bell makes him start. He raises his hand to the man pushing open the bank's outer door. He aims his finger. This is what a person does when he has been unfairly treated. He points to his malefactors and names their crimes.

"Don't you laugh at me!" Norman shouts. "I am a customer! I have a right!" He watches the man leave, sees him float, legless, past the bank's large blank window. "I am a customer!" Norman shouts at him.

❧❀❧

The flaking paint on the front door of Margaret Bray's squat three-storey walk-up apartment building just off Roncesvalles Avenue seems to achieve a new level of expressionistic eloquence every time Norman visits, and he marks each change in its matte-brown curls and cracks as if watching the autumn leaves turn.

As he opens the door and steps inside, he glances over the folded newsprint flyers stacked on the edge of the radiator and checks the slit in Margaret's tin mailbox. It is always better, when asking his sister for money, to render some small service in advance. He opens the box with a spare key and finds (to his slight chagrin) six pieces of mail, including two actual letters. He lifts them out, closes the box again, and starts up the stairs.

At Margaret's apartment, he raps hard three times, shoves in the key, and enters before she has time to register the knock. "Hello?" she calls through the bathroom door as he walks in. "Who's here? Is that you, Philip?" Philip is the building's superintendent, a man in his seventies who has apparently taken to visiting Margaret for a sherry before supper two or three times a week.

"It's me, Margaret." The mention of Philip has reminded Norman that he could use a drink. He heads for the tiny kitchen.

"Norman?"

"I've brought your mail."

A pause. Then, irritated, "Leave my sherry alone, Norman. I'm expecting Philip in a few minutes."

Norman has no intention of touching her sherry. He opens a veneered cupboard door, shoves aside the bottles of Dubonnet and vermouth and Paarl Golden Medium and latches on to a two-thirds-full bottle of gin, itself not so far removed from womanish territory but at least drinkable. He pours three fingers' worth into a highball glass, then opens the freezer, finds a dried-out ice-cube tray and dumps a handful of ice wafers into his drink.

"What are you doing here?" His sister's voice, slipping across the bathroom tiles, sounds quarry-cut, immutable. Norman swishes the gin over his teeth, swallows, and sets himself to the task.

"You've got some letters," he calls pleasantly. "Shall I read them to you?"

"Don't you dare," she calls. He can hear her muttering to herself, padding around, fumbling with rolls of paper and little plastic pots of face cream, furious with him. As he shuffles the envelopes, she emerges around the corner, draped in a flowered lavender caftan – the "company" caftan – her grim, puffy face topped with fine blond hair brushed into a cloud.

She snatches the letters out of Norman's hand. "Your services are not required." She begins to shuffle away towards her TV chair – a graceful, stuffed emerald throne with its back to the kitchen – and says, without looking at him, "Of course, I don't suppose you've come to tell me you can spare a moment in one of your busy, busy days to take me to see Dr. Stanton."

Norman pours down another freshet of gin, holding his breath, hating the sweet juniper fragrance of it. "What's that, Margaret?" he says distractedly, checking his watch.

"What do you *want*, Norman?"

He sets down the glass and pats his pockets for cigarettes as he follows her into the living room. Then, as if it's just come to him, "Gillian's children, you remember Amy and David? They're coming for dinner tonight. I thought you might like to join us." He pulls a cigarette from its pack with tight lips and fishes for his lighter.

Norman's sister tsks audibly as she settles into her chair. "Why would you think that? I've barely met them." She waits and, when Norman fails to respond, half turns. "I've barely *met* them." She sighs, shakes her head, and begins to rip open the first of her letters with pale, tuberish fingers.

Having started a little fire at the end of his cigarette, Norman inhales quickly, waves the flame out, then talks through the smoke escaping his lungs. "No, you've met them. I remember they quite liked you. And why not? You're –" He's aware of the passage of time, but it's a delicate thing, getting to the crux. "You're a generous woman."

In her chair, Margaret leans forward and puts a hand to her mouth. "Oh, my God."

Norman is in the midst of retrieving his glass from the kitchen. He pokes his head through the doorway. "Bad news, is it?"

"Sophie Mather's nephew has won a scholarship to the Royal Conservatory of Music." She leans back in her chair, closes her eyes, and lays the open letter across her face for a moment, then lifts it away and sighs. "We'll never hear the end of it now."

At this news, Norman straightens, purses his lips for a moment, and holds the gin glass snug against his breastbone. "I could have gone to the Royal Conservatory," he says, swaying back slightly on his heels.

"What?"

"It was one of my options."

Norman's sister shifts around in her chair. "That's a complete crock. You were never going to the Conservatory."

Norman comes forward. "It's not a crock. You just don't remember. I thought very seriously about the Conservatory."

She regards him stiffly. "I don't know where you've come up with that one." At a knock on the door she brightens instantly and motions Norman away. "That's Philip. Go let him in."

But Norman stands still, his jaw prow-like, and juts his fisted glass towards her. "I *went* to the Conservatory for an *interview*."

39

His sister rolls her eyes and trills out a singsongy "Come in, Philip!" that Norman manages to decipher as disturbingly flirtatious.

The sound of a joggled knob. "Can't," comes the muffled voice. "'S locked."

Margaret looks up at Norman darkly, a face that says, *Stop this idiocy and behave like a normal middle-aged man.* "Norman," she says firmly. "I don't care one way or the other. Please answer the door."

"You all right in there, Margaret?" Philip's muffled voice again. "You want me to go get the master key?"

"No, Philip," she calls sweetly. She makes a fist and pounds the arm of her chair. "Now, Norman," she commands, her yellow hair shimmering. "Go and let him in!"

"Not," he begins, squinting at her, "until you admit that I'm right."

She stares at him silently for a second. Then she closes her eyes. "All right, Norman. Yes. You went for an interview."

"Ah-*hah*!" Norman is candescent. He strides triumphantly to the apartment's door and opens it with a flourish. "Helloooo," he says, finishing with a smeary grin. Before him stands an elderly, pot-bellied man, slightly shorter than himself, with long strands of silver hair combed back on his head, wearing a checked short-sleeved shirt with reading glasses tucked in his breast pocket, clean dark-green work pants, and plaid slippers. Heavy-faced, extraordinarily jowly, he holds a large jar of something burgundy-coloured and seems unhappily startled by the sight of Norman.

"I'm, uh, I'm Philip," he offers gravely. "I live there in the basement."

40

"Yes, please, come in," says Norman, smiling broadly and motioning towards Margaret's living room. But as Philip steps awkwardly through the doorway, Norman stops him by putting a hand to his shoulder. "What's that you've got?" he says, looking down at the jar Philip is clutching. "Is that homemade jam?"

"That's beet spread," says Philip, holding it up. "It's a thing my family – my cousin made it."

"Isn't that marvellous!" exclaims Norman, taking it from Philip's grip. He wheels and proceeds down the hall and through the living room towards the kitchen, along the way calling, "Philip brought you some homemade jam, Margaret."

"He did? Well, let me see it."

"My cousin's beet spread," says Philip, making his way into the apartment. "I brought some down from Cornwall."

"Oh, Philip, that's so nice of you." She calls, "Norman, put some out with crackers. I want to taste it!"

In the kitchen, as he refreshes his glass, Norman can hear them murmuring. He catches snippets of conversation: the word *brother*, Philip's *staying* and *dinner*, Margaret's *haven't a clue*, and takes pleasure from all of it. "Norman," he hears his sister trill, "since you're there, would you pour Philip and I a sherry?" He opens the cupboards, bypassing the glasses and bottles of sherry, and latches on to a small box of rye squares. He takes out a handful, then opens the jar of beet spread with a pop, sinks in a knife, and lifts out a dark-red pebble of jelly.

When, after a minute, he emerges from the kitchen with his cheeks full, carrying nothing but the opened jar of beet spread in one hand and half a cracker in the other, he sees that the stolid Philip has pulled a chair close to Margaret and settled

41

himself in. Eventually they both turn towards him, and as they observe him with puzzlement, Norman works the bite into something to be swallowed and acquires a look of mild concern. Finally he says, "I don't think it really goes with gin."

Margaret smacks the armrest of her chair. "Norman!" she exclaims.

Norman, perplexed, extends his hand in a plea of innocence. *What?*

"Honestly, you're such an ass sometimes."

Philip stands up. His feet don't move; he doesn't take a step or even adjust his stance. He simply rises from his chair on stanchion legs, with his hands at his sides, and looks directly at Norman. But his jowls are vibrating.

"That beet spread is for Margaret."

Norman hears the rumble in Philip's voice the way the sound of hollowed-log drums must have met the ears of the first explorers, full of portent, but inexplicable. He smiles warmly. "Yes, I know." Then it occurs to him that Philip, having brought a gift, might be looking for appreciation, or even praise. "It's fine," offers Norman, nodding encouragement. "We just need to figure out what it goes with."

Philip's face darkens. He seems to expand.

"It goes with sherry," he says.

"Oh." Norman absorbs and processes this information, squeezing it through the flushed passages of his awareness. What he says next he intends largely as a guilty admission – he, as a non-sherry drinker, is incapable of fully appreciating the qualities of Philip's cousin's beet spread. Part of him also hopes to leave the question of the beet spread behind so that he might proceed to figure out a way to ask his sister for fifty dollars, which after all is why he's here. At the same time, another part of him wonders whether he might be able to manage a pleasant, seemingly offhand remark about the beet spread – something about its being worth at least fifty dollars to a sherry drinker – and, from there, segue into asking his sister for the money. These are the notions with which Norman wrestles before he says, "Well," and with a sharpness he doesn't quite intend, "that's not much of an enticement for me."

Sadly, before he can skip ahead to the offhand part, the pleasant part about the beet spread being worth fifty dollars, and so on, Norman becomes aware of Philip's slow progress towards him on his plaid, foam-soled slippers. He sees his sister lay her face in her hands. He hears what could be Gregorian chanting on a distant radio but is, more likely, the sound of his own blood rushing through his ears, because in the last several minutes he has consumed about six ounces of gin. He then realizes, with ferocious clarity, that Philip is standing before him, with a thick, scaly, building superintendent's finger pressing hard into his breastbone.

"Give that beet spread back."

For a moment, it seems to Norman that Philip wants him to give back what he's *eaten*. What a strange thing to say, he thinks. What a strange man.

"That wasn't yours to take," Philip is saying, with an oddly deep voice, low and burbling. Molten. "You didn't ask for it. It wasn't offered. So give it back."

"Philip." Norman's sister is standing beside her chair. "Norman, you should apologize to Philip."

"Wait," says Norman, holding the jar up out of the way until he can explain. "I don't think you understood. I was about to make, you know, sort of a little joke."

"You were going to make a joke about my cousin's beet spread?"

"Yes. Well –" Philip pushes his finger harder into Norman's chest, and the pain cuts him short.

"Look, now, I take to most people," says Philip, "but you're a rude man. You grabbed that jar out of my hands and helped yourself, and you didn't give any to your sister there, the person I brought it for. And then you say it's not good enough for you."

"Listen –"

"And now you won't give it back."

"Yes, but you don't see –" Norman tries to stop, but he can't contain himself; it's nerves, it's the gin, it's Philip's jowly face inches away from his, he can't help himself. He begins to giggle.

"Norman!"

Philip removes his finger from Norman's breastbone and walks away towards the kitchen. Norman, giggling, trying to stop, watches him go. Watches him emerge from the kitchen a second later holding – now he can't help himself, he knows it's wrong, he guffaws, he belches laughter – a large spoon. Philip walks up and takes the jar out of Norman's hand. Tears are running down Norman's cheeks.

"Norman, please!" His sister sounds far, far away. Oh, God, he can't stop. He can't stop laughing. "Norman, Philip's cousin is *dead*."

Oh, my. It's hard to stop, but, oh, oh, yes, he can feel it draining away. He's getting a grip. Oh, Lord. That felt good though. Yes it did. He relaxes against a pale painted wall, still grinning broadly; the gin has made his face muscles sticky.

"She died of cancer two weeks ago," says Margaret, holding tightly to her chair. "They were very close."

Okay, thinks Norman. Now I see. I really must be serious. He clears his throat, looks Philip straight in the puffy red eye – and bursts out giggling again.

"You want it so badly," says Philip, fitting the spoon – a large, silver one, for serving heaps of casserole – into the jar's wide mouth and scooping out all the beet spread it can hold, thick and shimmering and purplish red. Norman, not quite believing what he's seeing, watches it come towards him. He tries to back up, and finds himself pinned against the wall. "Then you're gonna eat this," says Philip, aiming the spoon at his mouth, "and act like you like it."

Norman feels the touch of cold metal on his lip and snaps his head back reflexively against the wall, a jolt of pain adding to his gin confusion. He closes his eyes and holds his hands up defensively, but before he can do more, he hears a shout – "Philip!" – and a thwack. Norman opens his eyes, blinks, and sees the older man standing ashamed before Margaret, who has a rolled-up TV-listings magazine in her fist. Glops of beet spread slide from Philip's spoon to the carpet, leaving blood-coloured clots.

"Norman," says his sister sternly, "that needn't have happened."

"No," Norman heartily agrees.

"I want you to apologize to Philip."

Norman's eyes widen. "What?"

"Apologize to him. You insulted him. You insulted something his dead cousin made with her own loving hands."

"I didn't!"

"I heard you."

"But that's not what I meant." He thrusts an arm in Philip's direction. "And he attacked me!"

"Well, if he did you could hardly blame him."

This is too much. "I will not apologize." He stands up straight. "But I will say this – you can both shove the beet spread!" He spins and, dizzied by the gin, strides towards the apartment's front door. Before he opens it, he turns to face Margaret and bellows, "Can I borrow fifty dollars?"

"Absolutely not."

Less loudly. Pleading, really. "It's for dinner tonight. Gillian's kids."

"No!"

He slams the door behind him.

⟡

Why do this now? she wonders, putting a hand to the black band she uses to tie back her sandy, in-between-length hair. Why wait until now, when I've been sitting here three minutes with the engine running, to have a conversation with the doorman? She watches him, nodding and leaning back with laughter in the lobby of his Walmer Road high-rise, waiting for him to shake himself free from a conversation with someone he barely knows so that he can get in the car and go visit someone he should know better. She watches and then begins punching the radio buttons to find an FM station that doesn't make her heart palpitate. What she doesn't need, just at the moment, is a driving bass beat, she doesn't need a sixteen-year-old's electronically buffed vocal searing into her ear, and she certainly doesn't need the commercials, most of which, as a private in the army of Young & Rubicam media buyers, she can recite from memory. She needs calm.

Come on, David, David, David, we're already late enough. (Punch. Hip-hop.) Chatting with the doorman is something you do when there's nothing to do. (Punch. Classic rock.) You don't wait until your sister arrives, late, to take you to dinner, and think, oh, now, this minute (Punch. Easy rock), I'll have a heart-to-heart with old Sol.

She watches him, tall, lean as a sculler, starkly handsome under his dark cap of hair, a face of highlights and shadows. What's he wearing? A charcoal-grey suit with a paper-white shirt and a burnished-gold tie. It's like he's deliberately being provocative. To establish distinctions. She goes the other way, on occasions like this. She tries to blend into the walls. She sees him sip from the can of club soda in his hand and finally nod goodbye to the doorman. She watches him leave the building, then pause to toss the can into the recycling bin by the entrance. That's when she beeps, when his back is turned, just to see him jump. As he approaches the car he shakes his fist, mock scowling.

"That was an important conversation to have just now, was it?" she says as he slides in.

He turns halfway towards her, as if his neck is stiff. "Why, are you in a hurry to get there suddenly?" He's freshly showered, pristine, clean like a knife scoured and wiped.

"Well, we're late."

He waits until she's out of the circular drive and on her way. "Someone's in a bad mood."

"No," she sighs, "someone's fried from having to call seventeen stations today to lift all the Shopper's spots because of a twenty-cent price change on toothpaste nobody told her about, and then having to sit in a car waiting for Godot."

"I see." He adjusts the seat belt across his chest and motions towards the radio. "You listening to that?"

"Why not?"

"I dunno. It's old."

"It's not that old. It's not classical." She doesn't want to defend her choice. It's her car, he's getting the lift. He could just as easily have driven himself, though she's glad he didn't. She doesn't like arriving there alone. Two months ago, after David bailed at the last minute, she endured three hours of Norman by herself, sitting on the edge of the faded brown couch next to the piano and staring at the walls as Norman, sunk into the yawning puce easy chair that supports him twelve hours of the day, talked at length about the nuances involved in portraying a taxi, particularly for an audience of children, who lack the instant shorthand an adult brings to the subject. Children have no fundamental appreciation of the taxi's societal role, not to mention its station, Norman was saying, while she looked at the walls. Finally, when she heard a pause, she said, "Norman, you still haven't painted the living room. Mom tried to get you to do that for six months before the accident."

"Oh," said Norman, refocusing, "well, I really haven't had time. I did have this marvellous realization though. Did you know that in Hong Kong, taxis outnumber regular vehicles?

They're a fixture. Here, you see, they're more of a luxury –"

"Those pieces of tape on the wall," persisted Amy, "that would have killed my mother, letting those stay there, collecting dirt."

Norman smiled impatiently, seeming determined to push through to his conclusion. "When I realized that I knew I had to get across this idea, the *specialness* of Timmy. I had to get across his –" he waved his hand in the air, as if feeling for the word "– his peculiarity."

Amy was looking past him, at the small tin ashtray sitting on the piano, surrounded by little grey stalagmites of spilled ash. "She was a fastidious woman, Norman."

Amy had learned long ago, when she was still living at home, that her mother's cohabitant, this actor, would often respond directly when his name was inserted into a question or statement. It was a trick that her brother refused to apply; he expected Norman to have the decency to listen to him when he spoke, and became righteous and blatant and repeated himself, gradually raising his voice, until Norman responded or reacted in kind. Amy endured frequent bouts of this shouting while they were all living together, through the last bit of high school and her university years, before she and then David finally fled to their careers. And so now, whenever she is intent on getting a response, she inserts Norman's name, and frequently gets some small, brief satisfaction.

"Was she?" Norman stared at her forcefully, apparently searching his recollection. "That was never my impression. I mean, academics – I played a professor once. You remember – well, I've spoken of it – it was a quite good Prairie Theatre production of *Goodbye, Mr. Chips*. I played him as fairly untidy."

49

"So," says David, turning away from his window, "do you wanna lay bets?"

She brushes a stray hair from the curve of her cheek (a legacy of her father's, these hateful round cheeks of hers, at least according to pictures). "No. I don't want to bet."

"Come on. How long before he asks either one of us how our jobs are going? Or whether we're seeing anyone? Or any expression of actual interest in something other than himself?"

"No." She slows to fifty going past a girls' private school.

"I say two hours, around dessert. And then he'll cough it out, like it hurts him."

At a red light, she taps her fingers against the steering wheel. She finds it hard to settle her breathing. She glances at herself in the rear-view mirror: she's wearing a cream silk camisole under a vintage lace blouse, below that a short, caramel wool skirt. Should she have worn something less casual? Or more? David establishes his visual stance – overtly successful – without any hint of anguish or torment. For her it's the same debate every time, and a ridiculous one because Norman would hardly notice if she came wearing a clown's baggy pants and big-foot shoes.

"Why do we do this again?"

Both hands on the wheel through the intersection. It seems predestined that he would ask this question – she's been wondering herself – but she hates that he expects her to answer it. He could figure it out if he wanted to, use his cunning junior economist's mind to find the trends and the leading indicators. But since she started the routine – a single visit two months after Gillian's death; it wasn't supposed to transmute into custom – it's her justification that's required. She sighs to buy herself time.

She knows what her answer will be: Because Mom loved him. Which contains all these things: a sense of loyalty to her; an assumption, a hope, that she would want them to maintain this connection; a worry that her mother's presence in her own home is being obscured by Norman's smells, his ashes and skin dust taking over every surface; a fear that losing contact with Norman would mean drifting farther from her. They don't care, particularly, that she left the house in the name of a man who never married her, who simply lived with her, off her, for the eight years before her death. What rankles is that he assumes it as his right, and seems oblivious to their annoyance.

"Because Mom loved him," she says.

He waits a moment, staring out his window. "I suppose."

Fifteen minutes to get there, through Little Korea. Through the wrought-iron Portuguese neighbourhoods, past the thickened wives hosing down their patches of sidewalk, two gallons of water to wash a gum wrapper over the curb. Through dusk, coming later here, in the sloping shoulders of the city, than it does downtown. There is no reason to think Norman would miss them if they stopped coming. What would they miss?

"You know," he says, beginning something, stopping. She waits, thinking, let this be about his job. Let him want to talk about market gains or interest rates.

"What, David?"

He breathes in and out, deliberately. "I'm not sure I want to do it any more."

"The visits."

"It's not clear to me why we bother."

A sense of dread comes over her, a powerlessness that frustrates her. The little tower of building blocks she's stacked up is weaving in the air. She wills away the idiotic tears gathering in her eyes.

"You're saying, 'Because Mom loved him.'"

"Yes, that's right." Someone's horn blares. Is she driving too slowly?

"But *we* don't love him."

It's hard to hear this; she wants David to have love, to forgive easily, to be generous, though Norman feeds off generosity, which makes it a challenge. And she's not sure it's true, that they don't love him. Maybe they fear loving him, fear investing with such slim hope of returns. But mainly what David says is hard to hear because it takes so much effort to keep up the connection, and she doesn't want to do it alone.

"And he sure as hell doesn't love us."

If this is so, then all the wrong things are possible. It is possible to live with someone through six formative years and make no impression, sink no hooks in, have no more bearing on his life than the men who sweep the streets at midnight. And that can't be right. So he gives cheap, ill-considered presents at Christmas, garage-sale tchotchkes and bargain-bin stationery. So what? She refuses to extrapolate. So he doesn't call and doesn't ask, or sometimes does but never seems to hear the answer. You can't read so much into so little. She wants David to believe that you can have expectations and have them met, that someone who had influence on your life should in turn be influenced. A man cannot act as a parent without care. A child must make an impression.

"I think, David," she says, brittle, "this is a really bad way to begin the evening. You know?"

Along Dundas, over the tracks, then just as the road swings away north, she finds the corner that always gives her trouble, a doubling back and down, into Sorauren, as if the two roads were never meant to be joined but someone forced the issue. "I think," she says, aware of the flaking in her own voice, "it would just be miserable if you stopped coming."

He leans towards her with a theatrical brow. "Now, Amy," he says, full of Normanesque gusto, "how's that job of yours going?" And when she pulls up in front of the house, she's giggling with relief.

Twenty minutes later, having gone to the house – still the prettiest Victorian semi in a neighbourhood that David chooses to describe as "torpid" and "what parts of Detroit must be like," though he has never been – having knocked on the ornate wood-and-etched-glass front door, which Gillian found behind a leaned stack of old doors at a flea market north of the city on Highway 7 and painstakingly refinished, having knocked and heard no answer and then sat in the car for twenty minutes, David slaps his thighs with both hands. "Maybe I'll take a walk." She looks at him. "Just around the block. I won't leave you here."

Fine, she thinks. "Fine."

"Five minutes."

She waves him away. Go.

"Well, where the hell is he?"

"It's all right, David. Take your walk. I'll stay here." It's already difficult enough; better that he not start the evening feeling cooped up and frustrated.

He searches for the handle, finds it, and swings the car door out across the sidewalk, but before he gets out the two of them hear a hollow croak, the sound of a screen door opening, and then a rattly slam, from one of the nearby houses. They twist in their seats towards the sound and see a muscular, swarthy man in jeans and a fringed leather coat, with a swept-back mane of black hair, storm out of the turquoise-painted porch and down the steps of the house directly across the street. He is stuffed with rage, clenched and seething. Passing by the eaves spout that dangles from the roof, he discovers a metal garbage can, grabs the warped lid and smashes it like a cymbal against the side of the porch. Even he seems shocked by the sound, and he drops the lid with another cymbal crash and pounds off down Sorauren, towards Queen. David and Amy watch him go.

"Well," she says, after a moment.

"Those garbage-can lids need a good ass-kicking sometimes."

"Absolutely."

The two of them sit quietly for a moment, and then without a word, David reaches out and pulls the car door shut. It takes a little while longer before Amy can feel herself breathe.

❀

It's another ten minutes before Norman strides up the sidewalk, carrying a small plastic bag in one hand and a cigarette in the other. He walks past Amy's car without noticing it and starts up the porch steps, and only the sound of two closing car doors makes him turn.

"Oh," he says, distractedly, "you're here."

He flicks the cigarette over the side of the porch and fishes for his keys, as Amy and David share a look.

"Was there any problem, Norman?" says Amy, pulling down the edges of her lace top.

"No, why?"

"You're, like, an hour late," says David.

"Actually" – Amy lifts a hand as if directing trouble somewhere else – "it's not quite forty-five minutes. But we were wondering if we should start worrying."

"Oh, no," he says. "No need to worry." He fumbles his keys twice, then opens the door and steps over the threshold. "Come in, come in."

After he switches on the hall light, Amy hands him a bottle of wine. "Ah." He examines the label. "*Rosso Conero,*" he says, "*Imbottigliato da La Vite,*" pronouncing the Italian with a flourish of rolled *r*'s and trapeze-act inflection. "Yes, that will be fine."

Amy follows as he walks into the kitchen and flicks a dead light switch. "Oh yes," he says wearily. He sets the wine on the counter, along with the plastic bag, which he slowly empties of its contents: a small cellophane package of white mushrooms, a garlic bulb, three dusty baking potatoes, and a large sirloin steak bearing a manager's sale sticker.

"Have you had that wine before, Norman?" David says this loudly from the hall, where he appears to be rooted, his voice already carrying the agitated edge to which Norman invariably reacts with befuddlement.

"Ah, no," says Norman, smiling awkwardly. "But I'm looking forward to it."

He opens the fridge door and bends to see inside, pulls out an aged zucchini and inspects it, then moves on to the cupboards, opening and closing doors. When he has opened and examined every space, he finally leans forward with his palms pressed against the counter and cocks his head at an angle, as if there's something not quite right.

Amy scans the room. "Is there no other light in here, Norman?"

Still in the hall, David catches her eye and makes a "drinking" gesture, then taps a finger to his nose.

"Is anything wrong?" she says.

"Well, I've had kind of a crazy day, to be honest." Norman opens the fridge door once more. "And I don't seem to have enough vegetables. I remember now that was something I should have bought."

As he stares into the white-lit interior, Norman grips and regrips the handle of the fridge door, like a weightlifter priming for the clean and jerk, appreciating the metal sternness of it. Behind him, Amy moves towards the window of the kitchen door that frames what was once her mother's garden, where she grew spinach and carrots and, on occasion, peas.

"It doesn't matter," she says.

"Certainly it does." He lets the refrigerator door carry his hand as it shuts.

"David doesn't like vegetables anyway, do you?" She lifts eyebrows at her brother just now edging into the kitchen. He shrugs.

"No, we should have vegetables." Norman purses his mouth and stares off dolefully. Then he brightens. "I know, I'll go next door and borrow some."

"Oh no, Norman."

"Of course."

David's expression turns skeptical. "It's not really something people do, is it?"

"Well, it's the sort of thing *I* do," Norman chuckles, already halfway out the front door. "You know me."

The door closes behind him. "Yup," says David with the same lilt, "we know you." He goes to the living room and kneels on the couch to peer out through the half-curtained window. From this vantage he begins to call out a running commentary.

"He's going to the house on the left, with the white porch."

Amy, from the kitchen, searching for light bulbs: "I don't care, David."

"He's up the steps. He's ringing the bell. He's waiting. Now he's feeling for his cigarettes. What has he done with his cigarettes?"

"They're here on the counter." She has found a sixty-watt, deep in a drawer, and now pulls a chair into the middle of the room.

"He's waiting, waiting. There's no answer at the first house. They're either not home, or they know him too well." Silence for a moment. "Still nothing."

"We have light," Amy says.

"All right, he's giving up on the first house. He's down the steps. Now, he's crossing the street."

She comes into the living room with her arms folded. "Don't watch, David. It's not polite."

David turns towards her. "No, I think he wants us to watch. He's being him." He turns back. "Oh shit, he's going to that house on the other side of the street, the one the garbage-can crasher came out of."

"Oh, God. Do you think he's come back yet?"

"He's at the door. He's ringing the bell!"

◈

On the steps leading to the turquoise enclosed porch, Norman can feel the gin vacating his head, leaving a residue of sensation, a scraped and hollow feeling behind his eyes. He has already put from his mind most of what occurred at his sister's apartment; the sting of her refusal to lend him money remains, but not the reason it happened. Were he forced to think about it, he'd conclude it was just her being her obdurate, judgemental self, a product of her advancing age, no doubt, and this fatigue situation, which he only half believes. However, vegetables, and not Margaret, are his immediate concern, and so he has the comfort of ignoring the fact of Margaret entirely. He is about to ring the doorbell a second time when he hears a click and a rustling, sees a shape moving through the darkened porch towards the screen door, and presses a neighbourly smile into his face.

The shape hesitates for a moment, inside the porch, then comes forward and reveals itself in the screened street-lamp light, a small woman, about five-foot-three, in her mid-thirties, with dark, springy hair – Mediterranean hair, Norman decides – tied back, away from the fine features of her face, its smooth olive skin, precise nose and jaw framing a wide, sculpted mouth, and deeply brown, deeply worried eyes. She pulls a black cardigan tight around her, searches Norman and his smile and the street, up and down, with these eyes, before pushing on the screen door, which sings as it opens.

"I'm sorry to trouble you but –"

"He has done something?"

Norman is briefly marooned. His focus, to this moment, has been vegetables, his need for them, his anticipation of finding them. Now comes this sudden, unexpected question, faintly accented and unfathomable save for the fact that it has nothing to do with vegetables.

He can only shake his head.

The woman frowns at him. "You are not here about my husband?"

"No, no, I'm, I'm a neighbour. I live just there –" Norman points across the street.

"What do you want?" The sharpness of her voice further unsettles him. She seems about to pull the door shut and he has an impulse, which he barely resists, to put his hand out and hold it open. She is not giving him the time to present his need – that is, himself – properly.

"Vegetables!" he blurts, regretting it instantly.

Her head snaps back and she moves to pull the door shut.

"Please." Norman grins desperately. He motions with an open hand to his house. "My wife's children" – easier to say "wife" just now, though he hates to mislead – "my common-law wife, who's dead, actually, her children" – he sees her growing more concerned – "they've come for dinner, you see. Dinner." She flicks a glance once more down the street. "But the trouble is, I have no vegetables." He holds his empty palms out for her inspection, the gesture of a man bereft of produce. "I went shopping, but I forgot to get vegetables, which was silly, I admit" – he gives his head a wry shake, touches his forehead, smiles: *See?* he is saying, *I am charmingly addled, not dangerous* – "and now, to be perfectly honest, I'm . . . in a bit of a spot."

He stops there, looking up at her for some sign of sympathy or forgiveness, and What Will Come Next means more to him than is possible to imagine. Norman sometimes, and especially when brandy or, in this case, gin has swelled his artist's thalamus, takes these encounters, the transactions of strangers, to be signifiers of the health of the universe. If she is a woman of the world, some part of him thinks, and if the world in its balance is just and kind, she will understand him. If she is a woman who meets life openly, is made ready by some sweet music of the spheres to see the possibility of goodness in all things – even a strange man arriving at her door asking for vegetables – she will give him what he needs. But her face betrays nothing, except for a slight crease that transits her forehead.

"I'm Norman Bray," he says, holding out a hand to shake hers and then, when she keeps her arms wrapped tight around her, using it to motion across the street. "I've lived there quite a while, actually. A number of years." He pauses, searching her dark eyes, and then – this is his final gambit – he tunes his voice to a noble melancholy. "Please understand that I am trying simply to give these children a good meal. I have failed in my preparations, and I ask for your help. Asparagus would be too much to hope for, but some spinach, broccoli perhaps, even frozen peas would do." He hopes the light from the street lamp is catching the moisture in his eyes.

The small, finely etched woman looks far down the street behind him and puts the heel of a hand to the tight hair above her ear. Then her expression softens slightly. She lifts a finger at him – "You will stay here" – and holds it there until he nods his confirmation. Then, "Let me see."

She disappears into the house and returns a moment later holding a used plastic bag, which she opens for him. "I meant to go shopping tomorrow. I have only these." Inside the bag is a small mound of pale yellow beans. She sighs at the meagre offering. "You may have them."

Norman receives the bag from her narrow hand. "Ah," he says expansively. "The children will be very appreciative."

"And you?"

"Oh," he hesitates. "Yes, of course, I . . . as well."

She folds her arms around herself again and nods towards the bag. "You should cut off the ends and boil them for –"

Norman lifts a hand. "It's all right" he says, leaving. "I cook."

❧

Out of its Styrofoam tray, stripped of its plastic wrap, Norman's slab of reward meat shows what appears to be a green bruise that was conveniently hidden by the sale sticker.

"Don't mind that," he says as Amy and David lean in for a closer look. "That just means it's well aged."

"It's the colour of mucus," says David.

Norman lofts an eyebrow. "I promise you that spot will be more tender than all the rest. True steak lovers would fight over that part. I'm happy you don't want it. I couldn't be more happy." The potatoes are baking. The mushrooms and onions are sizzling in the pan. Norman sprinkles salt and pepper on the meat (a little extra on the offending patch), and plops it in foaming butter. While it fries, he rummages in a drawer for the corkscrew, finding it amongst a clutter of stained, bent spatulas,

dull knives, fondue skewers, and old corks. He hands it sideways to David.

"Would you do the honours?"

As he stands over the steak, prodding it now and again with
his fork, Norman hums a tune.

"What's that from?" says Amy.

He glances sideways at her. "You don't know 'To Dream the
Impossible Dream'?"

She shrugs.

"*Man of La Mancha*," intones Norman. He lifts his fork
and thrusts it towards her, sabre-like, as he arcs his left arm
high over his head, his eyes glinting. "'Beware the Great
Enchanter, Sancho,'" he booms. "'For his thoughts are cold
and his spirit shrivelled. He has eyes like little machines, and
where he walks the earth is blighted. But one day I shall meet
him face to face. And on that day . . . !'" He lunges and sticks
the fork lightly into Amy's lacy arm.

"That's cute," she says.

"I did it first in 1986, at the Prairie Theatre," says Norman,
his attention once more on the steak. "Pete Trainer was the artistic director. Flagrantly gay. For many years he lusted after me,
and when he realized I'd never succumb, he stopped inviting
me back." He lifts his hands beseechingly to the sky and sighs.

David selects three wineglasses from the cupboard. "That
was the reason, was it?"

"My Dulcinea that year was Rosie Fallingcourt," Norman
continues. "Too stiff-limbed for the role, really, but she possessed a lovely soprano." He flips the steak and adds to the pan
a slice of butter that sounds to him, as it slides and foams,
vaguely like applause. "To my mind, Sophia Loren, who played

Dulcinea in the movie version, was closer to perfection. Full in the chest, and she had a slightly lascivious quality."

"Lascivious?" says Amy. "Sophia Loren?"

"Well, she was playing a whore!"

Amy's eyes widen at him.

"I do know what I'm talking about, you know." He stabs at the meat. "I was in the damn play."

"Here, Norman." David holds out a glass of wine. "Have some more to drink."

Norman accepts the glass dejectedly and sips, focusing the whole time on the pan in front of him. "That's nice," he says, grudgingly. "Peter O'Toole as Cervantes and Quixote, of course, I could not abide. He lacked Cervantes's necessary masculinity." He lifts the steak out of the pan onto a large plate. "Amy, would you set out the cutlery please?" He takes a knife and slices the steak, brown and glittery with butter and fat, into three sections, which he deposits onto plates. "His personality was too thin, O'Toole. He was too effete." He spoons out helpings of steaming yellow beans. "A musical lead like *La Mancha* . . . well, any of them, *Guys and Dolls*, *Camelot*. Good God, Richard Harris." He shakes his head and emits an appalled throat-clearing sound. "It demands something most movie actors don't have." He turns to Amy. "Do you know what that is?"

She shakes her head mutely.

"It's *balls*." He says it deliciously, cradling the word in the low sling of his voice.

"Weren't you in another production of *La Mancha*?" says David.

"Hmmm?" Norman bends to open the oven and transfers three potatoes to their plates.

"Right around when Mom was killed?"

"Oh," says Norman, carrying his plate into the living room. "I'll have to think about that."

❦

They array themselves around the oak dining table – a thing of panels and sections inserted and overlapping each other like playing cards – that Gillian discovered at a country auction and refinished over a summer in a stain so densely brown it was, and is, almost black. They eat quietly for a while. But then as Norman carves into his sirloin, pulls each slice through a puddle of meat juices, and reminisces aloud about the famous steak dinner he enjoyed as a twenty-two-year-old during a New Stages tour stopover in Lethbridge, Alberta – "Two inches thick, I swear to God. What is that, seven, eight centimetres?" – Amy sees David watching her. He eyes her steadily, mildly, as he chews, and so she chews back at him defiantly. *What?* she asks, with her eyes and her working jaw. *What are you saying to me?* And it irks her that he smiles slightly, as if he's proud of himself, as if he's convinced that she already knows.

Norman segues from his beef recollections into a familiar story about a group of Calgary city councillors who tried to shut down a 1971 production of *Hair* because of its nudity. The words "I have found Albertans bizarrely conservative in other areas, however" mark the precise point of transition.

Amy slices her wax beans into thumb-long exemplars of the French style, the diagonal cuts perfectly aligned. She watches David push the debris from his buttered potato into a dike against a tide of rare steak juices. After a minute of "not for

64

a second" and "can you believe" and "prudes, every one of them," David brings a paper napkin to the corner of his smirk, sips at his wine, turns his head to Norman for the first time since his monologue began, and speaks over top of him, "Do you ever think about Mom?"

Norman hears the question, Amy can tell, because his face registers a distraction, as if a car horn had just blown. But as usual the Calgary *Hair* story has lifted him into a high realm of pique, and his momentum is too strong to be stopped.

"– they actually walked in, *in the middle of the second act*, and started heckling the performance. Shouting things out" – he cups his hands around his mouth and bellows across the table – " 'Shame! Shame!' "

When Norman reaches for his wineglass to take a restorative sip, David waits out the pause. Amy can't help but acknowledge and admire his restraint: he holds off until Norman's mouth, clear of wine, looks about to open, and then jumps in. His timing is athletic.

"Norman?"

"And so as a gr–" Norman blinks and hesitates. He turns to David, as if Gillian's son might also be wondering where the distraction is coming from. But David only smiles at him politely.

"Uh," Norman continues, "so as a group, we decided to do something that – well, it was perfect. Really marvellous. I don't know who came up with the idea. Might have been me. Was it? Could have been Simone Gantry. But no, it's really more something that I would think up. Anyway. What we did" – in his delight, the corners of Norman's mouth coil up like pill bugs, and he suppresses a giggle – "we –"

"Norman."

"*What?*" He slams both hands onto the table so that all the plates and cutlery jump and land with a clatter, the wineglasses wobble and rest. "What the hell is going on here? I'm trying to tell a fucking story!"

"I was trying to ask you a question." David's voice is calm; he's smiling. But the quality of his smile suggests some sharper intent.

"You can wait, can't you? I'm in the middle of a goddamn story."

Calmly: "We've heard it."

"What?"

Amy fork-handles pale yellow parallelograms across her plate. No doubt she could stop this. No doubt she should.

"We've heard the story. Maybe five times already. Amy will vouch for this. Is it five, Amy?"

Amy says nothing, just looks at him.

"Anyway, we've heard it. You mooned the politicians. Right? Everybody clapped."

"Cheered." Norman's eyes are sharp, under eyebrows arched like scythes. "They fucking cheered. Split the goddamn ceiling."

"Right, sorry. But the question I asked – and I've asked it before, by the way; I asked it last Christmas, and I asked it the first anniversary of Mom's accident, and you have yet to hear it. You have *yet* to hear it. Or if you have, you haven't bothered to respond."

Norman deep-breathes like a sumo champion and looks down at his plate.

"So that's three times, Norman, that I've asked you this question, and I have yet to get an answer." David leans forward, his elbows on the table between Norman and Amy, his hands clasped into a ball. "Can you answer me, Norman? Do you ever think about Mom?"

Norman turns his wineglass slowly by the stem and clears his throat as a formal prelude to what he's going to say. He winches his jaw tight. "Let me tell you about my day," he begins, his voice thick with aggrievement. David sighs and tips back his head and Norman lifts his voice another notch in intensity. "It started with a woman I didn't know, a waitress, lashing out at me for no reason. Then, at the taping today, I was accused of sabotaging the production by deliberately ignoring my call time, which was an absolute lie."

Amy eyes David, whose face is turning red. She lifts a small hand. "Norman."

"Let me finish. Then they stripped me of the role I had originated and developed for two years. Stripped me of it!"

"For missing your call time?"

"I've no idea. It's possible. It's not Robert's show any more. The whole thing is in the hands of some cable-channel executive child who has no idea what it is to put your fucking heart on the line."

David is tapping the knuckles of one hand firmly against the table, and each rap makes Amy feel more like a sparrow trapped inside a cathedral bell. "But I think what David –"

"*Then*," roars Norman, "when I went to get some money to buy tonight's dinner, my bank locked its doors and refused to serve me. Absolutely refused! Out of what I can only assume is sheer malice, because there were tellers there. I *saw* them. And finally" – he's bellowing now, as if he's trying to reach the back row, making their ears actually ring – "in my own sister's apartment, some hulking lunatic I'd never met before tried to assault me with *a jar full of beet spread*!"

David has stopped his rapping; he and Amy stare at Norman in wonderment.

"And so, David, yes" – Norman's voice mellows to an oak-barrel baritone – "today was a day, one of many, that I did think of Gillian." He lifts his face towards the spot on the wall, above the buffet, where there used to be a picture of a smooth-skinned, smiling, forty-seven-year-old Gillian, as if his plan is to speak in reference to the image of Gillian to give the moment the weight it deserves. But the picture isn't hanging above the buffet, hasn't for two years now, not since an Alberta relative claimed it. Norman, it's clear, doesn't remember this, and with a glimmer of alarm he slides his gaze around from one wall to the next, until he tightens his mouth and carries on as if nothing were amiss, his voice collapsing into a hoarse whisper and his eyes beginning to glisten. "She understood me, you see. She understood who I was." Then, as though stabbed clean through by their doubt, he lowers and narrows his gaze towards his wineglass, which he lifts and empties with the air of a man who knows he has done the moment justice.

David stirs a last fork-speared morsel of beef through the coagulation on his plate, his face bearing a complex fusion of anger, frustration, and appalled gratification. Norman reaches out to heft the wine bottle and pours the last of it into his glass.

"I'll take the dishes in," says Amy, rising.

David starts, "You don't –"

"Thank you, sweetheart," says Norman gravely. He offers up his plate with his knife and fork already tucked in. "There's soap under the sink."

David stands as Amy stacks his plate on top of Norman's and carries them both into the kitchen. "I'll help too," he says.

What to make of any of it? She sets the dishes down next to a couple of envelopes on the kitchen table, the feeling gaining on her of being outside the emotional loop, of missing something important. She plucks a fermenting cloth out of the sink and starts the hot water as David walks in and stands in the middle of the kitchen with his hands on his hips, as if waiting for her to look at him.

He's going to scold me now, she thinks, for removing myself, for not mixing my issues into the pot. But with David's anger and Norman's anguish already crowded in, where, she wonders, is the space for my puny anxieties and doubts? Still, he wants his chagrin officially noted, he wants her to see him acting peevish, so she obeys, looks up at him with her hands in dishwater, and sees the big, dark, angry eyes.

"Do you believe that performance?" he says, clench-jawed.

"Shhh," she scolds him, smiling. This isn't about her at all.

"I mean, my God." He grabs a cloth and starts drying glasses. "How did she fall for him? That's what I wonder. How did she buy any of it?"

She whispers, "I don't think he was this bad then. I think he's gotten worse."

David shakes his head. He's silent for a moment. "No," he finally says, "it's always been show."

Amy sets a fistful of wet cutlery in the rack. "Maybe for her it was like going to the movies. Maybe she suspended her disbelief." She reaches out with sudsy hands for the plates and,

lifting away, pulls one of the envelopes off the table. It pirou-
ettes to the floor. David picks it up.

⊸●⊷

In the dining room, Norman revives his spirits by savouring the
last of the wine. It's a moment that never fails to give him
special pleasure, even when he's downing the final mouthful of
a nine-dollar bottle of Italian red. At this moment, as he fingers
the stem and swirls the dregs in the bowl, if he were asked,
"Norman, you look contented; what are you thinking about?"
he would say the following: "I am thinking about dedication to
craft, how it is underappreciated, except" – here he would raise
a finger – "except by those of us who are equally dedicated.
Even a small sip of wine can, I say *can*, reflect this love and
commitment, in the same way that a single moment in a performance can reflect the true artist's devotion. It's not a stretch
to say that, as I have dedicated my life to creating beautiful
moments, this winemaker has dedicated himself to creating
beautiful sips." And the listener would nod, satisfied, because
Norman would be satisfied. In this reflective mood, he hums . . .

> *I am I, Don Quixote, Lord of La Mancha,*
> *My destiny calls and I go!*

Perhaps he would be even more eloquent, more expressive;
he would share with the listener examples of those occasions
where his dedication to craft became especially important, as in
those very difficult, very challenging days during rehearsals for
*Man of La Mancha* at the Beverly Dinner Theatre. My God,
what he was up against there. He'd never trouble Amy or David

about it, of course, but any casual observer would be amazed at how he endured.

He half sings, the words forming approximately from the tune, like shapes in cigarette smoke . . .

*And the wild winds of fortune shall carry me onward*
*Oh whithersoever they blow*

He wishes Amy had brought a second bottle of wine. Maybe she did and didn't tell him. Perhaps he will ask her. He feels . . . expansive.

*Whithersoever they blow*

Boom it out. Let them hear it. Oh, here's Amy now.

*Onward to glory I go!*

Norman hammers the table for a crescendo effect – *du-du-du-dum!* – and smiles heroically at Amy standing at the entrance to the dining room. David, beside her, holds an envelope in his hand.

"Norman, what's this?"

Norman focuses on the envelope David is holding out towards him, blinks, then turns to Amy. "Amy, dear, did you happen to have any more wine in the car, I was wondering?"

"Sorry, no."

David comes forward stiffly and lays the envelope on the table in front of him. "This is from Mom's bank, Norman. Do you know what it is?"

The envelope is a rotted fish laid in his lap. Norman registers it with distaste.

"I assume it's a flyer of some sort. A credit-card application. I was going to throw it away because, as you know, I don't believe in credit cards."

"No, it's an official foreclosure notice. You can tell by these markings. It's supposed to scare you. Open it up."

When Norman hesitates, David does it himself, forcing his finger through the envelope, busting it open. He lays the envelope aside and opens the letter, glancing at it – with a look back at Amy – before handing it to Norman.

"Read it."

This tone of David's, this presumptuous, authoritarian director's tone, makes Norman bristle, but he takes the letter nonetheless. It's signed by Howard Cantor, director of personal-loan management:

Dear Mr. Norman Bray,
It has come to our attention . . .

Norman stops reading and tries to conjure up the sort of voice a loan-management director would use. He realizes he has no foundation for it; he has never heard a loan-management director speak, nor any bank employee other than a teller, for that matter. It would be austere though, Norman is sure, devoid of passion, suggestive of a life shadowed from the warm light of art. "It has come to our attention," he says out loud, thinly, austerely. That sounds right. Already he pities this man. He reads out loud:

Dear Mr Norman Bray,

It has come to our attention that the mortgage account for your home at 102 Sorauren Ave. has fallen dramatically into arrears. . . .

Norman stops reading out loud and refocuses his eyes. He continues silently.

Though we have attempted to pursue this matter with you in order to seek a solution, we have not received any reply to the number of notices we have sent to this address. The account is now in default by the sum of $7,476. . . .

Norman reaches reflexively for his wineglass and, finding it empty, sets it back down carefully.

As a result, it becomes my unfortunate duty to begin the process whereby this bank will legally take possession of the property at 102 Sorauren Ave. exactly three months from the date given above. I regret that we have been forced to take this action. Should you have any questions, you may of course contact me at any time.

Sincerely,
Howard Cantor
Director, Personal Loan Management

Norman again reaches out for his wineglass and finds it, again, empty. He tries to think of something to do. Something decisive.

He decides not to believe it. The world of commerce is so foreign and suspicious to him that any statement it delivers is as close to a lie as any other. Nothing it tells him can alter the truth he knows – the house is his. He sees something in David's eyes he doesn't like, a squinty condescension.

"I'm sure it can all be straightened out," he says, laying the letter on the table.

David picks it up and scans it, then shakes his head slowly. "It's not the kind of thing you straighten out, Norman."

"What happened, Norman?" Amy says. "What's going on?"

"No, the question is, what's he going to do?"

Norman notices that his fingers are prickly. So are his legs. He feels strangely cool around his chest and throat. He picks up the letter again, finds the word "default," and wonders at it. "By default" is a phrase he understands, but "in default" doesn't sound right. Can default be a location, a state? Norman decides he objects to this use of the word. Gillian would no doubt agree. She would at least take his point.

The two young people are standing over him like police constables, David in his hard shirt and tie, as if dinner were a business meeting, Amy in some sort of vaguely religious-looking lace tunic. "It's an obvious error. Gillian left the house to me. I own this house. I *earned* this house."

David makes a sound halfway between a cough and a bark of laughter.

"David," warns Amy, the lace shuddering rhythmically above her breast.

"In what way earned?" says David, not looking at her, looking at Norman.

Norman narrows his eyes at the long, dark face, the sharp chin and bony cheeks, and something sinister occurs to him. It's possible, perhaps even probable, that David is trying to take his house away from him. Not Amy; Amy is not the sort. But David is an economist, one of the moneyists, living a life of ledger. It is not at all unlikely that he could be in league with bankers to strip him of what's rightly his. He stares potently at David.

"I earned her love."

꧁꧂

Norman wakes in the dark and sees a red glow racing across his bedroom ceiling. It flows down the wall and disappears beyond his feet, chased by another, and another, a constant repetitive red flash that could be the light of a fire truck, an ambulance. He lifts off his covers and swings his feet down onto the bedroom's cold wooden floor, feeling caught in the middle of a crisis, a world of emergency. The flash beats on him like a headache. His bedside clock says 3:36. Still half-asleep, he jerks himself upright and plods unsteadily, naked, to his window and sees a police cruiser parked on the sidewalk across the street, two wheels up on the concrete, nudging the grass. He lifts the window as much as he can and bends towards the three-inch gap as two blue-shirted police officers, a man and a woman, emerge from the front door of the house directly across from his. For a moment, in his slow-dispersing fog, Norman imagines they are David and Amy, come back to arrest him for his great crime of ignoring a bank.

Then, no, he sees that these are real police officers, and they have come for someone or something in the house with the boxy turquoise porch. The house of the dark-eyed woman who gave him beans. Norman bends forward, leans his elbows on his knees, and hears the female officer speak over the cruiser's idling engine. "We should get keys to this place," she says.

He shivers slightly in the November chill and walks back to bed, avoiding the cold heads of the nails hammered into the floor boards. Now there, there was a crime. Someone, years ago, ramming a hundred nails into good wood because, why? They couldn't bear to hear the floor squeak? Things should be left as they are, damn it. Things should just be allowed to be.

Norman slides back into bed, curls up, and pulls the sheet and the quilt over his shoulder. In a moment, the red flashing light vanishes and the room falls back into darkness. Every emergency is, by its nature, temporary.

# ACT II

Sunlight is colder at 8:30 in the morning.

Norman notes this fact noncommittally as he rises according to his clock radio's command (a half-hour spent, after the late TV news, familiarizing himself with its controls: What is *this* button for? What if I turn this knob *that* way? Ah-hah!) He moves slowly, with ragged determination, as if his environment at this early hour might present unfamiliar dangers. He makes himself a full pot of coffee, putting one scoop more than he normally does in the small metal basket to ensure his alertness, without acknowledging to himself what he needs to be alert for. He pushes two halves of a frozen English muffin into the toaster and when they pop, crisp and browned, he paves them liberally with peanut butter and spreads on dollops of the currant jam he has had in his cupboard for almost a year because he has been saving it for an appropriate time.

In the bathroom he keeps his attention similarly narrow. When he showers, he ignores the greying soap film coating the tiles, the black mould adding contrast and definition to the corners of the tub, the brown rust stain running up the middle, between his feet. He concentrates instead on the sensations of soap and skin. Rinsed, he stands, head bowed, and lets the water sting the back of his neck, focusing on this small discomfort and imagining that he must have some ideational link with the penitent Filipinos he once saw on television beating their backs bloody with sticks. Shaving, he's careful to pull tight the fleshy skin under his chin and razors away the white foam in even strokes. Swiping on deodorant, he barely registers the acrid note underlying the scent of the no-name brand and, so far as he does, considers it an intentional element in the fragrance and actually pleasant.

It's as he dresses that Norman first begins to think of what lies ahead. After the briefest internal debate, standing in sock feet before the open door of his closet, he settles on Commandingly Confident as the impression he will seek to make and chooses slimming black trousers, a cream shirt frayed only slightly at the collar, and a tweed sportcoat that Gillian gave him for his forty-eighth birthday, which still fits remarkably well if he keeps it unbuttoned. He forgoes a tie because it would be too great a concession to a banker's expectations.

Fully clothed, armoured in choices, he mentally rehearses the coming encounter, imagines Cantor standing before him: a tall, thin man, humourless, attentive to detail and convention, but *persuadable*. He shakes the man's hand, tells him firmly that what he is doing, this foreclosure business, is wrong, and that it must be put right. He applies the full force of his evident atypicality – he is an artist; there must be allowances, means of compromise – and gradually pushes Cantor, though reluctant and constrained by custom at first, towards an appropriate resolution.

In his kitchen, lit meekly by the back door's square window through which Gillian, cup in hand, would look out onto her small garden and sigh, Norman checks the letter for the bank's address, then slips it into his breast pocket and unfolds a crackling transit-system map to determine his best route. When he lights a cigarette, he finds his hands are shaking and thinks, it's the coffee. He switches on the small black radio that sits on the table and then, finding the noise and chatter of it unsettling, turns it off. In the rising silence he sips his strong coffee, sucks on his cigarette. Looking around he thinks, this is a good, serviceable kitchen. I want nothing more than this.

On the Queen streetcar, eastbound, Norman recites to himself the monologue he will use, editing it, tweaking it, and reciting it again in each new form. He likes its emerging shape; it's a compelling speech, both gracious and forceful. He can see Howard Cantor in his mind's eye and knows, despite the disparity of their backgrounds, that he will convince the man to do the best thing. Words, thinks Norman. Artfully employed words will save him. The closing is the trickiest part. "Mr. Cantor," says Norman softly, aloud, "you cannot let yourself be bullied by routine assumptions. You cannot let yourself be ruled by rules." (That's good.) "Money, Howard, does not make right!" (No, that's awkward. But use the first name; nail him with it.) "Money, Howard . . ." (Is what? What is money?) "Money, Howard, can be a tool, but it shouldn't be your boss." (He should use "ruler," Norman thinks, but he's used "ruled" and "rules" already. A third time would sound idiotic.) "Money, Howard, can be a tool. Don't let it be your . . . master." That's it. Howard Cantor will be left spongy and speechless.

"Were you speaking to me?"

Norman, startled, turns in his seat to find a small Ethiopian woman sitting next to him, holding a sleeping child wrapped in a red-and-pumpkin tibeb against her chest, her frail face regarding him with something approaching fear.

"No, I'm sorry." Caught by this woman's eyes, Norman feels inexplicably shy. He finds himself unable to look at her, and turns away to the window at his shoulder.

"The streetcar is very slow," the woman says, hugging her bundle.

"Yes. Yes it is." Norman rubs his knees and watches the storefronts crawl past, the buildings that house them seeming to compress, to grow denser, like spectators along a parade route, as the streetcar whines towards downtown. There are seventy stages in the city and forty-seven productions mid-run, at least according to the reports in his Equity newsletter. Norman could not, if you asked him, name more than two of the directors involved. He has not performed in a union production for twelve years, not been to an audition for twenty-three.

He turns back to the woman, searching for something to say, and she helps him by offering, "I am taking my son to the doctor."

"Oh," says Norman, his mind working. "The doctor. Yes." He nods, for lack of a follow-up, and then some small thing clicks. His eyes light up. "I have to take my sister to the doctor soon." He shakes his head at the woman. "Not this morning, though. I managed to avoid that." As the streetcar slows to a stop, Norman waits through the driver's repeated clanging of the bell, then continues, "This morning I have to talk to a banker." He sighs and shakes his head slightly. "You can imagine" – a moment of eye contact, full of shared knowing –

"it's not a thing I would *choose* to do. But there are times when circumstance forces the issue." The woman stares back at him, and Norman feels he has made a connection.

A moment later, as the streetcar sways through an intersection, and physics press the woman lightly against Norman, she says, "Would you pull the cord for me, please?" And when he has done so and she has grasped hold of the metal pole with one hand and pulled herself upright, she indicates her bundle.

"My son has a hole in his heart."

"Ah," says Norman, startled. He squints, as if pained by glare from the window, and for a flickering second he regrets having spoken to the woman. But then he sees, it becomes clear to him, that this circumstance is meant to be enriching. The woman could have shared her burden with anyone on the streetcar, and she chose him. As the doors open to a view of the Osgoode subway entrance he feels the need to offer some sort of response. "Thank you," is what he finally says. But the woman has already descended the metal steps, the doors are closing, and she doesn't hear. The streetcar whines aggressively as it pulls away from the stop, and through the windows Norman watches her make her way down the steps to the subway that will take her and her bundle north, to a hospital that fixes holes in hearts.

When he himself climbs down from the streetcar, moments later, Norman still carries some of the glow from his encounter and finds himself encouraged. He attacks more heartily the task of finding the bank. Every building in this section of downtown strikes him as modular, machine-stamped, and unfit for human habitation. He thinks of them as solid. What it must do to someone, he thinks, to spend hours, days on end, compressed within these structures. He feels a brief surge of woe on behalf of the occupants.

The bank he's looking for, he discovers, is a tall white building of concrete and metal, an enormous stone milk carton. Inside, amid a geometry of counters and cubicles that momentarily overwhelms him, he spies the customer-service desk and approaches it. Behind the counter sits a young woman – really just a girl, he thinks – with dark lips and small hoop earrings, dressed in a deep-red pantsuit, straightening documents to be stapled.

"Good morning," says Norman, hitting three distinct notes with the force and clarity of a mallet-struck vibraphone. The girl's head jerks upright and her hand darts halfway to her breast. A shapely breast, he can't help noting. "I'd like to speak with Howard Cantor. Is he here?"

"Um" – she has to catch her breath – "probably." She lifts up the handset of one of two phones in front of her. "Can I say what it's about?"

"My home." That's good. Raise the moral stakes immediately.

She punches in a three-digit number. "Sorry, your name?"

He smiles neatly. An abbreviated row of teeth. "I'm Norman Bray." Twenty years ago, perhaps, under the right circumstances (a show running at a theatre nearby, for instance), hearing his name might have tweaked the frontal lobe of a young woman like this just enough to make her pause. But now she merely nods and says into the handset, "Norman Bray is here about his loan."

"Actually, no, my *home*."

She covers the mouthpiece. "I'm sorry? Your –"

"Just say my home."

"Sorry, it's your home loan, right? Howard's the loan manager."

He sighs. "Yes. Essentially."

She lifts her hand away. "Right, his loan." Her smile strains. "I'm not sure."

Just now it occurs to Norman that he might have been expected to make an appointment. What if Cantor makes him wait? That would undercut his moral authority appreciably. A banker would be just the sort to try that kind of gamesmanship. He decides not to let it happen; he will insist on being seen.

The red-suited girl hangs up and points off to her left. "He'll meet you at that counter over there."

Norman pulls himself straight. "Where?"

"That counter there. See? He's coming up right now."

Howard Cantor, to Norman's instant delight, is a diminutive man of maybe thirty-five with oval glasses, a pale-grey suit, and a crescent-shaped bald spot at the top of his forehead. Norman watches the banker advance with small, apparently anxious steps, and he can feel victory in the soles of his feet. His only task now is to strike, precisely, the demeanour of the righteously aggrieved, the Christian shackled with Roman iron. To find the perfect pitch of outrage, so that every syllable, every twitch, suggests a barely contained force that would be terrible in its wrath, should circumstance cause it to be unleashed. He waits and lets Howard Cantor approach the counter some ten paces away, lets him look out in the direction of the red-suited girl's counter, lift his chin as a greeting and call softly, "Mr. Bray?"

Norman waits one split second more (the adversary is remote, restrained by dignity), and then he lights his eyes – now, it begins – and starts forward with a firm stride. It would all be perfect, would set exactly the right tone for the proceedings, except that other bank customers, unaware of the blocking Norman has worked out for his production, continue to move about of their own accord, and one, an elderly woman in a lambswool coat, pushing a folding shopping cart, happens to venture into Norman's intended path at just the wrong moment. Norman crashes into her little pushcart, catching his shin on the top wire edge, feels a great slash of pain, and roars a loud, sharp "SHIT!"

The old woman shrinks back with a hand to her face, so startled that she begins to weep. But Norman has been through similar adversity before – he sprained his ankle in the midst of a sword-fight scene in Bracebridge in 1972 and no one, not even his fellow cast members, knew – and he summons the same fortitude now to straighten up with a grim smile and carry on, despite what is very likely a nasty gash, without any trace of a limp, indeed with no further reference to the event. He makes it to the counter and begins to speak, "Yes, I'm – ," when he notices the horrified look on Howard Cantor's face as the banker stares past him.

"Is that woman all right?"

"Oh." Norman glances back at the elderly woman just now being ministered to by the red-suited girl and two customers who'd been standing nearby, one of whom turns the toppled cart upright. "Yes. Yes, she's fine. But now, listen, I'd like –"

"You ran straight into her." The banker, his brow deeply furrowed, can't seem to move past this little mishap.

"Charlotte," he calls. "Does the woman need to sit down? You can bring her into my office."

*No, no,* Norman thinks, this isn't right. This old woman is traipsing all over my moment. But to his relief, Charlotte, who is bent to confer with the woman, straightens and waves Cantor off with a smile, and the banker's furrows subside.

"Well, that was a little drama, wasn't it?" He scratches his bald spot with a trimmed fingernail and softly whistles his relief. And then Cantor finally seems to see and acknowledge Norman standing in front of him. "Mr. Bray," he says. "Now we get a look at you." And he pauses for a moment, almost studying him. "I assume you're here because of my letter."

"That's right, I am, and what I'd –"

"Excuse me." Cantor, smiling pleasantly, holds up his hand. "I believe this is best discussed in private." He points towards an opening at the end of the counter. "Please, if you wouldn't mind, follow me."

They proceed down a corridor past a series of glass-fronted offices, each of them inhabited by a young man or woman staring intently at a computer screen, hand resting gently on a mouse as if it were the head of a pet. Norman wants to stride, stride, but Howard Cantor takes only small, measured, infuriating steps. So he stops for a moment, to let Cantor gain some distance, and as he does he looks at the inhabitants of these offices and thinks: There is no joy in their faces. One can tell they regret their choices in life.

He feels genuine pity for them.

They enter the last, nearly empty room on the right, its windowless walls devoid of ornament except for a small impressionistic painting of some sort of flower, or possibly a poisonous mushroom. Its furniture consists of a simple maple table and four square-cut wood-and-vinyl chairs. Cantor extends his hand towards one of these.

Norman, attempting to take some measure of the man from his environment, and finding it difficult, eases himself into his seat. "I see that you keep a very neat office."

Cantor sits opposite Norman and lays his hands down on the table, one flat on top of the other. His face becomes still. He gives off the scent of something woodsy-citrusy, like a decaying orange. "My office is down the hall, actually. This is just a room we use to meet with clients."

"Ah."

"There isn't even a phone."

"Ah." Norman becomes conscious of the feeling that he is floating. The room, this table, nothing seems quite firm. He has the panicky sensation of lifting away, as if he were filled with helium and had nothing to grab onto. Soon Cantor's head will be very small and he will have to shout to be heard.

"Mr. Cantor," he begins, the sound of his own voice making him feel instantly better, "Howard, actually, if that's all right."

"Yes."

"As I tried to make clear to the girl, out there, what I am here about is" – he pauses exactly – "my *home*."

"You'd like to talk about the letter."

"I'd like to talk about the *entire situation*."

"Well, that's good. That's wonderful." Cantor smiles very briefly. "It's a shame you couldn't have come in before, when it might have done some good. But fine, let me just get your file" – he rises – "and we'll discuss the details."

It would be very useful, Norman thinks, to have something to look at. Something to study intently, a book, say, or a picture of Cantor's family. To look very hard at something is to appear concrete, a man in control, marshalling his mental forces. To stare off into blank space is to appear abstract, confused, a man all but lost. Yet this room is only blank space.

When Cantor re-enters with a blue legal-sized folder, Norman is bent around, craning his neck, to study the painting on the wall behind him. He says, "I find that quite an interesting painting."

"I'm glad," says Cantor, without seeming to be glad at all. He lays the file on the table and draws his chair up to it as if it might be breakfast.

"It's a picture of a deadly mushroom."

"Is it? Oh yes." With the flat of his fingers, Cantor presses down on his crescent bald spot, or perhaps on the hair around it, then opens the file and begins to sort through its loose pages.

"Yes, you can tell from the markings. They're a sort of warning, in a sense. I find the natural world fascinating." Norman is aware that a series of points about mushrooms, or nature in general, is not precisely the direction to be taking. But seeing the blue file out of the corner of his eye has provoked another bout of weightlessness, and he is groping for any handle. "Fascinating in that poisonous things are often the most beautiful. That nature, in a sense, equates beauty with danger. Predators, for example – jaguars and tigers and that sort of thing – are quite handsome in a way." What he must do is get off the subject of dangerous beauty altogether or turn it to something tangible and relevant to the situation. "But this isn't restricted only to wildlife." Norman sees Cantor bent hard over the file, studying it intently, *marshalling his forces*. "For instance," he says faintly, "your bald spot is strangely beautiful, and yet —"

He has lost all advantage.

The banker lifts his head.

"Now, Mr. Bray," he begins.

&#x2766;

Gillian's office was once Amy's bedroom, but after her daughter moved out she claimed it as her own and made it her workspace away from the university. She would mark papers here and immerse herself in totem stacks of books, her ever-steaming cup of tea always resting nearby. When she was alive and installed in this room, Norman never entered it, largely because he was a bit player in here, a spear carrier. The stars were her students, the papers they worked on, the thoughts they struggled to articulate, and it was all he could do to get her to lift her head from their scribblings. After she was killed he piled her belongings in here: boxes of her clothes, her notebooks, the woodcut prints she enjoyed that he never took to, the piles of decade-old *Harper's* magazines she refused to throw away. He had felt cramped in this house before she was gone – too many of her things, her children's things, too little space for him. After the event, the debris of her life weighed on him even more heavily, though he could not have said why. Two months after the accident, after he had spent a fevered day relocating her remaining effects into this small room, Norman went through the house singing "If Ever I Should Leave You" at the greatest possible volume.

Now he's on the phone to Amy at work, asking for her help in cleaning everything out.

"Right away?" she says. "I have plans tonight, Norman. Can't it wait until the weekend?" She listens as he explains that he has no choice, that it's the bank. The bank is being very hard. He describes Howard Cantor's stern, almost inhuman demeanour. Mechanistic, he says. It was all he could do to stand up to him.

"There's always a bit of the world against you, isn't there?" she says. "There's always something you're up against." She can tell by his hesitation he's surprised; she's a little startled herself. Cynicism is David's territory; hers has traditionally been chronic, chaotic indecision. She types out a fast, flattering e-mail to the brand manager responsible for a spot she didn't particularly like (changing "really funny" to "kooky" before settling on "rich") as Norman works on her equally reliable sense of obligation – her mother's things; still family; how little he asks – until finally she agrees to come.

"I'll probably get there around seven," she says and hangs up, and realizes then she never asked how he was doing.

❧

The facts, as Howard Cantor reviews them with Norman, are these:

Gillian Swain bought the semi-detached house at 102 Sorauren Avenue from James and Dora Craigleaf in 1989 for $287,000. She put 15 per cent down. She lived in the house for eleven years, refinancing her mortgage twice, and renewing it at an interest rate of 8.5 per cent in 1999. After her death in a car accident in the fall of 2000 ("My sincere sympathies"), she left the house in Norman's name. As stipulated in her will, her personal retirement savings account, valued at $103,000 at the time of her death, was applied to paying the ongoing monthly property tax and mortgage instalments of $312 and $1,557 respectively. This money ran out in July of this year, and since that time the bank has been attempting to engage Norman in a discussion of how he was going to assume the monthly instalments until, after four months, and an unpaid sum of $7,476, it was determined that the mortgage for 102 Sorauren Avenue was irrevocably in default. At which point the process of voiding Norman's redemption rights for the property began.

Norman – who has been receiving these specifics through a fog of indignation – raises a hand just then, in the belief that he may be able to take control of the situation by, on some level, fathoming it. "I just want to be clear. What you are telling me is that I owe this bank $7,476. Is that correct?"

Cantor, eyes on the file, purses his lips. "I'm afraid, no, the amount you are *in default* is $7,476." With the fingertips of one hand he shifts the papers in front of him in search of some other sheet. "The figure you owe the bank, that is, the outstanding mortgage principle," he draws out the piece of paper, "is $132,849."

Cantor pauses for a moment as Norman thinks, Ah, this is what it's like to be pillaged.

"But I own the house."

Howard Cantor, for his part, seems willing to allow Norman to absorb the information at his own pace. "If you mean, Mr. Bray, that you are the current holder of the title on the property, then, yes, that's true."

"I signed something. I remember signing something that gave me the house."

"Yes, you signed a transfer of ownership. This is the document here." Cantor holds up the transfer of ownership.

"Exactly! That's my signature."

"Yes, it is."

"All right then." The facts, as Norman sees them, seem pretty clearly in his favour. Obviously he's missing something.

"You understand, of course, Mr. Bray – I mean, I don't have to explain the concept of mortgages, and mortgage payments."

"No. No."

"Because I'm happy to do so."

"No, that's fine." He has to admit that Gillian was always very adept at this sort of thing.

"You have to keep making mortgage payments, or control of the property reverts to the lending institution."

"Yes, I understand."

If only Gillian were here.

◦●◦

Amy, direct from work, wearing her crisp olive suit and her hair pinned back, looks around her former bedroom and barely registers that it was ever hers. She listens, arms crossed, as Norman explains that the tilting towers of bulging cardboard in front of her must be gone through and sorted, to see what can be thrown out or given away before the rest is moved to the basement. Out of one box at her feet she hauls up what appears to be an instrument of torture, a kind of spring-loaded sling with two black-painted wood handles linked by four long silvery coils.

"What about the bank, Norman? What did the bank say?"

Norman is distracted by the task of flipping up the flaps of boxes and looking inside. He picks up a paperback. "Oh look," he exclaims. "Here is my David Niven." He holds up Niven's autobiography for Amy to see (*The Moon's a Balloon*, observes Amy, circa 1972). He slaps his palm with it. "An excellent read."

"Norman, what did the bank say?"

He glances at her. "That's a chest exerciser. We'll keep that. Put that whole box in my bedroom."

As she bends down to pick the box up, Amy sees to her left what looks like an old metal toolbox, or something used for fishing tackle. She undoes the clasp and swings open the lid, and a thick, suety smell billows up at her. For half a moment, she sees layers of greasepaint in rows, thumb-thick tubes of reds and browns, of sky-blue, of flesh colours in deepening shades; she sees brown pencils, a metal disk of pancake powder, powder pads and sponges; she gets a glimpse of small, thin brushes, a fist-sized jar of Pond's face cream, and a loose ball of what might be hair. Amy sees all this in the moment it takes her to realize what she has opened and to close it as swiftly as she can. She stands up, away from the box, and waves a finger at it.

"You're keeping that, right?"

"Yes, yes, that stays."

From the David Niven carton Norman pulls other things of apparent interest and provides a running commentary for

Amy's benefit. A twenty-five year-old package of sandalwood incense sticks that, he reports, "still have fragrant potential." A paperback copy of *Zen and the Art of Motorcycle Maintenance* from a young Halifax actress "whose name, I think, was June." (He checks the flap: "Cynthia.") His Sammy Davis, Jr., which he holds up (*Yes I Can*, observes Amy, circa 1965). Six old copies of *Oui* magazine (September 1973 to June 1975). An ebony letter opener in the shape of a naked and extremely long-legged woman, "which your mother never liked, for some reason." An Yves Montand songbook.

A third of the boxes are clothes, and going through these isn't as hard for Amy as she expected. There are only a few things – the odd sweater, a favourite pantsuit – that she can imagine her mother in, and these items don't give her pause. What troubles her more are the signs of living – the worn shirt cuff, the faded tea stain – that she finds on pieces of clothing she doesn't remember at all. For more than a minute she holds in her hands a limp cotton blouse, the plum faded to lavender from repeated washings, before she recognizes it as the present she gave Gillian the Christmas before she moved out of the house into her first apartment.

The pauses seem to make Norman impatient. "We have to get these out of here tonight," he says, making a sweeping motion with the hand that also holds the Sammy Davis, Jr. "Do you think it's necessary to go through every box?"

"I don't know what you expected, Norman," she says, not looking at him. "You figured I'd just haul it all off to Goodwill without a second thought?"

"No, that's fine." He opens the book at random.

"Just toss it into a dumpster?"

"Hmmm," he says, intently reading.

Five white banker's boxes, meanwhile, hold Gillian's files, most of them research papers she'd read and collected over a dozen years as an assistant professor of literature, though she wrote some herself – on the sacred writings of twelfth-century Italian monks, for instance, and the poetry of fourteenth-century French courtesans (collections of which, her mother had told her, Norman could sometimes be found thumbing through after two in the morning, with a Duff Gordon lifted in his hand).

"This stuff should have gone back to the university," says Amy, more to herself than to Norman, who sits reading and nursing a glass of the Merlot she brought and hasn't yet tried. Her watch says nine o'clock. She was supposed to have been taken to dinner tonight by the engaging Grant Dekker, an account rep who works two floors above her. This dinner – at the pricey Xipe, a vegetarian place on Church Street – was the culmination of two weeks of e-mail flirting. Now, she figures, it'll take another week just to get the mood back.

She lifts the lid off the fifth white box and sees something different: forty or more green and black notebooks packed like a compressed accordion. The first one she pries from the box is dated "Nov. 1996 to Feb. 1997." The second, a hand's breadth away, says "April 1993 to Aug. 1993." Amy opens the first one and reads a page at random:

"Dec. 12: Can't decide what to get David for Christmas. He wants to believe himself a man, but how does that manifest itself, here and now, at age 19? Do I get him a briefcase? That seems absurd. A bottle of scotch? Even more so (though I must remember to get Norman his bottle of brandy). I suppose, given his accumulation of girlfriends, a year's supply of condoms would be most appropriate, but I couldn't bring myself to do that. Amy will be a waltz by comparison. A pretty, intelligent young woman with no self-esteem – it's almost criminally easy to satisfy her. One of these Christmases I have to spend some real time and money on that girl." Which must have been the impetus for the plane ticket for Seattle, a city Amy had forever wanted to visit, the following year.

She flips the pages and sees references to the university, to colleagues of Gillian's she'd met, finally having it confirmed that Phyllis Grant was indeed a lesbian, and that Peter Lamar, one of the history faculty, inspired in her mother feelings of physical revulsion, with his hot breath and sweaty neck and tendency to stand too close in conversation. Why then, Amy wonders, was he always invited to their house for dinner? She glances up at Norman, who is in the middle of reading something out loud to her from his Sammy Davis, Jr., and it comes to her instantly – because Lamar was the only one willing to sit still at the dinner table and listen to Norman's endless monologues on things like his preference for furniture covered in natural materials other than leather, while the rest of them fled to the kitchen to wash dishes.

"Huh, that's funny," says Amy when she senses Norman is finished reading, hoping that it was, in fact, funny.

"It's not funny at all, it's tragic," says Norman, offended. "It is elaborately tragic. Did you miss the reference? Maybe I should read it again."

"No, you're right, it's tragic. I got it."

"*As I felt pain –*" he reads.

"You're right, Norman. It's not funny at all."

Norman sighs and takes his book and his glass of wine out of the room.

Fishing several notebooks out in sequence Amy sees that they're packed into the box in chronological order and she decides, without really thinking about it, to pull out the very last notebook, dated "October 2000– ," last and thinner than the rest because her mother's accident occurred on November 26, while driving to Norman's opening night at the Beverly Dinner Theatre. She opens to a page near the front, dated "October 12," and begins reading:

"I don't know if I can take this any more."

◦━◦

"What is it you do, Mr. Bray, if you don't mind my asking?"

Norman doesn't mind at all. He sits straighter in his chair. "I'm an actor."

"Oh!" says Cantor suddenly, throwing his head back. "Oh! Wait. It's coming to me. 'Actors' – what is it?" He stares at the ceiling. "'Actors are loved because they are unoriginal. Actors stick to their script. The unoriginal man is loved by the mediocrity because this kind of artistic expression is something to which the merest five-eighths can climb.'" He drops his gaze back to Norman. "Sorry, that's a thing I learned years ago. By an Irish poet named Kavanaugh. But an actor. Well, well." Cantor seems mildly hopeful. "You act in movies, do you? There's always some movie or other being filmed around here. I thought I saw Meg Ryan last week."

"No," Norman says patiently. "I'm a stage actor. Musical theatre, for the most part."

Vivid disappointment. Cantor's face slackens, the mouth and eyes droop, even the ears decline slightly, as if sliding back on the wax that holds them to the head. To say "stage actor" and "musicals" to someone under forty is, so often, to watch an enactment of the first moment of death. Not that Norman finds the reaction of the over-forties much better. Their response is almost always, word for word, "Oh, you mean Broadway!" No, he is forced to explain, he does not mean Broadway. Broadway is a place. It is in New York. There are musicals there, to be sure, but he has never performed in them. Broadway is not what he does. He is an actor concerned with matters of craft, of emotion and meaning. He creates truth. Broadway, like all of New York, exists to create money. So, not only has Norman not performed on Broadway, he would never perform there.

"I have, however, done some television."

This seems to intrigue Cantor slightly. "Television? Oh, that's interesting. I never watch it, because I find it depresses me. But my daughter is an avid viewer."

"Your daughter!" Possibility rushes in. "Then your daughter may very well know my work!" He leans forward slightly. "Until recently, you see, I was the lead on *Timmy Taxi*."

The banker's eyes become opaque. Two blue peppermint breath mints.

"It's a children's show," says Norman. "For toddlers. On Sunday mornings. You must have –"

"Oh, I see." Cantor smiles politely. "My daughter is fourteen, actually. So she probably –"

"No," says Norman, crestfallen. "It's not likely she would have seen it."

"Unless she happened past it at some point."

"Yes." He is beaten. "Maybe then."

For a moment, Cantor gives his attention to the pages strewn in front of him. When, finally, he lifts his head, he seems bewildered. "Can I ask, Mr. Bray, why you never responded to our letters? Before now, I mean. I think someone from our branch may have even left a message for you once, asking you to call. But you never did. If you'd contacted us, you see, we might have been able to arrange something, adjust the payment schedule or . . . Why did you never respond?"

Norman opens his mouth and hesitates. Part of him intends to say it was a mistake, a lack of understanding, a kind of misadventure of reason. He wants to explain that until now there had always been someone else to deal with these things, someone like Gillian, and that he has only just come to see that without her in his life these everyday worries have fallen to him. And that, although he still feels it is wrong to impose these oppressively ordinary demands on an artist, he is still willing to seek a compromise. He is willing to ask for a second chance.

He opens his mouth to say this, or some of it, but he holds a breath and sees Howard Cantor still leafing through his mental files, searching for some image to correspond with the name *Timmy Taxi*, or the notion of an actor who has not appeared in movies with Meg Ryan, and he finds himself unable to get these words out. Instead, extending his hands and staring at them dumbly like a man trying to discern his left from his right, he says, "I could not . . . find the time." And then Norman, realizing this answer's vast inadequacy, slumps back in his chair.

Howard Cantor gives a soft click of his tongue and for a moment scratches his bald spot with the end of his pen, raking it across his scalp and leaving a pattern of thin white lines. Norman hears him say the word *prisoner*. "I'm sorry, Mr. Bray. I'm as much a prisoner of the system as you." He says other things Norman doesn't quite recognize, foreign phrases, occluded, fog-obscured words that only suggest meaning. And one of these may have been the one he dreads most. The word that changes everything.

"I'm sorry," Norman says. "Did you just use the word *foreclosure*?"

"Well, yes." Cantor gives a turtle-head shrug. "Yes. I said that. It's unfortunate. Did you want to review these documents?"

It was a sneak attack. The banker slipped in the word when he wasn't ready. "No, I don't want to review the documents. Yes, I do. Give them here." Norman grabs the papers and stares at them, waiting for the lines and bars and curlicues of black ink to make sense. He looks for the figure $132,849, wants to face it down and denounce it for the fraudulent artifact he knows it to be. But he can't find it. Can't find $7,476 either. He feels his testicles constrict. He racks his mind madly for the speech he honed, that perfect lance of words. Failing at this too he searches for the reason it's all happening, the grounds for the great injustice. And here, at last, he seizes on a single, solid thought.

"It's because I'm an artist, isn't it? An actor." Cool serenity washes over him, the calm that comes of knowing why. "You people have always mistrusted us."

"Not sure what you mean by 'you people,' Mr. Bray. But no, not at all."

Norman, however, has found his truth. "We actors are used to persecution, frankly, used to being shunned. In ancient Rome – did you know? – only slaves could be actors. Acting was *beneath* a Roman. Citizens were often jailed for appearing on stage. Soldiers, on the other hand, were beheaded."

"Mr. Bray."

Norman clears his throat, hardly noticing whether Cantor is listening, and decides to stand. "And later, on this very continent," he says, looming over the table, "when an actor died, he was buried outside the boundaries of consecrated ground, beyond the walls of the church. He was interred amongst the witches and the insane." He begins to move about the small, glassed-in office. "I've heard that sometimes the body had a wooden stake driven through its heart." He touches his chest as if fingering an old memory. "People who had seen the actor perform – who had watched him bring characters to life – thought that he'd been possessed. Once he was dead, they were afraid for their own souls." Norman glares at Cantor and makes his voice fill the room. "Are you afraid for your soul, Howard Cantor? Is that the reason I'm being persecuted? Would you, if you could, have me buried with witches? *Would you drive a stake through my heart?*"

The banker gapes at Norman, standing above him, eyes shining, fisted right hand pressing into his chest, staunching the flow from an apparent wound made by his own rampageous theory. And then, of all things, Cantor's expression changes. He smiles with something like approval.

"Is this what you do?" he says.

"I'm sorry?"

Cantor shakes an open hand at him. "This! This! Is this the sort of thing you do on stage? Because it's quite good."

Norman falls back on his heels, stupefied. Does this man understand nothing? Does he not recognize sincerity? That wasn't acting, he thinks. It was all me.

Still, he can't help but be pleased by the compliment. And in its glow, Norman begins to feel some warmth for this banker. Perhaps he is different from the rest of them, a moth among wasps.

Just then Cantor excuses himself and steps into the corridor where, for several minutes, he confers with a colleague in murmurs Norman can't make out. When he returns, easing himself into his seat with a rustle of wool blends, the banker considers Norman for a moment. "Tell me plainly, Mr. Bray," he says, finally, "do you have any sources of income? What jobs have you lined up in your field?"

Norman hesitates.

"Anything?"

"Well, the *Timmy Taxi* show," he says. "That's really a regular job. Although of course it's called *Tiny Taxi* these days. And there is a woman involved. But you know there couldn't have been a Tiny if there hadn't been a Timmy, no matter what his gender. As I'm certain Robert would agree."

Cantor shakes his head as if to clear it. "And that pays you how much?"

"It's non-union."

"Yes?"

"And I'm" – Norman swallows – "I'm on hiatus at the moment, although I can return at any time."

Cantor says nothing, waiting.

"It's, about, two hundred dollars a show."

"I see."

"That's only for four hours' work, you understand. So it's fifty dollars an hour. That's a very high rate of pay."

Cantor is rubbing his temple. "What I'm getting at is this. You seem like an intelligent man. And perhaps you are talented. But you have gotten yourself into a difficult situation. And let us remember that under no circumstances would the bank ever have entered into an arrangement with someone of such . . . intangible means. It's anathema to our entire way of thinking. It –" The banker brings a hand to the delicate skin at his neck, breasting over the stiff white collar of his shirt. "It disturbs us."

For a moment, Cantor's gaze wanders over the shiny, pale surfaces of the room; he appears lost in anxious thought. Norman, considering his options – which include describing for Cantor the ridiculous mental image that has just occurred to him, of Tiny Taxi in a dress, with a pair of womanish reading glasses dangling from his grille – makes what is for him a startling choice. He says nothing.

When the banker finally refocuses on Norman, he seems brighter, almost buoyed. "And yet we want to be entirely fair, now that we find ourselves in this position. We are, as I have been reminded, known as 'The Fair Bank.'"

"Fair?" For Norman, *fair* is a king among words. Excepting *artist*, there is no other greater. All he wants is to be treated fairly and judged the same way. In a fair world, he can't help but succeed.

"It's part of our marketing strategy," says Cantor. "We own 'fairness.' Another bank has 'flexibility,' so" – he shrugs – "we're ramping up on 'fair.'"

Norman feels the need to grip the edge of the table. He had been wavering in his assessment of Howard Cantor, torn between the likelihood of his incarnating all evil and the hope that he possessed a single shred of humanity, but leaning, if the truth be known, towards evil the whole way. Now it seems he is being asked to whip right over to shred-of-humanity with no warning. "I'm sorry," he says to Cantor. "Could you explain what's happening?"

"I am being persuaded to give you an extra ninety days, Mr. Bray, to cover your default. Since this is the first time you and I have actually spoken, we've decided it's the 'fair' thing to do."

"Well," says Norman, completely unfastened, "because I –"

"However, there are conditions." Cantor prods the crescent of scalp once more with his pen. "We can't possibly enter into such an agreement with you without some real, concrete assurances of your earning potential. So" – he sets down the pen, leans forward, and presses his hands against the tabletop – "let's reconsider this acting business."

"He doesn't listen to me. He never listens to me." Amy is reading. "It makes me question, constantly, the value of what I'm trying to say. I find I doubt myself more than I ever have. In my most severely addled moments, I sometimes wonder whether I actually exist. Perhaps I have vanished, become a non-being, and all that remains of me is my penmanship. But then no, I remind myself, his not listening has nothing to do with me. He has convinced himself that the only voice that matters is his. It's not a spiteful thing, he doesn't mean any harm – he believes it. My role here is to be his audience. I'm sure he would prefer a thousand hands applauding him, but he has me and so I will do. There, right now he's going on about some act of effrontery in the supermarket, something to do with out-of-date milk. This is what six years without work has done to him. He is gripped by the mundane, because his life is filled with it. And because it involves him, it must be important, and if it is important, then there is no need to seek out anything greater in life. No doubt this singular knack of his has saved him from years of depression, but he has lifted himself onto such a pedestal that he has stranded himself. He is trapped by his own self-regard."

Amy has read through most of her mother's entries for the month of October 2000, and she's found that nearly all of them concentrate on the same subject. Norman. Norman's intransigence. Norman's constant, childlike need for attention. Norman's inability to hear any voice but his own. From what she's read it was an abrupt change, this concentration on all matters Norman; he was a relatively minor character in the earlier journals, where her work, the politics of the university, and her children figured more prominently. And when he was mentioned, more often than not, it was with affection. Equipped with the buffers of David and Amy, and dinner guests, Gillian was able to see his manner as charming, even entertaining. But here, almost two years after David has moved out, two and a half since her daughter left, Gillian has reached her limit.

As Amy turns the pages, the entries seem to get more desperate. What at first reads as comic becomes sour, angry, until

Amy begins to feel a gnawing anxiety in her stomach. "He is driving me slowly mad," she reads in her mother's entry of October 27. "But can I get him to hear this? No! His own needs are so important to him, no one else is allowed any. I love him, but I hate that he makes me feel this way about him. He is, I know, a good and gentle man. He can display such sweet sensitivity, to moments of beauty, to acts of kindness. But he is sucking the kindness out of me. When he's off on an errand, or at the library, I have the exhilarating sensation of being able to breathe. When he walks into the house, my heart sinks. His self-acceptance is suffocating. My mind turns violent. Sometimes, after he's been talking to me for half an hour about something utterly meaningless, I realize I've been digging my fingernails into my forearm, raking the skin. I've actually drawn blood. Yesterday Tina, the department secretary, asked if I'd gotten a cat."

Amy notices that Norman hasn't returned to the room. She picks up the faint sound of the television downstairs, and occasionally the not-so-faint sound of Norman's snorting laughter. Outside the half-curtained window it's dark, and she checks her watch: 9:25. She still hasn't had dinner, and she realizes Norman probably expected her to order something in for both of them.

She reads on, and discovers the tone of her mother's journal changes dramatically in the entry dated November 2. "Thank God," she wrote. "Thank God he finally has a job. They called him this afternoon from Beverly, desperate because Joe Chaput (who hasn't half Norman's talent but is well liked and works steadily), has come down with bacterial pneumonia. They want him up there by the end of the week. At first Norman acted uninterested. It's only dinner theatre, he said. What if he commits and then something bigger comes along? Incredible. His first offer in six years and he's worried about tying himself up. I didn't say that to him, of course, but I did say, 'Norman, it's a show. A show!' I told him, 'Norman, the children have never seen you perform. Do it if only to prove you are what you tell them you are.' I begged him to take it. Literally clutched his hand to my chest."

This was the doomed *Man of La Mancha* production in Beverly, Ontario, that David asked Norman about at dinner. Neither Amy nor he ever saw it because it closed as soon as it began, apparently in the wake of her mother's death.

Amy sets down the journal for a moment and walks softly, in ankle-socked feet, down the narrow hallway to the bathroom. She leans over the' sink and splashes small handfuls of cool water on her face, then dries herself with an old but clean yellow hand towel she pulls from a pile in the corner. All the time she avoids her image in the mirror, because these days she feels her cheeks are too puffy and just now she doesn't want to confront them, though she knows the whole thought process is ridiculous, which makes her feel worse. On her way back, she stands at the top of the stairs and hears repeated, manic applause coming from the television downstairs and decides against calling to Norman about dinner.

Back among the boxes and reading the entries after November 2, Amy finds that Gillian's desperate tone returns. Whatever she'd been expecting from Norman's employment, she'd been disappointed. "This can't continue," she wrote on November 4. "I thought I could hold on. I thought getting work would change him. I thought that having a purpose would make him a man of purpose. That his sights would be raised, if not beyond himself then at least to what else he might accomplish. But the central fact of Norman doesn't change – what he is seems to be enough for him – and I can't bear it any longer. Easily said, of course; I've nursed that thought so long without acting on it. But it's suddenly clear to me the only thing I can do is get out – out of the whole thing."

After that it's as if she shut off. Amy flips through the pages and sees that most of the entries between November 9 and 25 are one or two lines, little stammers of frustration. November 12: "Norman called from his motel room in Beverly. Hates the bed." November 16: "Norman finds the director 'ineffective.' Is taking over." Of those that follow, however, Amy finds three that she feels the need to read over several times. November 18: "Very sweet tonight on the phone. Said he can't survive without me. I forget this part of him. Maybe I'm wrong." November 21: "It's decided – I will wait until after the run is finished, and no longer." November 25: "Opening night tomorrow. Again I'm undecided. So much of him is love."

Her mother used to talk about this loving side to Norman. "He's heartfelt," she would say. But Amy, who considered Norman's emotionalism maudlin and overdone, particularly after three glasses of brandy, had always assumed she said these things in an attempt to kindle some affection between the two of them, the way she herself now seems to be doing with David. It has never until this moment occurred to her that maybe Gillian simply believed it. Amy frowns and slaps the journal back into the box. She's never before considered her mother gullible.

She picks up the box and carries it downstairs, into the living room where Norman is watching TV. She drops it on the floor beside his chair. Norman's eyes don't leave the set.

"Norman."

He lifts a hand, his eyes still fixed. "Just a minute. I'm interested in this." On the screen, two men in chef's aprons are opening cans of tomatoes as fast as they can. The camera cuts to a close-up of their twisting, clenching hands. The view changes to show an audience of about twelve people, leaning forward, rapt. Back to the men, halfway there. Music charges along in the background like Pamplona bulls. Each of the men is desperate to open his tomato can first! And when the man in the yellow apron does, the audience cheers! One man in the crowd pumps his fist! "It's awful," says Norman. "But it's fascinating."

"These are Mom's journals, Norman. Have you read them?"

"Wait now." He actually points to the television, as if perhaps she hasn't noticed that it's on.

She looks at the TV. "It's an infomercial, Norman."

He shifts agitatedly in his chair and leans forward, to suggest his sudden inability to hear what the television is trying to tell him. Noting the empty bottle of wine on the coffee table, and knowing that Norman after a bottle of wine is generally less susceptible to petitions from the rational world, Amy goes to the kitchen, as the audience cheers madly again. In the fridge, she finds a wizened apple and wipes it with the damp cloth draped on the handle of the refrigerator door. When the light coming from the living room flares brighter and the sound jumps, she knows the commercials have begun and she leans against the sink, eating her apple, waiting for Norman to walk in. Which he does, after a moment, his hands in his pockets.

"All done up there?"

"Honestly, Norman."

"Have you thought about dinner? Maybe we should order something in."

She tosses what's left of the apple into the garbage pail under the sink. "I'm going home soon. Did you hear what I asked you?"

"What's that?"

"Those are Mom's journals in the box. I wanted to know if you'd read them."

"No, I haven't." He shrugs the indistinct shrug of a man unsure whether he should be offended by the suggestion. "I didn't even know she wrote a journal."

"Maybe you should take a glance." Even as she says it, Amy questions her own impulse in pressing this point. She can't tell whether it's an act of peevishness or a desperate attempt to help a blind man see.

"Well, I think the important thing right now is to get the boxes out of that room." He turns half-heartedly towards the staircase. "So how's it going up there?"

"I thought we were doing this together, Norman. You said you wanted to clear the room out, you didn't say you wanted me to do it."

"But you're doing such a good job."

"I'm not, though. I've been reading her journals for the past half-hour. In fact . . ." She hip-bounces away from the sink and walks past him into the living room, where she opens the box and pulls out the last, thin booklet. She brings it into the kitchen and hands it towards Norman. "Here's one you could read right now."

"We should finish that room off first, though, don't you think?"

"You'll enjoy this, Norman." She pushes the booklet into his hands. "It's the one you star in."

◦⬤◦

The banker wants him to get a job as a community-college music teacher. Or a stadium announcer. Or perhaps a hawker of peanut-butter samples at regional food fairs. There are lots of jobs for people with talents such as his, Norman is told, and he should go about acquiring one of them immediately.

Norman is squeezing his kneecaps with his hands. "You realize you're talking to someone who was given a Mirror Award?"

Cantor, who has been scribbling down a phone number for Norman on a robin's-egg-blue Post-it note, raises his head. "What's a Miro award?"

"Mirror. Mirror." Norman gathers himself. "I was given the Mirror for my efforts in a production of *Man of La Mancha*."

"That's a play?"

God damn all bankers everywhere. "It's a famous musical. Absolutely famous. *Everyone* knows *Man of La Mancha*."

"I've never heard of it."

"It was even a movie, for Christ's sake, with" – he shuts his eyes and exhales – "Peter fucking O'Toole."

Cantor purses his lips for a moment, then tears off the Post-it note. "Sort of like *The Lion King*."

Norman feels a tingle of superiority that erects the little hairs on his arms and on the back of his neck. "No," he says, "it is not at all like *The Lion King*." He enunciates as if biting through parsley. "Because that, you see, was a musical adapted from a movie. *Man of La Mancha*, on the other hand, was a musical adapted *into* a movie."

The banker reaches across the table and sticks the blue paper down in front of him. "This is a phone number."

"Do you understand the difference though? Do you see? Because it's important."

"It's for an employment counsellor."

"I don't need an employment counsellor, because I am an actor. That is my job and I do it very well."

"The engagement of an employment counsellor is a unique feature of our fairness program, Mr. Bray. I expect you to call him first thing Monday morning and arrange to meet with him, so that he can then direct you to opportunities that will allow you to fulfill your obligations to this bank."

They would leave him his home, but take away his life. "This is ridiculous!"

"If you don't call him, this bank will assume that you are irreparably in default and will begin the foreclosure process immediately."

"Do you not see how wrong this is? Because it's very, very clear to me."

"Also, Mr. Bray." Cantor waits for Norman to look him in the eye. "I recommend that you empty one or perhaps even two rooms in your home and start renting them out right away. This is not necessarily in the best interests of the bank, since a house with tenants can be harder to sell, but it is in *your* best interests and I advise you to do it."

Norman feels uncharitableness descend upon him like hot shower mist. A cleansing, relaxing, moistening event. "If it is not in the best interests of this bank," he says, "then of course I will do it immediately."

# ACT III

He spends Saturday according to his custom – morning, of course, in bed; the hours between noon and two in his bathrobe; mid-afternoon in the library, flipping through the pages of out-of-print biographies, with particular attention to a thick life of Picasso that he finds fascinating and yet troubling for its relentless focus on the artist's financial history ("What does it matter?" he keeps demanding out loud, to the consternation of those in nearby chairs); late afternoon walking through his favourite park, a forested enclave with a pond and, he is sure, though he has never seen them, fish; the five-o'clock hour in his padded puce chair, silently tolerating his TV's snowy, cableless reception. Whenever thoughts of what occurred the previous day, or of what's to come, begin to slip into his awareness, he focuses his attention on something immediate – the combed cloud streaks spreading across the sky, a black poodle being walked by a red-haired child, the white fur of dust on a library shelf, the woman with the pierced cheek at the checkout desk – and finds it, them, her so remarkable that his absolute mental fealty is required. And in this way he manages to pass much of the day with barely a single, fully formed thought about what might become of him.

At around six o'clock a general uneasiness begins to make itself known in Norman's midsection. He puts it down to hunger – he cleaned out the fridge at lunchtime, finally resorting to the ancient bacon, which he then decided tasted better for having been aged and pledged to age all bacon before eating it in the future – and yet hunger is not the reason he goes to his bedroom, sits on the edge of his bed, and opens up a knee-high box that Amy shoved against the wall.

It's a box of old clippings and correspondence. Here are copies of contracts. Publicity photos. A file thick with reviews. He pulls this one out and begins to sort carefully through the fragile strips of newsprint, lifting each by its edges and laying it lightly onto his lap. Each one has a phrase or a sentence under- lined with a fine ballpoint pen – "Bray is dashing as Nick"; "Bray's voice is a sweet fulfillment of longing"; "But by far the most praise belongs to Norman Bray" – every one of them like an old friend waving from a street corner: *Hello, Norman! It's good to see you again! You're as handsome as ever!* And here is a lovely picture he'd forgotten, torn from the *Toronto Star*, with Norman as Sid Sorokin and Louise Manly as Babe in *The Pajama Game*, 1968, when he was still young enough to handle a modified tenor (though naturally that meant Louise had to come down a notch too, which did not make her happy. "I hate this!" she wailed in rehearsals. "I sound like Greta fucking Garbo!"). He loved this shot for the way the light caught the corner of his upturned eye, like a little star, while Louise's face lay buried under his chin.

After twenty minutes or so, Norman returns the file to the box feeling somewhat better, and fingers through the rest of the contents, continuing his search for the thing that will comfort him most. It's then he comes across something he doesn't expect – his Miriam Ashacker file.

For a time in the 1980s, Miriam Ashacker was Norman's agent, responsible for getting him a toothpaste commercial and two regional pool-maintenance spots (as well as, she would remind him, a salted-cracker commercial he could have had if he hadn't been such a complete asshole about a simple wheat-stalk costume). She was always a robust and heartwarming creature, especially during the winter months, when she would spend a great deal of time at Ouzeri, a large Greek restaurant on the Danforth, eating plate after plate of thick, sweet bougatsa.

The file bearing her name in Norman's broad block lettering is a thin file, containing mainly copies of a few letters he sent to her, several of them about the wheat-stalk-costume issue, which he persisted with for months after the fact because the very idea that she had put his name forward for that job troubled him and suggested, he said, that she understood neither him nor the qualities that made him unique. Did she appreciate that he was not a "costume actor"? Could she please write back with her own description of his talents and qualities so that he could be sure that she did? The file contains her one response to his letters on this subject: "Dear Norman. The costume thing was last summer. Please shut up about it." It also contains a few bits of administrative flotsam, including a change-of-address notice, the last thing he received from her, announcing the agency's move from the Danforth area (why she had ever located way out there in the first place Norman could never fathom, unless it was simply for the bougatsa) to a small space closer to the production companies she was trying to supply with talent, downtown in the St. Lawrence Market district, on Frederick Street.

In spite of the wheat-stalk conflict, he has mostly fond memories of Miriam. He remembers her as a good listener. She would sit with him in her office, her cheek resting on the heel of her hand, receiving his every word, sometimes – and this suggested to Norman extreme concentration – with her eyes closed. Then finally, when she had absorbed everything he had to tell her, she would lift her head with a sigh, pull her telephone towards her, and say, "Thank you, Norman. Now I think I can face the twenty-three people out there who want to hear what *I* have to say." He liked her, and it was a great shame when she announced one day that she could no longer represent him because, as she said at the time, there was "too little work, and too much you."

Sitting on the edge of his bed, Norman toys with the idea of calling Miriam. He pulls the change-of-address notice out of the file, finds a phone number printed at the bottom, and begins to underline it with the edge of his thumbnail as he grapples with the implications of reaching out to her. Having needs and making sure they are met is not the same thing as being in need. The dynamic is altogether different. Making sure his needs were being met during his years with Miriam was part of what Norman considered his responsibility as an artist and as a client. Being in need, on the other hand, is far less appealing. To the extent that Norman recognizes the state of being in need, he does not like the idea of going to Miriam Ashacker in it. He imagines calling her and knows just how it will go. She will ask him questions. She will wonder what he has been doing with himself and how he let himself get into this fix. She will prick him with doubts and plague him with inferences. He can hear it all now, in his head.

Even so, he considers another, equally good possibility – that Miriam will be glad to hear from him. If it's true that he wasn't her most successful client, in financial terms, it's only because he was highly selective. At the time, he believed that his choosiness helped make her more discerning and served to raise her agency's general standard of quality, but perhaps this lack of "financial" success became a source of regret for her. Agents measure achievement in terms of money; perhaps she looks back on it all and feels that she failed him. The more Norman thinks it through, the more convinced he becomes that Miriam will be grateful for his call, and for the chance to make amends (to say nothing of the entire wheat-stalk-costume difficulty, for which by now she will certainly be feeling contrite).

He lifts the handset of the phone by his bed and dials the number, then clears his throat several times as it rings and rings and rings. His first words should be strong. *Hello, Miriam*, he will say. *I thought I should give you a call. It's been a long time. When shall we get together?* Something of that order, gracious and direct. He'll get to the point quickly – *I'm eager for a challenge* – and make it clear he's choosing to call her because he respects her ability and for no other reason. She'll appreciate that.

The phone won't stop ringing. No assistant answers, not even a machine. It's Saturday, of course; that may be it. Frustrating, though. Norman had assumed that, because he was ready to make the call, someone would be there to answer it. The way a toaster is always ready to accept a slice of bread. He waits through another three rings, then a fourth, and hangs up.

"Damn it."

Now that he's ready to talk to Miriam, he wants to talk to Miriam. He doesn't want to sit there till Monday.

He goes in search of the phone book. It should be near the phone, but isn't. He looks around, he looks around, and it is nowhere. Maybe he never got a new phone book. Maybe the phone people never delivered it! No, that's not right. He got one. He remembers liking the new design.

He finds the phone book in the bathroom. He had wanted some reading material one morning, and there was only the phone book at hand, and he had grabbed it and made the best of it (Ah, yes, the time zones. The emergency-service numbers. Good to know).

But the phone book has no listing for ASHACKER M. Norman looks backward and forward through the A's, as if the phone company might have misplaced it somewhere among the Abrahams or the Augustines. He looks in the Yellow Pages under "Talent Agents" and finds nothing there either.

"God*damn* it," he says, and slaps the phone book shut.

Miriam had an assistant. What was her name? He can't remember. He closes his eyes and tries to picture the assistant in Miriam's office – the large, cluttered desk, the tall plant in the right-hand corner. Ficus? The swooping art-decoish lamp, the shelves of books and awards (Miriam was always being distracted from her work by some charity or other), the pictures of her clients on the wall (his third from the end, going for a stern yet romantic, open-necked, white-Othello look – he sees it clearly). He tries to place the assistant somewhere off to the side of all this, sitting at her desk. Tries to recall her hair colour, the shape of her face. He clamps his eyes shut, forcing himself to remember. And . . . nothing comes.

Wait, though. Norman recalls that among the administrative scraps in his Ashacker file was a letter signed on behalf of Miriam by her assistant. He checks the file again and, sure enough, finds the signature of Bernice Chen.

He has no memory of this woman. Doesn't even recall that she was Chinese. But he forges ahead because he is sure she'll remember him, and after twenty minutes spent calling most of the fifty-three CHEN B's in the phone book, he finds her and proves himself correct.

"Oh, yes," she says evenly, once he has introduced himself.

There is silence from Bernice Chen's end of the line as Norman explains his wish to reach Miriam, and the silence continues for some time after that as well. There's a moment when Norman wonders whether the line has simply gone dead. But then Bernice says, "You know, I'm not sure Miriam would be very happy to hear from you."

"Oh?" he says, surprised. "What makes you say that?"

"Whenever you called her, she would hang up the phone and do this –" Over the phone Bernice inhales deeply and then makes the sound of a balloon loudly going flaccid. When he says nothing, she continues. "Anyway, Miriam isn't an agent any more."

Norman's mind is still gripped by the appalling image of Miriam making loud rubbery-lip noises at his expense. He manages to cough.

"She has been very ill."

"I'm sorry," he says, having some difficulty following. "You said Miriam isn't an agent?"

"She's too sick to work. She has cancer."

Norman says nothing.

"She had it in her spleen," continues Bernice. "It was a spleen problem first. You didn't know?"

"No, I didn't." Norman lets out a sigh that encompasses all frustration.

"Eventually they removed it. That's when she closed the shop. But the cancer moved on. It became a bowel problem."

"I see." But Norman doesn't see at all. What is happening? What is happening to the world? A bank problem. A spleen problem. Now a bowel problem. It's as if there were an insidious plan at work. "But she's alive," he says. "She's able to talk."

"Yes."

"She's able to move around."

"Yes."

It seems to Norman that this notion of Miriam no longer being an agent is somewhat suspect. "Well, I'd very much like to speak to her."

"Hold on."

The silence again. The Bernicean silence. Norman resolves to wait it out. Silence works for him. Some of his very best moments on stage were silent ones, because his silences were *deafening*. It has to do with the power of contrast, he would explain to directors, the vivid connection between what is said and what is unsaid, what exists and what does not exist.

In this case, of course, the continuing existence of the Bernicean silence highlights the non-existence of any sense whatsoever. What is the issue? Why can't an actor have his former agent's phone number? Or her address? Her address would be better, thinks Norman, because then he could go and see her, and avoid any more of the flaccid-balloon nonsense. Is he supposed to wait for Bernice Chen's answer to one request before he can submit another? Why this endless silent mulling-over? He doesn't mind the silence; the silence isn't the problem. It's the mulling. What is there to think about? The problem is he can't see Bernice Chen's eyes. If he could see her eyes, he could tell whether she was silently thinking, or silently forget-ting he's even here, waiting. But he can't see her eyes, her eyes also are non-existent. And outside his window the day is dying, the light is failing. Soon the light will be as non-existent as Bernice Chen's eyes and Bernice Chen's sound, and Saturday will be non-existent because it will be Sunday. Soon Miriam herself may be non-existent if she's really so sick. What is the *issue*? thinks Norman.

"What is the *issue*?" he says.

"What?"

"Sorry?"

"I was on the other line," says Bernice.

"The other line?"

"I have two lines. I wanted to check with Miriam to see if, you know, she minded me giving you her number."

"Actually, I'd prefer her address."

"Oh . . . well, I don't know."

"Did she say I could have her number?"

"Yes. Reluctantly."

"Then I'm sure she wouldn't mind."

"You're not really in a position to know, though, are you?"

"I'm fairly sure she wouldn't mind."

"Hold on."

After another five minutes of Bernice Chen's non-existence, Norman has Miriam's address. And he is utterly spent.

&#10086;

Not appreciably nicer. This is Norman's view of the Moore Park area that Miriam Ashacker calls home. Not appreciably nicer than Parkdale, he thinks, as he walks from the Yonge and St. Clair subway station to Miriam's Garfield Avenue address. Perhaps there are a few more trees. Possibly the homes are somewhat larger, and in slightly better repair. But really, it's hard to tell in the half-light of early evening. Poor illumination can conceal a great many flaws.

Miriam's house itself – two square storeys of white stone, centred on a small platform of clipped grass like a cheese cube on a cracker – does, however, take Norman by surprise. Not that he had expected something different; he'd expected nothing at all. He'd never pictured Miriam in a house of any kind. Beyond being an agent, and eating bougatsa on the Danforth, she was intangible to him. She lived in a Greek restaurant for all he knew. Seeing this solid proof of her being is as startling to him as finding a family of refugees living in his own basement.

So is seeing a man open the door . . .

"Yes?"

. . . a man of about sixty by Norman's estimate, a little haggard, greying slightly, and apparently unused to having visitors, judging by his harassed frown and the way he keeps a grip on the door frame.

"Oh, hello," says Norman. "Actually I'm here to see Miriam." He leans forward and lifts his foot to step past him and into the house, but the man doesn't move.

"My wife is asleep."

"Yes, but –" Norman tries to see past the obstacle.

"Who are you?"

"I'm Norman Bray. Miriam is expecting me."

"I don't think so."

"Oh, yes! Her assistant –" Norman snaps his fingers to wake up the name. "Chen! Something Chen! She gave me the address. She checked with Miriam and Miriam said it was all right."

The man – the husband – still doesn't move, and gives no indication of intending to. Rather, he gives every indication of wanting to stay right where he is, in the way, stuffed like batting between Norman and the solutions Miriam could offer. Beyond the blockage, Norman can see the hallway with its carved wall fixtures crying tears of light, he can see a large living room the colour of chamomile tea. This is a house promising comfort and salvation. But the man will not let him inside.

"You're an actor, aren't you," says the man wearily. "First of all, Miriam isn't working any more. She hasn't worked for ten years at least. Second of all, as I said, she's sleeping. And I'm not waking her up."

"But you have to."

"I don't have to do anything. This is my home."

Norman's hands clench in a seizure of shared understanding. "Exactly! That's exactly it. This is your home. This is –" He hesitates, groping for the perfect balance of urgency and reasonable argument. "This is where you can be yourself, where you can *just be*, without any interference or judgement, and no one can make you do anything you don't want to do. And you're trying to protect that."

"Right."

"Well, that's what I'm trying to do." If he stares hard enough, Norman thinks, if he bores deep enough with his diamond-tipped truth, then he will get to the man's heart, and the door will fly open. "And Miriam – who, I would like to say again, agreed to see me – is really the only one who can help."

Gradually, the frown slides off the man's face, replaced by something less readable. Norman opens his mouth to speak but stops when Miriam's husband puts up a hand. "I'm going to close the door."

"They won't let me be!"

The man pats the night air with his raised hand. "Just listen. I'm going to close the door and go upstairs." His demeanour has softened to something almost fatherly. "If Miriam is asleep, I'm not going to wake her up. You can come – you can *phone ahead* and come back another time. But if she's awake, and she chooses to come down, then that's fine. All right?" He closes the door with a clump before Norman can answer.

In the twilit cool on the concrete landing he sighs and adjusts his bearing and pictures himself being seen by Miriam after so many years. He imagines the impression he will make, the warmth she will feel at seeing him so little changed. And what goes through his mind is a memory, not of the last time he saw her, but of the last time he willingly subjected himself to this sort of scrutiny and estimation, the last time he declared himself in service to whim.

It was an audition, twenty-three years ago. He was in his early thirties and the situation was this: he had gone eight months without work and was beginning to tire both of the constant entreaties from his wife, Amanda, to find "a real job, God, anything" and of the deepening dismay evident on the face of his late mother every time he asked to borrow a hundred dollars, as if the fact of needing a hundred dollars cemented his spiritual ruin. The other aspect of the situation, which rings even more brightly in his mind, was the substantial interest he'd developed in a young actress acquaintance by the name of Simone.

Simone was a girl in her mid-twenties with thick, restive hair who wore torn jeans and men's flannel shirts to rehearsals, and when she sat still or arched her back or did nothing at all but stand there on stage holding her script by her thigh, her significant breasts would press like two pound cakes against the fabric of those flannel shirts. It was Simone who, during a chance, sticky-August meeting in a bookstore, had tipped Norman off to the casting call for a new play called *The Commission* in the rundown Conquest Theatre on Bathurst Street. *The Commission*, she told him – peeling humidity-jazzed hair away from her face – was a four-hander about a destitute sculptor by the name of Duncan who sold his integrity to a corporation in the first act and killed himself heroically in the second. Simone was going for the role of Tina, the corporation's impressionable young PR representative, and she thought Norman would be perfect as Franklin, the sharp-minded executive who convinces Duncan to sell out. From her loamy description of the role, Norman had gathered that Franklin was really the central figure of the play. Once he'd read the script, however, he could see that Franklin was a thoroughly subordinate character, present in barely a fifth of the pages and that, in fact, Duncan was the lead, which meant, of course, that Duncan was his role. That the casting call specified for Duncan an actor in his early fifties was hardly a problem – Norman knew his presence carried a maturity beyond his years and the director would see that instantly.

As it turned out, the director – an astringent redhead named Herbert Wheaton – was not moved by the maturity of Norman's presence at all. He was completely blind to it. When Norman approached him at the foot of the stage and said he wished to read for Duncan, Wheaton glanced sideways at him and asked, "Have you read the script?"

"Oh, yes," Norman said, rapping his copy with a knuckle. "I think I've figured this guy out." This was, on the one hand, merely something to say. He couldn't honestly claim to have figured out the character of Duncan because he had only skimmed the script twice. But Norman had a steady voice in his head that told him he could play anything, if only he were given the opportunity.

"That's impressive," replied Wheaton, turning to face him head-on. "Have you figured out that he's a man of fifty or fifty-five? Because I've met at least one idiotic young actor who missed that part of it entirely." He said this with such lemony irony, and made the thrust of his judgement so clear, that Norman temporarily lost the voice in his head. He excused himself to the washroom and lifted cold water to his face until it returned, then found a side door wedged open for ventilation and slipped through.

On Miriam's front steps in Moore Park, Norman gives his arms a few warming slaps and assesses his present circumstances. In the time since the door was closed on him the evening has turned so decidedly chilly he seems to have crossed into another season altogether. A season of bitter disappointment. It was a mistake, he broods, to think Miriam would want to help him. A mistake to think her help would be useful or suitable. As an agent, as someone who operated for so long on the periphery of art, whose talents were the hard talents of money and profit and persuasion, she is obviously someone whose soul long ago lost its suppleness. She has a stiff, stale-bread soul. And the reason she isn't coming down is that she is afraid to look at him, because to see him will be to see someone whose soul is as moist and limber as ever.

After five minutes more, Norman checks his watch, and it occurs to him that perhaps she is making him wait, as a long-awaited retaliation for some injury he caused her years ago and can't now remember.

It's just the sort of thing Miriam Ashacker would do, Norman thinks. There was a huffiness to her, he remembers now, a judgemental quality that he never liked. She was always quick-tempered, and her anger seemed to bloom instantly, like a hot popcorn kernel, at the smallest perceived slight, or the tiniest complaint from him about the quality of service she was providing. She was, in her hypersensitivity, quite manipulative. It's interesting how these fragments of memory get lost and then, when you least expect them, shine like bits of tin in the grass. She played games, did Miriam. Oh, how she played games. Trying to rope him in to taking jobs that weren't suited to him, trying to undermine his integrity while fattening her agent's purse. He sees it all so clearly now he considers it a wonder anyone would ever be seduced into spreading their mind's legs for the things Miriam Ashacker had to say.

Norman sinks so deeply into his new understanding of Miriam that when she finally does appear at the door, her head wrapped in a kind of turban, her face shadowed and papery, her body halved in size and vigour, he can only think, *What game is she playing now?*

She smiles minutely, a thin line-drawing of a smile, and opens the door wider to let him in. "Norman Bray," she says, like a professor naming a particularly fraught period in history. "Come in." She could be asking the Cold War to come in, or Conflict in the Middle East. Her voice sounds remarkably strong, he thinks, for someone so apparently sick. As he steps warily inside, she lingers on the threshold to inspect the evening beyond him – "It's gotten cold, hasn't it?" – then lets the door close and faces him in the hallway. She has, it seems to him, become a small-scale likeness of herself made with cheaper materials. She is no longer Miriam, she is Miriamesque. "I'm sorry you had to stand out there for so long, or at all," she says. "But John is very protective and it takes me a while to get dressed –" She shrugs at her T-shirt-jeans-terrycloth-robe ensemble and smiles up at him. "Such as I am." Her eyes are larger than Norman remembers, larger and more green, as if all her energy has gone into them as her last, best hope for survival.

She guides him into the chamomile living room, where there is no sign of the husband, and motions to the left of a gas fireplace, towards a white sofa that looks soft enough to be made of meringue. "Please," she says. "Can I have John get you something?"

"Well . . ." He sinks deep into the sofa, which is even softer than it looks, and clears his throat. He has lost his certainty about Miriam's soulless manipulation, but whether this is a tell-tale sign of her seductive power, or the lack of it, he can't be sure. He knows that, for the moment, he should tread carefully, but not so carefully that he declines their hospitality. "Yes," he says, and then, warming to his opportunity, "I would love a Miespejo brandy. If you have it."

"To be honest, I don't really know if we have any alcohol in the house at all." She tightens her robe and shoves her hands in her pockets. "Oh, Norman, don't look so stricken. I'm sure we have something. But I don't drink any more so I just don't know what. Let me get John to look." She steps into the hallway and calls. "John? *John?*"

John descends the stairs in heavy sock feet and enters the living room. When he sees Norman, he stops.

"Oh."

"John, you've met Norman. He'd like a drink. A me-something – what did you call it?"

"Miespejo."

The husband's expression turns skeptical. "I'm not familiar with that."

"It's a very fine Spanish brandy. Miriam, I'm sure I've told you about it." He waits, hopeful. "But if you don't have it," he says eventually, "I'm quite used to making do with something else."

John tips his chin upward. "We don't have it."

"Well, that's fine. Whatever you have the most of is fine. I wouldn't" – he laughs quite good-naturedly – "want to drink your last ounce of something."

"Don't worry."

Miriam gives her husband's stomach a rub. "Thank you, John." And when he's gone she comes farther into the living room, looks at Norman, and then veers past him towards the carved mantel of the fireplace. She reaches up for a picture, admires it for a moment, then brings it over to him. It's an image of the younger, rounder, more complete Miriam, beaming under a crown of small white flowers, beside a less grey, less weary John. "We were married fourteen years ago. We met at Tanglewood, the music festival near Boston." She lowers herself into a firm-looking black leather armchair. "He's a composer."

"Oh," says Norman. "You mean jingles, that sort of thing?"

Miriam's eyebrows tent upward. "No." She shakes her head. "He composes concertos, and symphonies for large orchestras. He's in the same class as John Adams."

"Ah," says Norman, having no idea who John Adams might be, and wanting anyway to get on with other topics that have less to do with Miriam's husband and more to do with his own pressing situation. He looks for a place to put the picture Miriam has handed him, and decides on the floor.

"I'm sorry, Norman. Could you – ?"

"Yes?"

"If you're done with that could you set it back up on the mantel?"

"Oh." He bends over with a fraction of the effort he knows it will take to get out of the pillowy sofa completely, and picks up the picture. "I could just leave it here," he says, meaning the cushion beside him.

"Well, we might forget about it, and then someone could sit on it."

"All right then." With exactly the ungainly struggle he expected, Norman hauls himself to his feet, chuckling pointedly throughout the ordeal, and finally returns the picture to its approximate home.

"We were so lucky with the weather that day," says Miriam, somewhat dreamily. "It was November, but you can see the sun on the trees."

Norman hesitates, confused by the past tense, and for the briefest moment wonders whether Miriam's illness is so grave that she does not know it's still November. Then he understands: she means the picture. "Yes! Yes you can." He stands at the mantel, peering in at the image for, essentially, the first time. "Quite a lot of sun there." He looks steadily at the photograph, awaiting further inspiration. "But not on your faces."

"I think the photographer put up a diffuser."

"Ah, yes. I've seen those used." He nods assuredly. "For publicity shots."

"Speaking of which, Norman, I wanted to ask you –"

"You're in luck." John has appeared bearing an old-fashioned glass holding two fingers' worth of something the colour of tea. "Light rum," he says, holding it out to him. "I never liked the stuff."

Norman never did either, but he takes the glass with both hands. "I hope I haven't exhausted your supply."

"If you mean do we have more, the answer is yes. A bit."

"John." Miriam smiles at her husband. "I was just in the middle of asking Norman . . ." She puts a hand to her mouth. "Now I can't remember." She stares off. "Oh, I hate this. I don't know whether to blame age or the meds. I don't know which is worse."

"You're just tired," says John.

Miriam shakes her head. "Does this ever happen to you, Norman?"

Having used Miriam's memory glitch as an opportunity to pour down the hateful rum in one smooth dose without raising anyone's alarm, Norman now has all eyes on him. He swallows.

"Not really."

"Well, good."

"Yes, I'm happy to say" – Norman taps his temple – "it's all quite vivid." Idly, he hefts his empty glass. He can feel the leading edge of the drink's warmth now and, craving another, he lets his gaze drift down to what he holds in his hand.

John clears his throat. "Did you need something?"

"Oh, no . . . I'm just . . ." Norman raises his glass and, shyly, wiggles it. "Would it be all right if I topped this up?"

"Here, I'll do it." John strides past and takes Norman's glass with an audible huff. Then he turns to Miriam. "How late were you planning on staying up?"

"I don't know." She looks at Norman. "We'll see."

John resumes his march out of the room, saying as he goes, "You shouldn't stay up too long. You were in bed, after all."

As the rum infiltrates Norman's extremities and he antici-pates the pleasure of more, he begins to feel somewhat at ease. The sensation so contrasts with what he was feeling just moments ago he realizes that what he was, before, was ill at ease. It seems silly to him now, to have felt ill at ease in the company of a woman who used to work for him. He walks to Miriam's living-room window and looks out onto Moore Park.

"It's interesting you bring up memory." He puts a finger to his upper lip. "Because I seem to recall taking the bus past here, as a teenager, on my way to a summer job at one of the local tennis clubs."

"Did you?"

"I cleaned the courts, which was a hell of a job. And it was around here, I think . . ." He pauses for a second. "It was around here somewhere, in the early seventies, that they held an outdoor Gershwin festival – just a one-day event – that I had a part in."

"That must have been High Park."

"No, it was near here, I'm sure. I remember there was a group of girls, off in the distance" – Norman waves his hand slowly in the air, pulling his recollections into the room, filling the room with himself – "about four of them, and in the middle of some song I was doing  I guess it was 'Summertime,' that was the big song – these girls, eighteen or nineteen years old, started taking off their shirts." He shakes his head, astounded at the memory. Then he grins to himself, chuckles faintly, and slips in a small confession. "Two of them came to my dressing room later." He'll leave it at that, he thinks, moving a hand to the back of his head and down the hairs of his neck. Better to leave it there, better story, since he seems to recall that nothing ended up happening with those girls. They had boyfriends.

John re-enters the room with Norman's glass and hands it to him grimly. "There's not much left, so I'd make that last." He bends down to place a kiss on Miriam's temple, cupping her shoulder with his hand. "I'm going upstairs to work, all right? Call me for any reason."

Norman watches him go. And once John is fully gone, the urgency of the situation seems to disappear too, as if urgency had been John's companion and simply accompanied him out of the room. Norman is alone now with his need and the person who can fill it, and he has his drink, so he can take his time. In the silence – because Miriam is saying nothing, simply watching him – he feels something, perhaps himself, shift within the landscape of the living room. He feels taller. This is what gives him the confidence to raise a particular disturbing point.

"Miriam," he says, "I'm curious about something."

"I hope this is connected to why you're here, Norman. Because the suspense is strangling me."

"When I was chatting with your assistant before, a woman named . . ." His gaze slowly levitates towards the ceiling.

"Bernice?"

"Yes, Bernice, thank you. When I was chatting with Bernice, she mentioned something about you not . . ." Norman takes in and expels a slow, contemplative breath. He's suddenly not sure he likes this road he's begun to travel.

Miriam leans forward in her seat. "Not what?"

"Well . . . not . . ."

"Not being well?"

Norman says nothing. He takes a safety sip of rum.

"Well, she's right. I'm not well at all. That's apparent from looking at me." She settles back. "I appreciate your noticing, though, Norman. I guess you've changed."

Now Norman is in a quandary, and he has to take another big gulp of rum about it. Because in fact the issue he had meant to raise was not Miriam's health at all – anyone can see she's not well – but the suggestion that, according to Bernice, she never liked him. That's the thing that troubles him. Now he doesn't know how he's going to bring the subject up.

❧

She is in a mood. It is a hard, abrasive mood and there's nothing she can do about it and it's ruining her date and she knows it, which irritates her all the more. And the engaging, account-reppish Grant Dekker, who chose a lovely onion-yellow silk shirt for the occasion, and did his best by rescheduling after she cancelled last night and tried throughout dinner to make conversation about her work, which she hates, and has acted the whole time as if nothing was wrong, can do nothing now but drive her silently home without the faintest idea of what's bothering her. Because how do you explain to someone you're in a shitty mood because three years ago your mother died?

That's not precisely it, of course, but that's what he would hear. *Why are you in such a lousy mood?* Well, last night I was forced to go through my dead mother's things. *I'm terribly sorry. When did she die?* Three years ago. *Oh.*

That three-year span sits there like a hard lump in a plate of mashed potatoes. Somebody missed something, obviously. Somebody wasn't doing their job. *Your mother died three years ago and you never sorted through her stuff?* That's right. *You just left things unattended to, left them to linger and fester?* Absolutely. *Why did you do that?* Because I enjoy letting things fester. I feel it makes me more attractive. *And you're in a bad mood now because the enjoyable festering period is over?* You seem to understand me. Would you like to come upstairs?

"I'm sorry for being in such a crappy mood," says Amy, hands layered in her lap, as the engaging Grant Dekker turns onto Queen's Quay towards the waterfront's metallic condominium towers. "There are reasons, but I don't want to go into it."

"That's all right. I hadn't really noticed."

"You mean you think I'm like this all the time?"

"I meant that even your bad mood is strangely charming."

"Ugh. That's just too smooth for words."

"There you go again."

She huffs and stares out the window, at the towers rising like auto parts against the cold night sky. Having met Grant at the restaurant, she has to direct him now. "I live in the one that looks like a spark plug," she says. "There, see it?"

"In all its glory."

It looms over them as they approach and Amy watches it with a kind of fascinated horror. "I suppose you're wondering what possessed me to live here."

"Nope."

"Well, if I were you, I'd be wondering."

He downshifts into second and turns his Boxster into the drive. "I just assumed you liked it."

She waits until he stops in front of the building's entrance. "You mean you would willingly go out with someone who likes these buildings, and this one in particular?"

"Why not?"

"So, if this hypothetical girl was walking along by the water and saw this thing, and she said, 'Wow, that's a really great-looking building. I want to live there,' you'd say, 'Hey, there's a girl I want to date.' Is that right?"

He turns off the ignition and shifts around in his seat to face her. "My position would be that a choice of residence wasn't the only thing that defined you. I would assume there were other aspects to your personality. Just as, if I drove a Ford, you wouldn't automatically condemn me."

"I don't know about that. Which Ford?"

Impending drollery makes his face go smooth. "A Taurus."

She gives him a sour-candy look. "I could accept a Taurus on the condition that you poured the rest of your money into rare books and original art."

"You have a big heart."

She opens the car door. "Well, it's a good thing you didn't say a Mustang. A Mustang would have been the kiss of death. Frankly, you're pushing it with the Boxster."

"There now, see?" he says, leaning against his door. "You've gone and saved the evening."

He gets out and walks her to the building's entrance. "So why do you live here?"

She peers up at him solemnly. "A few years ago, I was walking along by the water, and I looked up and said, 'Hey, that's a great-looking building. I want to live there.'"

"Seriously?"

"Don't worry, I'm only renting."

"Well," he says, kissing her lightly, "you seem to be surviving the experience. No visible scars at least."

She pats his arm in mock approval. "Mr. Dekker, I would say that you have lived up to your billing. And if I felt at all friendly tonight, I would ask you up."

"What's my billing?"

She opens her door. "You're the Thoroughly Engaging Grant Dekker."

"I am?"

"I added the 'Thoroughly' in light of your extra-hard work this evening." She lets the door close between them as she gives him a small wave. "I'm available for testimonials."

In her apartment, reasonably pleased with herself despite her mood, Amy shrugs off her jacket and hangs it up in the hall closet. Standing at a mirror she inspects her teeth for any incursions of cilantro or poppy seed that the E.G.D. would have been forced to witness and, finding none, goes to her phone and checks for messages. One of them is from David.

*"Hi, it's the male Swain. Call me when you get in. I've got some news you'll find interesting."*

"The male Swain?" she says when she reaches him.

"You're the eldest Swain; being male is my only claim to status."

"How does being male give you – ?"

"You're so easy to get. It's like dangling rabbit fur in front of a dog."

She'll give him that; she is easy to get. "All right," she says, on simmer. "You seem to be bursting out of your little cage. Does this have something to do with the house?"

"It does."

"And . . . ?"

"No, just the house, that's all."

This couldn't be more annoying. He's waiting for her to ask him. It's a power game he's played since he was ten. Why does he have to hold on to these things as if they were food rations?

"David, I'm not going to ask you."

"That's okay. It can wait."

She sighs, bends down to pluck a precious *New Yorker* off her couch (precious because, as a magazine with no client ads that might have been mis-positioned or given too much cyan, it delivers pristine, anxiety-free reading), sends it seagulling across the room, and sits down. "Look, I'm in a pissy mood. So I don't really care if you tell me or not."

Like a good younger brother he asks what's bothering her, and like a good older sister she says she's not sure. But she's willing to review the chain of probable cause and effect. Her Saturday afternoon was spent downtown, catching up on work too boring to do during the week. ("So you figured you'd spend your free time doing it. Excellent plan.") Her Saturday evening, although nice enough, didn't go as well as she'd hoped, because her date's charm was out of proportion to her own. ("I thought you'd have gotten used to that.") And her Friday evening was spent alone in the company of Norman, going through boxes of their mother's history.

"Well," says David, after a second, "I can't think of anything flip to say to that, can you?"

"No."

"So that's probably it."

"I was thinking."

During the momentary silence that follows she takes the phone with her into the kitchen to pour herself a glass of whatever she has. Pinot Grigio it turns out.

"What did you find?"

"Clothes mainly, and some departmental things. A bunch of Norman's old stuff too. He must have just shoved it all in there together and closed the door on it." Amy notes with detached, almost professional interest that she doesn't tell David about the journals.

"What did you do with it all?"

"His stuff I just shoved into his room. Her things mostly went into the basement. Some I put out on the porch for Goodwill. I guess I'll have to call the university about her papers." She passes up a second opportunity to mention the journals. Intriguing. "Norman, as you can imagine, was a huge source of comfort and assistance. Not unlike yourself."

"So what prompted this sudden burst of activity?"

"The bank told him to rent out a room. The word he used was 'suggested.'"

"Oh." The fact that David says nothing more to this tells Amy he wants to say a great deal – whatever made her choose media-buying over behavioural science? She decides to sip delicious Pinot Grigio and wait. "I guess," he says eventually, "I should probably tell you my house news then."

"Only if you want to, David. My night's sleep doesn't depend on it."

"I was talking to a guy I know, a lawyer." For some reason he hesitates, as if he expects her to interject. "I, uh, found out that we might be able to contest Norman's ownership of the house."

He waits again for her reaction, and she doesn't know what to say. Outside her kitchen window, she can see the glint of ferry lights on the lake.

"Hello?"

"Why would we want to do that?"

"Because he's obviously fucking up and he's going to lose the house."

"But, David, you never wanted to live there anyway. I don't want to live there either."

"Doesn't matter. This was Mom's house and it's not right that he's going to lose it because he's so fucking out of it."

She hears a tremor in his voice she hasn't heard since he was sixteen, when not being allowed to use the car on a date was the cruellest thing he knew. She sets down her glass and walks back into the living room. Movement seems important.

"David, you know what? It sounds to me like you're doing this out of anger."

"*Of course* I'm angry. I mean, shit."

"So, what's your plan? You're going to get ownership of the house, which probably means assuming Norman's debt, and then what? You'll sell it?" It's good she's in the living room now; she can pace in a wide, continuous circle.

"I don't know. Maybe."

"Who is this lawyer anyway – some articling student you play hockey with?" What was that? Nothing more than older-sister snarkiness. Deadly accurate though, given his silence. Still, she has to find something better. "I just think it's a stupid idea." Oh, insult him. Now that's genius.

"Well, I don't know what else to do."

"Maybe we could help him." As soon as she says this unpremeditated thing she knows it's going to cause trouble.

"*Help* him?"

"Well, isn't it" – she's rolling her eyes at herself already – "isn't it the right thing to do?"

"How should we help him – financially? Forget it. If he was sick or something then maybe. But he's totally healthy."

"We're both doing okay though."

"No. *No*. Why should you have to give your money to Norman instead of putting it into your RRSP? Or travelling somewhere? Why should we have to hand over our savings to someone who can't be bothered to work for his own?"

All these reasons are valid, thinks Amy, but she wonders if a better, or a more honest, argument is simply that Norman, by choice and by chance, is the parental figure, and isn't the law of parenthood explicit? Doesn't it stipulate that *his* role is to help *them*, if not financially then some other way? By offering up his benefit of years. By being interested. By doing what he can not to pervert the system because he accepts that it's his responsibility, that he is supposed to be the water and not the boat. Even as she thinks these things she wonders how and when she became such a familial fundamentalist. And now that she is, she wonders whether the laws and responsibilities of childhood, whatever they might be, are quite so absolute.

"I don't know, David. I just think trying to undermine Norman on the house is wrong. Do you really want to get into some legal thing?"

She hears him sigh at the other end. He manages a snicker.

"Boy, when you say it like that, 'legal thing,' that's just devastating. What the hell was I thinking?"

"David."

"I'm so ashamed."

She smiles. "Maybe we should just think about it for a while. I mean, let's not do anything sudden. Okay? Can you, for now, just sit on this whole weird house thing?"

"Ooh! Ow! 'Weird house thing'? Stop it with your verbal bludgeoning."

Grinning. "I'm deadly, deadly serious."

"Don't worry, sister, you've won. You've wiped the floor with me."

"Shut up and goodbye." She hangs up and lets her grin dissolve. Clearly it's impossible to convince someone of something when you don't know yourself what to think.

❧

"What the hell is he doing?"

"I don't know, John. He seems to be sleeping."

In fact, he is not sleeping. He is lying down, with his eyes closed, on the carpeted floor of Miriam Ashacker's living room. For the simple reason that, having had very little to eat all day, and having managed to slip into the kitchen for a third glass of rum, he had begun to feel a tad woozy. And so, while he and Miriam were talking, he very politely said, "If it's all right, I'm just going to stretch out while we talk," and did so. He chose the floor because it was firmer than the couch and thus better for his back, not to mention for the purposes of staying alert, because he never had any intention of going to sleep in the middle of their conversation. Although, now that he thinks of it, he probably did, only for a moment, because he has no memory of John entering the room.

"He just laid down on the floor? While you were talking?"

"While we were talking."

"Well, that's ridiculous."

"It's a very Norman-like thing to do."

He tries not to smile, because he's rather enjoying lying here and letting them think he's asleep, and listening to them talk about him. It's very calming. All things considered, the whole Miriam visit has gone pretty well. Especially the moment when

147

she touched her forehead and said, "Now I remember! I wanted to ask you how it's been going for you, Norman. What things have you done lately?" And he was able to use his favourite answer to prying questions like this – "I've been keeping body and soul together" – an answer that, in its suggestion of artistic purpose and sacrifice, its allusion to the struggles of a life lived in pursuit of meaning, managed as usual to say a great deal, and say it well, while saying nothing whatsoever.

"But," Miriam persisted, "have you been *in* anything?"

Typically, in Norman's experience, once the body-and-soul answer is given, the listener drops the issue. That's another of its chief virtues. But in this case, unfortunately, Miriam required more, and he was forced to get into detail. "I've been doing a great many things," he said. "A fine children's show, for instance, which I did for love more than money."

And still that wasn't enough. "It's been almost two decades," she said. "Give me names of shows, directors you've worked with. I'm curious about your development." It seemed, really, as if she were trying to shame him. He had to give her something significant, something that would sink her into her seat and tip the balance back in his favour. So he brought out the big guns.

"One thing I'm very proud of is the work I did in a recent production of *Man of La Mancha*."

"Well, that's good!" she said, leaning forward. Interested.

Norman hesitated for a moment. "It was a dinner theatre." He coughed. "In Beverly."

"Beverly."

"A pretty tourist town about an hour and a half away."

"I've been there. Did it go well?"

Did it go well? He considered the question. "It didn't start well," he began. "I had to work very hard." Then, after a moment, he found his thrust. "What I had to do was take this unseasoned, inexperienced troupe" – he had his hands out in front of him, strangling the air – "and I had to lift it up! Almost single-handedly." He held his arms high, such was the difference he had made! Then he relaxed in his seat. "I did everything I could."

The expression she gave him at that moment struck him as – there was no other word for it – sly.

"I'm sure they were thrilled."

Norman straightened up as much as the meringue sofa would allow. "They were, actually. As a matter of fact, I was given an award."

Miriam was astonished. "An award?"

"The Mirror Award. Given to me in recognition of, I think they said, 'extraordinary effort.'"

Miriam seemed genuinely pleased. "I'm very impressed, Norman. Good for you." While she smiled at him, he finished the rest of his third drink. Then she cocked her turbaned head to the side. "When you say 'they,' Norman, who is it you mean?"

Norman regarded her stiffly. "I don't understand the question."

"Who gave you the award? What organization? I don't think I've ever heard of the – what did you call it?"

"The Mirror Award."

She shook her head. "I don't remember that at all."

"Well, your memory isn't" – he cleared his throat – "completely reliable these days, is it?"

It was just about then, when he saw the look on her face, that Norman felt the pressing need to lie down.

"I don't like this, Miriam," John is saying. "I don't know this man. And now he's sleeping on my floor."

Norman hears a change in the tenor of John's voice and thinks it best to speak up. "I'm not sleeping," he murmurs, his eyes still closed. "I was just feeling a bit dizzy."

"He said he hadn't eaten much today. And then he had all that rum."

Above him, John is breathing intensely, like a man under duress. "Do you want me to get him a sandwich or something?"

"Maybe some crackers and cheese," says Miriam.

Norman brings his hands to his face and rubs his eyes. "This is a very comfortable rug," he says. "You must have excellent padding under here."

"Would you like some crackers and cheese, Norman?"

He pushes himself into a sitting position, smiles, and throws a hand up helplessly. "I'm at your mercy."

"Good," she says. "And while John is getting them, you can finally tell me why you're here."

Within a few minutes, John – obviously a good man – has brought out a platter of crackers with Jarlsberg and havarti and, separated from the rest by a dam of celery, a few fresh-cut slices of cold roast beef. And Norman has largely explained his situation, to the degree that he wants to get into it – the somewhat fallow period of the last couple of years combined with a serious desire to try something new, and his very real sense that there are interesting roles out there for men of a certain age who still have a vibrancy about them. He's thinking of stage work, of course, but he doesn't want to confine himself. Television? Certainly, he would consider something there. He could see himself playing a wealthy rancher, for example, or an outdoorsman of some sort. Even a police captain. Something requiring strength and resolve, but with a worldliness, and an element of humanity. Not that he would turn down a villain – a villain could be great fun. But anyway, these are just ideas, and she knows the kind of thing he's capable of.

Throughout this, Miriam appears to concentrate intently, nodding in the appropriate places, once or twice offering a "right" or an "I see." And at the end, as Norman bites into a delectable-looking Jarlsberg-beef roll-up he's made for himself, Miriam says, "I guess you've come to me for advice, then, have you? A plan of attack?"

His mouth full, Norman nods enthusiastically.

"Well, it seems clear to me that, if it's acting work you want, your first step should be to get yourself an agent."

It may be that the Jarlsberg-beef roll-up is not as delectable as he first imagined. There seems to be a piece of gristle.

"I know many of them are listed in the phone book."

"But Miriam –" It was almost as if the gristle had been placed there for him, a little orchestration of disappointment. "Miriam," he says and swallows, "*you* are my agent."

"No, I'm not. I'm not an agent at all." Miriam has a severity about her that seems incongruous. How can such a sick woman sound so rigid? "I haven't been an agent for a long time, Norman."

"I understand, but –"

"And even if I were an agent, I would hardly have you as a client. Ask me why."

"By the way, this cheese is quite good. Although I'm not sure about –"

"Ask me why."

He's never had a tougher line. And it's just one word. He blinks – the mechanics of his jaw seem to be ossifying – and says, "Why?"

"Because I have already had you as a client. I know what you're like."

Norman clears his throat and levels his gaze. "That's not enough information."

"What do you mean?"

"I think if you're going to dismiss me so . . . so definitively, you should give me some grounds. What is the basis for your decision?"

"You're an incredibly difficult man."

He breathes in and out as evenly as possible, runs his hands back and forth along the tops of his thighs. Yes, inescapably, yes, he is difficult. But people don't understand that there are always *reasons*. People continually focus on the wrong *things*. "So because of that you've decided to abandon me?"

"I'm not abandoning you, Norman."

"I've come to you for help, and you're turning me away."

Miriam shifts in her chair and adjusts her head wrap. "I'm really tired, Norman. I think it's time for you to go."

Norman looks down at the platter John brought out for him. Where is that hospitality now? Where is the common bond? He picks up a cracker and considers it suspiciously.

"What brand is this?"

"Norman, please. It's late for me. If you want, we could talk a little on the –"

He has brought the cracker to the region of his nose for close inspection. "I wonder if this is the same brand you tried to get me to do that commercial for. The one with the ridiculous wheat-stalk costume."

"I don't remember."

Norman takes a bite of the cracker. "I think it is." He chews and tastes. "There's a mealiness to it." He bites into it again. He is a fury of chewing and tasting. "I remember that mealiness. I remember not *believing* that you wanted me to humiliate myself for a mealy cracker."

"Well, maybe you're right." Miriam gets up and walks towards the hallway. When she gets there and turns around as if to direct Norman towards the front door, Norman is standing tall and rigid beside the couch, his arms raised to a point above his head, his face struck with an expression of wide-eyed wheatish sincerity.

"Hullo, I am a wheat stalk," he says in a low, loopy voice. "I have been made into a mealy cracker." He toddles stiff-kneed into the middle of the room.

"Norman."

"Can you imagine my chagrin," he says, still in his wheat voice, "being forced to become such a terrible cracker." His eyes mournful, he drops his jaw and sucks in his cheeks, to affect a wheat stalk's dismay. "When I could have been a bun."

"Norman, stop it. Stop!"

He can hear the pounding of John's sock feet racing down the stairs.

"Miriam? What's going on?"

Norman totters into the hallway to greet him, his hands still pressed into a wavering peak. "Hullo, John. I am a wheat stalk." He begins to hop awkwardly from one leg to the other. "Oh! Oh! I am being harvested by the thrasher!"

John freezes. "Miriam?"

"Please make him leave."

"I ask you, John," says Norman the Wheat Stalk, still hopping, "what sort of agent would suggest an actor take a role like this?" His face goes long with misery. "Could I be any more pathetic? Can you see why I'd feel betrayed!"

"Mr. Bray?" John holds up his hands in semi-surrender as Norman hops. "Mr. Bray, please."

Norman hears the title, which he takes as a small indicator of respect, and stops hopping. He lowers his hands.

"You've made your point, Norman," says Miriam quietly. "I'm sorry I can't help you. Now I want you to go."

Slowly Norman sinks back into himself and heads towards the front door. Once he reaches the front mat, with his hand on the door knob, he tilts his head and says to Miriam in his saddest wheat-stalk voice, "It was good of you to see me."

Then he opens the door and steps into the evening.

◈━◈

The fall months were always a time of restoration for Norman. After a draining season of summer stock, or eight hot weeks in a tourist theatre near some attractive chunk of landscape – an ocean, a mountain range, something that drew people and then disappointed them enough after a few days to make them look elsewhere for their entertainment – he found the waning temperatures, the edge to the air, invigorating. It was always a paradox to him that he felt most alive at a time when, in his experience, there was the least work. Summer was for musicals; fall was generally the province of serious theatre. When he finally got the call to come to Beverly, to rescue their production of *Man of La Mancha* (An aging musical in the fall? Only in a dinner theatre) it had been nearly twenty years between autumnal performances. Was it any wonder he had an excess of energy?

But now the timing is auspicious, because the city has shed its drape of summer humidity, the air has a quickening bite, the November sky is magnanimous, and Norman feels brimming with potential at just the moment he has a project at hand.

At 11:30 Sunday morning, he is awake, showered, and dressed, and full of amazement at himself. It doesn't occur to him that his early wakefulness has anything to do with anxiety over the night before or the days ahead. Rather, blinking into the sunshine coming through the living-room window he thinks, I must somehow have found something new within me. I've discovered a new way to sleep more deeply than before, making the final hour of sleep unnecessary. He considers writing down his theories about this new development, in case they might at some point be of help to others. But then he remembers he has a great deal to do.

He retrieves his favourite, capacious mug from the cupboard, given to him by Amy years ago, pours himself coffee, adds three heaping spoonfuls of sugar, and searches his refrigerator for table cream. When he finds he has no cream, he resorts to milk and considers it, this morning, only a minor setback.

Beside the coffee cup, on the kitchen table, is a square of cardboard cut from one of Gillian's boxes and a thick black marker. Norman is making a sign. He uncaps the marker and for several minutes holds it, poised, above the square, as he debates with himself whether to make the sign read "Actor's

Room for Rent" or "Room for Rent with Actor." There is no doubt in his mind that including that one detail will make the property more desirable. One can, any day of the week, rent a room in the home of a pharmacist, say, or a librarian. But how much more rare and intriguing an experience it would be, he thinks – and therefore how much more valuable – to rent a room with access to the talents and insights and aura of a professional performing artist. As he marks out the large black letters, however, he discovers that the cardboard square is only big enough to accommodate the words "Room for Rent." He sighs and decides to leave it at that. Should anyone question why he's charging a rent several hundred dollars a month higher than those listed in the newspaper, he knows he'll easily be able to explain the room's intangible benefits. *Are you*, he'll begin, *a lover of the theatre?*

A little after noon, he puts the sign in the living-room window. Wearing his flip-flop slippers and old forest-green velour robe, worn down to a film at the seat and elbows, he goes outside to inspect it, finds it well positioned and clearly visible from both sides of the street, and considers his work done. Before he ventures off the pavement, he finds his large silver lighter in the pocket of his robe along with a cigarette, and uses the first to ignite the second.

At 1:30, Amy calls from her apartment. "Have you read the journal yet, Norman?"

"Actually, I've been busy. I've been making a 'Room for Rent' sign."

"Oh. How long does that take?"

"These things," says Norman, "have to be done properly." He walks with the phone to the hallway; from here he can see the sign, leaning up against the windowpane, doing its work. Beyond, in the street, pedestrians pass by on the sidewalk, and Norman watches their eyes, expecting them to glance over. To be intrigued.

"I really think you should read it, Norman. Mom says some things there I think you should hear."

"Why?" On the other side of the street, as he watches, one of Norman's neighbours, the dark-haired woman who gave him beans, comes out of her turquoise porch with a plastic bag and stuffs it into the metal garbage can resting against the side of the house. She stands there a moment, wearing sandals, a thin black sweater, and an orange sarong tied at her waist, looking furtively up and down the street. It's the sarong that catches Norman's attention. It makes him think of the billowing cottons worn by men and women of exotic cultures – Pakistani? Indian? Thai? – that he has seen on TV. He resolves to ask the woman where she got hers, should he get the chance. He imagines that it's quite comfortable.

"Never mind," Amy is saying. "If it's too much trouble, don't bother. But I'd like to get it back. Maybe I'll come by tonight and pick it up."

"No, no. I plan to read it." The woman seems to be staring at his sign. "I would like to read it, as soon as I get the chance."

"I'll come by tonight. I have to go to a client event later."

"Oh, Amy. By the way. Do you know anything about the whereabouts of my Mirror Award?"

"Your what?"

"The award I was given in Beverly, for *Man of La Mancha*. I've been searching and I can't seem to find it anywhere.

I thought perhaps you or David might have thrown it away for some reason."

"Is that what you were looking for when you kept rifling through boxes in Mom's room, which you then left for me to sort through?"

"Among other things."

"I don't know anything about it."

Norman's eyes are on the woman. Is she coming closer? Or is it a trick of light, the breeze buffeting her sarong?

"Wait, did you say Beverly? That doesn't sound right."

"Anyway," he says, "you're coming over later?"

"About seven."

"Good, then. Could you – ?"

He was going to ask her to bring over some cream, but she has hung up. By the time Norman has replaced the phone and returned to the window, the woman is gone.

Some two hours later, Norman has managed to move Gillian's journal from the kitchen counter to the small oak table by his chair in the living room. In this way, he feels he is showing deference to Amy's hope that he will read it. He has made an effort – is, in fact, acknowledging its importance – which any reasonable person could see.

The challenge for Norman is that every occasion of physical contact with the journal is a profoundly uncomfortable experience, because it is a corporeal representation of Gillian. Each touch of its paper cover feels to him like touching one of her dry, thin bones. Part of him knows this is absurd, but he can't quite shake the shivery sensation.

So before he can actually take the enormous step of picking the journal up and opening it with both hands – essentially cradling her skeleton in his lap – Norman decides to attend to other things.

Money, of course, is a pressing matter. He decides the time has arrived to confront Margaret about his need for funds. And not fifty dollars either. She has some money stashed away, he knows she does, and she will have to be convinced to contribute a good lump of it to his cause. He dials her number, vowing to himself that he will be even more polite than usual.

The phone rings until her answering machine clicks in. *Damn.* Margaret is not home to hear his politeness. "Oh, Margaret," he says when her machine beeps. "Yes, it's Norman, actually. Ah . . ." He never feels comfortable leaving messages on answering machines. They always catch him unawares; he feels startled, and he wishes he could take back every word that he speaks. "Well, I was hoping you'd be in, just now, you see, because I wanted to say, ah, to come over actually." All he wants is to sound like the professional communicator he is, but these awkward circumstances make him sound ridiculous and amateurish, and he yearns for the ability to reach through the wire and pull the tape out of the machine. Although half of them aren't even tapes any more, they're digital wisps in some centralized facility. Well, then, *he wants back his wisp.* "But since you're not there, which surprises me, I have to say, I mean it's, what, one or two in the afternoon on a Sunday –"

The machine beeps and the line goes dead.

⊶⊷

"Margaret," Norman says into the intercom, his voice echoing around the tight, tiled confines of her building's vestibule. In his determination to get here, to talk to Margaret, he has forgotten

159

his keys, and now he is forced to call up. "Margaret," he says again, leaning in and pressing the button to her apartment, unsure whether he is supposed to press then speak or press and speak, and finding the whole exercise, and the buzzing of the button when he presses it, and the echoing of his voice and his helplessness and the fact that he is out of cigarettes all very unnerving and dispiriting.

When it's clear Margaret won't answer, he retreats out onto the front steps of the apartment building and weighs whether to shout up to one of her third-floor windows. She must be there; she never goes out. The only explanation is that she's avoiding him, turning her back on him when he needs her most, and that can't possibly be true. To get a better vantage, to see which room of the corner apartment she might be in, he steps farther out onto the property, onto the weedy grass. The late-afternoon sun glints off dirty windows into his eyes and, though he shields them, they begin to water. He heads back towards the building, into the shade.

He hears a sound. A faint sound he can't immediately identify. It's not a distant whining horn or the howl of a far-off dog, not the bleating of a television or a radio's muffled yammer, but a faintly insistent human sound. He hears it as he makes his way, wiping his eyes, around the building, looking for Margaret's window. He keeps looking up and around, but the sound, fervent, almost angry, is coming from below, from deep in the crook of shade at the base of the wall. Confounded, Norman edges forward towards its source and comes eventually to a small rectangular window below ground level and protected by a cuff of corrugated metal. The sound is coming from here.

Norman gets down on his knees at the grass's edge and leans out, over the hole, towards the window. What he sees through the thick, drabbled glass in the dim light of the basement he can't, at first, comprehend. It looks to him like a vast, multi-vaned windmill slowly swaying in the windless air. He leans farther towards the window, licks the palm of his hand and smears away some of the caked dirt, and realizes with horror that he is looking at two people having rampant, ululating sex, and that one of them is his sister. His aged, white-limbed sister is roiling beneath a dark, lumpen splatter with thick arms and grinding legs that Norman suddenly recognizes as Philip. And that's when Norman abruptly draws back his hand as if singed, and falls into the hole.

"Ahhh!" he yelps, his shoulder instantly lodged in mud and garbage, his legs and feet waving above ground level, his arms trapped and useless behind and underneath him, and one paired cheek and eye pressed against the cloudy glass, forced to stare at the image he was trying to escape, unable even to blink away the sight of his pale sister consorting with the man who attacked him. A small grey spider, its legs like eyelashes, crawls onto Norman's nose, and inside, on his bed, Philip lets out a guttural roar.

Very shortly, amid their heaving exertions, Margaret and Philip seem to become aware of a frantic presence outside their window. But when they look over and see Norman they react as if he's more monster than human. Margaret screams, rolls halfway over, and begins weeping uncontrollably, while Philip seizes a heavy leather boot and hurls it towards the glass.

"Sons of bitches," says Norman, still trapped and writhing, certain that all this indignity was laid out for him. He watches

Philip cursing as he awkwardly pulls on his clothes, then fixes his eye on Margaret, now on her knees behind the bed, pawing at the blankets. He sees Philip clump around furiously until he retrieves his thrown boot, shake a fist at the window, and then storm out of the apartment. Margaret, still terrified, but curious too, clutching a yellowed sheet to her breasts, rises and begins to come slowly forward. Then, frowning up at the window, she seems to hiccup, and her eyes go wide. She says, mouthing the word without sound, "Norman?"

Norman hears a door slam and footsteps, and then he feels a hand grab his ankle and pull, scraping the shin he injured on the old woman's wire cart against the corrugated metal. Quickly Norman finds himself out of the hole and on his back on the grass, with Philip waving his arms above him.

"What the hell are you doing, spying on us? Jesus Christ –" Philip bends down, grabs handfuls of Norman's shirt, and hauls him onto his feet. "First the beet spread, boy, now this." He shakes Norman roughly and sends his own jowls aquiver, then fixes on him a resolute stare. "I don't care if you are her brother," he says, and swings a fist into the side of Norman's face.

❖❖❖

A few minutes past seven o'clock, when the last of the small, freezer-emaciated ice cubes have melted against his cheekbone, Norman wrings out the cloth he's been holding to his face and lays it on the side of the sink. The edge of Philip's fist caught the cheekbone square, and now a patch the size of a poker chip has risen up pink and doughy. He inspects himself in the bathroom mirror, prodding the spot delicately with his fingertips. "That's going to bruise," he says.

He can't remember the last time he was struck in anger. Probably in school, he thinks, when the fourteen-year-old sons of metal workers and furniture salesmen decided they couldn't abide his light step in the hallways and his too-ready smile. But not since then. He doesn't count the time or two when a staged sword fight went awry, and a dulled épée found its way into a biceps or shoulder, or when a kick that was supposed to land against his upper thigh landed somewhat higher. Then, you can be sure, his professionalism was tested – and he always rose to the occasion. And afterward, they became great stories.

But this unprovoked attack leaves him with nothing. As he lay on the ground, his cheek throbbing, his vision scattered and sparkling, he saw the outlines of the lumpish Philip standing over him and he could think only of how to get away, how to avoid another blow. It was inexplicable, what had happened to him; it was beyond his comprehension. If he'd been younger, or better prepared, he might have jumped up and swung back. He might have insisted this bully stay far away from his sister. But neither of these things occurred to Norman at the time. His first and only concern was to get away. And now, in his bathroom, with the sounds of the water he has left running and a tune that he hums, softly, to calm his still-quickened pulse, he reviews all that has occurred to him in the past few days, all of the challenges and affronts, and wonders what good can come from all of it, what new undertaking the great, formless force of the universe might be preparing him for. "Something," Norman says, his chest filling, his eyes lighting in the mirror, "profound."

He dries his face with a clean towel, pressing it softly to his swollen cheek, and thinks he hears the doorbell. He turns the tap off. Waits. And hears it again. Who? he wonders. And then it comes to him. Amy.

⟡

"There was a woman standing outside your house on the sidewalk," Amy says, entering. "She walked away when I pulled up."

"Oh?" says Norman, his eyes on the paper bag she takes with her to the kitchen.

"Yeah, I think it was the woman from across the street." At the counter she begins unpacking the bag's contents. She has brought Thai, because she can no longer face his empty fridge. "I hope you haven't made anything."

"Actually," says Norman, "I was just putting my mind to it."

She observes him warily. "What happened to you?"

He touches his cheek. "The strangest thing." He hesitates. "I had an encounter."

"An encounter."

"That's right."

She narrows her eyes at him as he opens a cupboard. "You want to tell me any more than that?"

"Not really."

He lifts down two plates and goes hunting for cutlery while she pries off the lid of a plastic tub of green vegetable curry.

"Does it have something to do with the house?"

"No," he says. "Did you see my sign?"

Amy puts her hands around a tub of steamed rice. Feels the heat in it spread to a spot behind her ears. "Yes, I did."

"I expect some nibbles very soon."

164

They sit across from each other at the dining table, eating quickly. Amy listens to Norman compare the curry she's brought to others he's had, and declare it as good as or better than many despite the lack of bamboo shoots, which he always enjoys. Bamboo shoots are usually a standard ingredient, he says, and he suggests, good-naturedly, that next time she might want to try a different Thai restaurant.

"I'll do that."

"It's just a thought. Otherwise this is quite good."

Amy decides not to talk about David. "Norman," she says, "tell me more about what the bank said."

He pushes his plate aside as if he has suddenly lost his taste for the curry. "I'm doing what's necessary. There's nothing to worry about."

"But they're threatening to foreclose, aren't they?"

"No." He begins feeling his pockets.

"No?"

"That's right." He stands and moves to the front closet. "I simply have to pay them a small lump sum and then resume the payments as before. It's all under control." He digs in the pockets of his jacket.

"What kind of lump sum?"

"I was sure there was a pack in here."

"How much, Norman?"

"Seven thousand and something. I forget exactly." From the closet he moves to the stairs, headed for the second floor. Amy begins to follow.

"But that's what they said in the letter, right? That's the whole amount. Do you have that kind of money?" At the top of the stairs, she finds him looking through the laundry hamper. "Do you?" She waits as he churns through the clothes piled there, makes the shirts and underwear boil. "Norman," she says, exasperated, "What are you looking for?"

"Cigarettes!"

"Why would they be in the laundry?"

Bent over the hamper, he sighs.

"What are you going to do about the money?"

He straightens up, and for the first time Amy sees something pale and anxious in him. Through an open window come traffic sounds, a woman's shouts, and in all of these she can't help but hear a thin crease of panic, so she's sure her therapist would say she's projecting.

"Things will work out," he says, adding a late, pained smile. "They always do."

"How though?" She feels her baby toes being pinched by her hard, dark shoes, the fabric of her suit chafing at her wrists. There are times when, dressed for work, she feels like something constructed by and for others, slotted into duties and responsibilities she's not ready for, and this is one of them. "I have a little money I could, maybe, lend you."

He gives her a surprisingly tender look, says, "I'm sure that won't be necessary," and turns to go downstairs. Passing by, he puts a hand softly on her wool-suited arm. When she lived at home, with Norman and Gillian, he would give her massive bear hugs, regardless of his mood. They seemed, sometimes, desperate.

"Maybe," she says, "I should take back that journal of Mom's."

"Right," he says, distracted. "I was going to read that, wasn't I."

"Oh, you know what? Don't even bother. I wouldn't mind getting it back, though."

"No, I'll read it now. I think it's by my chair." He jogs down the stairs – lightly, it strikes her, for a man of his age. She follows after him.

"Maybe not, though, Norman." He's already moving into the living room, beyond her view. She hears him say, "Here it is." And when she enters the room, she sees him settle into his chair, take a deep breath, and pick up the notebook with the care of someone hoping not to leave fingerprints.

"It's thin," he says through his pained expression, folding back the notebook's cover.

"Most of them were thicker."

"Oh, yes?" He acquires a studious look.

"That was her last one."

"Mmm-hmm?" He's already reading, or appearing to read; she can't tell. She goes into the kitchen and finds a newspaper to look at. More speculation about a missing elementary-school French teacher in Halifax. Were David here he would offer up his theories – a lesbian rendezvous or a bloody death at the hands of the vice-principal – calculated to offend her, and she, finding them offensive, would tell him to shut up. Without him, her own theories surface. She imagines a clean escape, from one kind of life into another. Madame French Teacher, in class every day, a roomful of verb-reciting children before her, planning her next existence. Choosing her name, her hair colour, her past. Feeling the possibilities roll through her mouth, becoming intimate with a new, more comfortable truth.

As she reads she listens for Norman. Occasionally she hears him determinedly clear his throat and, once or twice, give a rueful, disapproving chuckle. Then, for a long while, she hears silence, nothing but the pages being turned.

❦

In the living room, sitting in his chair, Norman is coming to understand. Slowly, as he turns the pages and reads Gillian's neat blue script, he sees what he has never imagined before, what he could never have thought possible. At first, it makes him angry, it fills him with grief. But he comes to realize it's the only truth that makes proper sense of everything that happened.

Gillian should have told him. She should have tried harder to be heard. And no doubt, yes, he could have been more alert himself as to what was going on. He understands now how troubled she was, and if she had managed to make her unhappiness clear, if he had been able to recognize his effect on her, who knows what he could have done? Who knows?

He might have been able to get her some help.

Yet as hard as his discovery is to accept, it also, somehow, lifts from him a great weight. He reads the last page and, exhausted by what he's learned, he sits with his hands hanging limp from the armrests, and the notebook lying in his lap. Finally, he nods to himself, closes the journal, and rises. Clutching the book tightly now, he walks into the kitchen, and sees Amy bent over the newspaper.

"I hope –"

She jumps. "Oh, my God, Norman. You scared me. I was just reading about that teacher."

"I hope you understand what a shock this is for me."

Her face falls. "I'm sorry, Norman. I didn't want –"

"Because I loved her, you know. I don't want you to think I knew, and did nothing."

She hesitates.

"I couldn't possibly have seen it coming."

Amy frowns. She looks from Norman to the notebook in his grip and back to him. "Seen what coming?"

He flaps the journal. "Her suicide."

For a moment she simply squints at him, as if he's far away. And he realizes he's made too great a leap. Of course she doesn't hold him responsible; Amy's not like that. She simply had to share what she knew. And probably – of course, he sees now – she wants his help, to understand.

He opens the journal. He fans the pages. "You were right to show me this. The clues are all here. What's amazing is how well she kept things hidden."

"Norman, what on earth are you talking about?"

He pages through, trying to find the relevant entries. " 'My mind turns violent,' " he reads. " 'Sometimes, after he's been talking to me for half an hour about something utterly mean-ingless, I realize I've been digging my fingernails into my forearm, raking the skin. I've actually drawn blood.' " He looks up at her. "Your mother was having trouble, Amy. She was really struggling. Mentally."

Amy holds her head as though pained. "I don't get what you're saying, Norman." She scrapes her fingers through her hair. "You actually think Mom killed herself?"

He flips to another entry. " 'He is driving me slowly mad.' " Another. " 'This can't go on.' "

169

She puts a hand on his arm. "Norman, she was frustrated with you. Don't you see that? You were pissing her off!"

He raises his voice. "'I can't bear it any longer,'" he reads. "'The only thing I can do is get out. Out of the whole thing.'" He slaps the book closed. "*The whole thing*, Amy. It's as clear as day."

"No." She shakes her head steadily, a constant, metronomic back and forth. "No, you're just taking bits of what – she was talking about something else, Norman. She's talking about leaving you."

He begins to pace around the kitchen. She's resisting the truth. How can he make her understand? "It's tragic. It's terribly sad. But what this tells us is that she wasn't equipped to live with an actor. She was too fragile. She simply lost herself. It's no one's fault." He turns then, at the sink – it's this above all she has to hear.

"It's no one's fault, Amy. You must believe that I had no idea I was having this effect on her. Looking back on things now, it seems I should have had some inkling. But that's hindsight. The fact is I never knew. If she'd told me, somehow, I'm sure I could have done something."

Amy gives a short bark of laughter. "You would've had to listen to her first."

"God, it's sad." His eyes begin to tear up. "What a fucking tragedy."

She puts out her hand. "Norman, give me the journal. I want it back."

Norman presses it to his chest. "This? Oh no, I think I should keep it."

When she was nineteen, almost twenty, and Norman had for two years been fully entrenched in the role of Man of the House, Amy began feeling pain in her abdomen. For three days straight she moped around with a mild fever, and her period arrived ahead of schedule and twice as heavy as normal. After the appropriate tests their family doctor, Dr. Janice Neal, diagnosed her with pelvic inflammatory disease and started her on a heavy course of antibiotics. As it happened, her mother was spending that month in Edinburgh at a conference on eleventh-century folklore with an extensive evening program, which made it difficult for her to be reached. Amy was loath to leave word that she might possibly end up sterile on the hotel message system. And she said nothing to Norman. When after two days he came across her supply of antibiotics and wanted to know what was going on, she told him she had a fever, probably the flu.

"I don't believe in taking antibiotics for the flu," Norman told her firmly. "I've never done it, and I never would. I wouldn't do that to myself." The body, he explained, had to fight these things on its own, to build up its resistance, in order to achieve its full potential. He wanted her to throw the antibiotics out.

"I can't," she said. "The doctor said I have to take them."

She knew already it was not a good idea to resist one of Norman's heartfelt directives; he was too fierce in his beliefs. And indeed, when she tried, Norman became livid. The doctor, he informed her, was undoubtedly getting some sort of kickback from the drug company. The doctor knew how dangerous these antibiotics were. To ignore the obvious facts was ridiculous. To continue taking the pills was insane. Therefore, in order to protect Amy from herself, Norman took the bottle of pills and poured them into the toilet.

She watched it happen as if it were something on television. Watched him flush the toilet triumphantly. She opened her mouth to speak, and ran into her bedroom. That night, when David heard the story and confronted Norman about it, Norman was appalled. How was he supposed to know what to do if no one told him anything!

Now, in the kitchen, she fights the tremor in her voice and tells him again, "Give me Mom's journal."

"No."

"Give me the journal, Norman."

"I'm sorry, Amy. I have to keep it."

"Give me my mother's journal, *please.*"

He stands erect. "You obviously can't see how important this is."

Amy stares at him, still and silent, when she knows what she should do is scream. It's not as though she lives here any more; there's no cost to shouting at him, telling him precisely, irreparably, what she thinks. She speaks her mind with other people; what's so difficult about doing it with him?

She walks towards the foyer, suffocated by her own silence, thinking the words she wishes she could say (*If it's such a tragedy, Norman, why do you seem so happy about it?*). She jerks open the front door and stalks out of the house, wondering what essential ingredient in her character is missing.

At ten o'clock that night, sitting in his chair, with the light from a street lamp falling across his knees and his mind gliding over the landscape of his circumstances, Norman hits a strange and sudden trough. Perhaps it has something to do with a fleeting image of Gillian in her car, or an unexpected peripheral sighting of Cantor's Post-it note stuck to his refrigerator door, or maybe it's only the potent stillness of the air – but the thought seizes him, savagely, that he might be in very grave trouble.

When this happens, he lets out a long breath through clamped teeth, and leans over to turn on the white ceramic reading lamp at his elbow. The light calms him a little. After a moment, he gets to his feet and walks over to the brass standing lamp in the corner, beside the piano, and cycles its tri-level bulb past sixty and one hundred watts to an expunging, brilliant one hundred and fifty. From here, he heads to the dining room and slides the dimmer for the stained-glass library swag to full, and in the foyer and in the kitchen he thumbs the switches high to complete the flooding of the main floor.

With only the slightest hesitation he opens the door to the dirt-floor basement crowded with bits of old wood furniture and smelling of bog rot and disintegration. He stands on the top step and reaches forward, hand waving in the hollow dark, to grab the chain, which he finds and yanks as if it were a rip cord. Then he slams the basement door shut.

He bounds up the stairs, finds the switch for a frosted sconce he never liked and, turning it on, finds he likes it a great deal. The second-floor hall light goes on. He reaches around the bathroom door frame, paws the wall, and feels a tickle of pride at how readily his hand locates the switch: on! In his bedroom he flicks on the ceiling fixture and, behind the half-filled ashtray, empty cigarette pack, and mould-ravaged coffee cup on his bedside table, the etched-glass globe of an antique banquet lamp burns affirmatively golden.

A few steps along is Gillian's old office, freshly emptied. Norman switches on the ceiling light and leaves the door open so that the light spills into the hall. The last room, David's cramped former bedroom, filled with boxes "temporarily" stored here two years ago during one of his condominium moves, has a three-bulb fixture in the ceiling. He flicks this on with a final conquering swipe and discovers two of the three bulbs are burned out.

He closes the door to David's room. The rest of the house, every corner, blazes car-dealer bright, and the best thing, the easiest thing, is to imagine the same unwavering brilliance in there, behind the door. Because this is a game, he knows it's a game and he is in on the game, and this part of it, the imagination part, is the *best* part.

But now, in this klieg-lit house, his imagination is failing him. Behind this door, inside this room, it is dim. And it's not a soothing moonlight dim, as Norman tries to convince himself, not a starlight-on-fresh-snow dim, or a persuasive candlelight dim, but a weak, pallid dim, a dim suggestive of compromise and discouragement and the multiform causticities of a dark, imaginationless truth. And the dread he meant to force to the outskirts of the house begins to brave the light and encroach.

So he goes downstairs. He pulls on his windbreaker and checks his pockets. The change he finds here – two dollars and fifteen cents – was seed money for a fund he was building to buy a pack of cigarettes. What he will do, instead, is buy two light bulbs, and manage some other way on the cigarette front.

Outside, the evening has turned surly. An icy breeze bears down on his neck and he shoves his hands deep in his jacket pockets and compresses his lips and eyelids against the chill and tells himself that he is a man who enjoys the outdoors. He imagines an elderly clerk in the convenience store, commiserating with him over the sudden turn in temperature. "I like it brisk!" Norman will exclaim. "I could go camping in this!" He repeats it the whole way. I like it brisk. I could go camping.

Three blocks later the convenience-store clerk, a short teenage boy with hair like a mussel shell, does not look up when Norman enters, and says nothing at all about the weather. Norman stands inside the door for a moment and bats himself on the shoulders to get his blood moving while the boy turns the page of a wrestling magazine. Finally, he sighs loudly and heads down an aisle.

The store's stock seems to consist entirely of potato chips in bright metallic bags. He finds light bulbs on the bottom shelf of the farthest aisle, tucked in beside bottles of drain opener, which is very bad for pipes in certain older homes. People don't know this. Sometimes Gillian wanted him to use products like these, and it was all he could do to resist.

At any rate, the bulbs. Norman sees three boxes of four sixty-watt bulbs, $3.59 each. Beside them, a single replacement appliance bulb in a plastic bubble pack, $1.98. That is all there is.

He lifts his gaze over the facial tissue towards the front of the store. "Excuse me," he calls. "Do you have any more light bulbs?"

"Just what's there." The boy says this without looking up, because wrestling is so fascinating.

"There isn't very much here, though." Norman advances partway up the aisle, past the bottles of kitchen cleaner and long boxes of sandwich wrap, which are extraordinarily expensive here, so the boy can see him more fully. "I'm sorry, I didn't make myself clear. I'm looking for two light bulbs. I need two sixty-watt bulbs. Two hundreds – that is, two one-hundred-watt bulbs – would be better."

"Just what's there, sir."

The boy has not looked up even once from his wrestling magazine, as if the pupils of his eyes were stitched to the pages with long nylon threads. "Sorry to trouble you," Norman murmurs, loud enough to be heard, his voice all compassion on the surface, but with an underlay of scathing commentary. Not an easy thing to do.

Nothing. Was David ever like this? Norman can't remember. He thinks David was something like this; he was certainly a handful for a number of years, and Gillian dealt with him rather ineffectually, rather meekly, before he moved out. But he himself was never like this. He was a hard worker as a boy: he practised for choir, he studied assiduously; he had dates, certainly, but at all times he was devoted to doing things the right way. And he does not understand why the world is no longer devoted. He does not understand why ignorant boys are now given positions of responsibility and why convenience stores have no selection, any more than he understands why banks wish to do him harm and agents will not help him and children act as if he's somehow to blame when a terrible thing happens. He finds it all a mystery. And he lifts his eyes to the fluorescent tubes and white ceiling tiles above and shakes his head, sharing this sad, perplexing moment with God.

Then Norman makes his way back to the end of the row to deal with the problem at hand. In supermarkets, you can buy half a dozen eggs. If they have only dozen boxes, you can break a box in half and buy six. It's tricky sometimes; the boxes aren't as easy to break as they used to be. And people he encounters, customers and checkout clerks, often seem surprised, as if they haven't been properly informed that it is perfectly acceptable to buy only six eggs if that's all you need. But never mind; he does it frequently.

So he will buy two sixty-watt light bulbs.

He eases the rectangular corrugated section, with its two bulbs, out of the cardboard sheath. Why package them this way if the practice isn't acceptable? *Go ahead*, says this packaging. *No one's forcing you to buy four. Split the four into two if two is all you need.* Slipping the bulbs into his loose jacket pocket Norman says, not loudly but audibly, "Two is all I need." The rest of the box he returns to the shelf. Someone else who needs only two will be glad of the precedent he's set.

"Mr. Bray?"

Norman stiffens. Someone is going to accuse him of breaking the rules. People are always trying to stuff him into their little boxes of behaviour. He should have known this would happen.

"It is Mr. Bray, right?"

"Now, look –" Norman turns to see at his elbow a young woman in her mid-twenties wearing a grey tweed coat. She comes up to his chin; her hair, the colour of sunburnt grass, is tied straight back off a wide escarpment of forehead. She has an uneasy smile on her face. "What I'm doing," he says, "is perfectly reasonable."

"I was in Professor Swain's medieval-poetry class." She extends a small, limp hand. "My name's Helen."

He takes her hand carefully. "Helen," he says.

"Right, Helen Dougal. I came over a couple of times. Just to drop things off." She nods, as if to confirm the truth of what she's just said, as if he might have his doubts. "I think one time you were playing the piano."

Norman senses the ground firming up beneath him. "Oh, yes," he says, "I play a little." He doesn't have the slightest memory of her. He generally avoided Gillian's students on those rare occasions when they came over because, just in the way they stood in the doorway, or ran up the stairs with their arms laden with papers or books, they sharpened his sense of being – not old. Old is not the word. But something akin to it. . . . Tired.

But he smiles at Helen because she is pretty, in an unconventional way, and because just now, in her presence, he's not feeling tired. She doesn't seem to be here to make him feel bad at all.

"I thought you were really good. And I liked your singing, too."

In fact, she is here to make him feel better.

"Do you remember what it was?"

"Uh," she begins. "Oh. Pardon me?"

"The song. You said you enjoyed the singing so I thought you might remember what song it was."

"Oh!" Helen's face acquires a wide-eyed look of horror. "Gosh. No. I mean . . ." She shakes her head. "No." She squeaks a small laugh. "That was like three years ago." She checks her watch, then looks off in search of something or someone. "Oh, by the way" – she shoots out a hand to touch Norman's arm – "I'm really sorry about what happened with Professor Swain. I mean, that was just awful. We all felt really bad." She adds a follow-up nod of extreme sincerity.

"Three years ago."

"Yeah, I know. That was really just –"

"I might have been rehearsing *Man of La Mancha*."

Helen's gaze wanders off over the pickles and mayonnaise. "Sorry?"

He begins to hum. He watches her, smiling, with his *hum, hum, hum*. "Familiar?"

"No." She shakes her head. "Not really."

*Hum, hum* and *hum, hum* and "Keep thinking" and *hum, hum* and "Onward to glory I go! *Buh dum bum!*"

He smiles expectantly, his face hopeful and bright, as someone appears from the adjacent aisle and wants to slip between them to get something on the bottom shelf. A woman with long dark hair wearing a heavily insulated white coat. Norman backs away slightly, reluctantly, splitting his attention now between Helen, who has yet to dredge the song out of her memory, and the woman, who seems familiar. He can only see the side of this second woman's face, and that only from an angle, but it could be the woman who has been staring at his sign, the woman who gave him beans. He glances back at Helen, wanting not to lose track of her, and then at the dark-haired woman, and what the woman is grabbing hold of, because he anticipates both Helen's sudden remembrance of his song and the second woman's imminent discovery of a convenient two-pack of . . . *light bulbs*!

Norman feels, at this moment, like a man tinkering with omnipotence, dragging a finger through the sand of cause and effect. "That must have rung a bell," he says to Helen, as he notes, out of the edge of his eye, that the second woman is now shaking the box of light bulbs as if she were annoyed. She doesn't realize her good fortune.

"No, I'm sorry," says Helen. But Helen is also watching the woman in the overstuffed coat, and looks back at Norman now with something almost like fear.

The woman peeks into the half-empty box, makes a *tsk* sound and sighs. She holds the box up over her head – it *is* the woman he knows – and seems about to call to the boy at the front.

"Oh, sorry, that's mine!" blurts Helen, her eyes wide with fright. She tries to reach for the light bulbs as the woman turns.

"No! That was me!" barks Norman. "I did that!" In his excitement, his wish to make a small contribution to the life of the Mediterranean-haired woman who surely, if she under-stood, would be pleased to be able to buy just the number of light bulbs she needs, he jostles Helen aside and knocks the half-empty box from the woman's hands.

Helen, pressed now against the glass of the milk cooler, regards Norman severely. "I was just trying to help you," she says. "I thought you were shoplifting!"

Norman has no idea what to say. He turns from Helen, who in doing him a kindness has ruined everything, to the white-coated woman, who is astonishing in the convenience-store light, her skin the precise hue of his most perfectly creamed coffee, and who seems not to be concerned with either of them. With a hand to her throat and her mouth opened in alarm, she seems to be sunk deep in thought, as if the event has served only to jog an awful memory.

"I was going to pay," he insists. He shows Helen his two-dollar coin. "I only needed two bulbs! I was going to pay for them!"

Helen's face knots into incredulity. "That's just *weird.*"

Before Norman can say anything else, before he can defend himself or explain his rationale, Helen straightens and hurries away, past the other woman and the boy clerk, who has been roused by the commotion and has wandered down the aisle. He stops halfway and leans giraffe-like towards them. "Everything okay here?"

"Fine," says Norman, flustered. "It's fine. I was simply –" He stops when the woman lifts the hand off her throat and touches his shoulder. "Fine," he says with more confidence, smiling the boy away.

The woman bends down and rises with the fallen box of light bulbs. "Your house is so bright tonight. So much like hope." She turns the box over in her hands. "Our house seemed too dark."

He understands completely; to have inspired someone in this way seems only natural. But it pleases him all the same and helps him to think that, really, when he was racing through the house, turning on lights in a panic, it was this sort of greater consequence he intended. "How many bulbs do you need?" he says. "Because if it's only two –"

"No, four. Four." She returns the half-box to the shelf and picks up a full one.

"Are you sure? Don't let them force you into it."

She studies him. "Who?"

"Well," he begins airily, utterly helpless. Her eyes are obsidian, the darkest he has ever seen.

"I am going," she says with a shy smile.

As the woman with the Mediterranean hair turns away, he thinks to say, "The sign. You saw my sign." She tosses back a furtive glance and continues up the aisle. "Are you interested?" he calls. He follows tentatively and when he gets to the front she's gone, so hurried that she has left the light bulbs on the counter next to the boy, who's back to reading his magazine. Norman, checking to make sure his own bulbs are secure in his pocket, places his coin noiselessly beside the box and leaves. He has some faint expectation that the woman will be waiting for him outside. But when he opens the door into the cold, he finds no more than night.

⌖

At 9:02 Monday morning, Norman's telephone rings. The first ring prods him just far enough out of sleep for the second to terrorize him completely. His eyes burst open and his heart rabbits to a sprint. It seems certain he is being attacked, and he would cry for help if only he could fathom how. With the third ring he finally computes the no-less-startling fact of what's really happening – his phone is ringing – and what action is required. He is able to muster the wet-cardboard flop of an arm across his body, reaching the handset just as his downstairs answering machine kicks in.

"Hello?" he rasps.

From the far end of the line comes the percussive sound of a handset being plucked out of its cradle.

"*Hello, this is Norman Bray –*"

"Hello?" says a male voice.

"Yes?" says Norman.

"*I'm not here, except, you could say –*"

"Is that Mr. Bray?"

"*– in a manner of speaking.*"

Norman tries to blink himself further awake. "My machine –"

"*But to quote Sir Toby Belch –*"

"Would you like me to call back or wait?"

"*I will meditate the while –*"

"My machine is on."

"*– upon some message for a challenge.*"

"I'll wait."

"*Please leave yours at the beep.*"

To Norman, lying still, with his eyes closed, the second of silence that precedes the beep feels like a gift.

"I'm sorry," says a flat, numbing voice after the beep has come and gone, "I'll try again. Is this Mr. Bray?"

"Yes." His brain feels as if it's made of wet coffee grounds. Norman pushes himself up and back against the cold headboard of his bed. "Who is it?"

"My name's Rol Henninger, Mr. Bray, from the Willingston-Hanford Agency. I'm the employment counsellor working with Howard Cantor."

"Ron did you say? Or Raul?"

"I said Rol. R–O–L."

"Rol." The name, like the voice, makes Norman think of a viscous liquid.

"Where have I found you, Mr. Bray, in bed?"

"Yes." The word *bed* triggers a massive yawn that prevents Norman from completely hearing or understanding what Rol Henninger says next. From the fragments he gets, he thinks it might be *We're often a cold fart*, which strikes him as a surprisingly self-deprecating thing to announce.

"I'm sorry, could you say that again?"

"I said, 'Then we're not off to a good start.'"

"Oh." He clears his throat. "Why is that?"

"Because, Mr. Bray –" It sounds to Norman just now as if Rol Henninger might be leaning forward; that's what he would do if he were to say the words *Because, Mr. Bray* in the way that he hears Rol Henninger say them. "– the fact that you are still in bed during business hours tells me you are not taking your situation seriously."

Norman pulls his blanket up to his chest. "That's not true. I'm taking it very seriously."

"I put more stock in that statement, Mr. Bray, when it comes from clients who, at 9:05 on a Monday morning, are sitting alert and fully dressed at their desks, rather than lying in bed half asleep." Norman wants to object to that, and strenuously, but Rol Henninger keeps speaking. "What I think you should do now, Mr. Bray, is get out of bed, take a shower, get yourself dressed, and call me back. I believe you have the number."

The image of the robin's-egg-blue Post-it note, marred by Howard Cantor's awkward scribble, jumps involuntarily into Norman's head.

"I thought –" He grasps for indignation. "Wasn't it supposed to be me calling you in the first place?"

"It was," says Henninger. "I start work at eight a.m., Mr. Bray. I waited as long as I could."

⋯⋯

Driving north on the two-lane strip of Highway 27 early Monday morning, Amy pushes a CD into her Jetta's slot and lets the singer's thin-boned candour define her mood. She has a bagel with cream cheese in the seat beside her, and a black coffee in its Styrofoam cup, both of them bought out of a sense of obligation – don't drive on an empty stomach, Gillian once told her – and both untouched. She taps the wheel as she gets farther from the city and watches the short-haired fields and cowlick trees roll by.

Since the previous night, she's been dwelling on the past, and on the things she may have missed. Obligations she may have neglected, duties she may have shirked. She has asked the question, Am I a coward? And some part of her has wondered whether saying no is simply a way to delay coming to terms with the facts. She has resolved, for the time being, to think the worst of herself, to see where that will lead.

Nothing could have been expected of her when her father left; she was only seven, after all. There were reverberations for a few years, uncomfortable visits sat through and long, angry telephone calls overheard. And during these she would watch game shows on television – *The Price Is Right* and sometimes, with a child's grasp of irony, *Family Feud* – because it was the only time she could do so without being scolded. But never did she have the sense that she had left something undone.

Her mother's death was different. She was the eldest child, by then a young woman with a career and a residence of her own; her mother was killed and it fell to her to be the clear-eyed one, to see the things that needed seeing, to ask the questions that had to be asked, even if asking some of them might have been considered a betrayal of who she knew her mother to be. It was here, undoubtedly, that she had failed.

Why this road, for instance? Why would her mother take this old so-called highway on a harsh, dark November night, instead of the faster Highway 400, if she really was trying to get to the dinner theatre in time to see the lights come up on Norman's Cervantes? An easy question, surely – nothing too dangerous, unless you allowed it to lead you down a bleaker path. But then apparently, as Amy reminds herself, she is not so inclined.

Three years ago, late in November, two constables from the Toronto police, a man and a woman, came to her door at about 9:30 at night, asking if she was Amy Swain, daughter of Gillian Swain, to which she said yes, looking at their eyes. They were, they said – speaking slowly and evenly – very sorry to inform her that her mother had been killed in a car accident, "up on 27" near the town of Thornton, at approximately 7:55 p.m. They were very sorry, they repeated, their faces quite fixed. Amy stepped backward and they lurched forward, the two officers together, as she bumped her calf against the coffee table and seemed about to stumble. The female officer took Amy's elbow gently and drew her to the couch, sitting next to her on the edge of the cushion, not like an invited guest but someone with a task to perform. The male constable stood nearer the door, two hands holding his cap below his belt, and then, apparently distracted by the Mel Gibson movie Amy had been watching and judging that inappropriate, walked over softly and pressed a button to turn off the TV. The sudden silence, and the loss of the phosphorescent motion, seemed a kind of death itself, and Amy felt, for a moment, suspended in time.

After two or three minutes, the two officers explained that, unfortunately, it was necessary for someone in the family to drive to a hospital in Alliston where the body had been taken in order to identify it officially, for the record. Again, they were very sorry. They knew how difficult it would be, but did she feel up to going that night? She said yes, if they were asking her, then she would go. Was it possible, they said, for a friend to drive her? Yes, it was – Laura, her roommate, could take her. That would be no problem. My mother is dead? she said. Yes, she was told. And they said again, they didn't stop saying, how sorry they were. She asked if anyone else had been hurt and was told no, as far as they knew it was just the one car, a single-vehicle event. She asked if her brother knew and was told no, he had not yet been located. Would she prefer to tell him herself? Yes, she said, she would prefer to tell him herself, but then she thought about telling him, and how she would tell him, and what he might say or do and the things that could happen to his face that she'd have to see and she said no, actually, could they do it? Would that be possible? So that was the first test she failed, and immediately there was another. When Laura, who came home from her boyfriend's instantly when Amy called, asked tentatively, as if pressing the tip of a needle against her skin, if Amy wanted to go up 27, to see where it had happened, she said no. God, no. The 400 would be faster.

And as it turned out, she thinks, those were only the beginning. Now, three years after the event, as she drives up 27 through Nobleton, past Dunkerron and Bond Head and Cookstown, weightless little communities strung like Christmas lights on a wire going north, she ticks off the rest of the list.

What, beyond the obvious, happened? There was another, simple question, unasked. What actually caused her mother to smash into an embankment, and with such force that, as one of the medical staff in Alliston thoughtlessly said, she had flown from the car like a bird? Surely this was something knowable, a question that could be answered, even if others weren't. Questions like, what was her last thought? What final image stamped itself on her awareness – a tree? A McDonald's billboard? A house in the distance with its porch light on? Or had she fallen asleep? Was there music on her radio when her car met the embankment? Had she been singing along? Was she distracted by something, or upset? Did she – this one above all, this one not even considered let alone asked, and so proof of her total failure of courage – did she want to die?

As Amy approaches the junction of Highways 27 and 21, near the town of Thornton, she finds herself slowing down against the music's rhythm and it takes a second for her to understand why – it was in this area, somewhere through here, surrounded by these fields, that the accident happened. She was never told precisely where, and maybe she has already passed it, but now, as she drives along, every ditch and roadside tree becomes a possible accomplice in her mother's death.

An hour before, she'd lied to get off work, something she rarely did because she never found herself convincing. "I don't know, I think it's a migraine," she told Darla, her department head, over the phone, lying on her side in bed and pressing her painless temple for effect.

"Where are you feeling it?" asked Darla.

"Just in one spot," she knew enough to say, "behind my right eyebrow. And I feel really nauseous, too."

"Okay, well, that could be a migraine," said Darla reluctantly. "Just get some rest. We need you back here soon."

"Yup, thanks," she said softly and hung up, hating herself for feeling guilty.

It's 11:05 when she pulls into the parking lot of the Beverly detachment of the Ontario Provincial Police, a two-storey brick building housing the officers responsible for policing the mid-section of the province, from Orillia in the north to Tottenham in the south. She parks beside one of the white cruisers striped in blue and gold, turns off the ignition, and debates whether to take her small leather briefcase in with her. Because it makes her feel more substantial, more adult, she does.

Inside the front doors she's greeted by a female constable standing behind bulletproof glass, a woman no taller than Amy but, she thinks, fuller, a more serious presence. The constable, her long blond hair tied back from a not-unkind face, hears Amy's request through the speaking vent, the kind used in old movie-theatre box offices, and she seems to understand – doesn't smile, exactly, but doesn't look askance either, to Amy's odd relief.

"Do you remember the investigating officer's name?"

Amy thinks for a moment, gripping and ungripping the edge of her briefcase, her moist hand making a faint sticking noise as she does. "No, I'm sorry." She hesitates. "He was tall."

"That's all right, I'll find it." The officer nods towards a row of caramel-coloured seats lined up against the wall. "You can wait over there."

He was tall. Rolling her eyes at herself, Amy sits on a chair close to one end of the row and puts her briefcase on the seat beside her. She waits at least half an hour, during which three separate people come in to complain about parking issues. The OPP does not handle parking, each of them is told, that's the local police – another building, a different part of town. Each time, the person leaves more exasperated than when he arrived. Sitting there, she thinks of an aphorism ascribed to Woody Allen – that 90 per cent of life is showing up – and considers that he might have added "at the proper time and place." So here she is, finally, and she wonders only about her timing.

At a quarter to twelve, a brush-cut constable with thick arms and shoulders and a broad, wind-chafed face enters from outside and walks over to Amy's chair. She hears his hard shoes first and looks up from the "Parents Stealing Children" pamphlet in her lap. She was right – he is tall.

"I'm sorry, I was on the road," he says, holding himself firm and still in a way that makes her notice his grey eyes. He holds out his hand, a stiff blue cuff at the wrist. "Amy, right? I'm Constable Dixon. I think we met, you know, before." He pauses. "I'm sorry about your mother."

After being led to his desk, and accepting a coffee, she explains what she wants: to see the files, to know what happened, to find out what he really thinks. She has – not concerns exactly, but questions. Probably silly. She wants to resolve some things.

It will not be a problem, he says. And she shouldn't think herself silly; it's not uncommon for surviving family members to show up several years after a fatality, wanting to know the details they couldn't absorb at the time. "Gillian Swain," he says to himself. "I think there was an accident-reconstruction guy on that one." He excuses himself and goes to a bank of file cabinets in the hall, coming back moments later with a sizable green folder. He lays it on his desk and sifts through some papers at the top, and Amy can't help but notice his hands, his arms. They appear, to her, too momentous for paper. The pages sit too lightly in his grip, no more than air. "Yeah, there was. Constable Lanar, in Orillia. Well," he shrugs, "they're all in Orillia." He sits down again at his desk. "We used to have our own department here, but they centralized it." He shakes the watch at his wrist to see it better, and seems to think for a moment, with his eyes on her, on the briefcase she holds with two hands in her lap. Then he shifts his weight in his chair. "I can call him and get him down here in two hours, maybe less if we're lucky. All right?"

"All right," she says.

"You have someplace to go for lunch?"

"Um . . ." She glances over her shoulder, a nervous reflex.

"There's a Greek-Italian place pretty close." He nods crisply. "I'll take you."

"Oh, no, that's –"

"It's not a problem." He has already begun to dial.

◦━◗ ◖━◦

Norman's plan unfolds in the shower.

First, he will call Robert Chenowirth. He'll ask to see whether some arrangement might be made to pick up his favourite black scarf, which he can't seem to find and therefore must have left by accident in the Jarvis Street studio. And, of course, while this arrangement is being made, Robert will have a chance to apologize and offer him his Tiny role back. Once he has his Tiny role, a firm weekly commitment, he can call the odious Rol Henninger and inform him that, having found employment, he has no further need of an employment counsellor. He won't say the words *Go screw yourself,* but he will clearly imply them. All stipulations thus satisfied, he'll be able to return to other pressing matters of which he suddenly has no shortage. Such as finding a tenant for his room. And raising what he thinks of as "a lump sum of money," the actual figure being a thing that causes him a fair degree of stomach distress.

He towels off with the terry-snapping energy born of confident expectation and dresses in a dark V-neck and slacks – his action-wear from rehearsal days. He makes coffee for himself in the usual way, does a few light vocal exercises, nothing too stressful on the voice before four or five in the afternoon, but enough to firm up his diction and tone. Then he calls.

"Hello?" says Robert with a suggestion of irritation.

"Ah, yes, Robert. It's Norman here. I was wondering –"

"Yes, I know it's you, Norman. I've got call display."

"Ah. Do you? Well. I was wondering if, the reason for my call is to see if you, or anyone – perhaps Penny, or even Judith, might have run across my black scarf –"

"No."

This answer comes rather more quickly than Norman had anticipated. He'd expected Robert at least to search his memory, to roll the image of the scarf around in his mind's eye and, during that time, to produce the expected apology. The *By the way Norman I'm very sorry about what happened on Thursday and I've been thinking it over and you really are the best Tiny and so I've told that twenty-eight-year-old to go jerk off in the corner* mea culpa. Norman thinks it best to pause for a moment, to give Robert's tumblers a chance to fall into place. But Robert says nothing more.

"It's a black wool scarf," says Norman finally.

"No," says Robert. "Nobody found it." After a silent moment Robert sighs. "I'm sorry to sound rude, Norman, but I'm in the middle of something. Is that all?"

"Oh," says Norman. It's a rather potent "oh," carrying all sorts of layers and delivered, he's sure, most effectively. "Well, I guess so then." A small, knowing chuckle – again, many-layered. "Yes, I guess so."

"Fine, then," says Robert. "Goodbye." He hangs up.

Bastard, thinks Norman. He sips at his coffee, which now for some reason tastes horribly, cloyingly sweet. He pours it out into the sink and makes another cup with what's left in the pot and puts hardly any sugar into it at all, which makes it taste decidedly bitter and which suits Norman just fine, just fine, as he walks back into the living room.

There, through the window, he sees the woman from across the street, the woman from the convenience store – although she's wearing neither a sarong nor an overstuffed jacket this time but a black sweater and jeans and sandals. It's the same woman, though, no doubt about it. And she's standing right there on the sidewalk in front of his house, staring up at his window, with her arms crossed.

Norman can't define the expression on her face precisely, but it's not merry, it's definitely not that. She must be here about the sign, he thinks. But why? Is there something wrong with the sign? Do neighbourhood bylaws not allow signs like these and she has finally decided to tell him? Or is it some other sign-related trouble? The discomfort Norman feels at seeing the woman with the Mediterranean hair staring unhappily at his window mixes with all his other new discomforts to create an intense apprehension, although one entangled with a certain sexual interest, because the woman is quite attractive.

He's about to open his front door and speak to the woman when the phone rings. No doubt Robert, having found the courage to apologize, is calling back to make amends. Norman is momentarily torn, but the chance to hear Robert apologize is too tempting. He picks up the phone with one of his more magnanimous tri-note hellos.

"I'm getting a pretty clear picture of you, Mr. Bray." Rol Henninger. His voice flatter and harder than ever. "You're one of those undermotivated types."

"Now wait a minute," says Norman, "I was intending to call you but I had some things to attend to first. And it was my understanding that I could talk to you at any point in the day."

"That wasn't the instruction I left you with, though, was it?"

No, it wasn't. But Norman doesn't want to say that because to agree with Rol Henninger would be to give him the upper hand. What he has to do is treat this man as he would a director, with a combination of tolerance and contempt that leaves no doubt as to who is really in charge.

"I don't remember," he says. "I was asleep."

Rol Henninger makes a snuffling sound that suggests laughter. His voice, however, remains as lifeless as particleboard. "Here is what's going to happen, Mr. Bray. By the end of this week we're going to have you into a job. It will be a job that will pay you an amount sufficient to cover your regular mortgage payments as well as the basic necessities of living. Now I understand that you also have a default amount to pay of over seven thousand dollars, correct?"

Norman opens his mouth to respond.

"Well, that will be entirely your matter to sort out. But it is my job to have you gainfully employed so that you are able to meet your monthly commitments, even if, as I suspect, that will require some degree of attitude adjustment on your part." As Henninger dispenses these morsels of approved conduct into his ear, Norman has the sensation of being processed by him, of being sorted and stamped. *Basic necessities of living* – does that include joy? Freedom of choice? The pursuits of inspiration? Norman has the clear impression these necessities aren't on the list. And, standing in his own kitchen, listening, he folds into himself slightly, becomes smaller, as Rol Henninger's rectitude crawls over his skin.

"Now, what I would like to do is meet with you, Mr. Bray." The voice pauses, as if reloading. "I would like to meet with you today, and the only question is where and when. I would suggest that you come downtown, but that doesn't seem likely, based on our short experience, so my preference is to come to your house, and I've got an opening at two-thirty. How does that sound?"

Norman feels the advancing, heavy step of convention and holds himself very still, like startled prey.

"Two-thirty or three, all right? I'll make it your choice."

What can he do? What are his options? He can say no, I will not co-operate, but the consequences of that course seem dire. He can say yes, but not today. Rol Henninger, however, seems likely to use that against him. There is a satisfied tone in the man's voice that he finds both infuriating and terrifying, as if the future is established and already conforms largely to Rol Henninger's expectations. Norman takes a constricted breath. The inevitable can only be delayed.

"Three."

"Very good. I'll see you then."

He replaces the receiver and presses down on it firmly. In the last few days, with no warning, the world has become an angry and threatening place. And he can't help feeling that none of these currents would have been unleashed upon him if Gillian hadn't abandoned him. Frankly, he's a bit disappointed in her, in spite of her tragic death. Didn't she say she'd be there for him? Didn't she seem able and willing? She did. And now that he could really use her support, where is she? He picks up his coffee and sips, and his mouth twists into contortions. The taste is unbearably foul. Did he not put *sugar* into this? He goes to the ceramic sugar bowl, shovels two teaspoons into his cup, and, stirring, walks back into the living room, confident that the woman will still be there. Not just confident, in fact, but hopeful. All he wants from the world at this moment is a glimpse of the woman with the Mediterranean hair, standing on the sidewalk, looking up at his window.

And when he turns the corner, looks past the curtains and sees that the sidewalk is empty, Norman feels his grasp on what he can expect of the world slip just a little bit more.

◦●◦

She watches him tear his bread. Thick and crusty, it seems to give of its own accord, to rend itself, so slight is his effort. And though dumbfounded that she finds this entrancing, she is no less absorbed. He ignores the butter, just brings fragments of bread to his mouth with his face towards the window, the light it lets in glinting off the metal buttons and bars sewn here and there to his shirt. When he smiles, the hard flesh of his cheeks bulges into walnuts.

"Been to Beverly before?"

She glances over at the restaurant's faux-stone textures and Adriatic blue paint. "I've driven past it, on the way to friends' cottages. That kind of thing."

"Nice small town. Not much going on." He shrugs. "You're used to bigger."

She can't quite place his intent. "It's nice of you to do this. Shouldn't you be out patrolling or something?"

Walnuts at his cheeks again. "Not exactly."

The motherly waitress who took their orders now brings out lamb chops for him, linguini with shrimp in rosé sauce for her, and wipes her hands on her white apron. "Anything else right now, Walter?"

He looks at Amy. "You okay?"

She nods, half smiling, lifting strands of pasta dripping pink with her fork.

"We're fine," he says.

The waitress pats his shoulder as she leaves. "You enjoy."

Twirling the linguini, Amy wrinkles her nose. "Walter?"

His face planes to innocence. "What's wrong with Walter?"

"Nothing," she says. "It just sounds like thick socks and plaid slippers." She smirks at him, feeling a tremor of exhilaration at the risk. "A bit."

"I see." He grins.

It's that grin, that intimacy, that makes her think of her mother. Sitting across from Dixon, Amy sees this suggestion of something nascent between them and feels not pleasure but a faint blush of shame. She's here about the accident, she's here for her mother, and taking some coattail benefit from that suddenly feels as wrong as anything could. The grin is Dixon's offer of permission, and she can't accept.

"I suppose all the guys you meet are named Lance or Sean or Vince," he says with narrowed eyes, kidding her. But she's not playing any more. It has happened that quickly.

"No," she says, wiping the corner of her mouth with a napkin, "I'm sorry." She eats the rest of her meal staring mostly at the basil sprig on the rim of her plate, answering his questions in monosyllables, wishing to be done.

At the detachment, half an hour later, he suggests she wait at the front. He has some calls to make, he says. He has become formal and unknowable again, the walnut cheeks entirely gone, and she is both disappointed and relieved. When Constable Will Lanar arrives, a thin man with glasses and bony fingers and skin that collects the colour of things around it, so that his cheeks and chin have a faint hue of blue, Dixon's introductions bear no hint of familiarity. They are here to inform this woman of the details of her mother's death.

"Okay," says Lanar. "That shouldn't be a problem."

They proceed to a small, spare room with a worn wooden table and chairs where they sit. Lanar opens his black case, plucks out a large envelope, and slides its contents onto the table. He separates the documents into five small piles and touches each one at its corner, as if confirming its presence. At the end of this he sits back in his chair. "First thing I'd like to do, Miss Swain, is ask how specific you'd like me to be."

She looks at the piles, one of printed forms filled in with handwriting, a man's cramped script, one of photographs and diagrams that her eyes pass over quickly, one a jumble of pages covered with randomly scrawled numbers and letters, another pile of forms, several sheets of typeset text. "What do you mean?" she asks.

"I can be very detailed, tell you exactly what happened and when, and how I arrived at those facts." He doesn't intend to be brusque, thinks Amy; he's being professional and direct. That's fine – she's not here for a typical kind of comfort. "Or I can give you a general picture of what occurred, the essential details, and leave out the data. A lot of people find that overwhelming."

She nods, looking at the documents, not at him. They wait while she considers, while she bears down on the fundamental: she has come here to know what she doesn't already know. "Tell me everything you think is useful," she says.

Constable Lanar presses back in his chair, and Constable Dixon does the same thing, each of their chairs giving a dry crackle of wood, stereophonic strain. "I'll just go over the documentation first then," says Lanar. "This first pile is the accident reports, descriptions of the physical evidence, and so on made by the officer first at the accident site – that was Constable Dixon here." Constable Dixon filled out the forms. She imagines him standing near the beams of his headlights, looking at the scene, her mother's car here, her mother's body there, and translating these awesome truths into simple data, shackled within the spaces provided. Width, composition, and characteristics of roadway (two-lane asphalt, smooth and unbroken). Width and condition of shoulders (1.5-metre shoulders, packed gravel). Type of skid marks left by the vehicle (striated, scalloped).

Radius of yaw (250.1 metres). Grade of slope (8 per cent). Two pages on the car itself: make, year, model, odometer reading, type of brakes, steering, transmission. The make, type, size, tread, and pressure for all four tires, the condition of every door, every head- and tail-light. The status of everything the driver might have touched: seatbelts, cigarette lighter, windshield wipers, sound system. It must have taken hours. He might even have been standing there on the 27 with his clipboard and flashlight, breathing puffs of mist, while Laura drove her north to the hospital on the 400.

"You mentioned the sound system," Amy says. "Was she listening to the radio?"

"Yes."

"Do you know what station?"

The two men trade expressions. "We don't usually note that," says Dixon.

"But the volume was at 40 per cent" says Lanar, looking at the report. "Which is pretty loud." After a pause, he continues to describe the piles of documents: the thirty-four colour photographs taken at the scene, including twelve of the driver where she lay on the western embankment, five pages of scale diagrams and grid maps, four pages bearing the calculations used to arrive at the reconstruction, a pile bearing the medical examiner's report, the forensic-lab report, notes from two nurses who attended to the body, and last, two typeset pages of damage analysis and interpretation.

"This is what occurred," says Lanar.

On the night of November 26, Gillian Swain, sober and alert, was driving a 1994 Honda Accord south along Highway 27 at approximately 7:55 p.m. as she approached Innisfil Line 14.

The road was clear, the temperature quite cold, roughly two degrees Celsius. She had the radio on, loudly, perhaps so that she could hear it above the sound of the air flowing through the slightly open passenger-side window and the car's own roaring engine. She was driving approximately 130 kilometres per hour, fifty kilometres above the posted speed limit. As she crested the hill to begin her descent towards the Line 14 inter-section, something caused her to jerk the wheel abruptly to her right, possibly an animal or an oncoming vehicle that had drifted into her lane. Her reaction took the Honda halfway onto the shoulder of the highway, with both right-side wheels driving in gravel for a second and a half. When she corrected the vehicle left onto the asphalt surface, she did so too sud-denly, sending the vehicle towards the eastern shoulder and forcing her to correct again, which she did three-quarters of a second later in the middle of the road, turning the wheel sharply right. It was this turn that resulted in her death, causing her vehicle to exceed its critical curve speed and sending it into a long yaw, which ended when the vehicle travelled up a small embankment on the western side of the highway and struck a large black maple, the point of impact just in front of the driver's door, bursting the door's latch and, as the car continued to spin 340 degrees, launching the driver into flight out of the vehicle and across the highway, landing sixteen metres away, while the car slammed its passenger side into another maple twenty-two metres south of the first and slid from there to a stop. The driver was killed by one of a series of head injuries, beginning when she struck her temple against the driver's-side pillar, continuing with a blow to the back of the head where it hit the edge of the car's open, swinging door, which sent the body, which had not been restrained by seatbelts, pinwheeling along the highway, and ending with the impact of the front of the head against the hard-packed earth of the shoulder. The first blow would likely have knocked her unconscious, the second in all probability killed her.

Amy hears little of this beyond the first sentence. The first sentence had captured her and made her numb to everything else. She studies Lanar. "How did you figure out all this?"

He shrugs slightly, the gesture not devoid of sympathy. "There are a good many calculations involved, but it all comes down to Newton's first law: a body at rest tends to remain at rest. A body in motion tends to remain in motion. It's basic physics."

Amy sits back in her chair, her face flushed. "Well, I can't believe any of it."

The two policemen share another glance, and Dixon leans forward. "Miss Swain, nobody's better at this than Constable Lanar. I have a lot of faith in his version of events."

"But it's all based on a faulty premise. She was going north. She was going to see someone in Beverly, so –"

"No." Lanar is shaking his head quickly. "No, Miss Swain, I'm sorry. I understand you're probably upset, and maybe I shouldn't have given you all the details I did, you know, I make that mistake sometimes. But there's no question around which way she was headed. She was going south."

"There's no doubt about that," says Dixon, leaning towards her, as if trying to pin her down, stop her mental flailing.

"My mother was going to a see a play," she says. "She had a ticket for a play in Beverly. Her partner was in the play. I can see her going too fast in order to get there. But why, just before curtain time, would she be going *south*, never mind at 130 kilometres an hour?"

The policemen look down at the documents, at their shoes, at the scuff-marked floor, at her. "I can't tell you that," says Lanar.

"This is reconstruction, Amy, not speculation." Dixon's bulk seems oppressive to her now, his bridled strength no longer poignant but grotesque. "We use observation and mathematics to arrive at facts. Your mother was going south. Maybe it's confusing to you, but the marks on the road, the trajectory of the body, the damage to the vehicle –" As he says it, Lanar holds up a picture of Gillian's Honda, crumpled on both sides like something gripped in a great fist. "To us it couldn't be clearer."

"Car couldn't have been going north," says Lanar. "Simple as that."

"The marks could have been some other car's."

"No. You match them to the tires. This isn't guesswork."

She came to have uncertainties eliminated, questions resolved. And the opposite has happened. What can she believe in if not the things she already knows? Her protest, welling up in her, seems feeble and embarrassing. "It doesn't make any sense." She's ashamed to hear a little girl's tears in her voice.

"I understand it's difficult," says Dixon.

"It's hard," says Lanar. "Can be hard." He begins to collect his papers, until Dixon holds up a hand.

"Amy, do you have any questions, based on what we've gone over?"

All she has are questions, even more than before, and they can't answer any of them. Except, possibly, for one.

There's a point within her brief hesitation when she almost asks it, when the words very nearly take shape on her tongue. But so much of what she assumed to be true has been thrown into doubt she wonders if she can believe anything just now. She looks from one official face to the other and decides that whatever certainty there is to be found, it's one she'll have to ease into.

"No." She shakes her head. "Not at the moment." She smiles to reassure them. "But I can call you, right?"

They both nod. And Lanar closes his file.

⊶⊷

On the way back to the city, Amy takes Highway 27 again, but this time with her mother's eyes. Out of Beverly, something bursting in her, into the town of Thornton, the roads lined with homes. Gillian wouldn't have sped here; she would have waited. Amy can feel the frustration she felt, the urge to get out, to hit the gas, but she would have stayed to a responsible sixty until outside of Thornton, famous for its monster flag outlet. Around the time she passes a large gingerbread farmhouse on the eastern side of the highway, Amy thinks, here is where she would have pressed her foot on the pedal, let whatever she was feeling – Was it anger? Despair? – take over. Here is where she would have hit eighty, then one hundred, faster. The road still straight, the houses fewer, the fields bleeding into her view. Past a series of Innisfil town lines into Cookstown, famous for its salad greens.

Immediately outside Cookstown comes a sign for New Tecumseth. From here the road rises. Large red-painted, green-roofed barns on the left, the speed limit eighty but forgotten, the

204

car cresting the hill, the road stretching through fields beyond, down and up over a far hill like a sweater's zipper. Here the road falls away at its edges, with a steep ditch on the right, and a steeper ravine on the left, lined with wooden posts tied by cable and with trees. Something pushed her right, perhaps a car exiting the lane or a gust of wind, she hit the gravel shoulder, then swerved left to get out of that fix, then found herself heading towards the posts on the left, snapped the wheel right again, which sent her into a long crescent swoon . . .

Amy slows as she approaches the intersection of Highway 27 and Innisfil Line 14. She watches the trees pass along the roadside, sees them not as individuals but as a group. At the appropriate place she brings the car to a stop on the shoulder. She switches on the radio and scans the dial. Something classical, she suspects, knowing her mother, and when she finally hears Haydn she turns up the volume and lifts her hand off the knob.

A while later she continues south, past the Highway 27 Country Market and a cemetery on a hill. And a blue-and-gold sign announcing the proximity of an historical plaque for the Honourable William Earl Rowe, famous for something. She's certain her mother would know.

⊷●⊶

Norman awaits the arrival of Rol Henninger as he would a cue to enter the stage running. For the twenty minutes or so prior to three o'clock he paces the length of his kitchen, his pulse gradually achieving a sprightly *affrettando*. He knows what he has to do, and it is up to Events and Other People to accomplish their parts. Thus his agitation, because Events and

205

Other People have a way of screwing around. A person can't always count on the things he should be able to count on to do the things they are supposed to do. Even a person at the height of his powers can be let down by what he can't control.

In the case of Rol Henninger, all he has to do is appear at Norman's door and stay quiet long enough to listen. To allow Norman the time to explain who and what he is, and why these remarks about "gainful employment" and "monthly commitments" and "attitude adjustment" are inappropriate in reference to him. To give him a chance to describe the many other benefits, beyond "gainful," as Norman suspects he means it, that can come from employment of an artistic nature. To explain that commitment to a set of aesthetic ideals can be just as strict and reliable as adherence to some payment schedule, and why the attitude that really should be adjusted belongs to him, Rol Henninger, and to the rest of the societal hegemony that expects a man of rare and tender gifts to produce adamantine products like "interest" and "principle." To make it clear, in other words, why they should all take a minute and think about what they're demanding of him, and ask themselves whether the world would really be a better place if Norman Bray were drafted into the workforce's muddy trenches.

At 2:55 p.m., as he's deep-breathing under the archway between foyer and living room with his feet wide apart and his hands on his hips, Norman hears the crunch of car tires against the curb outside. *Shit!* he thinks, *I'm not ready!* Five more minutes and he would have had his heart rate down and his breathing under control and he would have been able to open the door smiling and *in charge*, and isn't it just like Events and

Other People such as Rol Henninger to mess up the timing and put him on the defensive.

He makes a quick decision to go to the door, open it, and take command of the situation with a great, pre-emptive *Hello!* But in the very act of stepping towards the door he changes his mind. He will not to go to the door and open it, but stand in the foyer and wait for the knock. Better to seem surprised at the curious lack of professionalism. *Oh, here ahead of schedule? It's a bit unfortunate, but we'll manage . . .* Yes! Establish authority through disapproval! Norman claps his hands sharply together. Turning on mental dimes like this exhilarates him. It's like brainstorming over a character's intent. He can feel his synapses flashing like sequins. Let the knock come, he's ready now.

He hears a few light steps on the walkway and imagines Rol Henninger's dim, unsuspecting face floating towards him. Then he hears the knock – far softer than he expects, as though Rol Henninger's hand (or his convictions!) were frail and yielding – and almost immediately, Norman can't help but notice, the knob on his front door begins to turn.

Rol Henninger is breaking in!

"Hold on there! Wait just a minute!" Norman lunges forward, his indignation at a pitch, and yanks open the door to find not the employment counsellor standing on his porch but Amy, holding her briefcase in front of her like a shield.

"Jesus, Norman," she says, peeking over the handle. "What's happening?"

"What are you doing here?"

"I wanted to talk to you." She drops her guard slowly. "Why are you charging around like Charles Manson?"

"I'm not!" He looks behind her, over her shoulder. "I'm just surprised. Do you normally try to just walk in like that?"

"I did all the years I lived here."

He periscopes around to look at her Jetta on the street. "Is that your car?"

"You've seen it before. Can I come in? It's cold out here."

"Oh. What time do you have?"

Amy frowns and checks her watch. "Almost three." When he says nothing her arms fall to her sides as though suddenly weighted. "Is there a problem?"

"It's just that I'm expecting someone any minute."

Her face sets unpleasantly. She says, "This won't take long," and steps forward with a foot on the threshold until he's compelled to move aside.

◦━◦

"How does that sign look out there?" says Norman, sitting in his chair and facing the window, with his eyes on the "Room for Rent" sign and the street beyond. "From the car, I mean."

"It looks fine." Amy sits at her traditional half-cushion perch on the couch, her briefcase balanced on her knees.

"I don't have a car, so I was wondering."

They both study the blank white back of the sign.

"Any interest?"

"Lots of nibbles. I see people pausing as they walk by. They look intrigued. I know faces, I'm able to read them. There's interest there."

"It might help if you cleaned the yard up a bit."

"Have you rented out a room before?"

"No."

"Oh. I thought perhaps you were an expert."

"Just a suggestion. I saw some bits of garbage."

"I've got the yard under control. I don't think you need to tell me about the yard."

"Fine."

There's a pause. The back of the sign.

"Well." Norman shifts forward and slaps his hands together. "I'm expecting someone, so . . ."

"Does this meeting have something to do with the house?" She knows it does; why else would anyone visit? But after a second of Norman lofting his eyebrows and apparently searching for an acceptable answer, she says, "Never mind, it's none of my business."

He looks out the window and rubs his hands together.

"Norman, I have a question to ask you."

"Oh? What kind of question?"

"It's about Mom."

"About Gillian? Yes. All right, well. Interesting. Go ahead." Saying this, he stands up and moves towards the kitchen. "Would you like some coffee? I can make you some. No cream though, I'm afraid. And I've used the last of the milk."

Amy shakes her head no.

"I know you prefer milk." He hovers under the archway.

"Can you just sit down?"

He hesitates a moment, looking towards the kitchen as if filled with a deep and sudden yearning to make coffee, then moves back to his chair. She waits for him to sit. To settle.

"I want to ask you about that night."

"Which night is that?"

She moves the briefcase off her lap. "The night she died. I want to know what happened."

Norman frowns aggressively. "What do you mean? There's not much question what happened. She killed herself in a car accident. That seems pretty clear-cut." He begins rubbing the tops of his thighs at a steady heat-making rate, then shifts from that to patting his pockets and searching behind pillows. "Do you see any cigarettes over there? Check behind, check behind there, the cushions, there might be a pack –"

"Listen to me, Norman. I'm asking about what happened *before* she died. What happened in Beverly."

Norman, his hands stuffed behind the seat cushion, stares back at her. Slowly he retrieves his hands, returns them to his lap. "What do you mean, in Beverly?"

"Something happened in Beverly. She wasn't driving *to* the theatre, she was driving away from it. Did you know that? Did you see her?"

He shakes his head slightly, a quiet, careful movement. "I'm not sure what your point is."

Frustration feels like rigor mortis. She slides stiffly to the very edge of the couch. "There's no point, Norman. I'm not saying anything. I just want to know what happened."

Across the carpet, in his chair by the piano, Norman furrows his brow, and his eyes cloud with mistrust. "I certainly don't know what you're getting at," he says, "but I think it's a bit strange, your wanting to go over that whole business. Not only strange but cruel, frankly. It's as if you wanted me to go through all that pain again, which I don't understand at all." With that, he pries himself from the chair and stands up as if all discussion were ended. But he doesn't bull from the room, as Amy expects; instead he faces out the window, his expression limp. And when she twists in her seat and looks outside she sees a tall, straw-thin man in a charcoal suit striding up the walkway, so bent forward with purpose he might be leaning into a gale.

◦━◦

A mannequin. This is Norman's first, almost comforting impression of the physical Rol Henninger when he meets him at the door. As a mannequin, prefab and without personality, Henninger seems markedly less dangerous at the moment than Amy, sitting cobra-like on the couch. Not only less dangerous but useful, as a distraction.

He follows from the foyer as Henninger's long mannequin legs swing through into the living room in the direction of Amy. "Hello," he says, his mannequin arm outstretched. "Rol Henninger. Am I meeting with you and Mr. Bray together?"

"No, I don't think so." She looks straight up at Henninger as she takes his hand and then briefly sideways at Norman, who has remained near the living-room entrance out of a sense of prudent foreboding. "Are you here about the house?"

As Henninger stands in the middle of the room, the wan light sifting from the window illuminates only his bottom half, giving him the look of having been dipped in skim milk. He turns to include Norman in the conversation.

"Not really," says Norman, easing into the room. "But we do have an awful lot to discuss."

"Are you a close relative?" Henninger asks Amy. "I'm authorized to discuss a client's case with immediate family."

He takes the opportunity to lower himself in Norman's chair, directly across from her. "In fact it's encouraged. We like to get everyone involved. In some cases" – he seems to make a point just now of sweeping Norman up with his gaze – "it tends to help."

She says nothing for a moment, as if considering the question, and her face crinkles slightly. "I don't know," she says finally. "It's hard to explain what our relationship is."

Standing just a few feet away, Norman suddenly feels separated from Amy by oceans. What exactly is so confusing? He opens a hand towards her. "Amy is the daughter of the woman who left this house to me." He speaks as if the words themselves were water, as if they might spill if spoken too quickly. "And to me she is *like* a daughter."

He was always fond of her, and he never disguised the fact, but he has never said this before, not even to Gillian, and can't remember whether he has ever thought it. Now, the notion having been spoken, it surprises him with its accuracy. He didn't say it simply to placate her, to make her less of a threat; he can imagine himself saying it, and believing it, no matter what the circumstances. It seems to be independently true.

And she appears to be pleased, if a little confused. She looks at him in the frowning way of someone trying to decide on a purchase.

"Close enough," says Henninger, who leans back in Norman's chair and rakes his flat, trim hair with stiff mannequin fingers. "I'm an employment counsellor from the Willingston-Hanford Agency. We have offices all over North America. In this case we've been contracted by the bank that holds the mortgage on this property." Here he sends Norman an even-toothed smile devoid of warmth. "And we are going to get Mr. Bray working."

Amy nods encouragingly as Norman's blood clots up into a solid, jellied mass. "Well, that's good, right?"

"Without a doubt," says Henninger. He leans over to unbuckle the large leather satchel at his feet and begins rooting among its papers.

She glances over at Norman, and he has the sudden sense that she is about to get up and leave, which sets off a new skirmish of conflicting dreads. Rol Henninger's devotion to duty versus Amy's need to rummage through the past – it's hard to know which is worse. Or are they, together, just one big air mattress of peril and he is doomed to push down on one side only to have the other bubble up at him?

"Mr. Henninger," Amy says to the mannequin, "do you mind if I talk to Norman alone for a minute? We were sort of in the middle of something when you got here."

"Not at all," murmurs Henninger, distractedly shuffling through a wad of booklets and printouts. "I'm not going anywhere."

Amy rises smoothly and ushers Norman, despairing on all fronts, with her into the kitchen, where she leans against the countertop and crosses her arms with an unsettling severity.

"That man" – Norman toggles a finger at the open doorway they've just passed through – "wants me to stop being *me*."

"I guess we all have to make tough choices, Norman."

He shakes his head firmly. "It's not right and it's not fair." He studies Amy to gauge her mood and her objective. Her mouth is set, her eyes are hard. It looks bad. "What I need is a gig."

"A gig."

"An acting job. I need something big, something substantial."

"Well . . . how likely is that?" She rolls her eyes. "Anyway, I don't want to talk about that. I came here to –" She huffs into the space between them. "I wanted you to help me figure out something."

"Well, all right, certainly, if I can . . ." His voice trails off.

"I know something happened in Beverly the night Mom died. But it's some big mystery apparently because you don't want to tell me."

"I never said that. I'm just not sure what you're referring to. Maybe if I had more information."

Amy refolds her arms aggressively. "Since you won't answer my questions, Norman, I'll have to talk to somebody else." She shakes her head at herself. "I don't know why I didn't do that in the first place."

"Well, but, now . . ." Norman feels the need to probe cautiously, as one might poke at a dangerous animal with a stick much too short for the task. "When you say, 'talk to somebody else,' who do you mean, exactly?"

"I don't know, but I'm sure somebody will help me." She begins walking back towards the living room, apparently to retrieve her briefcase – "I'll get out of your way now" – and it strikes Norman that she has adopted the tone of someone highly pleased with herself, someone who thinks she has solved a problem without anyone else's input. The effect is *infuriating*.

He charges after her. "Now wait one minute." Under the archway. "Just what are you accusing me of?"

He comes upon Amy and Rol Henninger, whom he'd forgotten about, standing together in the middle of the room.

"Here you go, Mr. Bray," says Henninger, holding out a thin set of papers for Norman to take. "This is a copy of the explanatory literature I've just given to your – I'm sorry, what's your name?"

"Amy," she says, holding a similar set of papers in one hand and her briefcase in the other. "Amy Swain."

"Amy. Thank you. It's just some background on our process and our goals that I thought would be interesting for you to read. Mr. Bray, you don't have to read it, necessarily, because you will be going through the process. But now everyone has their own." As Amy turns to leave, Henninger focuses with a certain relish on Norman and smiles his painted-plastic smile. "Shall we get started?"

Amy disappears around the corner into the foyer and Norman hears her curt steps on the tile. "Just one minute," he says and hurries to cover the distance. He hears the doorknob being turned and as he rounds the corner he readies his lungs for full bellow – he's going to cry *Stop!* or *Wait!* or *Why?* – but as he opens his mouth he freezes.

In the now-open doorway stands the woman from across the street, a vision of perplexity in layers of bright cottons topped by her white overstuffed coat, holding a small suitcase and lowering the hand she was about to knock with.

Amy smiles at her. "We enjoyed your beans," she says, then steps past the woman and continues down the walk to her car.

❦

This is not as Norman would have wished it. He imagined himself as El Gallo of *The Fantastiks* – a role he played twice in Victoria, in 1981 and 1985 – vaguely Spanish, dressed head to toe in black leathers, dark eyes and sly smile poised above a sharp goatee, a weaver of romance welcoming the woman into his realm, where he would sing "September" to her and watch her melt before him. Instead, he is under siege, forced to split his attentions three ways: between the compelling picture of this woman, now at his kitchen table, bringing a glass of water to her carved clay lips; thoughts of Amy, in her car, off to "talk to someone," about what he would rather not imagine; and Rol Henninger, in the living room, sharpening his implements of castration.

In the meagre two-minute breaks he manages to wrest from Henninger, Norman learns the woman's name, Karina Lares, and what she describes as her "situation" – that she is a dancer from Caracas, Venezuela, that for five years she has been married to a man who will not let her dance, "because he is a pig-faced crusher of dreams," that she is now thirty-two and has only a few years left in which to pursue the thing she loves. That for this reason she decided to leave her husband, but that because she was afraid of his terrible temper and his tendency to do crazy things she wanted to stay close enough to watch him, in case he should decide to, possibly, burn down the neighbourhood. When she saw Norman's sign it was, she knew, a gift from the gods. And though she had needed some time to summon the courage, last night she was truly convinced when she looked out her window and watched his house glowing. And now that her husband has gone for three days of work in Montreal, this is her chance. She has come here to live, starting today, if the rent is not too much.

To all of which Norman nods distractedly and says, "Interesting. I've done some dancing myself."

Back in the living room, Rol Henninger presents Norman with a wealth of background into Willingston-Hanford's employee-placement programs, describing the method by which Willingston-Hanford custom-designs its process according to the needs and expectations of its customers, being the banks, insurance companies, and prison-release programs that, through the sponsorship of federal and provincial agencies, endeavour to manage risk to their profit margins and/or the populace at large by fitting heretofore negligent and/or unemployable persons or person-groups into stable employment opportunities.

"We are particularly proud," Rol Henninger informs him, "of our inmate-placement program branch, which is the most successful of its kind in this country, with a retention rate of 68 per cent. Which is why we are able to use the slogan" – here he taps a blue-and-white brochure featuring the image of a thick-armed and smiling felon wielding a tire iron – "The Last-Chancer's First Choice."

Having numbed Norman into quiescence, Henninger draws out a sheaf of "assessment instruments," which, he explains, are designed to illuminate a client's aptitudes and temperament in order to hone the field of focus.

"Assessment instruments?" says Norman, his eyes on the crisp papers in Henninger's hand.

"Questionnaires is another word. What we're after is a tight fit. We want to know exactly what you do, and how you do it."

"I am an *actor*," says Norman. "I do it *very well*."

Henninger, apparently concentrating on the act of thumbing through the pages, says nothing to this.

"I have been an actor for more than thirty years."

Henninger pulls out two white sheets, stapled together, and lays them face down on the floor to the right side of his right foot.

"Would you like to hear some of the roles I've played?"

Henninger pulls out a packet of four stapled sheets and lays it, also face down, in front of his foot, at the toe.

"Because I would be happy to provide you with a list."

The employment counsellor draws out a total of six groups of sheets, varied in the number of pages, laying them face down at equal intervals in a semi-rectangle around his feet. The effect, to Norman's wishful eyes, is of the bared upper teeth of a canine mouth, swallowing the man feet first. Henninger then bends down to the foot nearest Norman, picks up the adjacent sheet packet – the right fang – and holds it up.

"This instrument," he says, addressing Norman for the first time in minutes, "is to determine your team orientation."

"Any production requires teamwork. I'm a very good team player."

"There is a series of questions," continues Henninger, "to which you may respond 'Completely True,' 'Mostly True,' 'Somewhat True and False,' 'Mostly False,' or 'Completely False.'"

"What sort of questions?"

Henninger checks his watch. "Completing the first instrument is to take no more than ten minutes, beginning –"

"Hold on!" Norman waves his hands like someone flagging down a car. Karina has appeared at the edge of the living-room carpet, her feet in stockings, her small fabric suitcase in hand.

"This is my tenant," Norman says to Henninger proudly, enjoying the word, and he steps around the spread of pages to reach her.

"It is all right now to see the room?" she asks him quietly. "I am very tired."

He gives Henninger a sideways glance, says, "I'm taking my tenant upstairs," and leads Karina to the second floor, grappling all the way with how to approach the issue of money. His plan had been to set the rent at exactly the amount of his mortgage payment. But now, with Karina Lares walking next to him, her dark hair tied back with an elastic band, her suitcase announcing her homelessness, and her dark voice and air hinting at ancient, unknowable wounds, a price of almost a thousand dollars seems too much for a single room. It's as he's struggling with this fact, and letting the door to the room swing wide until it bangs against the wall, that he realizes he has failed to install a single piece of furniture.

"It needs a bed," he says.

"Yes."

He feels the disappointment in her eyes like a brick on his chest and tells her not to worry, it will be taken care of. There is a bed, he thinks, in the basement. She walks into the empty room and goes directly to the window, and looks down at the house she has left. As she stands there, still holding her case, she says something too softly for him to hear.

He leans forward. "I didn't catch that."

"I am wondering if it is a mistake," she says again, still facing the window glass, the pale November light on her cheeks.

"No, no," he says, coming into the room. He cannot think how to continue. No, no is really the sum of his argument.

Karina nods slowly to herself, as if agreeing with some unspoken thought, and turns to face him. "Are you poor?" she asks.

Norman's mouth opens but nothing comes out. By any measure he is poor, and yet he has never felt poor until this moment.

"I mean you have not many nice things," she says. "And you asked me for vegetables."

"Well" – he points to the open doorway – "downstairs, you may not have noticed it, I have a very good piano."

She holds out a hand, smiling shyly. "I am sorry, it was wrong. I mean to say that I am poor too." Even her slight smile is a great river of smile, broad and full between the high plains of her cheeks. Norman marvels at this smile, and finds himself wondering how it would look if she were extraordinarily happy, even as he attempts to process the meaning of "I am poor too," which does not bode well for a rent of nearly a thousand dollars a month or anything remotely close to it.

He clears his throat. "When you say you are 'poor' –" he starts, without an inkling of what might come next. He sees her eyes drop, and her smile diminish. "Of course, I appreciate the life of an artist. I am, as it happens, an actor."

She brightens. "Yes, you have told me. I thought, when I saw your sign, 'He will understand.'"

"Yes, but –"

Look at this woman. Look at how the knowledge that he is an actor gives her comfort and hope. Is it possible that a beautiful, dark-haired (*not* Mediterranean-haired; must try to remember) woman such as this, a fellow artist no less (who better to understand him?), could choose to live in his house, sleep by any estimation *next* to him, and that economics, of all things, could make him turn her away? He has never lived that way before, and no banker is going to force him to start.

It occurs to Norman that had Miriam Ashacker not refused him help, had the bank not told him to rent out this room, had he himself not been slightly confused about the entire mortgage-ownership-payment concept, he would never have been led to this opportunity. There is indeed a plan at work, and it has been working for him all along.

God, it turns out, is an artist.

"Yes," says Norman more firmly. He thinks the scent coming from her must be cinnamon, or cloves. "Would three hundred dollars a month be all right?" He thinks the skin below her ear, by the turn of her jaw, would taste warm and sweet. "You'll have use of the whole house." He senses himself teetering on some kind of precipice. "The water pressure here is very good."

A voice rises sharply from below. "Mr. Bray!" Henninger calls. "I get the feeling that you are stalling."

"I'm coming, damn it!" On his way to the door, he pauses. "Later we can bring up your bed. In the meantime, if you need to rest, you're more than welcome to use mine." He hesitates. "The bed may need tidying."

She nods. "Yes."

"Mr. Bray!"

"Who is the man?" Karina whispers.

He sighs. "My executioner."

❧

She stands in the reception space, listening to the faint twitters of incoming calls, and watches dark-suited David move smoothly down the corridor towards her, stepping through anointments of halogen light.

"I'm sorry," Amy says when he reaches her.

"No sweat." He continues past her with an arm extended towards a closed door. "I think this one is free." He raises his eyebrows at the receptionist seated behind a curve of wenge veneer. "Okay?"

"Till Terry comes knocking."

They enter a wedge-shaped boardroom with a wall of glass looking east. "Uh-huh," Amy says, impressed. "Is this where you pat down prospective clients to see if they're rich enough?"

"Yes," he says, shutting the door behind him.

"I was joking."

"Don't worry." He grins, rolling two leather chairs away from the rosewood table. "They don't let me do the patting."

She has been thinking about what to tell him, which of the many questions to share. All she knows for certain is that anything she says will make him angry and upend his day, and that it's her job to worry about it.

The cushiony leather of their chairs wheeze as they sit. "Are you still looking into the house . . . issue?" she asks.

"Um . . ." He slides a smoothing hand down his back before he leans against the chair. "Possibly."

"What does 'possibly' mean?"

"I'm trying to find out what's involved. I have an appointment with someone tomorrow. A real lawyer."

"Okay," she says, in a way that asks for further information.

"I'll tell you more when I know more." His face and manner have gone serious, his contours more acute. She has an image, now, of what he's like in full work mode, having to establish himself as David the junior economist and not as David her brother. She wonders which version he considers closer to the truth and, if the former, which is likely, whether her disappointment in him would even matter.

She focuses on the hands in her lap. "Well, I've been sort of looking into some things myself."

"Oh?" He propels his chair forward with a hard heel to the carpet.

"I'm not sure how much to tell you." She faces him. "I don't want you to become 'inflamed.'"

His response to this – an extraordinarily goofy grin – makes her happier. Slowly she tells him everything: Gillian's journal, Norman's fevered theory, her trip to Beverly and the things she learned, and Norman's peculiar mention of an award for a play she was fairly sure had been cancelled. As she talks he goes to the window, and eventually leans against it, so that the sun falls over his shoulders. And she finds herself, because he has so casually set her at ease, worrying more about the remote chance of his falling through the glass than about the effect of the things she's saying.

❧

*When others in the group question my contribution, I react patiently.*

"It depends entirely on what they're questioning. Are they questioning my sincerity? No one can honestly question my sincerity without being driven by some hidden motive, and I would devote all my energies to try to get at the nub of that because that can be totally destructive. Are they questioning a suggestion I've made? That tells me they're unaware. They aren't experienced enough to really understand the value of the suggestion.

223

And so in that case I would try to give them some background and context that would allow them to view the suggestion with clarity. But if someone is questioning my performance, that suggests to me that their judgement is clouded by factors other than quality and integrity. That tells me they're compromised, possibly by the demands of profit or politics. In that case I try to remove myself from the situation as quickly as I can, in the interests of everyone concerned. I think that's only reasonable."

"Once again, Mr. Bray. Please. The statement can be Completely False, or Somewhat False, and so on up to Completely True. I can't write down these answers you're giving me."

"But there are nuances involved. Nothing is ever black and white."

"I'm going to put Completely False."

"No! You can't choose for me. I absolutely reject that."

"Then what is your answer?"

"What's the middle one? Somewhat False and Somewhat True? That's the only one that allows for an element of shading and texture. If you must put something, put that."

*When group members make mistakes, I report them.*

"No, I deal with it directly. You can't rely on the director."

"That would be Completely False."

"Fine."

*The cohesiveness and functionality of the group is more important than any single individual's achievement.*

"Again, that depends. Of course it's nice for everyone to get along. But people place too much importance on that. Sometimes an individual's achievement is so much greater than others' that it causes hostility. Does that make it wrong? Are you going to tell me you would rather have a happy group than one that produces something memorable? That's crazy! That's a complete abdication of your responsibility as an artist."

"Somewhat False, then. Do you see how it's possible to convert these long, discursive answers into the appropriate response?"

"Those responses are straitjackets! You can't know me or anyone from a two-word answer."

*I consider my role to be that of a leader rather than a follower.*

"Completely True."

"My God, finally. Do you see? It is possible."

*I am quick to notice failures in the contributions of others and try to overcome them.*

"Well, I do what I can. It's what I've always done. No one can say that I don't try, no one. I try as best I can. I make the hard decisions and I take the consequences. Even if no one is willing to support me. Even if I am *entirely alone*. That's what I have to do. That's my role."

"Is that Somewhat True or Completely True? . . . Mr. Bray?"

"I'm sorry, I was just . . . Yes. Completely. Completely True."

*During brainstorming sessions, I prefer to contribute my ideas last.*

"It often works out that way, you see, because usually it's my ideas that are accepted. It's not something I plan. But there's certainly no point in sitting there listening to a lot of unworkable ideas if you know exactly what should be done. So I generally give my ideas first, and they're the last ideas anyone hears."

*I hesitate to implement a group member's suggestion until it has been analyzed thoroughly.*

"I analyze. Yes, of course I do. Because I believe that's part of the artist's job. You must always question, always. You can't be afraid of it, and I'm not, and I refuse to apologize for that. Even though, generally speaking, it has brought me a fair amount of grief. Because many people don't want to do that kind of work, you see. And that's why some people have called me 'difficult.' And some . . . well, it hasn't been easy over the years, that's all. And I have to – well, I have come to accept that. As frustrating as it is."

⊶⊷

Rol Henninger makes a final mark on the page, bends forward to slip page and pen into his satchel, then inhales slowly and presses his face into his hands. When he sits back, he looks at his watch and then out the window where the November sun is settling, full-hipped, into the city's red-brick foothills, and sighs until his shoulders slump.

"Mr. Bray, we have spent an hour and a half on something that should have taken us ten minutes."

"Really?"

Henninger sweeps a backhand over the papers at his feet. "There are five more of these tests to go through. Abstract reasoning. Mechanical reasoning. Language aptitude. And some of them are *supposed* to take an hour and a half." He stares, apparently stunned, at the spread of pages.

"Well, if it helps," says Norman, standing up to stretch his legs, "I can tell you that I have a highly developed ability to reason abstractly, to come up with innovative ideas. I can't say the same, I have to admit, for the mechanical side. I've never been very good at working on engines, that sort of thing. And you can see for yourself that my language skills are very highly developed. I have no trouble in that area at all."

Henninger is shaking his head rapidly, minutely, as though he's sifting particles inside. "No, I'm afraid that doesn't help. Mechanical reasoning is not about working on engines. Abstract reasoning is specifically about problem-solving using shapes and numbers. And this –" He picks up the thickest packet, the left incisor of the canine mouth, and waves the pages at Norman from his chair "– this is an 'occupational personality projection.' This is meant to give us a complete psychometric breakdown of your behavioural tendencies and attributes to determine how your normative psychological patterns would translate into the working environment." He shakes the pages at Norman again. "This would take us *days*."

Norman watches Henninger stuff the packet into his satchel and begin to collect the pages around his feet. "I'm a thorough man. I can't help that."

"My suspicion, Mr. Bray, is that you are trying to discourage and derail this process by being deliberately intractable. That's my suspicion. And I don't know why you would do it." He stops, with a sheaf of pages in his grip, and shows Norman a surprisingly anguished face. "I don't know why. This is as good for you as it is for the bank. The bank wants you to keep this house, by helping you obtain the means to pay for it. And yet you won't co-operate."

"But I am co-operating." This man doesn't understand how painful all of this is. How terrifying. "This is me at my *most* co-operative."

Henninger has resumed packing, creating wedges of space with a thumb and forefinger and slipping each set of pages home. "I could have installed you in an ideal situation, perfectly suited to your talents and temperament. Now, instead –"

Norman feels a momentary chest suck of panic. "Do you mean you could get me an acting job?"

The man from Willingston-Hanford snaps his satchel closed. "No. No we could not do that." He rises from Norman's puce chair and unfolds to his full mannequin height.

"But that is what I'm suited for!"

Henninger's head jerks back. "We're not a talent agency, Mr. Bray. We're in the business of finding clients reliable, steady, appropriate employment."

Everything Norman has never wanted or hoped for, neatly packaged.

"So," he says, following Henninger to the front door. "What happens now?"

"Now," says Henninger, twisting the knob and pulling it sharply towards him, "you will take any damn thing I can find."

# ACT IV

At 10:35 Tuesday morning, Norman wakes to a ferocious erection – the first in recent memory – and a sharp, persistent knocking on his bedroom door. The juxtaposition of the two sends his mind spinning. He pulls a pillow towards him and scans the room for intruders. His erection grows as commanding as the knocking on the door and Norman has the very real and disturbing sense that his erection has summoned the police.

"Yes?" he finally coughs out. "What?"

"Mr. Bray," says a voice behind the door, "the phone is for you."

Does he know that voice? It's a woman's voice. What is a woman doing in his house? And then it comes to him: Karina Lares, his tenant, is standing outside in the hallway. Standing, as he imagines it, in bare feet and soft cottons. And he has a prickling pillar of concrete between his legs.

The night before, he and Karina retrieved her bed – David's old twin bed – in pieces from the basement, along with some linen, a small brass lamp, and an old pink chest of drawers that

Amy renounced when she turned seventeen. Norman even found an old skeleton key to Karina's room which he gave her, and which seemed to help her relax. He asked if she was hungry and luckily, since he had nothing to offer her, she said no. When he closed the door to her now-furnished room, she was sitting on the bed, looking out the window.

Downstairs, he plucked up his "Room for Rent" sign and placed it like a bookmark between the tissue pages of his *Complete Works of Shakespeare*. The placement was entirely random, and he set the book down. But then, looking for further signs of a plan unfolding in his favour, and in an effort to lessen the sting of the Rol Henninger experience, Norman picked up the book again and opened to the page he'd marked. He found nothing on that page, nor on the ones immediately adjacent. But twenty-six pages and half an hour later he discovered this, from Act III, Scene iv of *Twelfth Night*: "Nothing that can be can come between me and the full prospect of my hopes."

Well, he thought, closing the book, that is a very good omen indeed.

This morning in bed, as his erection lingers while his confusion and panic fade, it occurs to him that perhaps he should take the opportunity to invite Karina Lares into his room. He is a handsome man, she is a beautiful woman, and he has been visited by the manifestation of an indomitable biological force that means to be appeased. Alternatively, he could walk out into the hallway, as he is, and let the evidence present itself. It is, after all, his home; he should be able to move about at will, in whatever condition he deems best. Naked if he chooses!

Unfurled like a colour pike! And if Karina Lares finds this objectionable, well then, she is clearly no artist and not suited to living with one.

"Mr. Bray?"

With some difficulty, Norman manages to corral the most reckless and obdurate of these notions into a kind of mental holding cell – not entirely subdued, but neither allowed to roam wild – and pulls on his robe. He does not dismiss the possibility that the appearance of the erection is related to the presence of Karina Lares, that she has introduced some rogue element into the house that has found expression in his suddenly turgid member. He has sometimes wondered what constitutes a muse. Perhaps, Norman reflects impishly, it's the ability to inspire this sort of stiff resolve. Perhaps Karina is to become his muse.

"Mr. Bray, the man is on the phone."

Why didn't the phone ring in his room? He remembers why: he had visions of just this sort of thing happening – Rol Henninger calling at any hour – and he unplugged it. Now, he will not replug it. To replug it would be a kind of capitulation, and it would delay his seeing Karina, which he looks forward to doing as soon as he can manage to bind himself up, or down, with a well-placed knot in his robe's belt.

"Coming!"

Eventually he finds that, while not successful, the effort and distraction are enough to render the operation moot.

"Yes?" he says broadly as he opens the door and sees his tenant, freshly showered and dressed. The sight of her hair, loose and slightly damp, causes Norman to clench his toes.

"The man is on the phone for you," she repeats. "He is waiting a long time."

"Thank you, Karina." Norman smiles at her as he moves past, in a way that he hopes is welcoming and somehow suggestive of other, future possibilities. "Did he say who it was?"

"No," she says, following, "he is just the man who wants to speak to you."

Norman pads downstairs to the phone in the kitchen as Karina disappears into the living room. With the receiver in hand he pauses, conjures up an appropriate frown, and brings the phone to his ear.

"Hello, this is Norman Bray."

"Mr. Bray, it's Howard Cantor." Not Rol Henninger. Norman is so relieved that he briefly chokes up. He has to clear his throat before he can speak.

"Yes?"

"I'm calling to see how things are going with the Willingston-Hanford people. I assume you've met."

"Well" – Norman plots his course directly – "I'm not sure what you mean by 'people.' I know of only one tall, unpleasant man who is proposing to run my life." Not bad, he thinks, for so early in the morning.

He hears Howard Cantor shuffling papers, or possibly sniffling; it's hard to tell which. "If you're talking about Rol Henninger, Mr. Bray, you must understand that he's trying to help you."

"I understand that he doesn't know who or what I am, and doesn't seem to care. I understand that perfectly."

"Did you not complete the assessment process?"

"We did part of it. I thought it went as well as could be expected for something so, frankly, superficial and meaningless. For some reason he seemed disappointed."

More shuffling/sniffling. Norman has the impression he does not have Howard Cantor's full attention, which is as galling as having to speak to him at all, about any of this. "I'll tell you, Mr. Bray, I tend to bow to Rol's judgement on things of this nature." He catches the sound smear of a hand being placed over the mouthpiece, then removed. "He's a very dedicated professional."

Another smearing noise, as though Cantor is having a second, private conversation with someone in the room. And who could that someone be other than Rol Henninger.

"So," continues Cantor, "did Rol lay things out for you?"

It's as if the two of them are whispering behind his back. "What things are you referring to?" says Norman sharply.

"Did Rol stress that this process requires complete buy-in from you." Another sound, a dry snuffling that sounds to Norman a lot like . . . snickering. "That you have to be on side, and willing to take his direction." It's all too bloody familiar. The ignorant, untalented many always seek to ridicule the gifted, dedicated few. "That this is really your best and only chance."

He's had enough of it. He can't pretend to ignore this sort of insult.

"Quite a little time you're having there, isn't it."

A pause. "Excuse me?"

"You and Rol. It sounds like you're really enjoying yourselves."

"I don't understand, Mr. –" The hand over the mouthpiece again. "Enjoying ourselves how?"

He has to laugh. "I can *hear* you! Covering the phone so the two of you can tell your little jokes. Having a grand old time at my expense."

"Mr. Bray –"

"Fun to mock the actor, is it? Great fun!"

More muffled sound – some final hilarity. Then a sigh as Cantor brings the phone back to his mouth.

"This whole business," says Norman, "is one giant amusement for you!" He wishes Cantor could see the contemptuous look on his face.

"Mr. Bray." Cantor speaks in a voice ratcheted tight. "I could not resent more your implication that my efforts, on your behalf, have been part of some kind of practical joke. The fact of the matter is I have a virus. I have been coughing and sneezing since Sunday and I was trying to avoid making you listen to it." The muffled noise again, which, now that Norman thinks of it, does have a faint, wheezy-hacking quality. "I also have to say that this belligerent attitude of yours, this paranoia, makes me question, quite seriously, whether you are a good risk for this bank. I'll be speaking to Mr. Henninger."

Then Howard Cantor hangs up. And Norman, standing in his robe in the kitchen, facing out onto Gillian's old garden where the rage of dying dandelions and tall grass and horse nettle is stirring in a damp, heavy wind, considers the likelihood that he misread the situation; that he has made a serious mistake. The more he considers it, the more probable it seems. He takes a deep breath and hangs up the phone and thinks, well, mistakes are part of being human. And by now it must be clear to anyone that no one is more human than he.

He goes to the coffee maker with purpose. Norman has a vague theory that mistakes such as the one he just made get shuttled to a central clearing house of mistakes, somewhere out in the universe, and that this massive mistakes depot is connected to an equally large reparations depot, and what one does to make amends for a mistake is do something positive or thoughtful for someone else, and this kindness gets marked down on the central reparations ledger and cancels out the mistake on the other side in a roundabout and slightly magical but nevertheless rational checking system. So what he will do, to balance out his misreading of Howard Cantor's muffled snuffling, is make coffee, more coffee than usual, so his tenant might also enjoy some. The system, Norman reasons, doesn't pay much attention to the size of the gesture, but merely whether it is thought of at all.

He sets the filter and begins spooning in the grounds, and notes how lucky it was – or, who knows, how clearly part of the grand plan – that last night, after Rol Henninger's departure, he was searching again for cigarettes and found a ten-dollar bill. That allowed him to make a trip to the convenience store to stock up on coffee and cream, and now he has both the idea of doing a kindness, and the means. He also has – not least important – someone for whom to do it. The fact is, since Amy and David left and Gillian died, he has had fewer people in his life to help him balance the ledger. And any fair accounting would have to conclude that whatever mistakes there have been over the last few years have gone largely unchecked, mainly for want of opportunity.

When the coffee maker gives off its steam-chugging death rattle, Norman assembles a tray with two cups, a bowl of sugar, and a tiny carton of cream. He walks with it into the living room, where Karina is once again on the sofa, staring out the window at her house across the street.

"Coffee?" he calls, causing her to spin on a cushion, and then holds out the tray for her to take what she needs.

Unfortunately, as he bends forward with the words "This is just made. Please help yourself," he forgets the fact of his robe, that it loosens easily, and so it falls away, exposing his limp regions completely and precisely at her eye level.

Karina moves with extreme deliberateness, eschewing the cream but spooning up the sugar, hesitating with it for just a moment above her cup, then stirring it in. Throughout this, revealed in her presence and warmed there pleasantly by the faint light venturing through the window, Norman calms himself with thoughts of the time, thirty-some years ago, when he seriously considered becoming a nudist and would gladly have met every day, and every guest, in much this way, had his wife, Amanda, not objected to the idea with a bout of disconsolate shrieking and rending of pillow shams.

Finally, Karina sets down the spoon and lifts her cup with two strong, slender hands, allowing Norman to set down the tray and cinch himself up.

"Well," he announces, "there's certainly nothing wrong with the human body. And you're a dancer – I'm sure you've seen a great deal more than that."

She touches her lips to the cup. "More, yes." Then she grins very slightly and turns back to the window.

Seated in his own chair, cup in hand, Norman stares out at the same house and sets his mind to finding something to say.

"Was the bed comfortable?"

Karina shifts in her seat. "Yes. Thank you. Very comfortable."

"That bed used to belong to David, the son of the woman I lived with here."

"Yes."

"I might have mentioned that already." He sips his coffee. Which is ideal. "He left home a few years ago."

She smiles and blows softly into her cup, sending wavelets across the surface of the tiny black-brown pool.

"So did his sister, Amy. Whom you've met, actually; she was just leaving when you arrived."

Karina nods. She holds her cup high, next to her chin, and draws it closer to take each small sip. "Was she angry?"

"Who?"

"The girl, Amy. She had an angry face when she left."

Norman shifts in his seat. His knees seem bony in this light, and he tries to adjust the coverage of his robe with one hand. "I don't remember," he says. "It was very hectic here at the time."

"You had a . . . a fight?"

"No, I wouldn't say that." There's one side of his robe, the left, that he can't get loose. He can feel the terry cloth all bunched up beneath him. "Young people are easily agitated, it seems to me."

"Oh, yes." Karina nods. "You have some difficulties?"

Norman eases up his left leg and wrenches the robe free. "Amy is like a daughter to me. I told her that just yesterday."

"And where is her mother?"

"She died in a car crash three years ago."

Karina casts her eyes floorward and shakes her head.

"I am sorry to ask these questions." She leans forward to set her cup down. "I must return to my room. I have work in the afternoon." In the silence that follows she stands as if to go.

"Her name was Gillian," says Norman.

Karina, hesitating, sits back down on the sofa's edge.

"I'm afraid she found living with me rather hard."

It has just occurred to Norman that here, sitting across from him, is a woman who has found her own unique means of escape from a challenging relationship, a woman who therefore might be able to relate in some small way to Gillian's apparently tortured mindset. And here is also, miraculously, an artist, someone who might – he dares to hope – understand how he feels about Gillian's death. In other words, here is a woman with all the elements needed to help him quash the niggling thought that perhaps he was, somehow, to blame.

So he tells her. He fills in the details that seem material – her journal's revelations of a deepening disturbance, the hint of a plan. Amy's struggle to accept the hard but evident truth. And overarching it all, the obvious trials of living with an artist, which is no one's fault, just fact. He confesses to Karina that he had thought, mistakenly, that Gillian was equipped to deal with the peculiarities of the task – which, as Karina must know, is a bit like living next to the sun, regardless of whether the artist is working or not.

He lingers on this point – that an artist's nature is implicit, that an artist remains an artist, whether or not he is practising his art. Because it's true, isn't it, that being an artist is, first and foremost, a quality of mind.

He presents all this to Karina, and for these moments her eyes watch him with a pain that seems both real and remembered, and which says to him he is understood. As he draws to a close, she leans back in the sofa, against the grey window light, and combs the long fingers of both hands through her still-damp hair. Then she lets her hands fall against her thighs.

"I think, no artist should accept such misery."

Norman waits for the next thing Karina will say, the thing that will reassure him. Because while he's not quite certain of the meaning of this statement, it does not sound like reassurance. It sounds, in fact, like the opposite, which, after all he's said, can't be right. Her face gives him no clues: It's firm and smooth and she looks at him with a fixedness that could be read any number of ways, few of them unreservedly reassuring. So he waits.

Instead of saying the next thing, Karina stands up and walks away. He watches her move through the living room, into the foyer and up the stairs, until she's gone and he's alone with his coffee and "No artist should accept such misery." Which, as it stands, is not very good company.

As heavy clouds cement the sky beyond his window, Norman fingers the frayed cuff of his robe, teases the tendrils of cotton, and has a sense of being very tired. He understands that his schedule has been disrupted lately, that his rhythms are off, and he could put the sensation down to that if he wished. But it's a different kind of tired, he realizes; it's the fatigue born of someone else's disappointment.

Christ.

He tries so hard to make others happy. Some people have never understood this about him. But why else is he an actor? Doesn't it follow, if he's in the entertainment profession, that making people happy is what he lives for? Isn't it obvious? And yet every once in a while there will be someone in his life who exudes an obstinate, inexplicable something – disillusionment, dissatisfaction – some buried sourness he can't seem to do anything about. His first wife, Amanda, was one of them. Certain directors he's worked with. His parents.

He fears Karina might be another. And just now, in his reliable chair in his quiet living room, with so much endured and the day barely even begun, what he needs, he realizes, is the comfort of someone who is glad in his presence, someone who can't ever be disappointed.

⊷⊶

Where were the glasses? He opened and shut the cupboard doors in sequence and found the glasses, finally, in the cupboard next to the oven. That was very strange, he thought. No one should put glasses there. By the fridge or over the sink, but not by the oven – that's for plates. He would have to explain that to her.

He entered the living room bearing in each hand a glass of cognac with ice (unfortunately not his favourite brandy, another thing he would have to explain). He entered and saw her sitting on the couch expectantly, wearing an outfit of dark pants and a pinstriped blouse that complemented her forty-five-ish figure, and knew that she found him handsome. This awareness – he never quite took it for granted – helped him relax in unfamiliar surroundings.

"Here we are," he said expansively, setting the smaller glass on the table in front of her. "So," he said, easing onto the middle cushion, "you have children."

She smiled and lifted her eyebrows appreciatively. "Two. I can't say 'boy and girl' because they're teenagers. Young man and young woman." She took a sip from her glass. "So," she said, with an expectant smile, "you're an actor."

They'd met the night before, after the premier of an amateur musical adaptation of *A Study in Scarlet*, at an aftershow party in the hall used for rehearsals, darkened for the occasion and strung inexplicably with Chinese lanterns. Norman was the cast's lone professional – the community grant allowed one per production, at below-union fees – and Gillian was there as a representative of the university, which had helped sponsor the production, and because at the time she was something of a Sherlock Holmes buff.

She'd found him at the bar, finishing up a rather frustrating discussion with the bartender.

"Mr. Bray," she'd said, at his shoulder.

"Don't even try asking for brandy," he'd said crisply, turning to her. "All they have is Hennessy. Hennessy, for God's sake."

"That's all right, I mostly drink wine." She'd stuck out a hand. "Gillian Swain. I'm with the university."

"Oh, yes?" Half interested, still fuming. He was wearing a navy sportcoat over a white shirt, with a gold cravat tied loosely at his neck.

"You're quite a good actor," she'd said, at which his face had brightened. "And you have a very nice voice."

He'd smiled warmly then, his mood completely turned, and motioned with his unsatisfactory Hennessy to indicate the company around him. "Not a bad production at all, really. Good group of people, lots of enthusiasm, which you hope for in a situation like this – mostly amateur."

She'd recognized her cue. "You're a professional, of course." Then, while he detailed the last several years of his career, she'd seemed to listen intently. "Really," she'd said, jumping in at a pause. "Something I wanted to say though: I'm a bit of a Sherlock Holmes enthusiast, and I didn't entirely agree with your interpretation."

"Oh?" he'd said, a full two notes, down and up like a check mark, his face all seriousness.

"Not really. Far too sexual, I thought."

"Too *sex*ual."

"Holmes was an ascetic. He had too much going on up here." She'd tapped her temple. "He didn't pursue pleasures of the body."

Norman had barely been able to contain himself. "No. You're completely wrong. I won't say he pursued them, but he certainly appreciated them." This had been the thing he'd struck on in rehearsal: if Holmes could be passionate about a shapely and elegant idea, then why couldn't he be passionate about shapeliness and elegance in other guises – like that of a beautiful woman? By God, he could. He could be an appreciator of beauty in *all* its forms. And so he'd made Holmes a bit of a ladies' man, a font of admiring glances and playful, lingering smiles. And now here was this woman questioning his

244

innovation. He could feel the blood pressing against the backs of his eyes. "He may have been a genius but he was also a man. I played him as a man."

"I understand that was your concept. I'm saying that I disagree with it." Gillian had smiled throughout, despite the glares being thrown by people who'd had to reach around them to get their drinks. "It's not supported by the books."

"Well," Norman had said, lighting a cigarette, snapping his lighter closed, "the books are dead, aren't they. A hundred years old. Theatre is a living art, you see – we interpret things differently all the time. We force blood into them. But by all means, if you want an unchanging reality, if you don't want to be challenged by a new idea, then stick with the books." He'd been about to turn away – he was in the midst of doing so – and something had made Gillian touch his arm.

"I'm sorry," she'd murmured. "I did enjoy your singing." He'd left her then, with a coolly gracious smile. But an hour or so later, made magnanimous by the compliments from others, he'd found her and brought her a glass of wine.

So now here they were in her living room, on her sofa, the children having fled to the houses of friends. And Norman had a cognac in his hand, and Gillian had the same, and things were going as well as Norman could wish. Because in truth it had been a while. Since before his divorce, in fact. There'd been no one in the amateur *Scarlet* cast who'd seemed viable, really – housewives with husbands or college students whose brains were engorged with all things immediate and young and not really capable of seeing the value inherent in someone learned and appreciative of subtler pleasures. Not that he hadn't tried; he had. But he'd come away, if he were forced to admit it, slightly bruised. Penny Curtis, for instance, the young stage manager with ambitions in television – she'd seemed accessible, not unattractive if you didn't mind a soft, melancholy face, and not too high a mountain to climb. She'd tended to linger after rehearsals, in bulky sweaters or shapeless dresses – which for Norman suggested hidden joys and were always a source of intrigue – working with props or lighting. After the first dress rehearsal she'd brought several bottles of wine for the cast, a nice Cabernet that Norman particularly enjoyed, and he'd wanted to thank her, really, that was all. When he'd found himself with her in the wings, he'd merely gotten caught up in the moment. He'd found himself moving from thanks to flattery, because she had lovely ears that burned red whenever she tried very hard to make her case, to be heard or understood, and he'd wanted to touch those ears in that moment, to feel their heat, and he told her so, and, yes, he touched them, just put his hand out and drew his fingers along the rim of her ear. He'd meant it as a kindness. But she began shouting and accusing him of quite astonishing things, so that he'd been forced to back away with his hands raised, like a mugging victim, while the others came running. That's how it had felt – as if he'd been mugged. He'd left the party immediately, walked out into the drizzle while the others remained inside, and what they'd said about him then he could only imagine.

The official opening-night party, where he met Gillian, had come two nights later.

In her living room, nestled against the arm of the sofa, Gillian touched the glass of cognac to her cheek. "What are you thinking about?" she said.

"Oh, nothing," said Norman, relocating his charm. "Just that it's lovely being here with you."

The bridge of her nose wrinkled very slightly, even as her hand moved to her hair. "You don't have to say that, you know. You don't have to try so hard."

"I'm not. It is lovely."

She nodded at him. "I see this. I see it in students." She paused, smiled. "Why don't you take some of the pressure off yourself and ask me about what I do? Let me do some work."

Norman sat back a little and blinked. No one had spoken to him this way before. No one had ever understood the pressure he felt. In fact, he'd never really understood it that way himself until that moment. It was this that made him think Gillian was the one meant for him.

He was about to give this asking-about-her business a try, as an experiment, when the two of them jumped at the sound of thumping steps on the porch, and Gillian's sixteen-year-old daughter, Amy, blew in through the door, through the hall, and up the stairs, to the sound of one long, continuous, siren-like wail.

The two adults sat silently on the couch for a moment. "That was my daughter, Amy," said Gillian. She set down her glass. "I'd better see what's happened."

In the twenty minutes that Gillian spent upstairs with her daughter, in the stretches of quiet murmurs he could hear through the ceiling, punctuated by the occasional yelp of hurt and outrage, Norman made his way through two top-ups of cognac and a thickening sense of destiny. At first he was annoyed at the interruption. Things had been going so well he could taste the – not conquest, not in the case of a woman of maturity and experience – but *attainment*. And now suddenly he wâs forced to sit alone in a strange living room and contemplate having the whole thing called off or postponed because of some childish trauma.

Slowly, however, and then with increasing momentum, he came to perceive the interruption as a blessing. Because he did want to impress this woman who seemed to understand him, wanted to show her all that he was, give her, there in her living room, a chance to see not only his surface textures and hues but also the breadth and substance of his great, grand heart.

The quiet murmuring continued, and shrieks of "But he *does*! He *told* her!" and "You don't under*stand*!" pelted the walls of the hallway and stairwell and caromed down to Norman where he stood on the landing. Where, softly at first, he began to sing . . .

*You are sixteen, going on seventeen,*
*Baby, it's time to think.*
*Better beware,*
*Be canny and careful,*
*Baby, you're on the brink.*

On the floor above, the murmuring and the crying stopped, and Norman, whose baritone was rich and whole from the exercise it had had over the previous few weeks, not to mention the drinks he'd had that evening, sensed that he was having a delicate yet meaningful influence. So he continued, through the corny old lines about *young lads*, *cads* and *men* and *things beyond your ken*. He saw shadows move slowly in the hallway above him as Amy and her mother crept out of the bedroom, edging towards the strange sound they were hearing, and Norman, not wanting to break the spell, continued on, into the part normally sung by the girl, which required a nifty transition into his softest, most engaging falsetto, but it was all working for him, yes sir, and he managed brilliantly . . .

*I am sixteen, going on seventeen,*
*I know that I'm naïve.*
*Fellows I meet*
*May tell me I'm sweet*
*And willingly I believe.*

Now, as Gillian and lank-haired, skinny Amy appeared at the top of the stairs with, it had to be said, slightly bewildered, even anxious expressions, Norman sensed he was heading into dangerous territory, for coming next was the line *Bachelor dandies, drinkers of brandies*, which was not really the picture he wanted to conjure up now that he had altered the chemistry of the evening so masterfully, so he attempted a rewrite on the spot, cobbling together a line about teenage Randys and the eating of candies, which, although it was the best he could do, was not very good. And it came out awkwardly, in a sudden burst, injuring the rhythm and creating an image too vivid for either Amy or Gillian to ignore, so that as Norman tried to soldier on towards *"Timid and shy and scared am I"* they fell, Amy first, followed by Gillian, into fitful giggling, and then desperate laughter, as Norman's confidence dissolved and his voice trailed away.

"Well," he said, trying for a dignified smile amid the torrent, "at least you're not crying any more."

And then – this is what Norman remembers so fondly – Gillian, as if managing to see in Norman's act, or at least in the hurt evident in his eyes, just the thing he wanted her to see, came down the stairs and cradled his cheeks in both hands, held his face gently for a moment, and kissed him.

And within this remembered moment she is forever pleased, and not disappointed.

❧

With a little research, Amy learned that at the time of its production of *Man of La Mancha*, the Beverly Dinner Theatre was owned by one Bishop Meckling, now of Montreal. And since that particular production was the last musical Meckling tried mounting before deciding to sell out in favour of breeding seal-coat Birman kittens, he remembered it rather vividly when Amy reached him by phone. "Fucking nightmare," he offered.

When Meckling asked why she was calling, she hesitated, and glanced at the newspaper on her desk. "I'm writing a story," she said, "about dinner theatres."

"It better be a goddamn horror story," said Meckling. Unfortunately, he couldn't provide any details on opening night because by then he'd taken his family to Montreal on "cat business," which was an industry he assured her would make a far better story. But he provided the names and phone numbers of a couple of the people from the production, people with whom he still kept in contact because "They're people I understand. They like cats."

Which is how Amy finds herself now in a busy College Street coffee shop, her fingers stroking the sides of a hot chocolate, listening to the marble-skinned Liz Dube, the production's wardrobe mistress, equate Norman with an Australian cane toad.

"*You* know," she's saying, "the toads they shipped in to solve some grub problem, grubs eating wheat or some damn thing, and they ended up causing other problems far worse. Norman was like that." She takes a long sip of pinkish tea. "What did you say your connection with him was?"

Amy winces a smile. "It's hard to explain. Norman was with my mother."

"So that makes you –"

"I don't know," she says, standing up. "Would you like a muffin or something?"

Liz Dube, attractive in a sculpted, large-featured way, shakes her pearl-white hair which, assembled with some industrial magma of sprays and gels into shiny ropes, produces a rattle. "Muffins are about 40-per-cent fat. They're deadlier than cigarettes. But I'll take a biscotti."

She bends down to reach for her purse, a stiff taffeta bag resembling a vacuum cleaner insert, but Amy waves her off and heads to the counter. She returns after a moment with small white plates bearing an apple muffin and the biscotti, which Liz Dube places in her mouth like a kazoo, biting down aggressively behind pursed lips. She eyes the muffin with a combination of amusement and alarm.

"That's a Norman thing to do," she says, with a hand up to catch crumbs.

"What is?"

"To ignore. You know, to hear someone's input and then carry on regardless, as if they don't really exist."

"I like muffins."

"Of course you do. You're meant to. The mouth responds to all that oil and sugar, just like our brains want to believe a Hollywood movie. The entire entertainment industry is founded on that emotional need to swoon. A beautiful face, a grand gesture, some swelling music – we want to give in. Doesn't mean it's good for you."

Amy, with degrees in English and sociology, not to mention a belief in the sanctity of one's own diet, suppresses an urge to unleash muffin violence on this woman she has asked to coffee. Instead, she turns away to watch a young mother at the counter, with a baby girl in a stroller at her feet, lift a steaming cup over the child's head to her lips.

When it seems the little girl is safe, Amy turns back to the table and lifts a muffin half to her mouth, pausing. "I actually hate Hollywood movies." She bites down, the muffin giving like a sponge.

"Okay, well, there's hope for you." Liz Dube pops home the last of her biscotti, inspects the front of her shirt, and brushes her hands over the side of her chair. "Anyway, the point I was trying to make was simply that Norman was very much an ignorer, and you show some signs of his influence."

"I guess if that's the worst you can say about him, or me, that's not so bad."

Liz sputters a laugh. "Honey, really, that's the best thing I can say –"

A sudden serrated bawling from the counter pulls Amy half out of her seat. The young mother is bending towards her baby as a teenaged employee presses a fistful of paper towels into her hand.

"Was she scalded?" says Amy.

"No," says Liz, smirking, "she threw up all over her OshKoshes."

Slowly Amy sits back down. "The way you talk about Norman," she says, "it's like you're angry at him."

"I'll be honest, when Joe, who had the role first, got that ridiculous pneumonia and I heard it was Norman Bray replacing him, I seriously thought about quitting the production. I mean, he's talented. He is. Okay, so *that's* the best thing I can say about him. But it comes at a price. There are reasons he hadn't worked in, like, ten years." Amy watches as Liz looks down at her lap and attacks a patch of biscotti crumbs with a flurry of bristly fingers.

The child has stopped screaming. Amy spots her with her mother by a corner window, sucking contentedly on a cookie studded with Smarties.

"What I'm interested in finding out," she says, "is what happened in Beverly on opening night. Before the show."

Liz lifts her tea and sips. As she does, her eyes suddenly widen at Amy as if she has just scalded her tongue. "I guess," she says slowly, "it was your mother who died, in that accident."

"That's right."

Liz slides back in her chair. "We heard about it the next day. I'm really sorry." But something about her manner changes. Her ease, in the chair, becomes the ersatz ease of someone on a talk show; she becomes heightened, sharper, adrenaline pumping through her repose. "You know," she begins. "I'm not sure I can tell you much about that."

"Did something happen?"

"Well, it's hard for me to say." She frowns.

"I'm confused."

"Yeah, well," says Liz, nodding and staring blankly in the direction of her teacup. "Do you know – this is just a small thing – Norman insisted he was a size forty-two in the chest and he wasn't. He was a thirty-eight, a forty at best. But you could never tell him that. He'd just swell up like a balloon and start bellowing about how he 'knew his own goddamn body.' So I just stitched 'size 42' labels into his tops." She shakes her head. "He never noticed."

Amy leans across the table towards her. "Maybe it isn't clear what I'm asking about. I'm trying to find out if my mother was at the theatre that night, before the show, and if something happened. Something involving her. You were there, so I was hoping you could tell me."

Liz Dube swirls her finger in her cooling tea as if it were a toothpick in a martini. "I know what you're asking about," she says, with sudden intensity. "I just don't know what to tell you." She ponders Amy for a moment, a decision-making stare. "Is he important to you?" she asks.

"What?"

"Is he important to you, like a father figure or something? Is he someone you love?" She waits, while Amy settles on a realization that surprises her.

"I guess he is," she says. "My own father left when I was really young. So, yes, in some way he is."

The wardrobe woman nods. "Okay, well, then I have nothing more to say to you. Because I'm not going to be the one to mess with that." Abruptly she grabs her purse and begins to gather her things: a lip balm, keys, and a pack of gum from the table. "I'm doing some TV work now," she says. "They get hyper when you're late." Then she stands, pulls on a long black fake-fur coat, retrieves a filmy red scarf from its sleeve and wraps it twice around her neck. On her head she sets a large red hat, its wide brim a cascade of scarlet feathers. The ensemble, combined with the woman's pale skin and white hair, makes Amy think, as it did when she walked in, of an animal's chewed-off leg.

"By the way," says Liz Dube, "I think it's cool that you're doing this. I mean, looking into things. After three years most people would just let it go." She frowns. "Why *are* you doing it?"

Amy smiles very slightly and looks down at her muffin plate. It's hard to explain, she wants to say, and you haven't been enough help for me to make the effort. Then she remembers something. "Do you know anything about the Mirror Award?"

Liz Dube is adjusting her filmy scarf so that it bunches around her neck and lies against her coat in just the right careless way. "The Mirror Award," she repeats, looking satisfied at the result. "No, I haven't heard of that."

"Norman says he got it for his work in the show."

The woman's head jerks up, and she stares at Amy with an astonishment that seems tinged with concern.

"For what, exactly?"

"He didn't really say. But he sounded pretty proud of it."

The woman begins to drag on a pair of long black gloves, and as she does so she sucks up her red bottom lip. She glances up at Amy furtively. "Maybe I should tell you my theory about Norman."

Amy waits as she fiddles with the fabric encasing her fingers.

"I see a lot of actors who I think are headed for a fall. I don't mean their careers, I mean emotionally. People who are built on really fragile ground."

"You think Norman's like that."

She shakes her head. "My theory is Norman's already had his fall. I mean, I couldn't tell you when it happened – it may have been years ago. And it may not have seemed like much at the time. Sometimes these things happen quietly. But I think what happened in Beverly was like an aftershock. You know, the bounce."

Amy nods slowly and then, because Liz Dube appears ready to leave, stands out of a habit of politeness that feels more her mother's than her own.

"Anyway, that's just a theory. And I've no idea what's happened to him since." The wardrobe woman adjusts the angle of her hat. "I suppose I should ask. Is he well?"

Amy shrugs and in the same motion slides her hands into her pockets. "He's the same."

Liz Dube shoulders her bag. "I'm sorry about whatever mean things I said about him."

"That's all right," says Amy, feeling something spark in her. "I wasn't listening the whole time."

◦●◦

Norman becomes aware that the living room is cold. He has been napping, evidently for a long time. The cast of the sky and the fact that the street lights are flickering tells him he has slept away much of the day. And while he was out, the wind outside graduated into a fit of weather, a storm that is now forcing the trees into stiff-backed arcs and sending waves of rain like shovelfuls of fine gravel against the window glass. He sits in his chair looking out at the rain and the trees and what he feels is annoyance, at the weather, for rising up while he wasn't paying attention.

Listening to the wind, he finds he is able to make out layers within the sound. He can hear the resonant bass note that forms its acoustic body. He can hear the reedy, frictional tenor that acts as its shell. There's the percussive note from the collision of wind against window, and, incredibly – Norman is amazed by what his trained ears can perceive – a sound within all this sound that could almost be that of a human voice, belligerent and unconstrained. A woman's voice. Coming from upstairs.

"*Vaya al diablo! Te odio. Vete al carajo!*"

When he realizes it's Karina's voice, Norman gets to his feet. He steps as quickly as his wooziness allows through the living room and up the stairs in his slippers, his mind filled with the images of the coming confrontation with Karina's invading husband, who has somehow, obviously, come home from wherever he was, discovered his wife missing, and found his way here. It occurs to Norman only then, as he ascends in a series of stair couplets, that an arrangement involving a woman living in his house to escape a potentially violent man who lives approximately sixty feet away is a riskier proposition than he first realized.

"*Usted cabron! Usted hijo de puta.*"

He ventures up to the door; he hears Karina shouting but no one else. Only Karina, and the febrile wind and rain.

"*Soy bailarina, usted asqueroso! Maleton!*"

Who is she yelling at? Is she in danger?

"*Le bailaré a usted cabron. Usted no puede tomar eso de mí más!*"

If she isn't in danger, then he'll have to establish some house rules. He requires an atmosphere of calm, a general tranquillity conducive to concentration. Thinking back, it's apparent he did not make this clear.

"*Chinga tu puta madre. Soy bailarina, usted asqueroso!*"

All right then, he will knock.

"*Maricón! Jodete y aprieta el culo!*"

He knocks. "*Usted hijo de puta!*" He waits. He hears a sound, a banging he can't quite make out, and then Karina's voice again, but calmer. "Yes?"

He clears his throat. "Hello!" he calls, as if to someone aboard a ship, in the fog. "Is everything all right?" He waits.

The door opens, and Karina peeks out at him, sheepish. Her face is wet. "I'm so sorry. Have I disturb you?"

"I heard shouting. Is – are you all right? Do you need help?"

She smiles shyly. "I am feeling better. Thank you."

Norman finds this answer confusing. He was expecting something more along the lines of an explanation. "Yes, but, may I ask *who* you were shouting at?"

"At no one. I was shouting into the wind." As if it were the most obvious thing. "It's a kind of *terapia* – no – therapy for me. When a big wind blows, like now, I open the window and shout into the wind. And all the feelings inside me is come out. It feels very good." There's no guile in her face, no artifice. "Would you like to try it?" She opens her door wider for him and goes to the window.

Norman follows her tentatively. Already it feels different, smells different in here. It's no longer Gillian's room. Karina has placed silver jewellery – rings and bangles – on the dresser. On the bed lies something satiny and of a hue not unlike the fair, innermost meat of a cantaloupe. A picture beside her bed shows a trio of old people, two women and a man, in what seems to be a garden. On the wall she has attached a poster, with the words "Ballet Contemporáneo de Caracas" below a picture of the company on stage, mid-dance, shot from the theatre's balcony. Each of the dancers reduced by the distance to tiny squiggles of ink.

Karina thumps the heels of her hands against the top of the window sash to loosen it as Norman stares at the poster, trying to find her.

"This was your company, then," he says, and as he says it, as if on cue, the poster begins to vibrate, and then flutter and writhe against the tape holding its corners, and here in her room this sorcery seems natural to Norman. It's right that the poster should dance, and it's with faint disappointment that he becomes aware of cold air coursing around him and sees that, of course, she has simply opened the window. He turns to see her haul up a foot-high picture frame from the floor and snug it in roughly to hold the window up. Her wedding picture.

She points to a spot beside her. "Kneel down here," she says over the noise of the wind.

Norman does as he is told, kneeling next to her at the window, feeling the wind part and pull his hair, rip at his shirt, slap and tug at him. This is a hillside wind, he thinks, a coastal wind – how does a wind like this make it into the city?

"You must lean out," she says, putting her neck under the guillotine sash, rain sparkling on her face in the street light. "Lean out of the window, with your whole head, and shout at it all your anger." Her hair coming undone, lashing at her face, at her lips and teeth, she shouts, "*Usted hijo de puta!*" She laughs girlishly. "*Jodete y aprieta el culo!*" She pulls her head in, her face slick and glowing with rainwash. "Now you," she nods at him.

"What are you shouting?"

She laughs. "Terrible things. Terrible." Water flows from her hair and cheeks, it runs along the ridge of her collarbone, it follows the edge of her upper lip and drains into her sly smile. "'*Jodete y aprieta el culo*' is a Cuban saying. It means, 'Go fuck yourself.'" She shrugs and then motions him forward. "It's easy."

Slowly, Norman fits his head under the guillotine, leans out beyond the walls of his house, squinting against the pellets of rain, facing a neighbourhood aghast with storm, convulsing trees, whipping hydro wires, a dying cardboard box somersaulting across pavement that's running with water. The raving elements make him anxious, self-conscious, as if this tantrum has something to do with him. And it doesn't help that Karina is next to him, that her scent is buffeting him and he can feel the wet tendrils of her hair splay against his neck, flicking the edge of his jaw. That he knows she's waiting. And he can't find the words.

Damn it, he thinks, he has so many injustices to name, so many wrongs to declaim, and he can't find his voice! This should be second nature, shouting into the void, railing like, like – he grabs an image – like Lear against the elements. *King Lear*. Now there's majesty for you, to howl above the blustering of God Himself. That's balls for you. *Lear*.

"Blow, winds, and crack your cheeks!" he shouts. "Rage! Blow! You cataracts and hurricanoes, spout till you have drench'd our steeples, drown'd the cocks!"

He grins at her, he gleams.

"What are you doing?" she yells at him, frowning.

"That's Lear," he shouts. "On the heath."

Her face goes hard, she leans back abruptly, away from the window, and then rises and sits on the bed. He pulls his head in.

"What is it?"

"You are performing," she says.

"Well –"

"You are saying lines. Shakespeare. Yes?"

"That's right." He's confused, cold. "It's the perfect speech. He's with the Fool –"

She shakes her hand at him. "Please shut the window." He does, setting the picture down against the wall. The room, empty of wind, seems to ache.

"What's wrong?" he says. It's a question he can't remember ever asking before.

"I am being myself, you are saying lines from someone else." She shrugs. "That's your choice, okay. But is not the same thing." She rises and opens her door. "Anyway, I am tired now." She waits for him to leave.

"But I'm an actor."

"I'm a dancer. So?" Her hand on the knob, her jaw firm.

"Let me try again."

She shakes her head. "Some other time."

"But this wind," he says; meaning, when will *this* happen again?

She doesn't move though, doesn't shift or sigh. There's no retreat. He points to the wedding picture leaning against the wall, she in simple white silk, the man, looming over her, in black. "Your husband. Does he do it properly?"

She narrows her eyes at him. "What do you mean?"

He doesn't know what he means. He walks out into the hallway.

"I live here now," she says, and shuts the door.

❦

Norman touches his cheek with his fingertips and feels nothing. The rain has made his face numb. It's not an unpleasant sensation; he's past his storm-inflicted sense of unease and he reminds himself that he rather enjoys coming out on the other side of a battering from the elements. A driving rain, a January blizzard – surviving climatic fits like these makes him feel more alive. Tonight, having emerged from the storm, he is an artist-survivor. Soaked through and, on the whole, satisfied. And time will tell for what great new adventure he is being so thoroughly tested.

In addition to being an artist-survivor, of course, he is also an appreciator, an enjoyer of fine things, such as, for instance, a fine brandy. Which is why he has gotten dressed and braved the elements to come here, to this smallish neighbourhood LCBO outlet. He has in his pocket Karina's rent money, which she left for him on the kitchen table, and he wants a bottle of Miespejo Aguardiente. It seems like years since he has enjoyed a fine brandy. He will treat himself to a bottle of Miespejo because he is an appreciator and because he deserves it, and then he will buy himself food, and whatever is left over, only what is left, he will reserve for the bank. The bank will have to make do.

Here, though, is one small problem: He can't seem to find his brandy, even though he scans the brandy and cognac shelves thoroughly once, and then again. Even though he looks for it among the whiskies, and then the "specialty drinks," and doesn't give up until he could swear he has searched the entire spirits section.

"Excuse me," he says to a passing Liquor Board employee, a stern man in a pale-green shirt, "where have you put the Miespejo?"

"Huh?"

"Miespejo. I can't seem to find it."

The Liquor Board man frowns. "What is it?" he says. He seems in a hurry to be somewhere else.

"What is it?" Norman stares at him. "It's a brandy, for heaven's sake. One of the best."

"Sorry, I don't drink brandy." The man has already turned to walk away. He says over his shoulder, "Anyway, if we have it, it's on the shelf."

This won't do. "No, look," says Norman, hurrying after him. He puts a hand firmly on the man's shoulder. He's going to ask the man to stop and think. He's going to remind him that he works there and therefore he *must* know what Miespejo is, and where he has put it. He's going to ask the man, calmly but insistently, to help him find it. But before he can put any of this into words, the man grabs Norman's wrist, holds it high in an excruciating grip, and barks, "Don't put your hands on me!"

Norman shakes his head. "No, I'm –"

"I deal with crap from drunks all day. I don't need your shit."

An angular woman with long grey hair tied back, the checkout clerk Norman remembers nodding to on the way in, pokes her head around a display of vodka coolers. "What's the matter, Frank? What's going on?"

Frank, still holding Norman's wrist high, as if he were a child caught in the act of reaching up for a slice of pie, turns towards her. "This guy grabbed me."

"No," pleads Norman. "I was just trying to ask a question." Did he grab too hard? Did he wrench the man's shoulder? What has he done wrong?

The clerk comes halfway. "What do we do now?"

"I was just asking about brandy."

"Be quiet one minute," scolds the woman. "Frank, you want me to call the cops?"

Frank studies Norman hard for a moment and huffs a breath. "No," he says, releasing him. "Just make sure I don't have to see him again."

"Right." The clerk walks around Norman warily and presses her fingers into the small of his back, prodding him towards the front. "Wait here," she says when they arrive at the counter. She reaches underneath to haul up an old Polaroid camera. "Look at me," she says. And when Norman does, a flash goes off and the camera spits out a white square. She pulls a pen from her breast pocket. "What's your name?"

"Norman Bray."

She writes the name in block letters along the white strip at the bottom. "That Bray with an *a* and a *y*?"

"Yes."

"All right," she says, pinning the image to a corkboard above the register next to three others, "we've got your picture and your name now. You'll be recognized. So don't come back here. If you do, we'll transmit this image to every store in the city and you'll be S.O.L. Is that clear?"

Norman holds out his hands. "But what did I do? I was only –"

"I don't care what you were only. This is a government-run organization. We don't have to take nonsense from customers. Now I'd get out of here if I were you." She flicks a finger at the door.

"This is outrageous," blurts Norman, next to tears.

"I'll tell you what's outrageous," says the woman, who drops her voice a notch when another customer enters. "There was a Liquor Board clerk in Scarborough shot two days ago. Not dead but hurt. In hospital. So don't give me outrageous. We have a right to protect ourselves."

Norman turns away from her face full of anger to the pictures pinned beside his on the corkboard. Two greasy-haired delinquents, one of them nineteen or twenty and T-shirted, puffing for the camera, the other older, maybe thirty, with a blasted stare coming from under a Detroit Red Wings cap, and a dark-haired woman, chemically wired apparently, caught with her mouth open, mid expletive. Beside them, his own image is coming into view, a middle-aged man in an old wind-breaker, his wet hair smeared across his forehead, his face red, his mouth wrenched downward by torment, his eyes seeping like wounds. What an image to preserve. He reaches out towards it.

"Don't touch that," says the woman. "That's staying."

❦

Walking slowly up Sorauren Avenue after ten o'clock, his jacket scooped out like a lizard's cowl against the wind, Norman shifts the bag of groceries he's carrying from his left to his right hand, then catches sight of his house in the distance and presses grimly towards it. Getting closer he determines which window is Karina's and notes that her light is out, meaning she is asleep, or at least in bed and won't want to be disturbed, which is, to some degree, a relief. But as he comes to within half a block his gaze fixes on a strange detail. There is something in his mailbox, a package pushing up the lid like a thick manila tongue. He has no doubt the package is connected to Rol Henninger, that it is some new "assessment instrument" he's meant to use on himself, like the home blood-testing and urine-analysis kits he sees advertised on TV in half-hour segments at two in the morning. There is an unmistakable, almost bio-logical menace to the thing stuffed in the black box near the door. He keeps his eyes on it as he gets closer, hating the thing, whatever it is, because it is being forced upon him.

Standing on the porch, his house keys at the ready, Norman almost decides to ignore the package altogether. He almost decides to rush in and slam the door on it before it can lick out of the mailbox's orifice and somehow – he's not sure how – corrupt him. But turning his back on it, letting it remain there, strikes him as untenable. So he grabs the package by its upturned corner and, with the terrible resolve of someone ripping off a bandage, wrenches hard upward.

It comes out of the mailbox easily; in fact it's rather light. Norman equated ominousness with heaviness. He expected something weighted with doom. But it's light enough that all of his effort devoted to lifting it is transferred to sending it in an arc over his head, and by this one simple motion the flimsy brass-and-crystal porch light hanging by a thin wire and chain disappears, much like the head of a dandelion thwacked into non-existence with the swipe of a badminton racquet. The detached fixture lands with a munch on the wet ground, shards of glass sail briefly on the wind to the lawn's distant regions, and Norman congratulates himself on having properly pegged the object in his hand as evil.

N. BRAY it says in large, thick, black-markered letters and, up in the left-hand corner, as he suspected, a smaller *R. Henninger*. He sets his grocery bag down and probes the bubble-padded package with his hands, detecting the hard rectangular shape of a book. But it's too light to be a book. A box of some kind then, containing God knows what. He shakes the package, but it makes no sound. He turns it over and over in his hands, N. BRAY it shouts on one side and then blank on the other, again N. BRAY and then blank once more. In all this handling, the package begins to shed some of its potency, and Norman begins to regard it, though still warily, with some measure of scorn.

Rather than go in just yet, he sits down on the top step of his porch and lays the package off to the side. What he wants is to extend the delicious anticipation of escaping the weather. Out here is all frantic, near-freezing wind and the stinging remnants of rain being flayed from the trees, a jumble of atmospheric nastiness that seems to sum up very nicely the ridiculous trials he's been put through over the last few days. So he will sit here and revel in what he has endured, and then he will go inside, into his warm, dry house, and shut his door on it.

He reaches back to his grocery bag and pulls out a box of saltine crackers, and he sits there eating his saltines, defiantly, in the wind and rain.

⟡

It was, as Amy remembers it, the third day of a four-day drive.

This was nine years ago, in July, when she was seventeen, David was fourteen, and Norman was still a strange new presence in their lives. They had gone as a group to a place near Calgary to attend a wedding – Nanette, daughter of Gillian's older brother, Milton, married a sportswriter for the *Herald* – and now they were making their long way back.

At about nine in the evening they entered the outskirts of Sault Ste. Marie and began the search for a motel. The first they tried had only one room available and was rejected because Gillian, as she had throughout the trip, insisted on two, one for the adults, one for the teenagers. The second and third tries came up completely dry, and so there was mild debate about whether or not to return to the first, which Gillian shut down with a severe "It's not happening" and continued to stare out the passenger-side window.

Gillian had been severe since the night of the wedding reception. Amy understood why and so did David, and possibly Norman did too, although that was unclear since he seemed determined to act as though nothing had happened and Gillian's mood was merely a rogue, supernatural phenomenon that had no basis in fact.

What had happened was that from the moment they entered the ballroom of the newly furbished Macleod Inn, with its two-storey windows facing out onto the distant Rocky Mountain foothills, Norman had begun drinking the Okanagan Valley sparkling Chardonnay offered on trays by the inn's pretty, gingham-skirted waitresses. And he kept drinking throughout the evening, through the dinner and the speeches and the dancing and the circles of men with cigars, to the point that, around eleven, he began to get very excited. He started talking exuberantly about the event being an occasion for celebrating new beginnings and shared adventure, about the dramatic setting amid the foothills being the perfect place to make a grand, symbolic, *organic* gesture that would honour the bravery of jumping headlong into the unknown, and about how it would therefore be a tremendous idea, a really thrilling statement, if every member of the wedding party and anyone else who wished – the in-laws? the waitresses? – joined him for a joyful nude frolic in the Macleod Inn's large outdoor pool.

Most people had found this hilarious at first because it seemed harmless and strangely fitting. Gillian's new man, whom the Western end of the family was meeting for the first time, was an actor. Actors probably joked about this sort of thing all the time, and wasn't it a hoot? And although the laughter receded into thin smiles as Norman began tugging on the elbows of the best man and the maid of honour, trying to get them to come with him outside, they kept smiling right up to the point when Norman fiercely denounced them all as spontaneity-murdering prudes, stripped to the skin, and, in front of the gathered crowd of extended relations and assorted business contacts, attempted a naked backflip off the diving board, an attempt that ended as his back hit the surface of the water with a smack that echoed like a gunshot off the foothills. Two of the ushers had to dip their dress-shirted arms into the chlorinated water, up to the shoulders, to haul him up onto the dry concrete surround, while two great-uncles talked the assistant manager out of taking punitive action and Gillian apologized to anyone who would listen.

And now here they were in the car, three days of silent driving later, looking for a motel with two rooms where they could watch TV and not have to think about any of it.

"I think we should try Highway 550," said Norman, tapping the wheel as he waited for a traffic light to turn.

"Whatever you think," said Gillian, barely audible.

David, slumped in the back seat, picked at his fingernails and huffed a derisive "Why don't we just go to the place we stayed at before, on the way up?"

"That was the second place we tried, stupid," said Amy.

"No, it *wasn't*."

"Yes, it was. Don't you remember the moon sign? It had the big green moon."

"I didn't see any green moon."

"Well, like usual you weren't paying attention."

"Shut up!"

"David!" barked Norman as the light turned and he began to pull forward. "Don't tell Amy to shut up."

David had barely chirped out his first ripple of protest when Gillian, wheeling on Norman, overwhelmed it like a surge of surf. "I *wish* you wouldn't try to discipline my children," she said. Amy was sitting behind Gillian, but she could see when her mother turned that her eyes were hot and her mouth was cut into a scythe. "You don't have *any business* doing that."

"Well, you weren't saying anything."

"Lead by example, all right?" Gillian spat the words out like seeds. "Lead by example."

Norman stared ahead through the windshield and breathed. The car seemed to be filled with his breathing. "I do that every day."

Gillian snorted at that and, turning away from him, muttered a bitter, "In what universe?"

The car continued for a short while along a sparse commercial strip, and though there was no visible rain the tires hissed as if a shower had washed through these outskirts only minutes before and the pavement was still wet. Amy couldn't see the road from where she sat, slumped against the door, so it was a surprise to her when the smooth ride became bumpy and the sound changed and she realized Norman was pulling the car onto the gravelly shoulder of the road.

"Why are you stopping?" said Gillian.

"Because," said Norman, that was all, and from the darkness of his voice Amy gathered that he was pulling over because he was angry, although why that would make someone unable to drive she didn't know. It seemed unwise to ask.

He stopped the car between two mobile signs with fluorescent orange lettering announcing "TERRIFIC SAVINGS on DISHWARE" and "LIMITED TIME TWO for ONE" and turned off the ignition, and the four of them just sat there in silence, with minivans and Malibus hissing past, staring through their individual panes of glass at a place that looked like any other but was, in fact, unknown to them. And when Amy heard the sound of Norman's car door being opened and felt the insinuation of damp air, her instinct was to reach forward, to say, "No."

He paused as the door swung wide. "I'm just taking a walk," he said, his voice clotted. Then he got out and shut the door with a delicacy that would have struck them as ironic had they not already come to know that irony was out of Norman's range. That he was nothing if not a man who believed the things he expressed. And they watched as he lit a cigarette with his big lighter and walked out ahead of the car, his feet munching through the soft gravel, until he rounded a slight bend and disappeared behind the shadowy hull of a transport trailer marooned on its peg leg in a BF Goodrich parking lot.

At the time, she had been sequestered in a darkened hallway trying to decide whether to let herself be kissed by an eighteen-year-old math whiz from Spokane, so Amy saw none of what happened at the pool that night at the Macleod Inn, though she heard about it almost instantly from David and a few awestruck cousins who had witnessed fragments of the event. And whether her perspective was influenced by the fact that she had no stored mental image to keep the embarrassment fresh, or because it suited her just then to deem her mother harsh and judgemental, or because there seemed to be something actually vulnerable and wounded about Norman as he trudged into the retail-commercial distance, she refused to condemn him for what he'd done.

After ten minutes or so she began to get worried. Neither David nor Gillian had said anything, but she noticed rain had begun to baptize the windshield, and the cars speeding by on the left were raising hackles of grey mist. She was just getting ready to point this out to her mother, and to suggest that they go looking for Norman, when she saw him up ahead, jogging back to the car. He appeared to be carrying something.

He ran – carefully, trying not to jostle whatever it was he was cradling in his arms – until he reached the car and opened the door, and they could see that what he had was four opened bottles of Coke.

"There was a gas station a few hundred yards up," he said, sliding behind the wheel with the bottles against his chest. They could see the colour of his skin through his soaked white shirt, where it was pulled tight at the shoulders and across his back.

David already had a hand reaching over the top of the seat. "Thank God," he drawled. "I'm seriously thirsty."

"No, no!" Norman hunched away from David's hand. "These aren't for drinking. Not right away."

"Norman, let him have some," said Gillian, whom Amy judged to be as relieved as she was irritated. "We've been sitting in this car for twenty minutes."

"No! Let me tell you my idea!" Norman, still clutching the open bottles against his body, shifted around in his seat so he could see all three of them. He was almost shouting, and gleaming with Inspiration. "At first I bought these just for people to drink, but as I was walking back I had an idea of something we could do together. As a group!"

It seemed apparent to everyone but Norman that there was a limited supply of tolerance in the car. Amy's only hope was that he would get to whatever he had in mind before he used it up. "Each of these bottles is a note," explained Norman. "That's what I've been doing for the last few minutes although" – he looked at Gillian – "I'm sure it wasn't twenty." He held one of the bottles up. "This is an E." He blew across the top of the bottle and produced a mournful note. "You see? That's an E. I've been pouring out the pop bit by bit until I got the notes I wanted. Okay, that one is yours." He handed the bottle to Amy. "Don't drink it now or the note will be off and we won't be able to do this." He held the next one up and blew across it. "Okay, that's the D. Gillian, that's yours." He handed the bottle to her and looked at the remaining two. "I think this one," he lifted a third bottle and produced lowest note yet, "this one's the C." He handed it to David. "Please don't drink it, David. Do you promise?"

David took the bottle and slumped back in his seat with a sigh. "I should have gotten the E. The E has more in it."

"You can have mine when we're done, all right? But right now I want you to promise. Do you promise?"

David made his eyes go wide with exasperation. "I *promise.*"

"Okay," said Norman. "I've got the G. So now everyone try their bottles so you know how to get the sound. Just blow across the top like this." He demonstrated his G and the others, with varying levels of reluctance, joined in. Amy was the first to get it right, and eventually Gillian and then David tried and succeeded in producing a muddy note.

Norman's level of enthusiasm was now extremely high. "Now that we've all got it we're going to play a song!" he exclaimed. "There aren't many four-note songs but I did remember one. All right? So when I point to you, you play your note. And if I point to you three times in a row, then you play it –"

"– three times in a row," said David. "We get it."

"All right I'm just making sure. Ready? Go!" Norman pointed at Amy, then Gillian, then David, back to Gillian. Amy for three notes, Gillian for three, then Amy for one. By the time Norman hit his G twice it was obvious that what they were performing was a murky yet recognizable version of "Mary Had a

Little Lamb." They made it through all the way, once, as rain pelted the car, and Norman's only mistake was to be so encouraged by the result that, after a short bit of instruction on hitting each note just a little more crisply, he made everyone do it again. "For real."

Amy, Gillian, David, Gillian, Amy, Amy, Amy. Gillian, Gillian, Gillian. Amy, Norman, Norman. Amy, Gillian, David, Gillian –

Norman was already frowning when he blew his notes and now he waved his arm. "Stop! Stop!" He looked at David. "Blow your note."

Sheepishly, David puckered his lips and blew across the mouth of his bottle.

"Your note's off. That's not a C, that's closer to an A-sharp." Then Norman's eyes grew alarmed and his cheeks darkened. "You drank from it!"

"Norman, he was thirsty."

He stared, crushed, at Gillian. "You knew? You saw him do it?"

"My *God*," said David. "I just took a sip."

Norman didn't acknowledge that, didn't breathe. He turned his eyes to the road ahead of them and held his bottle in his lap. "I was trying to do something for us," he said quietly. "And nobody cares."

Gillian put a hand on his arm. "We got through it once, though. It was lovely. It was a lovely idea."

During the half-hour it took them to find a motel with two rooms, no one said anything further. And neither this Norman event nor the one at the pool was raised again, to Amy's knowledge. She remembers all of it now, staring out the window of her downtown office where she is working later than anyone has a right to expect. She remembers it because she's on the phone with David, who has tracked her down to report the findings of his recent investigations.

"There's no Mirror Award."

It was the issue of the Mirror Award that he had seized on when Amy came to tell him what she knew. It sounded wrong to him, he said, and of all the things she described to him, its wrongness seemed most provable.

And now he has confirmed it. He's checked around. He's talked to arts councils and funding groups. He's done Internet and database searches. He even called the top theatre critic in the city. No one has heard of the Mirror Award and no record of it exists.

"Norman's lying," David fumes. "I think we should confront him on it. He's always trying to make something out of nothing. It's the story of his life."

As she holds the phone with one hand and loads work into her briefcase with the other, she thinks about Norman crouched in the rain, on the gravel shoulder of a commercial road in Sault Ste. Marie, pouring Coke out of bottles until they made the right sound, and she wonders if this quality of Norman's might not be something to applaud.

# ACT V

In the morning a chalk sky sprawls above a city of scattered leaves and toppled sandwich boards. Newspapers, plastic bags, and gum wrappers are strewn generously across lawns. Norman stands at his window, draped in his comforter, and surveys the disarray. He feels the way he used to feel waking up the day of a dress rehearsal, the day he'd find out for certain what worked and what didn't, which beliefs and expectations had to be propped up and reinforced, and which ones abandoned altogether. He has no reason to feel this way today, particularly. It's just a sense.

It is now 8:30 and Karina is already showered and dressed. He knows this because he woke to the ringing of the shower curtain being pulled, heard the taps being turned and the hot water sputtering into a steady flow, and then he imagined her stepping into the stream and could not get back to sleep. He listened to her murmuring to herself as she showered, listened to the squawk and thud of her moving about in the tub, reaching for soaps and lotions, turning and arching to let water hit the tender recesses, and sometimes only standing, apparently, because there were times when all that could be heard was the sibilance of water droplets against porcelain and skin.

He heard her in the hall, walking past his door to her room, heard the door being closed and drawers being opened, hangers scraping roughly across the metal bar of her closet. He knew exactly what was happening by the sounds she made, as if he were listening to one of the radio dramas of his childhood – *The Shadow, The Cinder Block Gang, The Adventures of Karina Lares* – and imagining himself there, in the story.

But for a while now he has heard nothing at all. Specifically he has not heard the front door being opened and closed, the sound that would immediately precede the sight, as he stands expectantly at the window, of Karina Lares walking down the path to the street.

He decides to get dressed – actually dressed for the day, not just covered up by his robe – and as part of this decision he discards the idea of having a shower himself. It will take too long and, while he is oblivious to any noise but that of running water, she will leave before he's had a chance to talk to her. More than anything he wants to ask her about what she said yesterday. He wants to understand her message to him.

Once he's dressed, Norman makes a brief stop in the washroom. He runs his hands under the tap, wets his hair with his fingers and tries to stir it into some respectable shape. But this proves impossible and he decides he doesn't care; he has other priorities.

He's halfway down the stairs before he sees Karina on the living-room couch by the window, her legs curled up, her hands tucked beneath her. He stands on the stairs, watching her, until she turns away from the window and sees him, and the hurt in her eyes is so unexpected it makes him wince.

"Are you all right?" he says and knows instantly what a stupid thing it is to say. If it were a line in a play he would have it removed. When she says nothing and turns back to the window, he continues down the stairs, aware that now is not the time to ask her to clarify or explain, that, instead, the situation demands something of him. He is meant to offer support, say something that will help. But he can only think of what he would do if it were he at the window, looking back on an act or a decision that might have been wrong but now couldn't be undone, could only be reconsidered. Re-imagined.

As he enters the living room, Karina's chest heaves with a sudden breath. "I heard him last night," she says, her voice taut. "I think he is come back early. I heard him crying."

"Well, but," says Norman, searching for words, "it may only have been the wind."

She shakes her head.

"It was quite a wind, though." Norman nods adamantly. "And I've discovered that wind can contain all sorts of sounds."

"No." She turns and looks at him severely. "He was home and he was crying because I am gone. It is because of me."

She's being stubborn, he thinks, as if she actually wants to feel badly about herself. This is something Amy would sometimes do, before she left – come home from an exam and declare herself stupid. He could never figure out why but didn't want to investigate. In his view there was something risky about delving into another person's emotions. And there was always someone else around who was willing to try.

But there's no one to step in here, no Gillian to take this woman by the hand. So Norman, doing what he can, reaches for the straw of his own experience.

"When I'm upset about something," he starts, "sometimes I'll go and see a movie, or a play. Put myself in the main role, and imagine how I would play it – usually, I have to say, much differently." He tries to catch her eye, but already he sees her shifting, losing interest. "Or another thing –" He reaches for a book. "I'll read a good story and find the character that fits whatever I'm feeling. If I'm angry then it's the villain. I'll play him in my mind, and imagine an audience, out there, soaking it up!"

She's moving, getting up from the sofa, and he rushes through what he has left to say, his voice rising as he goes. "And this seems to help, you see, because the worst thing is to feel impotent, to feel there's nothing you can do. And if you can imagine –" She begins to walk through the living room, away from him, and he blurts out the rest. "What I mean is –" It seems so meagre an idea. "Maybe we could watch some ballet."

She stops at the edge of the carpet.

"We could go together. I could get some money for the tickets," he says. "Or I could . . . find something on TV." It's all he has to offer.

She smiles almost imperceptibly. "Maybe," she says, and draws a hair away from her eye. "Sometime maybe, yes." She looks sternly at him. "But not to imagine."

She begins to walk away. But Norman is very sure he has found the solution to her troubles, and he's determined to convince her. "I think you should, Karina." He picks up the

TV-listings guide. "I'll look. There might be something on right now."

"No," she says more firmly. "Now I go to work. Because this morning I have to open the shop."

"But I think this is very –"

"I am already late," she says, with a glance towards the window. "I should have left before, but I am afraid he will see me going."

"Does he know you're here?"

She shakes her head. "Not yet." Then she shuts her eyes and folds her arms around her waist. "It is a very big mistake to live here."

He extends a hand towards her. "No, it isn't."

She stares again out the window at the turquoise porch across the street. "I was thinking when I left, if I walk out the door, not to come back, that is leaving. If I go to another country or another city or another part of the city, it doesn't matter. If I walk out the door I am leaving. I am gone. So why should I have to go far away?"

"Yes. It's true."

She shrugs. "I thought maybe he should see me. Every day a reminder that he cannot make decisions for someone else."

"Absolutely."

She shakes her head. "Now I think I should be far away."

"Not at all." He has to stopper this flow of thought. "It's good that you're here, you see, because I'm here and I" – he smiles suddenly – "I have no other plans. So I can walk with you to the shop."

She hesitates.

"It's fine," he says, going directly to the hall closet to pull out his jacket. "I enjoy a good walk." He finds her overstuffed coat as well, a coat far too warm for the season, and holds it up for her. "Please." And when she slips her arms into the sausagey sleeves and he catches her now familiar scent of cloves, he finds himself wondering how many ways he might help her, how many things he could do.

⚬━⚬

The store, she explains, is called Essenshell, a shop selling cotton dresses and wraps in the colours of the sea, with sewn-in bits of shell and coral in small brooch-like designs. "So terrible," she says, her caramel skin darkening, a hand shielding her abashed grin.

They walk together – Norman keeping his strides to a manageable length – and she tells him selected details of her life in Caracas: her one-room apartment in the hillside barrios of El Hatillo, her daily commute aboard the raucous, careering *carritos*. She tells him that at the age of ten she found in her school's tiny hoard of books a history of ballet filled with colourful pictures. The most entrancing of these was a half-page photo of a Russian ballerina dressed as Giselle, which she tore out and kept. She decided soon after to become a dancer, but her parents, who worked a four-hectare coffee farm near the Andean village of Peribeca, were religious people who thought the only way to serve God was through physical labour. "Or maybe," she says wryly, "they believed it because this hard work was all they could do." Stranded in the desert of their belief, they refused to endorse her wish to "float around with music." Her father, she tells him, once tried to beat it out of her, and she left when she was sixteen.

It's this Norman understands. This last detail. He hears the rest, but he has no ready associations with life in Venezuela, so the particulars she gives him are all blank facts, like being told the sweetness of something is due to the presence of fructose. The notion, on the other hand, of being persecuted for one's uniqueness, of suffering to find an outlet for one's rare talent, this he can relate to, this he can feel under his skin. And he has a sense, too, that he might just have uncovered a clue to "No artist should accept such misery." That possibly what she meant was the misery of being misunderstood.

He races mentally down this *avenida* of connection and affirmation while Karina tells him other small details: the luck of finding a school of dance that would take her and, a few years later, getting a place in a small company in Maracaibo; the dream, finally realized, of winning a coveted spot in the Ballet Contemporáneo, where she met her husband, Diego, one of the painters of the company's lush, scenic backdrops. And the whole time she talks, Norman coddles his delicate new thought: *She's very much like me.*

She moves to the edge of the sidewalk to let past a man leashed to a stocky Doberman. "He is very talented," she says of Diego. "And very political." She continues on silently for a moment before adding, "I am proud of his painting."

They happen to be passing an electrical-parts store when Norman asks the question that seems most relevant.

"Why does he not want you to dance?"

When the question leaves his mouth she veers away and stares into the window, seemingly engrossed in a display of small motors stacked into a coppery pyramid, and Norman feels his nurtured connection being severed. When he clears his throat tentatively, she turns abruptly again and carries on.

"The store is here," she says a minute later, and pauses, rooting in her purse for a key, beside a window display of female Rol Henningers standing ankle-deep in sand and dressed in pantsuits the colour of kelp.

This is Norman's cue to leave, but staying seems necessary. Vital. He looks past her, into the shop, and asks, "Can I come in?"

"It is a stupid store." She draws out a dangly chain with a set of keys on the end. "I have many things to do." She slides one of the keys into the lock.

"I'm interested."

She sighs with a hint of frustration. But when she pushes open the door to the clatter of a steel sleigh bell and steps inside, he sees, to his relief, that she holds the door open to let him in.

Truly, the dresses are hideous – shapeless and ill-sewn, the fabrics oddly matched. "Very nice," says Norman as he scans the walls and racks, searching for something to praise. "That colour," he says, pointing to a pale-green dress hanging next to a mirror, "is what I would call aquamarine. Am I right?"

She is leaning against the counter with her arms crossed and one eyebrow climbing skyward. "You like these dresses?"

"Well," he wavers, "I can understand why some people would."

"Oh, yes?" she says, with an unruly smirk. She looks sharply from one rack to the next. "I can say honestly I would not wear one of these things." She waves a hand at the entirety. "This is all terrible junk."

"Then why do you work here?"

She considers this question with a slightly narrowed gaze, as though its real meaning must be hidden.

"What I'm saying," he tries again, "is that you're a dancer, not a store clerk. That's why you're not happy." Still she says nothing. In fact, she turns away, opens a drawer behind the counter from which she pulls a stack of red price tags, and begins to write on them with a black felt pen.

"I recognize the problems with your husband," he continues, "and you've done the right thing in leaving him, no question. Because no one should stay with someone who doesn't understand them, which" – he'll slip it in deftly, to see her reaction – "I think is probably what you meant before, when you spoke about not accepting misery." Nothing. No reaction. She doesn't even look up. "But what I am trying to figure out" – he speaks a little louder and raises his arms to indicate their tidewater surroundings, the fact of the store itself, the very idea of submitting to society's expectations – "is if you hate this place, why are you here?"

Karina straightens from what she is doing and sends him a look of pure exasperation. "I have to work. I have a responsibility." She launches a shrug so severe her shoulders threaten to consume her head. "I have to pay rent!"

Somewhere down the street a car alarm blares and Norman's eyes go to the window; he has a moment of wanting to share with her that he too is being forced to contend with the same rigid absolutes, the same *have-to*s and *must*s. That everything he values is being . . .

"These things," he begins. Then he faces her and tries to smile, managing something less than his best. "These things have a way of working themselves out."

"No. You have to make them."

In the distance, the car siren keeps wailing, and Norman moves towards the shop door and puts a hand on the metal grip. "Why is that necessary?" he says, mostly to himself. He stands at the closed door, looking down the street, and tips his head forward until it touches the cold glass.

"Please," she says quietly behind him. "I am late. Can you help me?"

He turns and sees her reaching towards him with a small stack of sale tags, each with the black-markered message: 40% off.

He cups his hands and receives the tags like spilled treasure. "What do I do?"

She motions for him to watch, then picks a coral-coloured polyester skirt from a nearby rack. "You tie this tag around the label, next to the price." She demonstrates, but what she does is not tying, it's something else, a curl-slip-tug manoeuvre, which her hands execute so quickly he isn't sure what he's seeing.

"Yes?"

"You'll have to show me that again."

She pulls out a second skirt and does the same thing.

"Ah!" Norman's head bobs. "I see now. This part goes up and through here. Like a dance step."

"Oh yes," she exaggerates, giggling. "A very pretty dance."

There are sixty-five tags, and she wants him to attach one to every piece of merchandise on the racks along the western wall. Once he has the hang of it, he finds it effortless, which allows his mind to consider other things, including a thought he finds troubling. In the middle of tagging his second rack, he asks, "What does your husband do, during the day?"

She's carrying a small ladder from a hidden storage room, and as she does this she frowns at him. "Why do you want to know about my husband?"

He hesitates. "I wondered if he might come here."

She places the ladder against a wall and climbs to reach an upper rack of white dresses with scallop-shell collars. "He does not know where I work."

"You never talked about it?"

"I told him I am selling dresses downtown. He didn't ask where." She waves her hand. "He was not interested."

Norman shakes his head at this, appalled.

After a few more minutes, when he has finished tagging a collection of turquoise pants and she has thanked him, Norman hovers for a moment in the middle of the store. Helping her, even with such a simple task, has given him a tantalizing taste of fulfillment. What if he could find something even more substantial? He claps his hands and rubs them together. "Is there anything else I can do for you?"

"No, thank you." She smiles, but it's a distracted smile. "I quite enjoyed this."

His tenant is waiting for him to go. He looks down at the floor, simply to buy time and avoid her impatience. And as he studies the smooth, tiled surface, he has an inspired idea. Why didn't he think of it before?

"This floor," he taps it with the toe of his shoe. "It's like a dance floor."

◦•◦•◦

Once, in a hotel bar in Vancouver, Norman had an argument with an older, moderately successful television actor over the relative indignities of their chosen milieus.

"Television actors don't lose their pasts," Norman insisted. "One's old work still exists. You sit someone down in front of a screen and you can say, See? I did this. It remains. A stage performance, on the other hand, retreats into vapour the moment it's complete. It has to be as right as it can be, and you have to *believe* that it's right. Because you have nothing else to look back on."

"Sweet impermanence," said the television actor wistfully. A man in his fifties, he argued that the stage was far more forgiving than television, because television preserved one's mistakes. "I have worked in television all my life," he said, "and when I watch the damn thing, I will inevitably see something I did twenty years before and hoped to God to forget. You flip around, to channels you hardly knew existed, and suddenly performances without any maturity, without any technique or understanding, assault you without warning."

"On stage," said Norman, "if you make a mistake, there's no escaping it. But in television there's always the chance for a second take, or a third. You can try things, and if they're wrong, you have the opportunity to do it again."

"But what if you don't know it's a mistake at the time? What if you realize it only later?" The elder actor nodded sagely at Norman. "Then you're fucked."

Each man paused to take a long, thoughtful sip of his drink.

"There is nothing so humiliating," said the television actor ruefully, "as to be accosted by the fetid flesh of one's undead past."

"There is nothing so challenging," said Norman, with effort, "as to craft a performance that, on its very first night, gets only bad reviews, and to have to go on stage, night after night for weeks afterward, trying to forget you've already failed."

The television actor finished his drink and rose, slapping his money onto the bar and his hand on Norman's shoulder. "But you, my friend, have the luck of time. Two years from now, or twenty, who's to say what really happened?" He leaned in and spoke in a practised whisper that could only have been picked up by a microphone, or an ear inches away. "No one keeps a bad review. So unlike me, you can't be held accountable for your failures and mistakes. The facts of them are, literally, neither here nor there."

◦━◦

He's going to soft-shoe.

He's going to shim-sham.

He's going to give Karina a performance to remember – not ballet maybe, but dance nonetheless – and he's sure that it's just the thing that will inspire her, because all imagination needs is a spark.

Here's a little sequence he remembers – brush, flap, slide, step, flap, *hitch* – from a '69 summer tour.

But Norman is saved in the dress shop, saved from himself, by the entrance of two women in their mid-twenties, spritzing chatter words like cartoon sweat, probably lured by the 40% *Off* sign Karina placed in the window. They push the door open, through the jangling sleigh bell, just as a look of concern flashes across Karina's face and Norman has a flicker of doubt.

This moment, this instant of early warning, has always been the most dangerous one for Norman, because it spurs him to feats of daring. From this juncture of uncertainty, without the interruption, he would have plunged ahead. He would have seen Karina's eyes turning anxious, her face darkening with alarm, and he would have grown more determined still. He would have whipped his fading enthusiasm on until Karina had complied with his wish to inspire her, until he had done what-ever it took to defeat his own misgiving.

This time, however, just as it occurs to Norman that what he plans to do might actually embarrass Karina and push her away, two shoppers in pursuit of savings appear. And he is saved.

When the shoppers point to a particularly ugly eel-green pantsuit hanging up near the ceiling, and Karina drags the stepladder closer to retrieve it, Norman catches her eye with a wave, and he leaves.

⊸⬤⊸

At 1:30, with a lunch of scrambled eggs in him, Norman is in the basement, rooting among the boxes and knick-knacks displaced by the earlier scrounging for Karina's bedroom furni-ture, when the phone starts ringing. He lets two rings go by until he remembers that Karina is not there to answer.

He tears through the basement and up the stairs as two more rings are born and die. At the door to the kitchen he hears his answering machine kick in.

"*Hello, this is Norman –*"

He grabs the phone. "Hello?"

"*– ay. I'm not here, except –*"

A scream of feedback pierces Norman's head.

"Mr. Bray, it's –"

"Wait!"

"– *ner of speaking. But* –"

He fumbles for the off switch at the top. The machine is shrieking at him.

"– Henninger. Are –"

The scream hits a sheering falsetto that makes Norman's insides twist.

"I'm trying to turn it off!"

"– *Belch, I will meditate* –"

He finds the silver plastic button on the side, of all places, and shoves it home. And the silence is, once more, a relief of spiritual purity.

"Mr. Bray," says Rol Henninger after a moment, "should I take it you're in bed again?"

"No! I was in the basement. I *raced* to get here." Where others would be gasping for air, Norman has complete diaphragmatic control over his breathing, but his heart is ramming like a tower bell against his ribs.

"I was speaking to Howard Cantor this morning." Norman awaits the inevitable crushing of his final tatter of hope, the hope that somehow all of this is going to go away and he is going to be allowed to live as he wishes. Here it comes, the arbitrary hammer of unreasonable expectation that has chosen to fall on him and everything he holds dear, and he can do nothing but listen. "He was not very happy."

"No, I suppose not."

"I have to tell you, Mr. Bray, that you are not doing yourself any favours. Do you understand what I mean when I say that?"

Norman, alone in his kitchen, feels the need to close his eyes. When they are closed, he feels the need to nod.

"You can be an extremely difficult man to work with. Extremely difficult. And eventually that has consequences."

He nods some more. He feels like a child being asked to agree with the concept of having his palm lashed with a stick.

"Did you, by the way, get the package I left for you?"

"I did."

"What did you think?"

"I'm afraid," he says stiffly, "I haven't had a chance to open it."

Rol Henninger pauses on the end of the line, and Norman hears him produce a glacial sigh that sounds like one of his own, layered with the incremental indignities of a life spent being underappreciated. "Mr. Bray, all I can say is that I am trying to help you. And what you are doing is kicking at, for lack of a better word, the machinery – the machinery that could get you a job and let you keep your house."

"I wish there were a better word."

"System, then."

System is no better. "I hear what you're telling me."

"You have been given a second chance. Like me or not, I am that chance. You will not get another."

"I understand," says Norman, exhausted from all this acceptance. "So what do I have to do now?"

Henninger explains that he has uncovered what might be an ideal opportunity, perfectly suited to Norman's "particular skill set." But they have to act quickly; he'll come by in half an hour.

When the half-hour is exactly up, a five-year-old navy-blue Plymouth pulls in front of Norman's house and its horn beeps, crisply, twice. Norman, wearing the same shirt, jacket, and pants that he wore to meet his banker, steps out into a November that seems to have shifted again, into something harder, darker, and more potently treacherous.

⊷●⊶

Rol Henninger drives as slowly as a man can drive. A yellow traffic light to Rol Henninger is a coal-mine canary, not a cautionary reminder but a portent of doom. In the passenger seat, Norman presses his foot into the Plymouth's clean black carpet – if he is going to be driven to his punishment, he doesn't want a lot of agonizing anticipation; he wants to get there in decent time.

Not that he is decided yet on whether he deserves to be punished. The question of deservingness remains open for debate. He's prepared to acknowledge, however, that some of the mistakes he's made may not be sufficiently covered by his blanket "being human" admission and a quick deposit in the reparations depot. Some of them may be a little trickier to redress.

He doesn't know whether it's coincident with this awareness or not, but lately a lot of people – people he feels obligated to listen to – have been remarkably sharp with him. Where has all this sharpness come from? Gillian used to speak to him so evenly; she seemed quite loath to upset him. The same was true with the people he worked with – even Robert, he realizes, just last week, tried to ease into his bad news. Now, because of some mortgage trouble, people seem to think they can say anything as harshly as they wish, with no regard for the way the words slice into him. Or maybe there were times when people said these sorts of things before and he was able to withstand them and now suddenly he can't, as if some invisible membrane that had once protected him from harm were missing. Norman's imagination allows him to picture vividly where this could lead. Membrane gone, then house gone. Tenant gone. Faith in the essential fairness of the universe shattered. He can see himself living as a boarder in the home of some tormented old woman. He can see himself living with Margaret.

He still feels weighted by thoughts of what Karina said to him. He feels oppressed. How can a person say a thing like "No artist should accept such misery" without making sure the listener has a full grasp of its meaning? For a while, over his lunch of eggs, Norman re-examined the ways in which Karina could have intended something ardently supportive and missed the mark solely because English isn't her native tongue. Then he remembered the look on her face when she said it. Sharp.

Out of the corner of his eye he watches Rol Henninger, steering them onto the westbound expressway with both hands on the wheel, and he thinks, there was a time this would never have happened. There was a time it was assumed he would drive, and if it wasn't assumed he insisted, because he trusted his own judgement and abilities far more than those of other people. When he saw *The Poseidon Adventure* with Amanda in 1972, he sat in the theatre thinking, I am Gene Hackman. I am the priest who takes charge and guides his followers to the hull of the ship. He has tried to be that way all his life, leading

people where they needed to go, whether or not they understood why. The opportunities have gotten fewer over the years,
but when he has had them, he hasn't flinched. Look at the last
time, in Beverly. What was he then if not Gene Hackman and
more, guiding a sorry troupe out of the depths and into the
fresh air and light of professionalism? And making the hard
choices, being responsible for the result – isn't that what it
means to be "the lead"?

And the only thing as consistent as his effort has been the
inability of others to appreciate his intent. It was as true in
Beverly three years ago as it was in the movie theatre in 1972,
when he leaned over in the dark, during the underwater swim-
ming scene, and whispered to Amanda, *I am Gene Hackman*,
and she rolled her eyes, and he knew it was just a matter of time
before that marriage was over.

And now he's sitting in the passenger seat. He's the one
following orders, and apparently Rol Henninger is Gene
Hackman. The thought, to Norman, is almost unbearable. It's
preferable to worry about Karina.

"We're about ten minutes away," says Henninger, allowing
another laden transport to pass.

"Ten minutes away from what?"

"If you had opened the package you'd know. What I can
tell you right now is I've done my best." His head wobbles
with a kind of bewilderment. "I think we've been blessed with
some luck."

Norman tries to remember what he was talking about when
Karina brought up the whole issue of misery. It seems to him he
was explaining that an artist's needs are constant, a fact of his

nature regardless of whether or not he's working, and how poor Gillian evidently had trouble with that basic, essential truth. It's possible then, Norman eventually decides, that she was referring to Gillian's misery. But if so, why the disapproval directed at him? If there were some suggestion that he knew of Gillian's misery, and then "accepted" it, he might be able to understand. But he didn't know. Her misery was insidious. Had it been obvious, there would have been no issue – when has he ever been still or silent in the face of obvious misery?

He has barely even formed this question when a face comes to mind. It's not Gillian's but the face of someone he has seen recently. He knows the face, sees the misery it bears, and because he feels ambushed he pushes the image away. He cracks open his window to lean into the stream of cold air, letting it massage his eyelids and cheekbones, hoping that it might, in fact, clear his head.

"I'm sorry, Mr. Bray," says Rol Henninger. "Would you mind rolling that up? The buffeting is distracting me."

Norman cocks an eye at him. "You're distracted by the buffeting?"

"Yes. I am."

Norman rolls up the window slowly, with evident disdain. As a driver, he welcomed buffeting. Open the windows! Let the outside in! Partly it was a way of dealing with the complaints of non-smokers like Amy and David who would start waving hands in front of their noses as soon as he lit up. But even so.

He sits back in his seat and the face appears again, like a postage stamp in the corner of his mind's view. And now that it's less of a surprise, Norman lets it remain. It's the face of Miriam Ashacker. Not the robust Miriam from years before but the pale, thin knock-off he saw just a few nights ago, her skin chalky and lined like a piece of driftwood.

The suffering in this face, the misery, is obvious. He is not in any way responsible for it, of course; unlike Gillian's, it has no tenuous connection to him. But neither can he say he didn't notice it at the time.

A person could argue, in fact, that he accepted it.

Norman pushes himself upright in his seat. There is a fluttering in his stomach he finds uncomfortable. He adjusts his seatbelt. Probably, he thinks, this wasn't the kind of misery Karina had in mind. She couldn't have known about Miriam, so clearly she was referring to something else. With her disapproval.

He purses his mouth, looks around through the windows. Plays his fingers against his knees. "Not much traffic," he says.

"Not much."

There's some problem with his breathing. There's a restriction. He can't seem to take a proper breath. He adjusts his seatbelt again and sucks air through his nostrils. His diaphragm is inexplicably tight. He blows out and tries again.

Rol Henninger glances over. "Is everything all right?"

Norman stares through the windshield, holding air in his lungs. He blinks.

"We'll be there pretty soon."

He exhales in a gust. "I need to make a phone call."

"Well, as I said –"

"No, I want you to pull off the highway and get me to a phone booth. I need to call someone immediately." To Norman it's conceivable that Miriam Ashacker is so sick she will die within the hour. And if he does not get to say to her what he must say, then he will never be able to look at Karina

Lares again without a lingering and enfeebling sense of shame.

"Mr. Bray, we will literally be stopping in minutes."

"I don't care. I have to communicate with someone *right now*. It's very important."

Henninger reaches into the breast pocket of his suit jacket, pulls out a small silver cellphone, and holds it out to him.

"You can use this."

"No, no," says Norman, waving the gadget away. "I don't want to use that. It's a private matter, I don't want to have the conversation with you sitting right next to me."

"You can speak quietly. It's a Kasai; it has very good pickup."

"No!" Norman can't blame Henninger for not understanding, but the fact is he doesn't want to be travelling when he speaks to Miriam. It seems to him that any words he would speak while moving along the highway, words that would then be digitized and reflected off some distant tower, would be less real than they should be, under the circumstances. He wants to hold on to a proper phone when he talks to her, wants his words to travel through a proper wire. And having solid ground beneath him seems important too; he wants to know, as it were, where he stands.

Henninger, sighing, puts the phone away and clamps the wheel again with his death grip. "We were going to be taking the exit after next anyway. I'll pull off there and if we see a phone booth before we get to where we're going, then I'll stop. Is that all right?"

"That's fine."

"Or I can just pull over and you can stand with the phone on the shoulder of the road as far away from me as you like."

"A phone booth will be fine."

When Henninger, a few minutes later, has steered the dark-blue Plymouth onto an off-ramp and circled back over the highway into a land of greyish, metal-sided boxes the general size and shape of buildings but with none of the visible features – windows, bricks, people – that one associates with buildings, Norman begins to wonder whether he's fallen for a trick.

"Where are we?"

"This is the Southwest Industrial Park," says Henninger.

Norman shoulders past the ludicrousness of the term "industrial park" and heads straight for the plain incongruity.

"What are we doing out here? I thought you were taking me to see about some sort of ideal job."

"I am."

Norman scans the faceless, nameless structures, secured like fortresses behind ramparts of parked cars and moats of clipped dried lawn. A phone booth – let alone suitable employment – seems as likely out here as a dolphin.

"This is a wasteland."

Henninger glances out one side window and then the other. "It used to be a wasteland," he says. "They reclaimed it."

"Well, whatever it is" – Norman presses back against his seat – "I want to make my phone call."

"We're almost there."

"You promised me a phone call." That this is the sort of thing prisoners say on television isn't lost on him and he jams the fact into the wad of dismay already stuck in his throat. "We're not going to find a *single* phone booth here."

"No," says Henninger, turning, as they pass each of the entrance drives, to eye the numbered concrete post sunk into the ground beside it, "I think you're right."

"Well then, pull up to one of these buildings and I'll go in and ask to use their phone."

Henninger allows the car to slow perceptibly as the road begins a lazy leftward arc and keeps craning his neck, searching. "One sixty-three," he murmurs softly. "One fifty-eight."

"Here. Pull in here." Norman targets a finger across Henninger's field of view towards a just-emerged and typically windowless building with the proportions of a giant shoebox, clad in white corrugated metal up a storey and a half to its flat, overhanging, lid-like roof. The home, according to a low brown sign set into the dying grass, of Vocem-Tech Ltd. Number 147.

Henninger takes in the view. "Well –"

"No," insists Norman. "Don't tell me how close we are. We've been 'close' for twenty minutes. I don't want to be dragged around any longer. I have to make a phone call and *this* is where I want to do it."

"All right."

"You obviously have no idea how important this is."

"Very good."

"I have to communicate something to someone."

"That's clear."

When Henninger has parked the blue Plymouth in the row of spaces marked for visitors, Norman levers the door open and notices the employment counsellor doing the same.

"Aren't you going to wait for me here?"

Henninger smiles thinly. "I thought I might come in."

"It's not necessary."

"I'd like to stretch my legs."

Out of the car, Norman charges across dusty asphalt towards what looks like an entrance to the shoebox, a space at one corner where a squarish piece of the building appears to be missing. The way in is marked with a lack of something. An absence. God, he thinks, to look at this blankness, day after day, this faceless, soulless void, would crush him.

He steps over the finger segments of concrete marking the limits of the parking area, walks up a poured-concrete path, and, in the shadowed section of missing building, the cubical dearth, finds a door in an expanse of smoked glass.

Henninger is behind him and Norman pauses at the door.

"I'll just be a minute," Norman says. "No need to follow me in."

The man nods and brings his hand to a tie that does not need to be straightened.

What he enters, a lobby of sorts, isn't a place, it seems to Norman, it's a non-place. Meant for non-people. Fluorescent light falls down from above like mist, without an obvious source. There is a hush in the air that feels unnatural, a processed negation of sound. Even the air itself seems synthetic, a kind of breathable plasma, something to fool the bodily systems, keep the lungs from shutting down, until a supply of real air can be found.

In the centre of the lobby, four objects constructed of stainless-steel tubing, bent and twisted into the shape of chairs, face each other around a low table made of slabs of greenish glass. In the centre of the table lies a single magazine, devoted to the minutiae of computer programming. In the corner of the lobby hulks a plastic tree in a cauldron-sized pot. Covering the floor in its entirety is a blue-grey carpet that mutes the fall of every step.

All the things constituting Hell.

At the far corner from where Norman stands is a door that might be made of steel or aluminum and, beside it, a horizontal panel of frosted glass in a smooth grey wall. Behind the glass moves the diffused shape of a dark head.

He goes to it, noiselessly.

As he approaches, the glass panel slides open, revealing a pretty woman with enormous brown eyes and – this is what captures his attention – short, dark hair encasing her head like grasping hands. The hair, he realizes, of Leslie Caron in *An American in Paris*. It's the one thing in this environment that makes sense to Norman, and he holds on to the notion like a talisman.

"I need to make a phone call," he says sternly before she can speak. "Do you have a phone I can use?"

The Leslie Caron–haired woman, sitting at a telephone console that takes up most of her small hidden room, attempts to smile even as she frowns, cinching her face into a bow of confusion.

"It's something of an emergency."

Concern flashes across the woman's face. "Is somebody hurt? Was there an accident?"

"No, nothing like that." Norman smiles impatiently. "It's more of a personal situation."

"I don't understand," says the woman. She leans forward until her head pokes halfway through the rectangular space in the wall and peers around as if she expects to find a bleeding accident victim leaning off to one side. Emergency was the wrong word to use. The woman has become distracted by his misuse of the word emergency.

"I shouldn't have said 'emergency,'" says Norman. "It's really just a very important personal matter." Urgent. "An urgent matter."

The woman sits back in her chair. "So it's not an emergency now."

"No. No. But I do need to make a call. It's very urgent."

She regards him suspiciously. "Do you have an appointment?"

Norman sighs. It's hard to imagine how someone who looks like Leslie Caron can be so unyielding. "I just need to make a phone call," he says. "Why do I need an appointment to make a phone call?"

A tinny chirrup emanates from the telephone console on the desk beside the woman and she turns abruptly from Norman to pick up the receiver.

"Vocem-Tech Limited."

She says it like a query — *Vocem-Tech Limited?* — as if she were unsure of the identity of her own employer, which doesn't surprise Norman in the least, given that its building and its grounds possess not a single identifying feature. Who wouldn't be confused?

"I'm afraid Mr. Landling will be in a meeting most of the afternoon," she purrs. "Would you like his voice mail? All right."

She presses a button, returns the receiver, and then, having given up all pretence of smiling, narrows her gaze at Norman in a way that he finds marginally accusatory. "Don't you have a cellphone?"

"No," says Norman, without satisfaction. "He does but I didn't want to use it. I wanted to use a real phone."

"Who?"

Norman stares at her.

"Who does? Who are you talking about?"

He shakes his head. "It's not important. Please." Maybe, he thinks, if he explained the problem with a great windmilling of his arms. "I wouldn't have bothered you, I would have been happy to use a phone booth, but there are no phone booths in the area. At all. Were you aware of that? None. Which isn't surprising because there don't seem to be any people. But it makes situations like this, when a person needs to make an urgent call, very difficult."

The Leslie Caron–haired woman glances nervously at her console.

Maybe, Norman thinks, if he shared something of what he's trying to accomplish. He leans closer, puts his face right in the rectangular space in the wall. "The fact is I'm trying to phone someone who's in pain. I wasn't very good about it before. Do you see what I'm – ?" He sighs. "I suspect there are a number of things I haven't been good at, over the years. I'm an artist, you see. We can be difficult. Because the responsibilities are great! But it was suggested to me, by someone I respect, that in particular I have been too accepting of misery, and I didn't understand that at first. But now I think I do, and I need to do something to correct that problem."

He waits.

"And I was hoping you could help me."

The woman has not moved except to draw in her limbs, to create a tight, defensive L with her forearms, and Norman smiles at her in what he hopes is a sincere and thoroughly non-threatening manner. People help those they like. He wants her to like him.

"Did you know," he says warmly, "that you have Leslie Caron hair?"

"I have *what*?"

Behind the woman, a man appears. Norman, leaning down, can see only his trim torso, his crisp white shirt, and the lower half of a blue-and-yellow tie, and he follows it as the man moves through the anteroom, past the telephone console and the woman, who looks relieved, to the steel door next to Norman, which opens to reveal a pleasant-looking executive in his mid-thirties with short sandy hair and an unmistakable air of anticipation.

"Norman Bray?"

Norman straightens up at the window. "Yes?"

"Would you like to come in?"

The man thrusts his arm out and Norman allows his hand to be shaken.

"I'm Bill Taschel. I'm head of the department."

Wonderful. Someone who can be of real assistance. "I was trying to explain to this woman that I need to make a very urgent phone call."

"Yes," says the executive, directing Norman down a mysteriously lit hallway. "Rol Henninger mentioned something about it."

"Henninger? You know Rol Henninger?"

"We've collaborated before. He called me on his cell. He said you wanted to come in by yourself."

"That's right. It's a private matter."

"I understand."

They have reached an intersection of hallways. In all directions Norman can see doors at regular intervals leading to what
he presumes to be offices, occupied by souls enslaved to
unimaginable drudgery, from which no sign of life escapes.

Bill Taschel steers Norman down the corridor on the right
and pulls on the second door they come to, which opens with
a vacuuming slurp. He props this door open with a hard leather
shoe in order to push open a second, inner door.

"Why don't you have a seat in here?"

Norman looks around curiously as he enters. "This is
a sound booth." He sees a chair on rollers sitting against a
counter, on which rests a set of professional-looking head-
phones with a snaking microphone attached.

"There's a phone on the stand behind the door," says
Taschel.

"Ah!"

"Dial nine to get a line out."

"Very good," says Norman. "Thank you so much." From
inside the little room he gives the obliging man a smile and
a collegial chuckle. "The woman at the front wasn't being
very helpful."

Taschel releases the doors and shrugs. "All you had to do
was give her your name."

"Oh." As the two slabs swing shut, Norman looks at the
disappearing executive with a bewildered awe. Enclosed in
silence, he shakes his head in astonishment.

That he would be recognized, in such a place.

Norman makes himself comfortable in the chair and surveys his surroundings. Quite clearly a sound booth of some

sort, very much like the one at the Jarvis Street studio, although smaller in this case, and walled entirely in soundproofing material, without the facing glass partition that allowed for vital interaction with the director. An isolation booth is what this is, thinks Norman, as lonely and bleak as the rest of the building. But not a bad place from which to make a difficult phone call.

And luckily, he kept Miriam's number in his wallet.

He reaches for the phone, which is indeed on a small stand, as Taschel promised, and pauses a moment with his hand on the receiver to gather and review his thoughts. Misery et cetera. Someone having mentioned it. Used to accept it. Don't now. Very much thinking of her. And so on.

He dials nine and the number. Clears his throat.

After three rings comes a fourth at a slightly higher pitch, and then a male voice comes on the line. "Hello –"

"Hello!" says Norman, leaning forward.

"– you've reached Miriam and John."

*Shit!* He waits through the "we're unable" and the "please leave a message" and feels himself heating up with a fever of unrelieved goodwill and personal growth. He is trying to show the world he is an artist who does not accept misery and the world will not take his call! He hangs up at the beep.

After a moment, Norman tries to will himself up out of his chair and into the hallway with the idea of returning to the blue Plymouth and submitting to the remainder of Rol Henninger's design. But he can't do it.

He dials the number again.

As the rings and the recorded greeting run their course, Norman stares at his shoes, girding himself for the usual answering-machine ordeal and reviewing again the points he hopes to cover regarding misery and his non-acceptance of it. But the beep comes more suddenly than he expects and he hesitates for just a second, and what he doesn't want, what cannot be allowed, is to leave the impression, recorded and replayable, that he is unsure about his message, that he is uncommitted to his purpose. Because he is *not*.

So he hangs up. And tries once more.

This time he waits out the rings and the dry baritone of husband John's greeting with the determination of a marathoner running through grinding pain. He will get to the beep. He will visualize Miriam's drawn face, her too-large eyes, and he will leave his heartfelt message. But just as he's about to take his readying breath, with the whole prospect laid out perfectly in his mind, the booth's inner door begins to open and he looks up in dismay as Bill Taschel pokes in his sandy head.

"I'm not done! I'm not done!"

"Oops!" Taschel gives a sheepish wave as he backs away and lets the door close. But the beep has come and gone.

It's with a special order of resolve, braided up with anguish and chagrin, that Norman makes what he decides will be his last attempt. He is beset with a profound fatigue, which he manages to hope – his optimism has always been a source of wonder to many – will lend a certain *gravitas* to his message, and he listens to the rings on Miriam's end with his eyes closed, steeling himself.

The greeting comes. The beep beeps. He listens to the enfolding silence that follows and opens his mouth to say all the things he intends.

And he realizes none of it is enough.

"Miriam," he says finally. "It's Norman." He sees her face staring at him, his shoulders rise and fall, and all that comes is, "I'm sorry." He lingers on the line for a moment, then puts the receiver back in its cradle.

As he stands, he hears a knock on the booth's outer door and the rush of air that tells him someone is coming in. As he expects, it's the eager Bill Taschel.

"So, Mr. Bray. Apologies about before. I've been watching the line to make sure I didn't interrupt you again."

Norman nods and edges towards the hall.

"Everything wrapped up satisfactorily?"

He squares his shoulders, giving Taschel a half-smile. "For the most part."

"Great!" Taschel slaps his hands together. "Well! Why don't we get started?"

—&bull;—

She finds the apartment at the top of three flights of paint-worn stairs in an old greystone building, one of several hidden behind the Caribbean-Italian merge of St. Clair Avenue West, amid the forest streets – Maplewood, Cherrywood, Pinewood, Humewood. And she wonders to herself as she waits on the landing where all the hume trees have gone.

The woman who comes to the door, Diane Ellard, is shorter than Amy expects, with mousy hair tied back off her face. Earlier, when she called to arrange the meeting, Amy had imagined her looking as dark and feral as Aldonza, the character she played in Beverly, because her voice had a dusky, shadowed quality. Now the reason for that becomes clear.

"Come in, but don't touch me," she says, watery-eyed and wrapped, onion-like, with layers of flannel peeling at her neck. She holds a balled tissue to her nose. "I've got some stupid bug."

She leaves the door open and pads through the hall, thick socks buffing hardwood, to a small living room smelling of incense and furnished with painted wicker, throw rugs, and hillocks of large firm cushions. "They said at the clinic it's just a cold, but I still should have told you on the phone," she says, lowering herself into a twiggy chair that crackles as she sits. "For the last two days my mind hasn't really been working."

"It's okay." Amy notes, only as she sets it down beside her, that she's brought her briefcase in with her again, like an anecdote she can't stop repeating.

"And nobody gives you any sympathy over a lousy cold any more." Diane freezes, tissue at hand, as if she anticipates some respiratory upheaval, but it doesn't come. She sighs and slumps deeper into the chair, head back and eyes closed. "Did you want anything? Sorry, I'm not much of a host."

"No, thanks. I'm fine." Amy slides her fingers back and forth along the seam of her jeans and wonders if she should wait to be prompted. An old flea-market cuckoo clock hangs dead on the wall. Outside, through a beaded curtain, the afternoon sky is turning the colour and texture of custard.

Diane coughs and makes a pathetic face. "Do you think – sorry – do you think you could get me a glass of water? I feel a bit dizzy."

"Sure." Amy rises off the couch and heads down the hall, the echoey clumping of her boots against the hardwood causing her to step more softly, to the galley kitchen, its parallel banks

312

of cabinets, above and below, all painted a milky green. She starts looking for glassware.

"And maybe a Tylenol?" Diane calls weakly from the other room.

The pills she finds on the kitchen counter, and when she fills the glass with water she hesitates for a moment, wondering whether she should let it get colder. She decides not to bother, and feels slightly shameful.

"You're great," says Diane, reaching out with two hands. "Oh, good," she murmurs, sipping. "I prefer it a little warm."

Amy can feel her cheeks burning pink. Diane flings the pill towards the back of her throat and gulps half the water in the glass, then lets her head loll against the back of her chair with her eyes closed and breathes heavily.

"So, you want to know about Norman."

"Just opening night, really." Amy pauses. "I realize it's maybe hard to remember things back –"

"No, no. It's all incredibly vivid. I mean, working with Norman is nothing if not memorable."

Diane brings a hand to her face and lets out a deep, croupish cough that conjures images of a cheese grater and makes Amy want to wipe her palms against the upholstery. Then the woman blows her nose, tosses the Kleenex to the floor, and pulls another out of a box.

"Before we dive right into it, though, I have to give you some context."

It began with the battered barber's basin.

It is the battered barber's basin – the battered *brass* barber's basin, in fact – that the character of Quixote, in his delusion, mistakes for the Golden Helmet of Mambrino, which he

313

believes makes a man "of noble heart" impervious to injury. Every production of *Man of La Mancha* requires a brass barber's basin sufficiently battered to be believable as a barber's basin, but not so battered that believing that it is instead something magical and brilliant stretches all credulity. And if, in locating such an object, you can have fun with alliteration – a game that actors adore – so much the better.

When Norman joined the cast in Beverly, with three weeks to go before opening night, one of the first things he did was demand to see the brass barber's basin. Was it, he wanted to know, believably battered? There were appreciative chuckles from many of the cast members scattered throughout the empty seats of the dinner theatre, where they preferred to sit eating dried apricots and Kit Kat bars when not required on stage, as well as from the prop girl hidden in the wings. The prop girl, Elise, was a boyishly small, wretchedly nervous young woman of no more than twenty-two, whose hands and neck were alive with eczema, and who seemed, in her ferret-like movements, always afraid of being struck. The fact that she laughed, back there in her alcove, gave everyone a warm feeling towards Norman; he was instantly accepted.

"It is brilliantly blemished!" someone shouted out, to more scattered chuckles.

"Beautifully banged up," someone else offered, to groans and a few polite titters. When no one else piped up it was assumed the air had gone out of that and the director – a thin-sweatered local man named Gerald Young who taught high-school English and who, because he knew the theatre owners, Bishop and Sandra Meckling, and regularly fed them corn and slow-roasted ribs at his once-a-summer backyard barbecues, had directed the past five Dinner Theatre productions – clapped his hands and said, "All right, let's carry on."

But Norman wasn't joking. "No," he said, a warning finger raised, "you don't clap your hands at me. I want to see the barber's basin."

Gerald, who was painfully good-natured – as a director this was his chief shortcoming – and simply wanted to keep things on schedule, blanched and squinted at him, and seemed at a loss for words. "Sorry, Norman," he finally said, shaking himself out of it. "I wasn't clapping *at* you. But we're – is it important to see the basin this minute?"

"Of course it's important," fumed Norman. "This play is a balance between the real and the imagined, and the basin is the central pivot point in that balance. It is the fulcrum. If the basin isn't right you screw the whole production."

This was certainly overstating the case, but at any rate out came the basin. Elise darted from her props alcove, practically trembling, and gave it over with livid hands for Norman's inspection. Since everyone liked this basin, had in fact remarked to Elise what a clever find it was – a second-hand kitchen-gadgets store, eh? Terrific – it was assumed that would be the end of the matter.

But not only didn't Norman like the basin, he clearly found it troubling. "This isn't right," he said, his voice a mixture of scorn and disappointment. He turned it over in his hands, staring at it as if he could not quite believe what he was holding. Then he faced the director and said in amazement, "This is a colander!"

Beside him, Elise, her head bent, mumbled something that no one could quite hear.

"This is a fucking colander," said Norman, his voice rising. "Does no one see why this is a problem?" He waited. "It has *handles*." He stared at them, all of them silent. "It has *holes*."

Elise again tried to speak, but her mouth was facing her chest and Norman was in the grip of his discontent. He slapped his forehead with his free hand. "I can't, frankly, imagine how anyone could think this would work. If this is indicative of the kind of thinking that's going on here, then this production is in a great deal of trouble."

"Norman, I think that's enough." Gerald's arms were crossed firmly and his mouth was set, which for Gerald was tantamount to pitching a fit. "Elise, you were trying to say something?"

Elise lifted her head partway. "Um" – her voice emerged in increments – "it's not really . . . done. I was going to . . . cover the inside with gold . . . sort of . . . foil."

"There," said Gerald warmly, "see? Problem solved. Now can we – ?"

"But the handles!" exclaimed Norman, shaking the colander in Gerald's direction. "What about the handles?"

"Elise?"

Elise had her hands tucked under her armpits, and her chin was pinned again to her collarbone. "Well I sort of . . . liked the handles."

"Yes, as do I," said Gerald. "Now is it all right if we leave it at that, Norman? We really do have to get on."

Norman stood on the stage shaking his anguished head, the colander dangling from one hand.

"We were going to do the bit with the Governor and the manuscript," said Gerald, ignoring him. "Sean, can you – ?"

"Right," said the thick-shouldered Sean, who played the Governor, getting out of his seat.

"No, wait, I'm sorry," boomed Norman, his arms raised in hold-everything fashion. "I'm sorry to do this, really, but I'm not rehearsing until I know this matter is going to be resolved in the best interests of the production." Then he turned and marched off towards his dressing room, pausing only to set the colander down with a delicate flourish at the edge of the stage.

There began a series of diplomatic forays by several of the more experienced members of the company to Norman's dressing room, each attempt to reason with him an exercise in swallowing contempt for the good of the group. Because they were trapped. There was no one else they could get to do the role, and do it for the money being offered, on such short notice. Norman was like an old, belligerent camel they needed to get them across the desert. There was no question of any of them wanting to work with him – his humiliation of Elise could never be forgiven – but for now they had to cluck their tongues soothingly and hope for the best.

Of the group, there was only one person who seemed at all sympathetic to Norman's behaviour and that, oddly enough, was Elise. Far from humiliated, she was entranced by how deeply he seemed to care about something that until then had truly interested only her. Naturally she wasn't happy that he had dismissed her efforts, but for an actor to risk the enmity of the entire cast over a *prop* – what, to a prop girl, could be more exhilarating? So she was thrilled when, three days later, she managed to find, on a cluttered table at a Saturday-morning flea market, a tarnished old brass nut bowl that would handle the basin/magical helmet job perfectly.

For the next two weeks Norman continued his systematic denuding of Gerald Young's directorial authority as though he were stripping needles from a sprig of rosemary. Blocking was questioned, line readings deemed wrong. It's not that he was doing it deliberately, he would explain to Elise in the privacy of her alcove. But his intervention was necessary to keep the production artistically on track. He was, after all, a professional actor. Gerald Young – nice man, give him that – was a high-school teacher. Was there any doubt about whose judgement should prevail?

Nine days before opening night, Gerald Young walked quietly into the owner's office of the Beverly Dinner Theatre and resigned as director. He did so without hysterics – according to the wardrobe assistant who listened at the door – but explained that during rehearsal he had, in his frustration, ripped a hole in the side of his favourite blue cardigan with his thumbnail. This, he determined, was a sign he couldn't ignore. Life was too short. And so his long and fruitful association with the Beverly Dinner Theatre came to its conclusion. He hoped there would be no hard feelings, and he extended an early invitation to next summer's barbecue.

At the cast meeting that followed immediately thereafter, Norman insisted that Gerald's departure was not nearly the crisis it seemed. In fact, he explained to the actors, whose gazes were fixed on the ceiling, their shoes, or, in one or two dark cases, on Norman himself, that eliminating the obstacle of Gerald's limited vision allowed for the free flow of ideas. Now the fun would begin.

The difficulty, though Norman was unaware of it, lay in the fact that almost none of the actors had any use for his ideas (with the exception of the elderly gentleman playing the Innkeeper, whose wife had encouraged him into acting as a way of enlivening his retirement from organic seed distribution and who found that at least he could hear Norman, whereas Gerald Young had seemed to mumble). Few of the cast knew anything about him; they were neither awed nor amused by his abilities; and his tendency to want to inject a strange lasciviousness into a play they regarded as a light comedy, for a venue they knew to cater to families, made them doubtful of his instincts. They regarded him, and even referred to him out of earshot, as the Necessary Evil. What does the Necessary Evil want now? The Necessary Evil thinks that since Aldonza is a prostitute, her dress should show more cleavage. The Necessary Evil wants the Moorish Dance to be more erotic. The Necessary Evil thinks the Governor character should be played as a pimp. Eventually they shortened the reference to Nec-E, which they pronounced Nessy, and began using it openly, confounding Norman by responding to his various demands or directions with "Yes, Nessy," or "I'll get on that, Nessy," or "Nessy, you're absolutely right." Norman clearly had no idea what they meant by calling him Nessy, but the pinch that developed in his face whenever he heard it suggested he was beginning to realize they were mocking him. When he asked someone whether they were under the delusion he was gay, he was told, no, it was a "Beverly term of affection," which placated him only briefly. And he appeared to be increasingly disturbed by the fact that no one was actually doing any of the things he asked them to do. Cast and crew members came later and later to rehearsal, some straggling in after lunch. His suggestions and encouragements to the actors – "That's not bad, but now *here* I think . . ." – were met with sighs or sly glances. Even the piano player the Mecklings had hired in lieu of a presentable quartet took to inflicting a crashing A-minor chord on his instrument whenever Norman proposed a tweak to the tempo. The production, in short, was disintegrating.

While Norman was rehearsing this imminent disaster, he stayed at the RestAll Motel, located five blocks from the theatre on the banks of a multi-lane expressway. The fee he was being paid should have afforded him someplace slightly nicer, something mid-range in the motel spectrum, but despite his own explanation – "I like the character of the place" – cast members suspected that he really chose the six-unit RestAll, with its grime-clouded cream stucco exterior, out-of-order Coke machine, and intimate highway view, so he could use the money he saved to maintain a steady supply of brandy. Whether or not this was the case, it was a fact that whenever Norman seemed to have absorbed one too many slights from the Beverly troupe, he would excuse himself with great dignity, leave the theatre, and seek solace in RestAll Unit #4, returning an hour or so later – unless someone phoned and apologized first – his voice thicker, his mood darker, and his judgement ("I think you're missing that cue *deliberately*") somewhat less reliable.

In Diane Ellard's apartment, Amy brings the cup of hot water and lemon Diane could not rouse herself to make, while the actress coughs wetly into her sleeve.

"Was everybody against him though?" Amy says. "Because Norman seems to think he was revered."

Diane takes the cup as she dabs at her eyes with a wad of Kleenex. "Elise," she says. "Elise liked him."

Diane became concerned for Elise one morning, three days after Gerald had resigned, when the young woman appeared in her dressing room before rehearsal began, resonating with something more than her usual anxiety. She wanted Diane's advice: Would it be okay, did Diane think, if she went with Norman that night to scout for props for her character.

"What do you mean? What sort of props?" Diane said.

"Well, Aldonza's really sort of a . . . prostitute . . . right?"

"Arguably."

"Well, Norman thinks she should have prostitute . . . things."

"He wants you to go with him to scout for *dildos*?"

"No, no." Elise's face and neck flared with a cranberry blush that overwhelmed her eczema, and Diane detected the hint of a frantic, guilty smile. "But, I don't know . . . maybe . . . whips or something."

"Elise."

"He just wants to look. He's not trying to seduce me if that's what you think."

"Elise, this is totally nuts." Diane got out of her chair. "I'm going to talk to the Mecklings."

"No! Don't!" Elise covered her face with her raw hands and Diane worried she might lose her. She sat back down.

"All right, I won't. I won't. But Elise, really. You can't go with Norman on a sex-toy hunt."

"But . . ."

"You didn't have to tell me this, Elise. You came because you wanted me to confirm what you already knew."

"He's so *lonely*." She had the baby-sad look of someone finding a puppy adorable. "He's really sweet, too. You don't see

321

that side of him. Honestly, Diane, I know you hate him, but he's a very good, very talented person." She sat down on an upholstered stool next to Diane and ran her thumbnail along the piping. "He says his, I don't know, wife or something, doesn't understand him."

"Oh, God, Elise." Diane began to laugh desperately. "That's classic. That's exactly what he would say to you. And you're acting like somebody . . ." Diane stopped.

"Like somebody what?"

"Never mind."

"No, like somebody what?"

"Well, like somebody" – Diane paused to finish the wording in her mind – "who's feeling a little lonesome herself."

Elise huffed and clasped her arms at her waist. "You're all being really mean to him."

"He's totally obnoxious."

"He's just intense. You weren't so great to me, either, when I started here."

Diane went back to setting out her makeup on a folded white terry-cloth towel she'd laid in front of her mirror. Today was the technical rehearsal to work out the lighting, and she wanted to find the right combination of hues. "That's not true, Elise. You hid in your alcove most of the time."

"The point is I know what it's like to be on the outside."

Diane filled in her lower lip with a maroon pencil, as an experiment. "There's a big difference between choosing to stay out and having no way in."

"I'm not sure I even get that."

The actress pressed her lips together and sat back from the mirror for a better look, then she set the pencil down and touched the back of Elise's chapped red hand. "I'm just saying you are appreciated and Norman isn't."

That seemed to hurt her more than anything Diane had said yet. "Well, you should appreciate him. He's trying to turn this production into something special practically all by himself."

"Is that what he says?"

"It doesn't matter what he says. It's what I say."

Diane could see the whole direction of this conversation had to change or she was going to alienate Elise out the door and into a sordid rubber-and-leather scavenger hunt. She had to present a winning argument. But all she could come up with was, "Please, Elise, don't go with Norman tonight. I'm worried about you and I don't trust him and I think it's a mistake." And that did not do the trick.

Elise stood up and struggled to make direct eye contact with her, which Diane knew was a bad sign. "I know that you care about me, Diane. That's why I wanted to talk to you. But I think you don't really understand Norman like I do, because you don't really listen to him. So" – she turned towards the door – "thanks anyway."

For the next two days leading up to opening night, Diane rarely saw Elise, and never for long enough or privately enough to ask her any questions. Nothing came of Norman's sex-toy idea, either because the *instrumentos del amante* were scarce along Beverly's cottage-town streets, or because Norman had decided against trying to scale the wall of Diane's disdain to press the subject of her character's untapped potential. The one prop he and Elise did find together was a hand mirror he judged perfect for the scene in which Aldonza begs Quixote to "look at me as I really am." Covered in gold foil, he said, it would add a hint of magic to a moment he insisted on adding, when she was to hold the mirror up to her face and imagine herself fleetingly as Quixote's fair Dulcinea.

But Diane's issues with this and myriad other suggestions faded in light of more pressing business, that being Norman's increasing inability – an inability that seemed to be growing in inverse proportion to the number of hours left before opening night – to remember his lines.

Norman, of course, refused to admit this. He would stand on stage in character, he would hear the line that the entire cast knew to be his cue, and he would stare at one of them – say, Richard "Dicky" Dirch, the short, earnest man playing Sancho – waiting for him to speak. Then Dicky would see Norman eyeing him and stare more intensely back, prodding Norman with his eyebrows. Then someone sitting out front would pick up a script, and shout out, "That's you, Norman. *'And for that wouldst thou have me surrender?'*"

"I *know* what the line is," Norman would exclaim. "I'm waiting for Sancho's reaction."

And Dicky would look astonished. "What reaction?"

"When Aldonza walks in bruised and tattered. You're sup- posed to react to that."

"Am I?" Dicky would turn to the others on stage. "Really? I didn't know."

The person holding the script would shout out, "It says, 'Unseen by the three, Aldonza enters.'"

And here Norman would shake his head as if at the folly of those who could not grasp what he understood so plainly. "Yes, that's what the script says, but we've moved *away* from the script here. I distinctly remember that we decided Sancho should react."

"When the hell did we decide that?" Diane would pipe up.

"No doubt on one of those many occasions you weren't listening," Norman would reply. And so it would go, until the fact that Norman had forgotten his line – that Norman was having an alarming amount of trouble with his lines – was lost in the debate over Sancho's failure to react, or Aldonza's need to reach for Quixote's hand on this beat and not that one, or the Innkeeper's loud and persistent throat-clearing, or the Governor's mistimed hesitation. And a growing sense of impending doom would descend on the cast only later, after Norman was secure and very likely drinking in RestAll Unit #4.

When a small delegation of cast members led by Diane tramped furiously upstairs to the theatre's administrative office, eight hours before the official dress rehearsal, to inform Bishop Meckling of their concerns, they found the office door locked. As they tromped wretchedly back down the stairs they were stopped by Paula the stage manager, who informed them that the entire family of Mecklings – Bishop and Sandra and their fifteen-year-old son, Jamus – had flown off for a week in Montreal to shop for seal-coat Birman queens of breeding age to offer up to their young Birman stud, Pompom. Paula the stage manager was a sharp-faced woman who favoured spiky black hair and jewellery made from nails, bolts, and other hardware and who made it quite clear that, while she enjoyed the theatre conceptually, she didn't much like actors and now shook her head in typical and vocal disgust at this group of people so divorced from the reality around them that they didn't know the

Mecklings had left for Montreal two days before and anyway what did they think those poor people would do one day before opening night, cancel the production? Honestly, it was no wonder the Mecklings were selling out of the business as fast as they could – or didn't anyone know that either?

The only option left to the delegation was to confront Norman directly, to leave him without a particle of doubt as to their concerns and their expectations – that he had better get a grip on his lines, that he stop his drinking or at least confine it to one or two post-show unwinders, and that he start singing like one of the choir instead of the choirmaster. That if he could do that, all of it, then they might all be able to endure the next seven eight-show weeks.

So the group of them – Diane, Sean the Governor, Robin Painter, who played the Duke and Dr. Carrasco, and Wilfred Tann, who handled three parts including the Barber – went directly from their mid-staircase dressing-down by Paula to the RestAll Motel five blocks away. It was 12:30 in the afternoon.

To the untrained eye of a passerby they might have seemed a fairly unintimidating band of malcontents – a group of four musical-theatre performers who walked lightly on their sneak-ered feet and who wore colourful scarves or sweaters tied around their necks and had, as they chattered angrily, a way of flicking their hands out as though trying to shake off an oily goo. But to anyone intimate with the theatre, their purposeful strides and collective focus would have presented a rather fear-some spectacle of determination, a knot of fed-up pacifists united in their resolve to confront an untenable situation before the situation took them all down with him.

They arrived at the threshold of Unit #4 on a foamy crest of ire heightened appreciably by Paula's condescension, and knocked firmly on the door, first Diane and then, when the door failed to open, Sean, with the meat of his fist. Still nothing.

"Norman!" someone called out. Someone else batted the window of Unit #4 with the heel of a hand. They stood there for a moment, wondering what to do and beginning to notice how unswept the RestAll property seemed, when Wilfred said, "Look," and pointed at the heavy cream curtain on the other side of the glass, waving slightly as if it had just been brushed by someone moving past. Their eyes then followed the brusher's imagined path inside Unit #4 from the curtain to the door and focused, like the guns of a firing squad, on the glassy eye of the peephole, through which Norman was undoubtedly looking.

"Let us in, Norman," said Sean, using a version of his pitiless Governor's voice. "We need to talk."

And then the door opened slowly and revealed not Norman but Elise. They simply gaped at her.

"What do you want?" she said darkly. She was fully dressed, including her battered Doc Martens, and did not seem – Diane breathed relief – groggy from having just been startled awake.

"Uh," said Sean. And everyone seemed to agree.

"Well?" said Elise, looking with remarkable steadiness at Diane.

"We . . . need to talk to Norman," Diane said.

"Why?"

"Come on, Elise." This was Wilfred. "You know."

"No, I don't."

Diane stepped forward gently and then turned to the rest of them. "Can I talk to Elise alone for a minute?" She didn't wait for an answer, from the troupe or from Elise. She simply pushed into the room and closed the door behind her.

Inside, Diane looked from the rumpled bed against the wall to the TV on its chrome stand to the single-burner hot plate on the white chipboard dresser. It was dim with the curtains drawn, the only light being what leaked in at the window's edges. There were no bottles visible. And no Norman.

"Where is he?" she said with a low voice.

Elise motioned to the closed bathroom door and sat on the end of the bed, leaving room for Diane beside her.

"Have you . . . ?" Diane started, searching her eyes up close.

Elise scowled at her. "He called me," she whispered. "About an hour ago. He said he couldn't breathe. I got here and he was all white and sweaty."

"Was he drunk?"

"*God,*" Elise said, scrunching her nose in disgust. "No, he was not drunk. He was totally panicked. I was with him for, like, fifteen minutes. And then he locked himself in there."

"Well, have you checked on him? Maybe he's . . ."

"No, he's fine. You can hear him deep-breathing." Elise motioned with her head for Diane to listen for herself, and Diane walked to the bathroom and put her ear against the door. She could hear a slow and rhythmic sucking and holding and blowing and sucking and holding and blowing coming from inside.

"Norman?" Diane called.

"Shhhh!" Elise hissed, furiously waving her away from the door. "You shouldn't even be in here." She pushed Diane away and leaned towards the door and called softly, "Norman, do you think you might be ready to come out soon?"

For a moment there was no sign that Elise's voice had made it through. Then came the wet catch of Norman clearing his throat and, after that, a softened-up, pummelled version of Norman's own voice. "Ah . . . ," it said. "In a minute."

"Okay," Elise called. She hesitated there, with a hand lightly on the door, then joined Diane on the end of the bed. "You know what he told me?" she whispered to her. Diane shook her head. "He said he hasn't been on the stage in nine years."

"Well, whose fault is that?"

"But, no. The point is he's –" Elise stopped when she heard the bathroom doorknob click. The two of them watched Norman emerge, his green bathrobe cinched tight, his hands shoved in the square terry pockets. His hair was damp with perspiration and precariously finger-combed into place. On his face was a crooked smile, a smile propped up with trusses and stays, a smile that collapsed as soon as he realized there were two people in the room.

"What are you doing here?" he said to Diane, with wounded, old-mannish bewilderment.

"We wanted to talk to you, actually."

He looked from Diane to Elise with the same kicked face.

"Not me," said Elise. "Her and –" She tossed a hand at the door. Norman turned and started towards it, and Elise reached out for his arm. "You don't need to talk to them now. Just forget about them."

"Who?" he said, pulling towards the door. He opened it, wincing at the sunshine and startling Sean and Robin and

Wilfred off their car-fender seats. "Yes?" he said, as if they might have been strangers selling Bibles.

"Uh," said Sean, flitting a glance at the others. "Is Diane in there?"

"What do you want?"

Wilfred crossed his arms severely. "We need to set some things straight, Norman."

"No . . . guys . . ." Diane was pushing herself outside. "Let's wait, all right? We can do this later."

"Do what?" said Norman in the doorway. His feet were bare and veiny, his face was puffy and suet-pale in the cold blue glare of November. To the people standing outside RestAll Unit #4, Norman Bray looked like a hospital patient.

"Yeah," said Robin. "We can talk later."

"At the theatre," said Sean. The three of them drifted off slowly and Diane drew Norman back inside.

"Well, that was very strange," he said, sitting delicately on the bed beside Elise.

"Don't worry about it, Norman."

"What were they here for?"

"Don't worry about it," said Elise, her hand patting his leg, mid-thigh.

But Diane could see Norman's eyes going wide and watery and his chin creeping towards a defiant thrust. "They said they wanted to set things straight," he quavered, "and I'd like to know what they're talking about." Then he looked up at Diane and, for the first time in the three weeks she'd known him, waited for her to speak. Elise waited as well.

"Just some blocking issues, that's all. We can work it out tonight at the dress."

"Oh," he said, visibly relieved. "We shouldn't really be working on blocking at this late stage, but . . ." His voice and gaze wandered away. He took a long deep breath. "Does anyone have the time?"

Diane's arms were folded and she glanced down into the nest of limbs. "It's about quarter to one."

He nodded to himself. "Well, I think I'd like to take a nap. I'm very tired." He stared off for a moment, and then – seeming to realize he wasn't yet napping – shifted on the bed, positioned a pillow for his head and lay down on top of the covers on his side.

Elise rose and motioned to Diane that they should go.

"Elise," said Norman, his voice sinking, his eyes closed, "are you leaving?"

"I'm just going to talk to Diane outside for a minute."

"All right," he said, snugging the pillow up under his head.

Outside Diane waited until the door was closed. "Now I'm really worried."

"Shhh!"

"Well, shouldn't I be?"

"I don't know." Elise was back to looking at her shoes. "But whatever you were going to give him a hard time about, I don't think you should."

Diane sucked in her cheeks and scrutinized the girl in front of her, cold in her jeans and T-shirt, hands in her pockets, elbows tight against her ribs. "If I didn't know you," she said, "I'd wonder about all this."

"What do you mean?"

"He's managing to avoid a slapdown that he fully deserves."

Elise's eczema seemed to flare. "Well, don't let me stop you. I mean, if your conscience can live with it, go ahead."

Diane exhaled slowly through her teeth and then turned and walked along the row of units, past the broken Coke machine. When Elise joined her she was looking down the street in the direction of the theatre, and they stood for a moment in what passed at the RestAll for silence, the only sound the hyper shouts of cars and transport trucks whipping by on the expressway some fifty feet away.

"First he's forgetting his lines. Now he's having panic attacks. This is not a good way to start a seven-week run."

Elise rubbed her arms for warmth. "I did wonder if maybe I should call his wife."

"No." Diane shook her head. "I wouldn't."

"I mentioned it to him and he said, 'Absolutely not!'" She thrust up a hand and approximated a Normanish obstinacy. "'What could you possibly have to say to her?'"

Diane rolled her eyes. Then she tipped her head forward confidentially. "Whatever happened that night, by the way – the shopping expedition?"

Elise grinned. "He got into a stupid argument with a salesgirl about whether some harness thing was made of real leather. We had spaghetti at that Greek-Italian place with the pink stone." She glanced towards the door of Unit #4. "He performed the menu for me."

Amy, in Diane Ellard's kitchen, breaks ice cubes into a plastic bag for Diane's aching head and wonders how many more duties she has to perform before they get to opening night. As sick and weak as she is, apparently Diane loves to tell a story.

She ties a knot in the bag and brings it out.

"Is this all right?"

Diane, her housecoat snugged tight around her neck, opens an eye. "That's fine," she says, taking the ice bag and laying it across the top of her head.

"I don't want to take up much more of your time."

"Oh, hell. Don't worry about that. I'm enjoying the company."

That evening, after his nap, a refreshing walk, and a late lunch of scrambled eggs, celery sticks, and saltine crackers (because his stomach was tender), Norman made it through the dress rehearsal with Elise in the wings holding a script ready to call out his lines. He seemed more confident, knowing she was there, and his memory lapsed only three times, but at the end, when he came off, she discovered he'd been sweating so profusely his costume was leaden with perspiration and left a beaded slick where he laid it on a dressing-room chair. She gathered it up, filming her arms and chest with a salty dew, and took it to the basement laundry while he stood in the shower.

She told Diane that, afterward, she'd collected the dirty clothes in his motel room while he unwound with a succession of brandies and recounted his story about *Hair* and mooning the philistines and then told her again, an hour and a half later, as a fresh recollection, while she lay sprawled across the room's one semi-upholstered chair wondering when he would fall asleep. And the next day, she had all of his clothes clean and hanging ready for him an hour before curtain when he arrived at the theatre with a strange sparkle in his eye and announced that he had discovered the problem.

"So," she said, uncertainly, "you're feeling better?"

"I am now!" he said, hanging his windbreaker on one of the brass hooks in his small room. He'd been thinking all day about the problem with the production, he explained, and the problem with the production was that there wasn't enough laughter. It had struck him during his afternoon walk through Balstead Park, the one with rows of chestnut trees, that the performances in the production were uniformly dour. How they had gotten that way he didn't know but the realization had struck him and thank God it had and now all that dourness had to go because it wasn't right at all. There should be far more laughter, Norman said – his voice bouncing off the painted cinder-block walls – and would Elise please gather the cast and have them meet with him on stage in fifteen minutes because he needed to explain what was required of them as soon as possible.

"No, Norman," she said.

"I'm sorry?"

She was standing in the open doorway of his dressing room because she'd been about to go and attend to her own tasks, but she stayed there and told him no, it was crazy, and she would not gather the cast.

"Well, fine, then I'll do it myself."

He started towards the door but she didn't move.

"Don't, Norman. It's too close to curtain." She looked directly at him, she told Diane later, scared that he might not really hear her. "It's a bad idea."

"Listen to me!" he barked. His eyes were fierce. "I've figured out what's wrong! I know what to do! I've got to talk to them!" But she didn't move, she said no, and stood there as firmly as she could, and she was relieved to see his intensity fade, if only slightly. He turned away from her and took several great, deep breaths, chest out and hands on his hips, as if he were demonstrating the technique.

"Are you okay?"

He waited until his exhale was complete. "Don't worry about me. Worry about this production."

"The production's great, Norman," she said to his back. "Really, it's fine." When he stood there shaking his head, not turning around, she said, "I have to go," and ran to her alcove to get her props in order. She made minor repairs to the gold foil covering Cervantes's makeshift scabbard, reswaddled the opening scene's manuscript in its cloth bundle, washed the stewpot and filled it with two cans of pork and beans for the tavern scene. Half an hour later, with still more to do, she went back to check on Norman. She opened his door and discovered the room empty, and heard, at the same moment, his voice explode somewhere down the hall.

"Goddamn it, this is important!" It was coming from the supporting men's dressing room, and Elise raced down to see Norman, dressed in the upper half of his Cervantes costume but with nothing on below his blouson shirt but underwear and rubber flip-flops, his hands balled up into fists, facing Wilfred and Sean and Robin and Dicky Dirch, who were all seated at their mirrors and seemed to be trying their best to ignore him.

"Norman!" snapped Elise. "You're supposed to be getting ready."

He turned to her with a look of crushed hope. "I'm trying to tell them, but they won't listen!"

"Never mind," she said. "Just get back to your dressing room."

"Yes, please, Norman," said Dicky, the only one who appeared more terrified than amused, clutching a towel to his throat. "We are all trying to get ready!"

Paula the stage manager popped her head around the door frame with a smile stretched across her hostility. "Thirty minutes!" She narrowed a glare at Elise. "What are you doing here? Is the stewpot done?"

"Yes."

"Is the trunk ready?"

It wasn't ready. "Yes," she nodded, struggling to keep from looking at her shoes, "it's done."

"Well, leave the actors be. They have a hard enough time getting ready as it is." Paula's head hung in the doorway, waiting for Elise to move, but Elise couldn't leave Norman there, half dressed.

"I just have to go over a few things with them," she said with faint desperation.

Paula huffed her annoyance. "Make it quick!" And her head disappeared.

Elise grabbed Norman's wrist and brought her face close to his. "You have to come with me," she said, then turned and dragged him behind her before he could protest.

"Norman," she said once they were inside his dressing room, "you really need to stay here and get ready. Did you hear Paula? Half an hour! You don't even have all your makeup on yet."

"Don't worry about my makeup," he said airily. "It takes me ten minutes to put on my makeup. I've been doing this for thirty years!"

"Well then, *do* it."

"The makeup is not what I'm concerned about. Those people need to understand –"

She laid both her hands on his chest and pressed into him. "They don't need anything, other than for you to leave them alone." He stared back at her, his lips rolled shut like a child holding his breath, something behind his eyes looking ready to blow.

"What's wrong with you, Norman?" she said. "What's going on?"

"It's not *there*," he seethed.

She had seen actors panic before, but it was always about something specific – they couldn't remember a line, they couldn't find their brown second-act shoes. Norman's fear seemed far more abstract. "What do you mean?" she said. "What's not there?" But he would only shake his head and repeat the words.

"Elise!" Paula shouted down the corridor.

"I have to go. You really, really need to get ready."

He grabbed her arm with both hands. "Do something for me!"

"What, do what?" she said, angling towards the door.

"Go out front." He pointed in the general direction of the stage. "Look and see how many people are there."

She drew her arm away. "It's full, Norman. I looked already. It's a full house."

His eyes went wide. He began to rub his hands as if they were cold. He turned and scanned the walls of his dressing room, nodding to himself as though he considered the structure sound.

"I don't have any choice."

She looked at him suspiciously. "Norman? What are you thinking?"

"It's the only way," he said to himself. "I have to do the right thing."

Elise tugged at the flouncy shoulders of his shirt. "Norman, curtain's in twenty minutes!"

His head came around and he regarded her in a manner that she could only describe as regal. He said, "I'm cancelling the performance."

She stared at him. Besides the absurdity of what he was saying, what she couldn't understand, she told Diane later, was that he seemed almost exhilarated. He was radiant.

"You're *what*?"

"I'm cancelling the performance! There's no other choice. I have to tell those people to go home."

From outside the door came Paula's voice, the words, "Only a second," and then the door to Norman's dressing room swung open and there stood Paula with her hand on the knob and, behind her, a woman in a camel-hair coat with a bouquet of good-luck tiger lilies clutched in her hand.

Elise rushed towards Paula and pulled her inside. "He wants to cancel the performance."

"*What?*"

"He says he won't do it. He says it's not ready."

"Oh, *fuck*!"

"Norman?" The woman inched forward, into the dressing room. "What's going on?"

"Fucking *actors*!" spewed Paula.

"I am not performing something I don't believe in," he announced, a hand thrust out by the heel to ward off opposition.

Paula was quick to recover herself. "Look, you –" She forearmed Elise aside and began thudding Norman's chest with two fingers. "*You're* not the one who decides whether a show is cancelled or not, *I* am. And *my* decision is for *you* to get on that stage when you hear your cue."

But Norman was luminous in his conviction. "It would be theft! We would be *stealing money* from those people!"

"Norman?" The woman in the camel-hair coat had come around Paula and now stood at his shoulder, her flowers still squeezed in her hand. "What's happening?"

For a moment, he seemed startled to see her. It was then that Elise figured out who she was.

"You're not seriously considering cancelling the show."

"Yes! That's exactly what I'm doing."

The flowers in Gillian's hand came down like an axe. "Norman, why?"

His jaw worked, his eyes welled. "Because I care about it too much!"

Paula buried her face in her hands and emitted a feral, growling sound. Elise was torn between Norman's obvious crisis and the things – the trunk, the goatskins of wine – she still needed to prepare.

Gillian had turned to the two women, her face rigid. "I think it might be better if I talked to Norman alone."

Paula, as if grateful for some action to take, nodded crisply and pulled Elise towards the hallway as Norman sucked air into his lungs.

"Don't try to dissuade me, Gillian!"

"Oh, I won't," Gillian fumed as they closed the door. "What would be the point!"

A few minutes later, Elise was rushing down the corridor with an armload of rope to be placed stage left when she hesitated for a second outside the dressing room. She was hoping for something encouraging to report to Paula; instead, she heard the oddest thing.

Norman was singing. Or at least, it was a kind of singing, though it was also a sort of keening battle cry. Over Gillian's pleading to "Stop it, Norman. Just stop," Elise made out a fragment of Quixote's song – *"and virtue shall triumph at last!"* – bellowed out in a voice stretched rigid with fury.

It did not augur well.

The ten-minute warning had been given when Elise, working frantically in her alcove, saw Norman stride past her, still in his Cervantes shirt, underwear, and flip-flops. She managed to call out, "Norman?" as he pushed aside the curtain and walked out onto the stage, where he announced, over the audible gasps of the ninety or so patrons who were tucking into their included-in-the-price coffee and choice of peach pie or apple crumble, that he required their attention. Elise was just getting to the lighting table at the near side of the stage when she heard Norman say – his voice strikingly loud in the sudden, wondering hush – that he was sorry to inform them that the evening's performance was cancelled. She was just pushing past the musty velvet, out onto the lip of the stage, as he addressed them, with a calm that did not match the agony on his face.

"We've worked very hard. I've done my best. But I'm afraid, in the end, I have failed you."

Later, Paula would report that her first clue something had gone wrong was seeing Gillian buttoning her coat as she marched towards the stage door at the back of the building. She was shaking her head and laughing miserably to herself, as if marvelling at some terrible joke. And when she reached the door at the end of the hallway, she threw it open and let out a whoop.

As the uproar grew, both front of house and backstage, Elise drew Norman back towards the safety of her alcove. That's where Sean and Dicky found them. Neither of the actors, in their astonishment, seemed to be able to speak. But then, on the prop table, Dicky spotted the mirror intended for Aldonza. He grabbed it and held it up in front of Norman's face, his hand shaky with rage, and said, "Here, Norman, this is for you. Take a good look at yourself. This is what it's all about."

Norman accepted the mirror Dicky held towards him and, while the two men walked away, studied his face for perhaps half a minute. Then he sighed softly, went to his dressing room, and closed the door.

◦—◦—◦

Amy watches Diane sip her lemon water quietly for a moment. She's happy for the small stretch of silence, the lack of story and the images to go with it. The sky outside has gone iron grey and, as Diane pokes around the chair for a lost Kleenex to use on her nose, Amy checks her watch-bracelet – 3:30. She should definitely be getting back to work.

"We didn't find out about your mother's accident until the next morning," Diane says. "Since the Mecklings weren't there we took a vote and cancelled the rest of the week. We all hoped that when they came back from Montreal they'd just can the whole show. Which, thank God, they did." The actress coughs twice. "I'm sorry I can't tell you more about what happened with Norman and your mother. But I guess it was pretty decisive."

Amy finds herself in the strange position of not having to say anything, of feeling no need, in this moment, to justify or explain or react.

"After you called and said you needed somebody to take you through what happened, I talked to Elise." Diane shoves the used Kleenex up her sleeve. "I wanted her to know what I was going to tell you, because a lot of it is stuff she told me." She pushes herself slowly out of her chair and shuffles in her slippers over to a tall bookshelf painted kidney red, the same colour as the streaks in the rug. With her back to Amy she lifts an object off the middle shelf and returns.

"So this morning she came over to give me this so I could give it to you." Diane hands her the prop mirror, a simple round makeup mirror covered in crinkly gold foil. Norman's mirror award.

"She found it in his dressing room. I guess he'd wrapped it up to take it with him, but in the confusion around what happened with your mother, he must have forgotten it."

As Amy turns it over, she sees a folded note taped to the glass. She peels it free and opens it. There's only a line, written in careful cursive: *He seemed a good man. But I did not know him. – E*

"It's a line from the play," says Diane.

Amy refolds the note and tapes it back to the mirrored glass. She knows this to be a conscious choice – she could as easily have crumpled the note or thrown it away. And she is aware that for the remainder of her time in this apartment, where she has found what she came for, she is free to do and think as she pleases. There are no expectations of her to do one thing or another. There are no mistakes to be made or questions to miss. Nothing she does will be wrong.

❦

Vocem-Tech Ltd. is a computer-software maker. Specifically – as Bill Taschel attempted to explain to Norman as he semi-listened, horror-struck, with his back pressed against the door jamb of the sound booth – it makes voice-recognition applications for the telemarketing industry. No longer will call centres be filled with unmotivated part-time labourers given the responsibility of generating sales for the leading telecom, cable, wireless, insurance, mortgage, and fabric-treatment industries. Once the technology is perfected – and Taschel was quick to reassure Norman that, thanks to Rol Henninger's glowing recommendation, he would have an important role in that process – outbound telemarketing software employing the latest neurolinguistic programming will be able to initiate calls, converse with prospects, and close sales more effectively and profitably than any human.

"At our current stage of development," said Taschel, "which is sort of C-phase, if you imagine J-phase as beta testing and L-phase as reaching gold-master status, what we need is a voice."

Norman, lodged halfway between booth and hall, where he had been trapped by Taschel's enthusiasm, understood the word *voice* and managed to nod.

"Specifically we need a professional voice. Most people don't have the stamina or the precision, but Henninger explained your background and that's why we're excited,

343

because what we're looking for is someone who can take a series of response modules, sometimes a paragraph long and sometimes just a few words, and say them the same way, over and over and over again, to train the recognition engine of the IVR system. We find it doesn't work to use a recording. There's no way to duplicate the aural dynamics of a live voice."

Norman attempted to etch on his face an innocent's chagrin, the sort of I-don't-know-what-you're-saying bafflement that served him well playing Antipholus in *The Boys from Syracuse* in 1983. But Taschel went relentlessly on.

"What we're trying to do is create a foolproof recognition-and-response tool, so that no matter what a prospect says or, within a range of emotional parameters, how he says it – you know, whether he's angry or interested or suspicious or just not sure, because doubt is probably the trickiest thing – the computer recognizes the words and the emotion and directs the input down the appropriate data path. To really, you know, hit them where they live."

Taschel grinned.

"Telemarketing is becoming a real art."

"Ah," said Norman. "Yes."

"By the way, what did you think of that bundle of personal-finance apps we passed on to Mr. Henninger for you? They're pretty kick-ass, I think. Mr. Henninger thought you'd appreciate them."

When he finally opened his mouth to tell Bill Taschel as politely as he could that, whatever "apps" might be, he was the wrong man for their job, Norman knew the decision would have ramifications. That his "chance," as it was defined by bankers and employment counsellors and people who worked in airless shoeboxes, would be gone. But it seemed to him he had no other option, that he was, for better or worse, what he was. The strange thing was that, at that moment, he took no particular pride in the fact.

"Thank you," he said, gripping Bill Taschel's hand and giving him a solid farewell smile. "And good luck with your . . . efforts."

Taschel seemed genuinely puzzled as he walked him to the front door. Norman couldn't help feeling badly for him. "Well," said the software executive with a limp wave, "let us know if you change your mind."

Rol Henninger, on the other hand, seemed not at all surprised. He spent ten minutes in the parking lot reviewing the dire consequences of Norman's decision. Then he turned the key in the blue Plymouth's ignition and headed back to Parkdale.

Now, with Henninger grim and silent behind the wheel, Norman sits in the passenger seat and replays the experiences of the last few days in his mind the way Londoners must have recalled the Blitz. He holds a cigarette out a sliver of open window because Henninger minds the smoke, and watches the city skid past with its back to him.

⊷

Amy, in her office, baton-twirls a pen between her thumb and finger.

"Beverly," she says into the phone at the prompt. Waits. "The OPP detachment," she says. She speaks evenly, dully, acceding to the computer's requirements. And then she dials the number it speaks.

When Constable Dixon finally reaches the line she rushes as quickly as possible past the gauntlet of niceties and says, "I wanted to apologize."

"Oh? Why is that?"

"I was rude to you. And to Constable Lanar."

"I don't know about rude."

"I was. I didn't believe you and I let my – anyway, I should have believed you, that's all. You were just doing your job, and you were doing me a favour on top of it, and I wasn't very appreciative so . . ." The plastic of her pen cap yields beneath the edge of her thumbnail. "I wanted to apologize."

"Well, don't worry about it." He pauses. "Everything's okay now?"

"I talked to some people and found out what happened. You were right."

"Yeah, Lanar's pretty good at what he does."

"The other thing I wanted to tell you" – and she tells him this because he was the first to see her mother, in the moments after, and it's important to her that he knows – "she was happy, I think."

At the other end of the line, in Beverly, Dixon hesitates. So she keeps going. "I think my mother was happy when she died. Something happened to her before she got in the car – something good for her, I think – and she was rushing home. That's why she was speeding, and had the music on so loud. She wasn't angry or upset or depressed. She was happy."

"I see."

"So it wasn't suicide or anything."

"Oh." He sounds taken aback. "No, I mean, that's always something we look at, but it was obvious from the yaw and the skid marks and all the other indications that she wanted to live. I thought we'd made that clear."

She smiles at herself. "You probably did."

"Good that you're sure, though. It helps to settle some things."

She lets a small pause come to rest between them.

"I'm glad you called then."

"Me too," Amy says. "So thanks . . . Walter."

She likes that he chuckles as he hangs up.

⟡

Norman sits in Henninger's blue Plymouth by the curb on Sorauren Avenue and reviews his predicament, which perhaps is not as bleak as it appears. The house will be taken from him? He will have to live the rest of his days in a single room furnished with a sagging cot? So be it. He's better off without the encumbrances of home ownership. As an artist he's meant to pursue a far less tangible reward.

Outside the car, across the street, on the front porch of what soon will no longer be his house, a large man with black ponytailed hair, wearing jeans and a fringed leather jacket, is screaming invective in a foreign language, apparently Spanish, and beating his fists on the door.

"Who is that man?" says Henninger.

"I have no idea."

Where else in the city, or even the country, Norman wonders, is there someone engaged in battering the door of an actor in this way? He imagines this to be the sort of thing that occurs in New York or Los Angeles. There is something cusp-of-the-abyss about it. Something . . . Leonard Bernsteinish. And it's with a vague sense of loss that he realizes there was a time, not so long ago, when he would have taken an odd sort of pleasure in the attention.

They were breaking down the doors.

Now he lets his head rest in the sling of his seatbelt strap, watches his front door being pummelled, and feels his fragile convictions draining away. He likens the feeling to giving blood – he has never actually given blood, but the draining and weakening sensations, he thinks, are probably similar. It would be good right now, in the face of this latest assault, to know that he had reached Miriam and said to her the things he wanted to say. To have been able to make a real difference in the life of someone in pain. There, he thinks, would have been a special kind of accomplishment, something to be truly proud of.

If only she had picked up.

"Maybe," says Henninger, "you should find out what he wants."

*Should.* What a word. He should, people said to him over the years, have worked harder, should have gone to auditions, gone to Broadway, tried movies, should have had children, stopped smoking, stopped drinking, should have been less demanding, should have given his attention, should have loved Gillian more.

"You should put yourself in their shoes, Norman."

This was something Gillian said to him in the dressing room, when he insisted on cancelling the performance.

"Whose shoes?"

"The audience, the other actors. You should try to imagine what it would be like for them."

He refused to hear her. "That's not my responsibility," he roared. "I'm *the lead*."

He would still insist now, if anyone asked, that being the lead is important. But in the same breath he would have to admit . . . he's beginning to wonder if it alone is enough.

Beside him, Rol Henninger reaches into his jacket. "I think it might be a good idea to call the police." He pulls out the cellphone and holds it between them. "Would you like me to do it?"

Norman sighs. "No." He takes the phone and holds it in the palm of his hand, a phone hardly bigger than his cigarette lighter, until Henninger reaches over and opens it for him.

"I have the numbers programmed. One is for my office, two is for my home. Three is for the police. Just hold down the number and it makes the call automatically."

Norman lets his thumb hover over the keys, but he doesn't press down because he's studying the man on his porch. He recognizes him now – it's Karina's husband – from the wedding picture he saw in her room. He watches her husband pounding on the door and shouting because – why else? – he has lost the woman in his life, and he finds he has no trouble putting himself in the man's shoes, imagining what that would be like.

He grips the handle of the car door.

Henninger turns slightly. "I wouldn't try to deal with this yourself if I were you."

"It's all right. I know who it is."

The employment counsellor looks out again at the man raging on the porch. "Do you know why he's so angry?"

"I think," Norman purses his lips, "he's probably angry at himself." He pushes the door open and climbs out of the car.

Henninger leans over and looks up at him. "Well, Mr. Bray, I wish things could have worked out differently, but I can say

349

with my conscience clear that I did all I could." He gives a brisk, stiff-fingered wave, says, "Good luck to you," and pulls the passenger door shut.

After the blue Plymouth has driven off, Norman stands on the sidewalk, puts a cigarette in his mouth, and tries to light it with Henninger's small silver cellphone. When he realizes his mistake he snorts and shoves the phone back into his pocket. Once he has his cigarette lit, he draws on it slowly and watches the man on his porch continue to rave. Watches him pound on the door that Gillian found and restored, take the door handle in his two hands and try furiously to twist it off, and then, finally, run off the porch, across the lawn still strewn with windblown potato-chip bags and leaves of newsprint, to bang on the window. Then Norman tosses the cigarette to the sidewalk, crushes it with the toe of his boot, and starts across the street.

At the edge of his patch of grass he spots a fallen branch, a long, filigreed twig about the length of a broom handle ripped from one of the trees on the corner, and, taking no chances, bends down to pick it up. He has a vivid memory of brandishing an épée during a run of *Two Gentlemen of Verona* in the fall of '67. He recalls that he was rather good. Now, as he walks up behind the lunatic man on his front yard with the wobbly length of maple flashing in his hand, he thinks to himself, *En garde.*

"Excuse me," he says.

"*Karina perra loca!*" the man shouts, banging his fist against the window glass. Norman steps closer.

"Hello there!"

"*Sálgase de esa casa. Usted no pertenece allí.*"

Delicately, Norman extends the branch and taps the invader with a woody finger on the shoulder.

"*Qué?*" The madman wheels, his leather fringes flying, and Norman sees his face up close for the first time. The man is – there's no other word for it – beautiful. He has eyes the colour of bitter chocolate, cheekbones high and polished like the crusts of hot rolls, and his nose is long and elegantly narrow, the nostrils a calligrapher's flourish.

"Who the fuck?" says the man, grabbing the end of the branch in one motion and wrenching it out of Norman's hand.

"This is my home," says Norman. Stripped of his weapon, he can only stand on his lawn in a way that he presumes is impressive. He makes a calming motion with his hands. "I think I know why you're here."

"*Mi esposa*," the man spits. "I come for my wife." He waves his arm behind him to indicate the house, then turns, raises the branch and begins beating it against the window, shouting. "*Usted me está volviendo una mujer loca!*" But the flimsy branch, swung mightily, only brushes against the glass and just as quickly he spins and focuses again on Norman, his face blank with fury.

"You live *here?*"

"Yes! Now –"

"*Hijo de puta!* You fuck my wife?" He holds the branch like a club above Norman's head.

"No, no! She's my tenant!"

The man's face clouds with thought. "Tenant," he repeats, eyeing Norman suspiciously. "You the landlord?"

"That's right."

He thinks about this, seems to roll it around in his mouth like an unpleasant taste. "You don't look like no landlord."

"No, that's true," Norman nods. "I'm an actor."

The man stares back dangerously, then his face splits into a sudden grin. "*Joto*," he laughs, and lowers the branch.

"Actor, that's right."

"*Joto* means 'faggot.' "

Norman bristles. "I'm not *gay*, damn you."

The man lifts a fringed arm and points it at Norman. "You have a wife?"

"No."

"A girlfriend?"

Norman hesitates. The man shrugs.

"*Joto.*"

"Now listen –"

Karina's husband tosses the branch away lazily, walks up to Norman and lays two firm hands on his shoulders. "I see my wife now." He smiles like an old friend. "You open the door."

"I don't think I can do that."

"Of course you can. *Of course.*" He squeezes Norman's shoulders harder in a way that might be affectionate if it weren't so threatening. "You have a key. You put in door. Turn. Is open. You give me key, I can show you."

Norman doesn't move. "She's not here now anyway. She's at work." Though she will, he thinks, be home soon.

The Venezuelan blinks, frowns. Then he leans forward and begins to survey Norman's features. "I am knowing this face," he breathes. The hard hand that has been battering the door now grips Norman's face – dark, callused thumb and fingers sinking into Norman's soft cheeks, turning it from side to side as he might check a roast for marbling. "*I am knowing this face.*"

"Well, I'm an actor," says Norman, anxious still but undeniably pleased. "You've probably seen me in something."

The man leers hard at him, and a spark of recognition lights up his eyes. "The liquor store! There is a picture of you – with the people *que está prohibida*. Why?"

Norman's face falls. "That was a mistake."

"Oh, *si*?" The man grins. "You must have done something very bad."

"I was looking for brandy! All I wanted was a certain kind of brandy, and they acted like I was going to shoot them!" Norman gapes at Karina's husband in amazement. "They thought I was some sort of *threat*. Can you believe it?"

The Venezuelan examines Norman up and down. "No," he says. "I cannot believe it." He turns and waves a hand towards the house. "Karina, when is she come back?"

It seems to Norman that the man is determined not to accept his loss, or at least not his role in it. Something about that should be admirable, he thinks, but he can't imagine what it might be.

The longer they stand here, though, the clearer it becomes to Norman that he has to draw Karina's husband away from the house. Karina will be here any minute. She could be walking up the street even now.

"I would invite you in," he says, "but I'm afraid I have nothing to drink." He waits for the man to react. "Do you?"

The Venezuelan looks at him doubtfully. "*Sí*."

"Well then." Norman's smile grows broad. "Why don't we go back to your house and wait?"

He studies Norman for a few seconds more, then seems to make a decision. "I have brandy," he says, then turns and heads towards his house. "Come."

◦━◦

"What's that?" says Amy's boss, Darla, as she looks down at her desk.

Amy turns away from her computer screen. "It's a mirror. A prop from a show."

Darla picks up the mirror and fingers a corner of the gold foil that's peeling away. "Wacky," she says, and sets it down. "How's your head these days, by the way?"

"Head's good." Amy moves her cursor and clicks. "Thanks."

After her boss, continuing on her rounds, has moved on to the office next door, Amy picks up the mirror. For a minute she tries to catch the light from her desk lamp and bounce it off the glass of a framed abstract on the wall. Then Darla reappears and proceeds down the hall, and Amy slips the mirror into a drawer. She goes to her printer, plucks out the page that's just emerged and examines it: a letter, neatly formatted and spell-checked, to Norman. A letter explaining what she knows, how she feels, and why, for the time being at least, he will probably be seeing less of her.

As soon as she sees the letter's cool, typeset professionalism she knows she can't give it to him. She returns to her desk and slips the letter into the wastebasket underneath, then pulls out a blank sheet of paper and a pen.

*Dear Norman*, she writes.

❧

There is hardly any light in this living room. What might enter from the street through the front window is belayed by the cluttered, shuttered porch attached to the front of the house. In a corner of the room, a table lamp sitting on the floor, burdened with a heavy velvet shade, gives off only enough illumination for the effect to be called a glow.

But there is enough light to see that the room is filled with paintings. Scenes of hillside villages, of farm labourers hauling rocks or sacks of what might be coffee. Images of protest and conflict in crowded streets, moments of violence between holders of placards and wielders of sticks, all of them painted in a furious, loaded-brush style. Perhaps thirty or more canvases, some small, many of them the size of an oven door or larger, stacked up on a path-worn wall-to-wall carpet, leaning against leather chairs and beige walls and a prickly upholstered couch.

"These paintings," says Norman, waving his hands generally. "You did these, did you?"

Karina's husband beams. "Yes," he says. "*Si.*"

"They're quite beautiful."

The Venezuelan's face goes hard. "Not beautiful. Important!" He beats the air with his arm at one canvas after the other. "All this paintings are about the workers that have no *esperanza*!"

He remembers now; Karina spoke about this. The Venezuelan painter is political. And his name – Norman smiles proudly to himself – is Diego.

Before his eyes have fully acclimatized to the cheerless gloom, something is shoved into his hands. A photograph in a heavy wood frame. "This is something beautiful," says Diego, pointing at Karina. "My wife, *si*? She is happy."

Norman tips the picture towards the meagre lamplight. Karina, in a buttery dress, smiles up at him from beneath the picture glass. His fingers caress the soft felt at her back. "Yes," he says.

"Who is this beside her?"

"That's you." In the picture, Diego wears a white T-shirt, its sleeves cut off at the shoulders, and the expression of a man too cheerful to know he is blessed.

"*Si.*" Diego leans in so close Norman can pick up the scent of anxiety on his skin, the old familiar tang of flop sweat. "The picture is say she is happy with me. I look there" – he taps the glass – "why should I think she is not happy? *Entiende?* Understand?"

"Yes."

He spreads his fringed arms wide. "So why she leave? Why is she live with you?"

Norman sets the picture down. "You understand, don't you, that she is a tenant? She is not actually *with* me." It pains him to have to insist on this fact.

Diego waves him off angrily. "*Si, si*, I know. *Joto.*"

He is about to take further issue with this when his eye is caught by a hidden canvas, shoved behind the couch. It's twice as big as the largest of the others, and done mostly (though the morose light, and the fact that three-quarters of the image is concealed, makes it hard to discern) in shades of orange and gold. It's also painted in a style that seems less angry than the rest and it appears, from the portions that are visible, to be a portrait of Karina.

Her face, turned to the left, shows no emotion; her neck is smooth, without obvious strain; and a foot, the only other part of her visible, seeming to have loosed all ties with gravity, is lifted high in front of her and pointed towards the top left corner of the canvas.

"That painting," Norman points to the image. "That's Karina, right?"

Diego's expression turns sullen. "*Si*," he mutters.

"Do you mind if I get a better look?"

Not waiting to find out, Norman begins to reach behind the prickly couch before he finishes asking the question. But Diego apparently does mind, because he shoves his leathered shoulders between Norman and the painting and lays a stiff hand on both.

"*Vete!* You no touch this picture!"

Norman backs away until he can feel the edge of a chair behind his knees. "Why not?"

Diego seems to falter for a second. He looks from Norman to the painting, brings a hand to the back of his head and grips his long hair tightly. Bits of paint can be seen lodged in the crevices of his knuckles, and around the nails. Then he waves at the painting. "Is not finish yet," he says, and heads off to his kitchen.

After a few moments, Karina's husband returns carrying two tall, celery-green plastic glasses that Norman can tell, from the dark, lithesome waveforms playing against their insides, are each roughly a third full. As the glasses come closer to where he sits on the couch, he detects a scent that's strangely familiar. The saliva coating the edges of his tongue turns involuntarily sweet. Diego makes as if to offer Norman the glass in his right hand, but before it has travelled halfway across the distance between them, it stops. Norman senses the man staring at him, but he is unable to take his eyes off the glass.

"Miespejo Aguardiente," purrs Diego. "Very fine." He smiles in a way that he obviously means to seem angelic. "You will let me see my wife?"

*Miespejo*. Like seeing the face of a never-forgotten love, the name invokes the same spasm of longing. *Miespejo*. It's been ten years at least, thinks Norman. No, fifteen. Why now? Why is this man the bearer of something so yearned-for, so precious?

The reason comes to him like an unobstructed breeze. Because he deserves it. Because he has been tested, and the trial is over, and this is his reward. His hand ventures out to meet the glass before he has quite clarified his thoughts on whether the pleasure it promises is the sort of thing that could rightly be exchanged for a key. But just before he touches the glass Norman's hand hesitates in mid-air. Miespejo fumes sigh towards him over the plastic lip. His mind receives an image of Karina's smile, in its full, rushing affluence, then watches it parch at this betrayal and disappear. With incalculable effort, he pulls his hand away.

"I'm afraid I have to say no."

Diego flares. "*Vete!*" he snaps and whips away the glass. He brings the tumblers together and tips one towards the other as if to pour Norman's brandy into his. But he hesitates as the edges meet and, with a sheepish glance, hands Norman back the glass. "Is no good to drink alone."

He lifts a canvas off a chair opposite Norman and sits, and the two men stare at their drinks in the false dusk. At Diego's feet is the picture of a happy Karina, and Norman considers it for a moment. Then he clears his throat.

"There's something I'm curious about. And I think you may be able to help me." He checks to make sure Diego is listening. "Your wife said something to me the other day, and I've been trying to figure out what she meant."

The husband looks towards the hidden painting. "My wife is say many things."

"Yes, but this was something specific, and it was" – he forces himself to chuckle as if it doesn't mean everything – "rather confusing." He hesitates. "I was telling her about my . . . about a woman named Gillian, who I lived with for a number of years. I mentioned that she seemed to find life with me difficult, even though I had, really, no idea. I didn't see it – like you." He gives Diego an eloquent smile. "I'm an artist too, you see."

When Diego fails to respond, Norman continues. "What Karina said was, no artist should accept such misery. I thought for a long time about that, and now I wonder." He pauses, and his gaze drifts from the brandy to the picture of Karina, then to Diego. "What do you think she meant?" He lifts the tumbler to take his first swallow of the Miespejo, and it is every bit the reward he expects.

For a long while, Diego stares into the gloom with eyes that seem not to see. "My wife she was a *bailarina*," he says eventually. "Very good. Very beautiful. Once she was in a dance call *La Perdida*. It means 'The Lost One,' about a mother who searches for her child. It was a new dance, very hard. But she was the star, so she work very much." Diego makes a fist and pumps it softly in the air. "All the time, she is try to be better."

He stares straight ahead, his fist in the air. "At one part she has to fall, on one knee, all her weight." He pounds his knee once, hard. "And she do it in rehearsal and she do it on stage, many, many times." As he talks, he pounds his knee rhythmically, with a force that makes Norman wince. "And I work there, on the sets, and I see this, every day, falling like this." He pounds. "Like this." And then he stops pounding and looks at Norman in disbelief. "They make her do this. She *want* to do this. And at the end, she gets big applause, the people stand up, they love her – but she cannot walk! She cannot go to the store, she cannot go to the kitchen or to the bathroom, except that she have a *bastón*, a cane. Or I have to carry her."

He drinks with one hand and swipes the air with the other. "*Capullos!* I say no more! Is no good for her to dance. She is very angry. She tell me, 'No, is not your decision.' I say to her, 'Karina, look at your knee. Your knee is like a football.' She say, '*Jodete y aprieta el culo!*' You know? 'Go fuck yourself.' She say, 'When I am better, I am dancing. That's all!'" He takes another drink and shrugs. "So we move here, to this city. I say to my wife, 'The doctors are good in Canada. They will help you.' But I know" – he taps his head – "in this city, she knows nobody. There is no dancing here for her."

Then Diego downs the rest of his drink, shakes his head with ungainly vigour, and stands. "I make some food," he says, and walks off dejectedly into the brighter light of his kitchen.

Norman finds himself alone in the half-light, with his fears and his questions unaddressed. He swirls the brandy in his green plastic tumbler then lifts it and swallows it all. In the silence, he closes his eyes. It seems strangely safe here, he thinks, almost like a cloister, although he realizes this has something to do with the Miespejo, which can work wonders to quell a man's unrest. He decides not to trust this feeling of safety but to enjoy it nonetheless, for the sweet moment it lasts.

From his corner of the living room, he can hear Diego in the kitchen. He opens his eyes and watches him shuffle from fridge to counter, carrying a platter of meat. He watches him pull a knife out of a drawer, then veer back to the fridge in search of something else. Lettuce perhaps. Or onions. He sees that bread may be involved. And mustard. He watches Diego begin to assemble something simple and filling. And Norman is happy, because he is very hungry.

"This is *capibara*," he hears Diego say from the kitchen. "Is a favourite thing of my wife."

Slowly, Norman begins to equate this waiting in the dark, observing someone else's illuminated movements, to standing in the wings, anticipating his cue.

"*Capibara* is like a guinea pig, only bigger," says Diego. "This you can only get from Venezuela."

The main difference is that, here, in this moment, he doesn't know his role. He doesn't know what's expected of him. He has come to this point, been forced to face things he's never considered before, been made to move from there to here, where there are no lines given, no cues written down.

And he doesn't know what to do. With this realization, a little rosette of shame blooms in Norman's chest. He should know. He is supposed to know.

"Most people say *capibara* is meat," says Diego from the kitchen.

He can't be meant to dwell in this strange uncertainty. Uncertainty and vagueness and ambiguity aren't playable. On stage, a man without lines reveals his emotions with gestures. But Norman doesn't know how to play the things he feels. Because what, after all, is the gesture for hopelessness? For a man's suspicions of failure?

What is the gesture for doubt?

"The Vatican say *no*." Diego laughs. "People in Venezuela love *capibara* too much. They want to eat it all the time, even on Lent. But on Lent, you cannot eat meat, so –" he crows, "*capibara is not meat!*"

Norman tips the glass again to his mouth, hoping for some small, final trickle of ease. And it's with the tumbler's plastic rim encircling his mouth, pushing up bulwarks of cheek flesh, that he notices again the hidden painting of Karina, behind the couch. The face, turned to the left and showing no effort, the dark hair painted tight to her head, as if it were braided or pinned. The bare foot floating limbless, above and beyond her. Karina, doing the thing she loves.

And the thought comes to Norman that this is one thing he could do – that if he failed Gillian somehow, by accepting but not seeing, then he could at least help Karina to be seen, allow her need to be understood, here.

He feels his breathing shudder and the palms of his hands go moist, because this small gesture, of hauling a painting into view, may not be enough. Or, in the case of Diego, it may be misconstrued somehow. He may not understand the intent.

But Norman has always trusted his instincts, and he sees no reason to dismiss them now, so he stands and steadies himself. He will give Karina the gift anyone wants, the thing he would wish for himself, to be seen and understood. He will lift the painting into view, and then he'll go back to his house, and tell her that he has seen it, or seen her. That he has seen what the . . . the . . . the words will come to him; he'll know what to say. The important thing is to do it. To take the risk.

He places a bracing hand on the couch's prickly arm, reaches over the back, and touches the canvas's top square edge. He grips the wood of the stretcher, brings the painting up – it's so magically light – over the couch, over his head, into view, and stands it against the smaller canvases along the wall, next to the shrouded lamp.

The velvet shade lifts off easily.

In the painting, Karina's body is sheathed in a long, sheer, blue-black dress, slit to the hip. She stands, tenuously balanced, on a slender left leg faintly visible through the fabric that caresses it, while her right leg – bare and ropy with muscle – is thrust forward across the long width of the canvas, its small pointed foot rising above all. Her arms reach forward too, the palms of her hands upturned and ready to catch the foot before it falls, as if the slender right foot, in Diego's mind or in Karina's own, is meant never to touch down.

Norman doesn't hear Diego come into the living room with a plate of crusty *capibara* sandwiches, but something makes him turn, and he finds Karina's husband, surrounded by paintings, staring at what he has revealed.

His face has dissolved into an expression that Norman instantly understands – it's in the slackened cheeks, the indolent mouth, in the lower lip giving way like ash, it's in the region of the eyes, in the brows skewed with awe, and in the shoulders sloped towards defeat. And it's all of these elements that Norman would attempt to marshal were he ever given the opportunity to express the inner cleavage of a man who has been reminded of all he has lost, and why. Norman witnesses Diego's long moment of sorrow and thinks, *I could play that.*

Diego drops the plate onto a chair and, without a glance in Norman's direction, goes to the painting. He kneels down in front of it, with the toes of his booted feet pointed into a V behind him, like a child saying his prayers.

"I paint this picture," he says hoarsely, "to remember her dancing." He spreads his hands out towards it. "I say to her, in this picture, you can always be a dancer. You don't have to go on the stage. You don't have to be hurt. You can be *una bailarina en su mente.* In your mind, I say to her. In your mind it is *better.*"

He shakes his head. He lifts his shoulders and lets them fall, not a shrug so much as submission.

"She say no. She say, 'Diego, I cannot accept *such* misery.' Then I go away to work. And when I come home" – he shrugs again – "she is gone."

The process of learning is a little like love, thinks Norman; it can't be rushed. Despite the influence of the Miespejo, or perhaps because of it, he begins to understand . . .

Karina hates this painting.

He goes into the kitchen, finds the bottle, and pours himself another brandy, then returns with it to the prickly couch. As Diego continues to face Karina's image, Norman sits and reviews what he actually knows.

He knows the people he sees every day, in restaurants and shops, on the sidewalks, waiting in their cars at stoplights, are not like him. They see the world for what it is. They look in the mirror and see flesh and bone, and maybe they like what they see, or perhaps not. But they seek and see the tangible above all. He, on the other hand, has always managed to see not what is there, but what could be. And sometimes the idea he holds in his mind seems a better, more compelling possibility, a thing more worthy of belief, than what actually is. He has always considered this to be a talent. A blessing.

However.

Gillian was not as happy as he believed. The idea he held on to, while better than the truth, was not actually helpful. And it contributed to events that, he thinks now, he should probably revisit. He downs a mouthful of Miespejo and lets his new observation sink in.

Karina, it turns out, does not want merely to think of herself as a dancer. Does not believe the image of her dancing is enough. That was an interesting idea, but not useful. She wants to dance, period. He takes another sip of brandy.

After a few minutes, Norman stands up. There are more facts to review, but he doesn't need to do it here. Nearby is the plate of sandwiches filled with a strange meat giving off a faintly humid aroma. He lifts one of the sandwiches to his mouth, sniffs it, and takes a bite. He moves the meat around in his mouth, not so much tasting it as registering the fact that this is a thing Karina loves. *Capibara*. Until today a meat he never knew existed, but now has on his tongue.

He leans down and picks up the plate; instead of telling her about the painting, he will take her these sandwiches. It is, without question, too small a gift, but it will have to do for now.

Diego is still kneeling at the painting, still lost in mourning, when Norman steps outside with the sandwiches into the darkening November day. Across the street, he's startled to see Amy's black Jetta, and inside, Amy herself, strapping on her seatbelt. He waves at her, and she seems to see him. But instead of getting out of the car, she pulls away from the curb and drives off.

Something tells Norman that, although it would be nicer to think that she didn't realize it was him, she probably did. He carries that thought with him like an extra burden towards the house until he looks up, and his spirits are lifted. There's something white sticking out of his mailbox.

Well, that's all right then, he thinks; she didn't have time to stay, but she left him a note. Sometimes the truth really is just as good.

With his hand over the sandwiches to keep them from blowing away in the wind, Norman makes his way up his front path. As he does, his eyes are drawn to the light from his window, and because he feels he knows Karina a little better now, it doesn't surprise him to see her dancing in his living room. Swinging her hands high over her head and twirling once. Twice.

Not imagining. Practising.

He watches her for a minute, maybe two, then begins to feel cold and decides to go in. It's when he gets to the foot of his front steps, plate in hand, that Norman thinks of another possible gift for Karina, something better than the sandwiches, that he has the means to give her. He pats his pocket to make sure he still has Rol Henninger's small silver phone. He does. Now all he has to do is press the one.

He takes a great, deep, bolstering breath.

What it will require, he thinks, sliding the phone out of his pocket, is that he make the best of a bad situation. That is not a skill that comes naturally to everyone, of course. But it's the sort of thing he happens to be good at.

# Acknowledgements

My thanks go to the many people who contributed in overt and subtle ways to the writing of this book: foremost among them my wife, Krista, who convinced me to think of myself as an artist (and take the associated risks), then dealt courageously with the consequences; Gary Stephen Ross, whose support was crucial personally and professionally; my editor, Jennifer Lambert, for her wise head, clear eye, and unstinting effort; Ellen Seligman, for her confidence; Helen Heller, for her commitment; Joe Chidley, who gave me the means to write fiction *and* stay solvent; James Hale, my first editor and fast friend, for his fine example; Retired Sgt. Al Redwood of the Manitoba RCMP, who advised me on the accident reconstruction; Carlos Ponce, who helped with the Spanish; friends in three cities – Toronto, Winnipeg, and Hamilton – for their interest and encouragement during the writing odyssey; and finally my father, Bill Cole, whose love of language fostered mine and who, by exposing me to the lives of actors, made this book possible.

Paul Orenstein

Trevor Cole's first novel, *Norman Bray in the Performance of His Life*, was a finalist for the Governor General's Award for Fiction and earned him the City of Hamilton Arts Award for Literature. Prior to becoming a novelist, he was best known as a multiple-award-winning magazine journalist. A former senior writer with *Report on Business Magazine* and author of an acclaimed satirical column in *Canadian Business*, he still contributes regularly to some of Canada's finest magazines.

Trevor Cole lives with his family in Hamilton, Ontario.